WHAT SHE DIDN'T KNOW

DOROTHEA ANNA

Philotimo Press

Print ISBN: #978-0-578-81206-9

Digital ISBN #978-0-578-81207-6

Published by Philotimo Press

Printed in the United States of America

Acknowledgments

First shout-out goes to God for giving me the gift to create fictional stories. Next, I must thank my editor, D.A. Sarac, for her fantastic editing and formatting services. She turns my manuscripts into magic. To my lovely family and friends, who have supported me throughout this endeavor. And last but not least, to my amazing critique partners, Trisha, Paul C., Scott, Ellie, Paul, and Michelle. Without your help, my story wouldn't have been finely chiseled into the gem it is today.

A big thanks to all!

For those precious souls who have stepped out of the dark, oppressive cave of their past and walked with strength and clarity into the light.

Praise for Dorothea Anna

"No reader would ever be bored with this story. A more zest soap opera than one could find on the boob tube. Lots of engaging characters and snappy dialogue, and a narrator telling us about the human condition."
—Robert T. Hunting, Retired Social Worker

"There's so much to unpack in this story, which makes it extremely meaty."
—Trisha Messmer, Author

"With all the sisters' flaws, they come across as three-dimensional, well-rounded individuals, and it keeps me, as a reader, invested in the story."
—Diane Farrugia, Writer

"The siblings are so clearly distinct that their differences alone are capable of carrying the plot."
—Paul Crocker, British University Lecturer of English

Chapter One

Ten Years Ago

Gloria's father towered over her, gripping his leather belt. His crimson face swelled with rage. "Ungrateful pig. You deserve to be grounded for three months. Hell, six!" His words slurred as he threw down the belt, its heavy silver buckle clattering on the wood floor next to Gloria's trembling body.

Tearstains streaked thirteen-year-old Gloria's cheeks. She'd only missed one homework assignment. She sucked on her bottom lip, keeping her gaze on the floor. He was going to kill her next time. Fresh tears spilled from her puffy eyes. She tasted blood at the edge of her swollen mouth as she tried to pull up her underwear and jeans to cover her exposed butt and back that burned like a wildfire.

"Gil, she gets it, for God's sake," Gloria's mother said in her raspy voice, her words garbled as she teetered back and forth on the living room rug. Her arms lifted to her sides as if trying to keep her balance.

"She doesn't get squat, Etta, and neither do you." Gil pushed

Etta out of his way, causing her to tumble into the nearest chair, and stomped out of the room. The front door slammed shut.

Welcomed silence fell across the room as Gloria rose from the floor, wincing from the pulsating pain in her rear. She zipped up her pants with a grimace. Seconds later, Gloria heard her mother's soft snores.

Now was Gloria's chance. Her father wouldn't get a next time to kill her. This was the opportunity she'd been waiting for since she was nine years old. Her bottom stinging and her eyes blurred, she crept from the room, ascended the stairs to her bedroom, and snatched her backpack. As she came out of her room, she nearly ran into her nineteen-year-old sister, Michaela.

"Jesus. What'd you do this time?"

Gloria wiped her mouth with the back of her hand. "Nothing."

Her sister's stare fell on her backpack. "Going somewhere?"

Gloria didn't answer, only tightened her grip on the bag's strap.

"Aren't you grounded?"

"Not anymore." Gloria rubbed her cheek, then hustled down the steps.

"You're making things worse. Going to piss Dad off even more," her sister yelled from the top of the staircase, with one hand on the banister and the other on her hip. She shook her head.

I'm done for either way. Gloria glanced at Mike, her eyes locking with her sister's briefly, before she ran out the back door.

Present Day

Michaela stood beside her mother's hospital bed, webs of leads pouring out of Etta's patient gown and connecting to a machine behind her. Etta's eyes were closed. She seemed to be dozing.

Michaela's younger sister, Fima, sat on the edge of the bed, holding their mother's hand. The antiseptic smell of the white space disturbed Michaela. She'd never liked hospitals.

Her mother's gray, sunken face didn't surprise Michaela. Etta suffered the effects of years of bad habits—drinking and smoking too much. True, she had scaled back on the drinking in the past four years, but she'd kept up the pack-a-day of cigarettes. Michaela pictured her mother's deteriorating liver and gray lungs. No wonder Etta lay stricken with double pneumonia.

She knew her mother's years of self-abuse were a coping mechanism against her alcoholic father's rough treatment toward her after Glory was born. She still remembered glimmers of happier times with her parents, but the darker ones sucked all the light out of those moments. His rage intensified and spread like stinging tentacles to her and Glory, but Glory especially. That was until Glory ran away, leaving her to deal with their fractured family.

"How many days is she going to be in here?" Fima asked.

Michaela shrugged. "Don't know. The doc didn't tell us yesterday when she was admitted, but maybe we can catch him this morning on his rounds."

Fima sighed and checked her watch. "I hope he's here soon. I've got to get to work."

Michaela waved a hand. "He'll be, Fima. Relax. You're always in a hurry."

"I don't want to get in trouble with my boss." Fima wrung her pink nail-polished hands.

The door swung open, and a doctor carrying a tablet, followed by a nurse, came in. The nurse walked over to the bedside and began checking the wires and monitor feed on the screen mounted above Etta's head.

"Good afternoon," the doctor said with a darting smile.

"Hello, Dr. Rappaport," Michaela said.

"Doctor, when do you think she'll be well enough to go home?" Fima wasted no time.

"A few days. The antibiotics take time to work through the system."

"So, you believe the meds will completely wipe out the infection?" Michaela asked.

"Yes, of course. She'll be fine." The doctor's stare flicked to Etta. "However, her overall health would improve if she'd quit smoking." With his chin lowered, he stared at Michaela over his reading glasses.

Did he know she, too, had that unhealthy habit? Michaela smoothed her short hair behind her ears.

He cracked another smile. "In any case, as I said, she'll recover and should check out within a few days."

"That's a relief. Thank you," Michaela said.

Fima rose from the bed, sliding the strap of her purse onto her shoulder. "Great news." She headed to the door, turned, and waved. "See you later."

Michaela flicked a hand in her direction.

The doctor and nurse left a minute later.

Michaela settled in a chair next to the bed. She rubbed her eyes. She needed to pick up groceries on her way home. Thankfully, her hours at the local consignment store were flexible. Being co-owner had its perks. Not only did it give her the ability to take time off when circumstances willed it, but also the position allowed her to support her and her daughter after she and Doug had separated two months ago.

"Michaela." Her mother's weak voice interrupted her thoughts.

"You're awake." Michaela smiled and took her mother's hand.

Etta's baby-blue eyes and pale face turned to look at her. "I'm not going to make it, am I?"

Michaela straightened in her chair. Had her mother been listening to what she'd said to the doctor when she'd questioned the efficacy of the antibiotics? "Of course you are. What crazy talk is that?"

"I haven't got much time. I know it." A garbled cough followed. When she recovered, she gave Michaela's hand a weak squeeze. "I need you to find Gloria."

Glory? Where'd this come from? Etta hadn't spoken of Glory in the past seven years—ever since her mother's estranged sister, Melina, who'd called admitting she'd taken Glory in when she'd shown up at her doorstep. But Glory left right after Aunt Melina had made that call and hadn't been seen since.

"Why are you bringing her up?" Michaela slid her hand from her mother's and stood. "You'd said years ago it was too painful to talk about her and had accepted she was gone. Now you want to try to contact her."

Etta sniffed, lifting her chin. "Yes."

"How do you suggest I find her, Mom?" She began pacing the floor. *Glory the rebel, the troublemaker.* She never did what their parents had told her to do. She'd skipped out on chores and homework and, Michaela suspected, played hooky from school more than a few times. Her sister's careless behavior stoked bonfire proportions to their father's already combustible rage. Everyone had paid for Glory's reckless attitude.

Etta drew out a long sigh.

With Glory's track record of horrible actions, Michaela believed she'd probably died. Otherwise, she'd have done the decent thing and come home long ago. But Michaela wasn't about to tell her mother that.

She turned on her heel to face her mother. "Where in the world do you suggest I look for her? Haven't the police already done that, even alerting the police department in Aunt Melina's area and coming up with no leads?"

Etta sputtered another coughing jag. She shook her head. "I don't care. I need to see her, talk to her, before I die."

Her mother was the most dramatic person Michaela knew. She'd missed her calling at the local theater. "Mom, the doctor said you're going to be fine."

Her mother sighed again. "Find her." Her eyelids fluttered closed, and she fell asleep.

"Easy for you to say," Michaela muttered and left the room.

Chapter Two

Michaela made it home before her five-year-old daughter Bailey stumbled through the door, bundled in a winter coat, with flushed cheeks from the cold outside.

Michaela waved to the bus driver through the kitchen window as the vehicle drove off.

"Hi, Mama." Bailey trotted into the kitchen, letting her backpack slide off her shoulders onto the nearby chair.

She held out her arms just as Bailey reached her, and they hugged.

"How was school, sweetheart?"

"We made big hearts out of heart candies, and the teacher let us eat some of them."

Michaela raised an eyebrow. "How many is some?"

"A little, I mean. We didn't eat too much." Bailey grinned wide, showing her missing front tooth that had fallen out the week before.

"Uh-huh."

Her daughter's bottom lip worked. "Okay, I had ten, but they were teeny."

"Was this before or after lun—?"

"After!" Her daughter pointed upward with gusto.

Michaela suppressed a smile. "Well, I guess you're right. They are small, and they were eaten after lunch, so they didn't ruin your appetite."

"Nope." Bailey looked around the kitchen.

"What is it, baby?"

"Is Gramma still in the hospital?"

"Yes. She'll be there a few more days."

"Is she gonna die?"

Michaela froze with a grapefruit in one hand and the refrigerator door handle in the other. She glanced at her daughter, set the fruit on the counter, and squatted in front of Bailey. She caressed her daughter's pink cheek. "She'll be okay, baby. She's got to stay there to rest so she can get better. The doctor said she'd be fine." She gave her daughter a reassuring smile.

"Good, 'cause I don't want Gramma to die." Bailey skipped out of the room.

Michaela nodded. Her mother would recover, no matter the nonsense her mother had spouted off at the hospital. She pulled out a package of celery from one of the grocery bags and put it in the fridge.

That evening, after her routine smoke on the porch, Michaela sat on her bed with her computer perched on her lap. Before she logged onto her browser, her last conversation with Doug invaded her mind. He'd begged her to let him come home. How many chances had she given him? Two. The third strike had him packing and out the door two months ago. He had left late that night, hunched over like a beaten dog.

She'd told him she wouldn't put up with his excessive

drinking. She'd seen enough of that in her childhood. She wasn't about to go through it for another forty or fifty years. *Then why'd you agree to marry him?* Her mouth tightened in a firm line. *Because I was young, stupid, and wanted somebody to take me away from my twisted family. And he wasn't drinking that much then.* Michaela reasoned with herself as she eyed the package of cigarettes on her nightstand. *Just one more.*

She rose from the bed, slid out a cigarette from the box, grabbed the lighter next to it, and walked to the bedroom window. Michaela raised its frame, and cold air swept into the room and across her face. She wedged the cigarette between her thin lips and lit it. Sucking in her cheeks, she popped her head outside before exhaling through her nose. The night sky held no visible stars or moon, just empty darkness.

Her gaze moved to the nicotine stick. She extinguished it in the makeshift ashtray—an old shot glass of Doug's he'd bought on their vacation in the Ozarks four years ago.

Doug had called a month ago telling Michaela he'd joined Alcoholics Anonymous, but Michaela didn't believe him. He'd said that before she'd kicked him out, and two weeks later, he was lit on gin, passed out on the den's recliner. The ache she'd felt in her heart each time that happened nearly destroyed her. But she'd gained courage through the support of Lena, her best friend and co-owner of their shop, who'd given her the advice to do what was right. Truthfully, the catalyst had been Bailey. Her daughter had seen Doug sloshed only twice, but that was plenty.

"Enough," Michaela chided herself.

She returned to her bed, logged onto her computer, and navigated to the search engine. Her mother had pleaded with her to find Glory. It seemed a waste of time to look for an adult woman who didn't want to be found or could be dead, but if she didn't at least try, tomorrow morning her mother would harass her for information.

9

The cordless phone on her nightstand rang. She picked it up. "Hello?"

"Mike." Doug's deep voice floated softly through the earpiece.

Sighing, Michaela gripped the phone. "Yes? Why are you calling at this late hour?"

"I was at a meeting and couldn't call until now. Would you tell Bailey I'll be at her school tomorrow afternoon for the Father-Daughter Valentine's Day luncheon?"

Michaela's brows met. Doug had missed several of Bailey's school events in the past, but now, suddenly, he was trying to make one. "You can't call her in the morning?"

A long pause followed. "Yeah, but she'd be racing to get to school."

"All right. I'll tell her when she gets up."

"Thank you."

Silence again.

"Mike, can we talk?"

"We're doing that."

"No. I mean—"

Michaela clucked her tongue. "Haven't we talked enough, Doug?"

"I don't think so."

"I do."

"I need to tell you about the progress I'm making in—"

"How do I know any of that is true? You've said that countless times in the past."

A faint female voice muttered something in the background.

Michaela's heart sped up. "Who's that with you?"

"She's a friend."

Michaela laughed joylessly. "Sure she is." She punched the End Call button on the phone and threw it on the bed.

Swallowing back bitterness, Michaela smoothed out her hair. He'd already found another woman in just two months. Who knew? It could have been many more months before that. Her thoughts only added to her misery, and she shook her head, willing them to leave her alone. Rubbing her temples, she focused on the computer screen and concentrated on finding a sister who didn't give a damn about her family.

Chapter Three

E arlier that evening, the light in the cylindrical capsule clicked off, and its lid rose. Seraphima removed her sun goggles and slipped out of the tanning bed, slick with perspiration. She put on her yoga pants, tennis shoes, and bulky sweatshirt. Turning to the square mirror hanging on the wall, she examined her flushed face with mascara smudges like tiny onyx raindrops dotting the skin below her bottom lashes. She put a finger to her mouth, wet it, and gently wiped under her eyes, managing to remove the dryer pieces of the eye makeup. She sighed and pivoted from the mirror to the chair adjacent to her. Only her boss, Linda, was still at the salon, so her gloppy, sweaty state wouldn't be a worry.

Seraphima grabbed her purse, slipped through the door, and scanned the short hallway with five other doors off of it that led to the reception area. She hastened forward when a young man shot out of a room and bumped into her. Thankfully, in the surprise encounter, the cleaning spray bottle the man held in his hand had squirted away from their faces.

"So sorry, Fima. I didn't see you." The man with too-blond

hair and a too-thin body dressed in jeans and a T-shirt smiled apologetically.

Seraphima had forgotten about Eli. Then again, why would she have remembered him? He was the cleaning guy. Technically, the salon's janitor, if she wanted to be blunt. She walked past him and said, "It's okay, Eli."

She heard his sneakers squeak on the floor behind her. The shuffling of his feet got louder.

"Do you want me to walk you to your car as usual?"

Seraphima was focused on stepping into a hot-as-she-could-take shower and had only half heard Eli's voice. She wanted to be fresh and clean for her boyfriend, Austin, who was coming over to her apartment later that evening.

"Fima?" His scratchy alto voice drifted over her shoulder.

She turned to face him. "I'm sorry. What were you saying? I want to get home and out of these clothes."

One of Eli's eyebrows rose.

Warmth spread through Seraphima's cheeks. "Uh, what I meant to say is that I need to go home and take a shower. I'm nasty sweaty from the tanning." She tucked a loose strand of hair behind her ear. She hadn't bothered to fix her messy ponytail after she'd left the room.

Eli let out a laugh that morphed into an embarrassing snort.

Seraphima looked away as if she'd not heard it.

"Right. Of course," he said.

She swung back around and headed to the front door.

"I'll walk you to your car," he said, setting down the cleaning solution and towels on a chair in the lobby.

She watched him from the corner of her eye as he squeaked over to her side and then stumbled forward to push the door open for her.

Suppressing an amused smile, she said, "Thanks."

"Sure." His chest rose and fell as he held the door open. The poor guy was a mess.

She crossed the threshold into the frigid night air.

Seraphima dug in her purse for keys, then hugged herself as she walked to her Honda Civic. Eli trailed behind her. His short breaths floated over her shoulder in tiny puffs of white. She unlocked the doors with her key fob as Eli opened the driver's side, waving his hand in a gesture for her to get in. This was a routine of sorts on the days that they worked simultaneously, and Seraphima knew those days meant something more to Eli than to her. His skinny frame hunched against the bitter breeze that fluttered through his hair as Seraphima sank into the driver's seat.

"You're a real gentleman, Eli. Thanks." She shut the door and started up the car.

As she drove off, she glimpsed in the rearview mirror Eli in the dim parking lot, hugging himself against the wind whipping around him.

Stepping out of the shower, Seraphima glanced at her lightly bronzed, petite body, and frowned. Her breasts were too small, her eyes and hair the wrong color, and her feet were too big. She folded her toes under as she stood naked a second longer before wrapping herself in a towel.

The door half opened, sending in a rush of cool air causing Seraphima to recoil.

Austin stood in the doorway, admiring her. "I'm here, gorgeous." He sauntered over, folded her in his arms, and kissed her passionately. While nibbling her ear, he asked, "What's for dinner?"

She playfully flicked his chest within the confines of his arms. "I just got home fifteen minutes ago. There's nothing made yet."

He stopped nibbling and released her. "Late getting out of the salon?"

"It was one of my tanning—"

"Oh, crap. I forgot about that." He ran a hand over her long, wet sable hair. His gaze traveled to her shoulders. "The tanning bed did its job." He brushed his lips against her shoulder, then turned and walked to the door. "I'll order something." He closed the door behind him.

Wearing comfy black leggings and a long, loose fuchsia sweater, Seraphima walked into the living room of her one-bedroom apartment where Austin sat on the couch, his socked feet resting on the coffee table. With his cell phone against his ear, he continued talking to whoever was on the other end. "Yeah, make that two orders of sweet-and-sour pork, five egg rolls, and a tub of fried rice."

Seraphima's stomach knotted. He'd ordered for her again. They'd been dating for six months, and he still didn't remember what foods bothered her blood sugar. "Austin, I can't eat sweet-and-sour pork. The sugar in them makes me ill."

He pointed at the phone and mouthed, *I'm on the phone.*

She sat down next to him and opened her mouth to speak once more, but he'd already wrapped up the order and ended the call.

"Our dinner will be here in thirty minutes." He leaned over and pecked her on the cheek.

She bit her lip, afraid to tell him what he'd not heard. So she didn't and just smiled.

Austin flipped through channels on her thirty-two-inch television, with little chance to see what was on each one. "What are you in the mood to watch?"

"I don't care. Whatever you want to watch." Seraphima snuggled next to him. He slid his arm around her shoulder and squeezed her closer to him.

"Okay. How about this show?" He flipped back to the channel he'd gone past a few seconds ago. The screen filled with a group of guys, two in one car chasing three in another down hilly streets in the heat of summer. The pursuers thrust their arms out their windows and fired dozens of bullets out of their semiautomatic guns at the reckless car screeching onto a side street ahead of them. A string of profanities shattered the already chaotic, noisy scene. Seraphima winced and looked away as blood splattered on a windshield.

"Whoa. No way that guy's surviving," Austin said and crossed his ankles.

Seraphima peeked from behind her hand and wished she hadn't. She squeezed her eyes shut and hooked her arm around Austin's thick neck. "Could we watch something less violent, please?"

"Oh, yeah. It *is* kind of violent, huh," he said and clicked to the next channel that displayed a chef cooking something in a large silver pot.

"This looks interesting," Seraphima said with urgency, not wanting the cooking show to go away for fear something more heinous, if that was possible, would follow it.

"Eh, if you're into cooking, but I'm not." He pressed the remote, and the chef and his fascinating pot of mystery food disappeared.

Austin spent the next few minutes surfing through five hundred channels, stopping every few seconds on car races, football, the bloody movie they'd been watching, and a home improvement show. "We'll watch this. It's just fixing up houses."

Seraphima nodded and snuggled against his side once again.

Twenty minutes later, the doorbell rang.

"The food is here," Austin said, untangling from Seraphima and popping off the sofa.

He flung the door open, snatched the bags of food, paid the guy, and rushed over to the tiny kitchen table. Taking out the egg rolls, pork, and fortune cookies, Austin sat down at the same time as Seraphima. For the next few moments, they ate in silence, enjoying the flavor of their Chinese cuisine.

But Seraphima didn't touch her sweet-and-sour pork. Austin pointed at it. "You're not going to eat that?"

Her face warmed. "I-I can't… because of the sugar."

"Crap. Forgot about that, Fima." He slid them toward him and continued eating.

"It's okay. There are the egg rolls."

"Yeah, and they're the best."

When they'd finished, they cracked open their fortune cookies. Austin snorted. "It says people are naturally attracted to you. Ha ha."

Seraphima chuckled. She unfolded the little paper. "Mine says you cannot love life until you live the life you love." She smiled and gazed at Austin. His dark brown, gelled hair, muscular arms and chest, and strong, square chin were that of an Adonis. And whenever they were together, it was pure ecstasy. The way he looked at her and caressed her washed away any of her self-doubts. He made her feel sexy and beautiful.

His green eyes darkened, and he took her hand. "Sounds about right."

Austin's cell phone rang. He left his seat and picked up the mobile from the couch. "Hey, Brad, what's up?"

Seraphima stopped eating.

"Yeah, I'm eating, but I'll be done in a few." He paced back to the table and crammed half an eggroll into his mouth. He glanced at his watch. "Sure. I can be there in fifteen." He nodded. "Okay. See you then." He set the phone on the table and shoveled pork into his mouth.

Seraphima's heart sank. She hated when this happened. She knew his job as a volunteer fireman had strange, unpredictable hours, but it didn't squelch her feelings of disappointment.

Austin put his large hand on her small shoulder. "I've got to go. I'm needed down at the station." Wiping his mouth with a napkin, he grabbed his phone with his other hand and jammed it into his back jeans pocket. He then sat back down on the couch and pushed his feet into his sneakers.

Seraphima rose from her chair and followed him to the front door. "Will I see you tomorrow?"

"Not sure what time I'll be off. If I get the chance to call you, I will." Austin put on his jacket, gave Seraphima one last soft kiss, and left.

She blew hair out of her eyes and gazed at the front door where Austin had been seconds ago. *When will you change your crazy schedule for more us time?*

Chapter Four

Seraphima pushed open the door to her mother's hospital room and walked into a conversation about Glory between her mother and her oldest sister. She hadn't heard Glory's name spoken by anyone in years. Anticipation swelled inside her, as she moved faster to reach her mother sitting up in bed.

"Seraphima, sweetheart." Etta raised her arms.

She hugged her mother, then moved to the chair next to the bed. "You're looking better today."

"Eh, I'm still very weak, and this cough is constant." As if on cue, Etta let out a garbled hack.

Seraphima caught Mike's rolling eyes in her periphery. "So, what's this about looking for Glory?"

"Yes. I asked Michaela to search for her."

Seraphima's heart sped up. She leaned forward in her chair. "Can I help?"

Before her mother could answer, Mike said, "Sure you can, but I doubt we'll find her. The police couldn't. If she's still alive, she doesn't want to be found. Otherwise, she would have come back years ago, saving Mom the heartache she's suffered the past ten years."

"Maybe she couldn't get back to us," Seraphima suggested.

Etta ran a finger over one of her eyebrows. "Yes, that's possible. She could have been hurt or didn't have access to a phone."

"For a decade?" Michaela's thin mouth folded in.

Seraphima frowned. Why did her sister have to be so pessimistic about everything? "Yes, Mike. I think she's still alive. She has to be." She brushed a long strand of hair from her shoulder. "Besides, you weren't the one getting beaten up practically every day by Dad. Yeah, he was mean and didn't care much about us, but that didn't compare to the whippings Glory got. He hated her, and I don't know why."

Her mother's hands fisted the starchy white hospital blanket covering her frail body.

Mike seemed to have seen her mother do this motion as well. "Let's not talk about Dad, okay? He's dead and gone."

"I just want you to find Gloria. I want to see Gloria." Etta's eyes brimmed with tears as her mouth turned down in anguish.

Seraphima covered her mother's hand with her own. "We'll find her, Mom."

"I've got to talk to her before I die."

Mike stood, folding her arms across her chest. "Didn't I tell you yesterday you're not going to die?"

"Everybody dies, Michaela," Etta whispered in a raspy voice. A wet cough followed.

Seraphima's stomach churned at the talk of death.

"Sure, but you're not going to for a while yet," Mike said.

Etta's hand traveled to her throat as she raised her eyes to the ceiling, as if she were contemplating her last days.

Seraphima gently patted her mother's arm. "It'll be all right, Mom. Mike's right."

"Find Gloria," Etta said again, but in a louder and steadier voice.

"We will, Mom." Seraphima and Mike's words overlapped each other.

Late afternoon, Seraphima sat at the beige reception desk of the tanning salon, the Bronze Booth. Its pastel-colored walls, large glass windows and door received yellow rays from the afternoon sun and orange pink beams in the early mornings and evenings.

Pop music drifted through the building at a low, pleasant volume—perfect background noise for Seraphima. It made the mundane workday go by faster.

She'd hated high school and dropped out of community college after a year. When she'd been offered this job, she'd taken it. It paid enough that she could live in her small, one-bedroom apartment on the outskirts of Denver. The discounted tanning packages didn't hurt either.

This job would do temporarily until her greater future plans came together. Not for a better career, but for marriage and children. Even though her parents had shown her a pitiful and destructive example of matrimony, she'd still yearned to wear the white dress, the ring, and be a stay-at-home mom.

Unlike her own mother, Seraphima wanted to be there for her children. Etta had worked off and on, and the sporadic years she wasn't working, she'd drunk too much, which had resulted in a lot of yelling and misery in the household. But her mother scaled down drinking once she'd divorced Seraphima's abusive father. With this positive change, Seraphima came to realize her mother had drunk too much to cope with her father's tyrannical behavior.

Since she was thirteen, Seraphima dreamed of being a dedicated wife and mother. Nothing would deter her from her goal. She knew what she wanted and planned for it.

Austin would be the perfect husband. He was attractive,

sexy, with dark, gelled hair, a muscular build, and admirable confidence—matching her criteria of the perfect guy. And when they came together, it was magic. No other man's touch sent her into ecstasy. Their intimacy would sustain their relationship forever.

They'd have three children and live comfortably relying on Austin's good job as a pro golfer, which was safe, unlike his firefighter job. He'd get over his excitement of fighting fires by the time they married. He was only a volunteer fireman, after all, and she knew his real love was playing golf. As hard as he practiced, and as much as he learned caddying for men who were more experienced, Austin was destined to become a pro golfer. Seraphima could picture his name first on the Leader Board at the US Open golf tournament. She smiled as she pictured her perfect family.

"Seraphima, could you put me in for another fifteen minutes tomorrow at two?" a female voice asked.

Seraphima blinked. Before her stood a heavyset woman with dyed crimson, curly hair.

"Oh, of course." She brought up the calendar on her computer screen and typed in the open square. "You're all set, Georgia."

"Thank you. Have a good night." The woman waved and walked out the door, her full figure silhouetted against the purple-pink early-evening sky.

"Fima, I'm going out for a few. I'll be back before closing." Seraphima's boss, Linda, an auburn-haired, thin woman with honey-colored skin walked past the front desk.

"Okay. See you later," Seraphima said.

She scanned the tanning booth squares on her computer screen. Two were highlighted in yellow. She glanced at the clock. Ten minutes until closing—the exact time left on both of the tanning beds. Tapping the counter with her pink nail-polished fingers, she imagined her and Austin in each other's arms.

"Hey, Fima, I've started to clean up the empty rooms." Eli's voice broke through her daydreaming. "I've got classes tonight."

"Classes?"

"Yeah, I have evening classes at my college twice a week— Tuesdays and Thursdays."

College? Seraphima's eyes widened. She'd assumed Eli cleaned tanning rooms from two to five thirty each day and somehow survived financially.

"When did you start college?"

"Last fall." Eli pointed with the spray bottle in his hand to the rooms. "So, I've got to finish up early and head out." He scuttled down the corridor.

The clock's long hand hovered near the twelve. Seraphima cleaned the counter and turned off the computer just before Linda sashayed through the door with a cup of coffee. "Got to grab a couple of things from the office," she said, trotting through an archway to the right of the main hallway of tanning rooms.

A minute later, Linda walked out the front door.

As she waited for Eli to finish the last tanning bed, the conversation her mother and sister had about Glory popped in her head. After leaving the hospital, she'd not been able to think of anything else until she'd settled in the chair at the salon and tended to clients. She'd allowed her mind to drift to dreams of Austin and her life together, but Glory sat in the back of her mind, like a steeping mug of tea. The feelings she'd had earlier resurfaced. The possibility of finding Glory and the happy reunion with her sparked warmth in her heart. And the excitement built knowing she'd be stopping at Mike's house after closing up the shop to help with the search.

"All done." Eli appeared at the front desk in his oversized jacket, looking like a thin tree with an overabundance of foliage spilling from its skinny branches. "Are you ready to go?"

"Yes." She slipped on her red wool coat, picked up her purse and keys, and followed Eli out the door, locking it behind them.

In the chilly night air, the sound of distant car motors and horns punctured the quietness of the evening. The smell of grilled burgers from the Dairy Queen adjacent to the Bronze Booth flowed like an aromatic ribbon in the breeze. The moon buoyed in the swath of black firmament, spreading its white glow over the asphalt and cars in the lot.

"It's not as cold tonight," Eli said as they reached Seraphima's Honda.

"Yes," she answered reflexively. Finding Glory filled her head.

She unlocked her door, and Eli opened it for her. "Thanks."

"Sure." He shut it firmly.

When Seraphima glanced up at Eli, dismay clouded his blue eyes. He then cracked a smile and waved at her as she slowly drove away. She shrugged. Maybe he'd been worried about his looming classes. Something she didn't have to worry about.

Chapter Five

S eraphima approached Mike's two-story brick house. Mike
sat on the front porch steps, puffing on a cigarette. She'd
started when she was sixteen and still hadn't quit. When would
Mike realize she was ruining her health? Hadn't she noticed
their mother's ashen skin, chronic smoker's cough, and extra
wrinkles around the mouth? Did she really want to follow in
their mother's footsteps?

As Seraphima reached the concrete steps, Mike squinted at
her and put up a hand. "Don't start lecturing me, little sister. It's
only my fourth one today."

"I didn't say anything."

"Yes, you did. Disapproval is painted in two bright pink
coats across your face."

Seraphima gave her sister a sheepish smile. "I forget how
easily you can read my emotions."

"You've never hidden them well." Mike's square-shaped face
split into an easy smile as she snubbed out her cigarette and
dropped it into the soda can next to her.

Grimacing at the aluminum receptacle, Seraphima turned her

focus on the front door. "Can we go inside now? It's chilly out here."

Seraphima followed Mike into the small living room with its worn plaid couch and matching overstuffed chair. Mike kicked off her mules and turned on the end table lamp while Seraphima removed her coat and sat on the sofa.

"Let me grab my laptop." Mike padded out of the room.

Across from Seraphima, a gold-framed school picture of her niece, Bailey, stood on the second shelf of a bookcase. Adjacent to the picture were two other silver-plated, framed photos of Mike with Bailey at her last birthday party and the other, an older picture of their mother with her and her sisters when they were children. Back when they were a family. Seraphima smiled and hoped they'd all be together again soon. Down a shelf, she raised her brows at a picture of Bailey sitting with her father on a lake's pier, fishing. Maybe Mike left the touching, sweet photograph there for Bailey's sake.

"I suggest you don't get your hopes up," Mike said, walking into the den with her computer.

Great. Her sister had already started with her usual mantra. Seraphima straightened herself on the cushion. "I always have hope."

Mike clucked her tongue and sat next to Seraphima. "Always the optimist, or should I say dreamer?"

"I prefer optimist." Seraphima grinned.

"I bet you do." Mike opened her laptop. "But I will tell you, I didn't find her on any of the social media sites out there."

Seraphima glanced at the picture of Bailey again. "Where's Bailey?"

"You know where she is. It's a school night, remember?"

"Oh, right."

"She needs a lot of sleep. Otherwise, she's a gremlin all day."

"I'll try to remember to get here earlier next time."

"That'll work."

Seraphima's curiosity about Doug and Mike nipped at her, but she ignored it as her sister brought up the internet browser.

"So, on to the silly search for Glory," Mike said.

Seraphima frowned. Mike couldn't help herself. "Geez, Mike. Can you at least *try* to show some interest, for Mom's sake... for *my* sake?"

Mike sighed. "I'll try the People Finder website."

"Don't you have to pay to get the information there?"

"Yeah, but it's only a few bucks." Mike pointed at her. "You were the one so gung-ho on finding our obstinate sister, weren't you?"

"Yes, and you should be too."

Mike gave her a sideways glance, full of *Are you kidding me?* "I hate having to repeat myself, but here I go. Glory is either dead or doesn't want to be found."

Goose bumps pricked Seraphima's arms. "My God, Mike, you say that with absolutely no feeling."

"I'm speaking logically, Fima." Mike threw up her hands. "Somebody has to."

Seraphima tensed. Her sister had grown so cold over the past few years. Maybe it was Mike's marital problems or Glory's decade of disappearance. Regardless, Seraphima didn't like the change in her sister.

Mike slid an arm around Seraphima's shoulders. "Sorry. I'm just frustrated."

"About Doug or about Glory?"

"Both."

It was Seraphima's turn to wrap an arm around her sister's broad shoulders. "I can't even imagine what you've been going through. I'm sorry too."

"You don't owe me an apology." Mike typed Glory's name in the search box in the People Finder website.

Glory's name appeared on the screen.

Seraphima gasped and leaned forward. "There she is!"

"Gloria Barstone," Mike read aloud. She pointed to the address box. "That was our address fifteen years ago."

Seraphima frowned. "I guess that's not helpful."

"Nope." Mike scrolled through the list of identical names with different ages until she reached the bottom of the screen with no subsequent pages.

"That's it?" Seraphima tugged on a strand of her hair. "No more information?"

"That's it. There's zilch in here to even pay a buck or two to look further." Mike closed the window, and the search engine page appeared again.

"What do we do now?"

Mike sighed. "Don't know. If her name's not coming up in searches, what do you expect me to do?"

Her sister was giving up already. Seraphima sprang from the sofa and waved her arms about. "This is ridiculous. Maybe try her nickname instead."

Mike stared at her with another *Are you kidding me?* look.

"Please."

Mike shrugged and typed in their sister's nickname. Nothing new showed up.

Seraphima folded her arms as her mind worked to think of something else, but nothing came. She tapped the side of her head with her knuckles. *Why can't you think of something?*

"Hell, she could've changed her name, for all we know." Mike punched the touchpad with her finger and closed the window on her computer. "I wouldn't put it past her."

A name change.

Her sister snapped her laptop shut and set it on the coffee table. Mike had come up with something without even trying. How'd she do that?

"You're right. She probably did. Great thinking."

"Sure. Brilliant." Mike's mouth lifted at one end. "So, what did she name herself?"

Seraphima pursed her lips. What would Glory have changed her name to? Her mind was a blank, and she frowned. "I'll have to think on that for a while."

"Of course." Mike leaned back against the couch cushions, raised her arms above her, and yawned.

"It's barely eight o'clock, and you're already sleepy?"

"Just stretching. Relax."

Seraphima grinned. Mike wasn't calling it quits yet. "Good. Would you grab some paper and pencils for us so we can write down ideas?"

"Why not?" Mike swept over to the desk by the bookcase and grabbed a small spiral notebook and two pencils. Tearing off a few sheets, she handed them and one of the pencils to Seraphima.

"Perfect." Seraphima slid to her knees by the coffee table and set the paper on its surface. She looked up at the ceiling as she tapped the pencil to her chin. *What could Glory have called herself?* "What about one of her best friends' names?"

"It's possible, but it would be stupid of her."

"Why?"

"Then again, Glory was never too bright."

Here she goes again. Fima thumped her pencil, eraser end down, on the table. "Why is it stupid?"

"Because. Don't you think the police would've already—"

"There's plenty of people who have the same names."

"This is getting us nowhere."

"Because you don't want it to."

"It's a stupid track to take."

Fima pointed at her sister. "You're the one who came up with name changes."

Mike raked her hands through her hair and leaned forward. "I don't know why we're doing this. She probably doesn't want to be fou—"

Heat crept up Seraphima's neck. "You've already said that a thousand times, and I still don't believe that."

"It's not a happy thought, but it's something we may need to face." Mike slid a book out from the bookshelf, then sat back down on the couch.

Seraphima ignored her sister and focused on the lined paper. "I'm going back to the name change." The one decent suggestion her sister had made. *Who had been Glory's best friend ten or more years ago?* Seraphima had only been almost eight years old then. How'd she remember who Glory's friends were?

"Okay, have it your way," Mike said in her raspy voice. "Got any names?"

"I-I can't remember Glory's friends. I was pretty young."

"You were eight then, weren't you?"

"She left two weeks before I turned eight."

"Right. Glory wasn't there for your birthday."

The painful memory came back to Seraphima. Her two friends sat at the kitchen table, staring at her as she sobbed and yelled at her mother, "Where's Glory? I want Glory!"

"...didn't bother to think how you or any of us would feel about her taking off like that," Mike muttered.

Seraphima scowled, pushing the awful memories aside. "I don't want to rehash old hurts, Mike."

Her sister gave her a sideways glance, then sighed. "Okay, back to this."

"I don't remember her friends' names... any of them."

"She didn't have many." Mike's tone reflected a touch of sorrow.

"She had a few. I do remember her going out—"

"That didn't happen much. Glory was grounded most of the time until the day she left."

Seraphima's lips quivered. Mike had nothing nice to say about their sister. Nothing.

"No, I only remember one girl, and we didn't see her at our

house much." Mike looked up from doodling on her paper. "But that shouldn't be a surprise to you."

Seraphima shook her head with sadness. "No." Their father's violent, alcoholic tirades had kept their neighbors away and had embarrassed Seraphima. Her family was a freaky sideshow.

"So, that girl's name was Penny Shaw."

"Maybe Glory used her name. Are you going to search for her in the People Finder?"

"I have no choice, do I?" A smile tugged at the side of Mike's mouth as she opened her computer. She typed in the name and waited for the results.

A few seconds later, a list of Penny Shaws appeared, one of which was the same age as Glory—twenty-three. Seraphima peered at the data on the screen. The address was in the Denver area, but no phone number was freely given. The bottom of the page displayed a cost of ninety-nine cents to get the information.

"Maybe we should just talk to her, Mike. She may know what happened to Glory."

"The police talked with Penny and her family after Glory skipped town. She was one of the first people questioned because of their friendship."

Seraphima gripped the pencil in her hand. *Maybe Glory confided in Penny and told her to cover for her. That's something best friends would do.* "Isn't it possible Penny lied to the police?"

Mike gave Seraphima a deadpan expression, as if her question was dumb. "That's a pretty dangerous thing to do. Do you think a thirteen-year-old girl would boldface lie to a police officer? Wouldn't she be afraid they'd find out she lied?"

"It wouldn't hurt to talk to her. Maybe Glory contacted her sometime later."

Mike shrugged. "I guess not. It's only a buck to get the info."

Seraphima dropped her pencil and clapped her hands. "Yes, only a dollar."

Mike used her credit card to get the information released in the following window that displayed Penny's phone numbers, both home phone and cell phone. "Excellent. We've got two numbers to try."

"Call her." Seraphima beamed and clasped her hands together. *Penny's the key to finding Glory!*

"Hold your horses. I've got to get my phone from the kitchen."

Seraphima jotted down the phone numbers under Penny's name.

Mike returned a minute later and dialed Penny's home number.

Seraphima chewed on the end of her pencil as she waited for Mike to speak.

"Nothing," Mike said, and punched in the cell phone number from the computer screen. She paced the living room then stopped and muttered, "Voice mail."

Seraphima gestured talking on the phone as if they were playing charades. "Leave a mes—"

"Shh." Mike held up a hand. "Hey, Penny, this is Michaela, Glory Barstone's older sister. I don't know if you remember me, but I'm sure you remember Glory. You two were close friends when we lived in Parker. My sister and I would like to talk to you about Glory. Please call me when you get this message." Mike left her cell number, then ended the call.

Smiling, Seraphima rose from the floor and slid the folded paper with Penny's numbers into her purse. "We found Penny."

"Yeah, and that's all the progress we'll make tonight, if you want to call it that." Mike set down her phone on the desk then hooked her thumbs through her jeans belt loops.

"I'll keep thinking up some names Glory could have used."

"You do that." Mike walked to the front door.

Stepping onto the porch, its yellow light above them and the cool night air brushing their faces, Seraphima gave her sister a hug. "You'll let me know as soon as you hear from Penny."

"Yep. Drive safely."

Seraphima walked down the porch steps and smiled inwardly. Despite her older sister's lackadaisical attitude toward Glory, they'd found Glory's childhood friend. Raising her chin, Seraphima approached her car with energetic steps. *Soon Penny will call, and we'll find Glory.*

Chapter Six

M ichaela entered her store through the back door and hung up her jacket on one of the wall hooks. Lena, her best friend and co-owner of their shop, was pulling out dresses from a donated box near the door.

"I hate Valentine's Day," Michaela grumbled.

"You're spending Valentine's Day with your daughter," Lena said. "What could be better?"

Michaela clamped her mouth shut. This was the first time in seven years she wouldn't spend Valentine's Day with Doug. But this wasn't her fault. He'd made the mistake of not controlling his drinking and destroying their marriage.

She headed for the coffee maker in the small break room. "You're right," she said over her shoulder. "Nothing could be better than that."

"Double the amount of coffee grinds this morning, Mike. I need the extra pick-me-up."

"You got it." She scooped the dark grounds into the filter cup. "What are your plans for tonight?"

"I'm going to my niece's dance recital."

"Sounds like you've got a fantastic night waiting for you too."

"Yep. I don't need a man... *we* don't need men." Lena's face split into a grin of coffee-stained, straight teeth.

Michaela snorted. "You got that right. They only end up being pains in the ass."

Lena laughed, and the two sat down for their morning coffee.

———

At lunchtime, Michaela entered her mother's hospital room. Etta was sitting up, with a natural pink color bathing her gaunt face.

"Michaela," she said in her gravelly voice.

Michaela leaned over and kissed her mother on one of her rosy cheeks. "You look like you're over the pneumonia."

Her mother produced a cough, covering her mouth with a tissue in her hand. "Well, it's a slow process."

"Looks like the antibiotics are doing the job though."

"I suppose." Etta flicked her gaze at Michaela's purse. "You have a cigarette for your mother somewhere in that bulky bag of yours?"

Michaela's mouth tightened. The process sure sped up. "Really, Mom? You want a cigarette now? In the hospital?"

"I can get out of bed and go down the hall to the courtyard."

"You're well enough to go prancing around the hospital?"

Etta sniffed with a raised chin. "It's a short walk and a quick smoke."

"How's that going to help you get better?"

"Don't be a hypocrite, Michaela. You've been smoking for years."

"Never in hospitals, Mother." Glaring at Etta, Michaela shoved her hand in her ample purse, blindly digging through the plethora of items until her fingers grazed the pack of cigarettes.

"Any updates on finding Gloria?"

"No— –"

The door swung open, and a nurse ambled to the bedside.

"Good afternoon, Ms. Barstone. Your lunch will be along very soon." The nurse smiled sweetly, her chubby face resembling cherubs depicted in Renaissance paintings. She glanced at the monitors, then to Etta. "You get to go home tomorrow morning. Won't that be nice to be back in your own bed?"

Etta's eyes grew larger. "Does the doctor really think I'm well enough to leave already?"

The nurse bobbed her head as she wrapped the blood pressure cuff around Etta's skinny arm. "He sure does."

"What about my medicine?"

"You can pick up the prescription at the pharmacy on the first floor on your way out."

"This is outstanding news, Mom." Michaela patted her mother's hand that played with the blanket covering her.

"I suppose."

"What do you mean you suppose? You're breaking out of here in the morning." Michaela grinned.

Her mother's bony shoulders rose. "I just want the doctor to be one hundred percent sure I'm well enough to leave."

"Don't worry, Ms. Barstone," the nurse said. "Dr. Rappaport isn't one to send his patients home prematurely."

"See? You're on the mend." Michaela couldn't believe the words coming out of her mouth. Where did all this spunk and optimism come from? Only a couple of days ago, she believed her mother was on the verge of death. Maybe the culprit was her little sister and her bubbly, dreamer outlook. Yep. Fima was to blame for infecting her. But her mother was getting better. Healthiness glowed from Etta's slender frame in that ridiculous hospital gown.

"All right, all right." Etta rolled her eyes. "You've convinced me I'm on the mend."

"Good." The nurse checked the blood pressure reading.

The door swung open, and another nurse entered with a covered tray. "Lunch, Ms. Barstone."

Etta grimaced at the mystery plate.

Michaela suppressed a giggle and moved toward the foot of the bed. "I've got to go eat too, Mom. I'll be here tomorrow morning to take you home."

A gracious smile lit up Etta's face. "Thank you, Michaela."

Michaela kissed Etta's forehead, then left the room, with her mind on work and a nice homemade spaghetti dinner, her little girl's favorite meal.

Chapter Seven

Tomato sauce simmered in a pan on the stove, its glass lid foggy with condensation. Taking out handfuls of thin sticks of spaghetti, Michaela dropped them in the large silver pot of boiling water.

"Mama, is it six o'clock yet?" Bailey asked. She stood on tiptoes next to Michaela and peered at the steaming saucepan.

Michaela glanced at the black-framed clock on the kitchen wall. "Look at the clock, baby. Where are the little hand and the big hand?"

Bailey cast a quick glimpse at the wall clock and shrugged. "Can't you just tell me?"

Michaela's eyebrows rose, and she put a hand on her daughter's blond head. "Getting off easy."

"Please?" Her daughter gazed up at her.

Those pleading blue eyes got Michaela every time. "It's five forty-five." She pointed to the clock. "See the little hand is on the five and the big hand is on the nine."

Bailey nodded. "I see."

"You didn't tell me you wanted to eat at six o'clock, but

you're in luck. It'll be ready by five after six. That's close enough, isn't it?"

"That's just right." Bailey grinned.

"Well, I'm glad you approve." Michaela chuckled and stirred the sauce.

Ten minutes later, the doorbell rang, and Bailey flew out of the kitchen yelling, "I'll get it!"

Michaela poured the cooked noodles through the strainer in the sink. Who could be at the door? Solicitors didn't usually come this late, and her family members were accounted for, busy with their own plans, or lying in a hospital bed. For a split second, Glory rapping on the door came to her mind. Laughing at such an irrational thought and again blaming Fima for it, Michaela listened for the footsteps on the hardwood floor—one set lighter and faster and the other slower and heavier.

"It's almost ready," her daughter's high-pitched voice swept into the kitchen before they did.

Turning from the stove, Michaela's jaw dropped. Doug stood just inside the doorframe, dressed in navy khakis, and a blue-and-green-striped sweater with a white shirt collar peeking out. His deep gray eyes, with their heavy lids resembling Paul McCartney's that had always melted Michaela's heart, stared at her with a mixture of fear and love. Her chest tightened, and she closed her mouth, pursing her lips together, willing away those fanciful feelings.

Bailey held Doug's hand, and her eyes darted from Doug to Michaela. Other than the bubbling of the sauce and the hum of the microwave warming up carrots, the room rocked in silence. Thick tension filled the atmosphere for what seemed like several minutes.

"Your expression tells me you weren't expecting me," Doug said, his tenor voice taking up the space in the suddenly smaller kitchen. He bent his head toward their daughter. "Bailey, I thought you told me your mother was okay with me coming over for Valentine's Day dinner."

No, I wasn't, and it sure as hell isn't okay. "Bailey." Michaela gave her daughter her narrowed eyes of disapproval.

Bailey stared at her socked feet. "I just wanted to eat my favorite dinner on Valentine's Day with Daddy too. All of us together." She peeked at Michaela, her eyes glistening with tears.

Michaela's heart wrenched in her chest from the hope coloring her daughter's precious face. Her husband wrung his hands as if unsure what to do. There were no signs in his having drunk large quantities of alcohol. He'd spoken clearly and stood with steadiness.

Folding in her lips, Michaela stifled feelings of wanting to flee from the room. *Get a grip. You're an adult. It's a simple spaghetti dinner.* "I wish you'd told me, Bailey, but since your father is here and I've made plenty of spaghetti—"

"And it's Valentine's Day," Bailey added.

"Well, yes—"

"When mommies and daddies eat dinner together because they love each other."

"Bailey, your mother and I—" Doug started to say.

"Sure, Bailey." Michaela interjected. "Would you please help set the table?"

Relief swept over Doug's face.

"Okay." Bailey trotted to the cupboard for plates and glasses.

A bottle of merlot sat on the counter, its cork stabbed through with the screw, lying next to the wine. Michaela had opened it for the special dinner with her daughter. She favored wine with most of her meals but had limited the drink to special dinners and social engagements. Just as she'd expected Doug to cut out his alcohol altogether, she'd reduced her intake to reinforce her ability to do so, even if she didn't have an addiction.

But seeing Doug sitting at the dining room table across from her with a glass of water, and not wanting to tempt him, she left the bottle in the kitchen and poured water into her glass. She noticed Doug watching her doing this, concern etched in his forehead, but his eyes were soft.

Throughout dinner, Michaela was grateful Bailey prattled on about school and the Father and Daughter Valentine's Day luncheon. Her cheery presence lessened the awkwardness hanging in the room.

As she carried the empty plates to the kitchen sink, Michaela's cell phone rang from the living room.

"I'll get your phone, Mama," Bailey called from the dining room. She slid into the kitchen in seconds as the phone continued to buzz and play its ringtone.

"Thank you, honey." Michaela took the phone from her daughter. "Hello?"

"Is this Michaela?" an unfamiliar woman's voice asked.

"Yes."

"This is Penny... Penny Shaw."

Michaela froze as the faucet flowed and filled up the right side of the basin. Penny, Glory's friend from childhood had called her back. She shook herself from her astonished state and turned off the faucet. "Penny, thanks so much for returning my call."

Peeking at her daughter sitting on her husband's lap and chatting in the dining room, Michaela snuck out of the kitchen and upstairs to the bedroom, closing the door behind her.

"I'm sorry it took me so long to get back to you. My family was out of town on vacation."

"No problem."

"You asked about Glory?"

"Yes. My mother wants me to find her. She desperately wants to talk to her."

"I'm sorry. I can't help you."

Michaela sank into the chair in her bedroom.

"I don't know where she is."

Michaela ran her hand over the wooden arm of the chair. "Did you ever?"

"Wha—what do you mean?" The steady voice broke.

"I mean, did you know where Glory went when she first ran away?"

Silence followed. Gripping the phone, Michaela strained to hear anything from the other end.

"No. I told the cops when they asked me that ten years ago."

"Was it the truth?"

"You think I lied to the police? Why would I do that?"

"To protect your best friend."

"Look, I'm not on trial here." Penny huffed. "I didn't do anything wrong."

"I know—"

"I called you back in good faith because Glory was my best friend years ago, but I don't have to take your badgering."

Sensing Penny was about to hang up, Michaela quickly sputtered, "Hey, I'm sorry. Can we start again?"

Stillness answered. But Penny's voice finally returned. "Okay, but I really don't know how I can help."

"Anything you can tell me would be helpful, Penny. Did you know Glory was staying with her aunt?"

The long pauses were becoming routine in the conversation.

"She did call me one time a year or so after she left town. She told me she was okay and staying with an aunt."

"So you *did* know where she was after she left home."

"Not when she left. As I said, that was over a year later."

"And you didn't tell the police."

"No. I figured she was with family, so she was all right."

Michael's jaw fell. She marveled at Penny's lack of consideration for Glory's immediate family. "You didn't think her mother and sisters deserved to know she was okay?"

"I figured she called you too." Her voice wavered.

Michaela wasn't sure if Penny's response was out of covering her own ineptness or if she truly was telling the truth. "I see. Well, she didn't."

"Oh."

Another patch of dead air followed.

"Have you heard from Glory since that time?"

"Yes."

Michaela straightened in her chair. "You have?"

"Yes, once after that call. She asked me if I knew if your dad was still around."

Michaela sat speechless.

"I told her I would check to see if his car was parked in front of the garage. I had noticed that he would park it there and later move it into the garage every day, except on the weekends."

Surprised at Penny's acute observations, Michaela said, "You were keeping an eye on what my father was doing?"

"Only if his car was at your house. I did this for Glory."

"Okay, so what did you tell her?"

"Well, the obvious. He was there every day like most fathers."

"And what did Glory say?"

"She thanked me and that was it. She didn't call me back after that."

"Never again?"

"Never, and my family moved two years later from the neighborhood, and our number was disconnected, so she wouldn't have been able to reach me. I didn't have a cell phone, and I'm guessing she didn't either."

"No, she didn't have one before she left," Michaela said more to herself than Penny. She rubbed her temple. "So, that's the last you heard from Glory? About seven years ago."

"Yes."

"Would you mind keeping in touch in case you hear from her?"

"I suppose that would be okay."

"Good—"

"Mama!" Bailey's treble voice carried through the hallway to outside the bedroom door. "We're eating cake!"

"Thanks, Penny. I've got to go."

Michaela shut off her phone and headed out of the bedroom. Doug and Bailey were at the bottom of the steps.

"Where'd you go, Mama?"

"I had a phone call." Michaela avoided Doug's stare. "So, you found the cake?"

"Yes. Daddy helped me. He got a piece for us. I already ate mine though." Bailey smiled apologetically and looked up at Doug with loving eyes.

"Your piece is waiting for you in the dining room," Doug said, tilting his head in the direction of the room.

"Thank you, but I'm not hungry. The spaghetti was enough for me, and it's getting late." Michaela checked her watch. "Time to get ready for bed, little one."

"Aww. But I want to sit with Daddy."

"I'm sure Daddy has to go to his home soon."

Bailey's bottom lip stuck out. "I wish Daddy could come back here and stay like before."

"I wish I could stay too, honey," Doug said, bending down to hug her.

Guilt ate at Michaela as she watched Doug and Bailey embrace. She pressed her lips together, realizing she'd nearly forgotten why she'd kicked him out. All right, so Doug hadn't shown himself to be a violent drunk. But he still acted loud, clumsy, and sometimes passed out. And there was that one time he'd actually pissed on the kitchen chair, thinking it was the toilet. She'd been left to clean it up.

No, he might be sober right now, but he wouldn't be in the coming days. Addictions didn't just go away. He hadn't admitted he was an alcoholic until Michaela sent him packing, and only did so then to pacify her. Until he could admit it to himself and get real help, they'd have to stay apart. Yet would he ever come to that realization on his own and want to make that step?

"Okay, give Daddy a kiss good night."

Bailey obeyed. "Night, Daddy. See you Saturday." She plodded up the stairs.

"Good night, sweetheart." Doug waved at Bailey and headed to the door with Michaela right behind him.

Michaela opened the door, moving to the side for Doug to pass. The familiar musky lemon spice scent of him teased her nostrils. She wiped her nose and stood straight as a board.

He stopped beside her, half a foot taller than her. "You know, it's not right to separate Bailey from me. I should still be living in this house. You saw it for yourself how she's hurting over this."

"If you wanted to stay in this house, you should've gotten help for your addiction when it started two years ago."

"Have some compassion, Mike. I've started making changes."

Michaela clutched the doorknob, looking away just as Doug's cell phone rang.

"Hello?" His face clouded as he listened to the person on the phone. "Don't worry. I'll be there in ten minutes."

Michaela eyed him and tapped her fingers on the doorknob.

He ended the call. "Sorry. I've got to go. Tina needs me."

"Tina." She echoed the name sharply with one eyebrow raised.

"Yeah, she's a member of AA and my sponsor." Doug opened the storm door and stepped onto the porch. He twisted at the waist. "Thanks for the delicious dinner. You've always been a great cook." He pulled out keys from his pocket. "We'll talk later. It's too important not to."

He was running off to be with another woman, and he still expected her to believe he cared about her. *AA sponsor? What a load of crap.* "Sure." Michaela smirked.

He walked off the porch to his car parked by the curb.

Michaela closed the door and headed to the kitchen to clean up the remnants of dinner. When she reached the kitchen counter where the bottle of merlot had been sitting, only half its contents were left. Raking a hand through her short hair, she blew out a frustrated sigh. *Damn it, Doug.*

Chapter Eight

The next evening, while Mike washed the dinner dishes, Seraphima ascended the wooden steps with Bailey by her side. They followed Etta into her large bedroom with its king-sized, four-poster bed. Seraphima helped her mother shuffle to it and slip under the plush maroon comforter. Exhaustion painted Etta's gaunt face. She looked much older than her fifty-three years.

Bailey stood by the nightstand where a stack of books lay. She picked up the top one and gave it to Etta. "Here, Gramma. You can read."

Seraphima recognized two of the novels in the pile—romances she'd read and recommended to her mother.

Etta gave Bailey a gentle smile. "Thank you, darling." She took the book and placed it on her lap.

Bailey moved to a cedar chest at the foot of the bed. She got down on her knees, opened the lid, and leaned over. "What's in here, Gramma?"

Seraphima walked over to the box and peered at the contents.

"It's your great-grandmother's belongings. Like a keepsake chest," Etta replied.

"What's that?"

"It's where you keep all the things over the years of your life that mean a lot to you."

"Wow. I haven't looked in this box since I was around your age, Bailey," Seraphima said. She squatted next to her niece and spotted her grandmother's black-and-white wedding photo tucked in a silver frame. "And this is one of the things I remember seeing." It lay next to a glass container with two ivory flowered and pearl crowns. A ribbon of the same color connected them. They stood out against the royal blue felt bottom of the box.

"What's that, dear?" her mother asked.

Seraphima held up the wedding picture.

"Ah, yes. Grandmother's wedding photo. She and your grandfather had such a loving marriage. It ended too soon with your grandfather's heart attack at fifty-one."

"So young." Seraphima frowned, looking at the two cheerful people in front of the huge church.

"Yes, well, medicine wasn't as advanced as it is now."

"My great-gramma's pretty," Bailey said.

"Indeed, she was. A real beauty." Etta smiled at Bailey. "You've got her eyes."

Bailey grinned and turned her gaze to the photo of her great-grandmother.

Mike appeared at the doorway with a glass of water. "Already settled in bed, I see."

"Mom wanted to rest." Seraphima set the wedding picture back on the blanket.

"Naturally," Mike said. "Pneumonia will do that to you, even when you're on the mend."

"What are those?" Bailey asked, reaching into the chest and tapping her finger on the glass container with the flowery hoops.

"Great-grandmother's and Grandfather's wedding crowns," Mike answered, eyeing them as if they were a foreign substance.

"They're beautiful, aren't they?" Seraphima gently rubbed Bailey's arm.

Bailey nodded.

Seraphima pictured herself wearing those beautiful crowns and a flowing white dress. "I'd love to have those at my wedding."

"You have to find someone to marry first, my dear." Etta chuckled, causing her to sputter a cough.

Seraphima beamed. "I have."

"You have? Why don't I know this?" Etta's stare bounced around the room, then returned to Seraphima. "Who's the lucky man?"

"Austin." Seraphima's fingers softly caressed the glass before glancing at her mother.

Etta rubbed her chin, then nodded. "Ah, yes. I remember—"

"The golfer?" Mike asked in a sharp tone, as if making a judgment on the man when she hadn't even met him.

Seraphima pushed aside any negative thoughts trying to creep into her head from her sister's usual pessimistic attitude. "Yes. I know he loves me, and marriage will follow."

"You know he does? Did he tell you?" Mike gave Seraphima one of her doubtful looks.

"Not exactly. He shows me in his actions. The way he makes me feel. I just know." Seraphima's mind filled with images of her and Austin intertwined in lovemaking.

"I'd make sure he tells you before running off to buy a wedding gown."

As if she had room to talk. Seraphima pursed her lips and stood. "Don't worry about us. You just worry about your own marriage."

Mike scowled at Seraphima before turning toward their mother. "Mom, you look really tired."

Etta sighed and rolled her eyes skyward. "I am that."

"I brought up your antibiotics and some water to wash them

down." Mike stepped over to the bed and handed Etta the medicine and cup.

"Thank you." Etta took the medications and gave the empty cup back to Mike.

"What's this, Gramma?" Bailey picked up a soft covered brown book with no title lying on Etta's bureau.

"That's my diary. Hands off."

Bailey hastily put it back on the dresser. "Sorry."

"Yes, well, it's all right. You know now what it is and not to snoop. Diaries are private things."

"Yes, Gramma." Bailey lowered her head, gazing down at her shoes.

"Didn't Grandmother have more books in here besides the one Bible?" Seraphima moved the pictures and clothes aside.

"Yes, of course. You know she was very religious. She had her three prayer bracelets, one of which was buried with her, her favorite book of prayers, a book on inspirational sayings and stories of saints, and her devotional journal."

"I only see one of the prayer bracelets and the devotional journal."

"Where are the other things?" Etta asked.

Seraphima dug around in the box. The book of prayers slid from between folded clothes. "Oh, okay. The prayer book is here."

Bailey plucked up the thickly threaded ebony bracelet and rolled it onto her wrist. "I like it." Her tulip mouth curled into a grin, and she got up and skipped out of the bedroom.

"What about the other prayer bracelet and the inspirational book?" Etta tugged on one of her scrunched-up sleeves.

Seraphima gestured with her palms up. "They're not here."

"It's amazing you remember all of that, especially the books, when I don't recall you reading any of them to us throughout our childhood, Mother," Mike said, standing by the chest with hands on hips.

Etta sat up. "What do you mean they're not there?"

"Come and see for yourself." Seraphima leaned her arm on the edge of the box.

Etta clucked her tongue, shook her head, then threw the covers back with a grand gesture as if she were attempting to crawl out of a sinkhole. She plodded over to the wooden container and peered in. "Well, when did this happen?"

"Beats me." Mike shrugged. "You're the one that keeps track of Grandmother's stuff."

"When was the last time you looked in this chest, Mom?" Seraphima asked.

Etta's eyes narrowed, staring at the items in the box. Her eyebrows lifted. "It's been years. I don't think I've looked in it since before Glory left."

"Well, there you go. That's a hell of a lot of years and plenty of chances for those things to go missing," Mike said. "And you have to admit you've never been good at organizing—"

"That's silly. The book and prayer bracelet are the only things—"

"I'm surprised there aren't mothballs in that box." Mike snorted.

"And why would anybody dig through this old chest?" Etta muttered, bending over the container for closer inspection.

Before the verbal tennis match could continue, Seraphima held up a hand. "Do you think Glory took them?"

"What would she want with them?" Mike asked.

"She loved to read," Seraphima pointed out.

"Very true. She read just about anything," Etta added.

"A religious book and a prayer bracelet when she's never prayed a day in her life." Mike crossed her arms. "She knew nothing about that stuff."

Negative Mike at it again. Seraphima grimaced.

Etta scowled at Mike. "You don't know that Glory's never prayed. We haven't seen her in ten years. Also, she loved

Grandmother very much, even though she only saw her the few times when Grandmother was able to visit."

"I can see why she pilfered five hundred bucks from Dad's stash in the bar downstairs, but a happy-clappy book, let alone a thing to wear on your wrist to randomly pray? Come on." Mike's sharp laugh stung with skepticism.

Seraphima glared at her sister and drummed her fingers on the top edge of the chest. "Can't say anything nice about Glory, can you?"

Mike waved a hand, dismissing her retort.

"Don't laugh, daughter." Etta huffed, causing her to release another cough. "Those books and bracelets were a great source of comfort for your grandmother."

"But not to you or anyone in this house. Otherwise, you would have read them and shared them with us." Mike smoothed out her shirt. "Not that I care about the religious stuff. It's the principle of it."

"I didn't get around to reading them. I had work and your father and you girls to take care of."

Mike pointed to the four books piled on the nightstand. "But you've had time to read a boatload of those ridiculous romances."

Heat crept up Seraphima's neck as she gripped the edge of the box. What was wrong with a little romance? A little romance might do Mike some good.

"They were quick reads and a good escape." Etta looked away from Mike's stare and shuffled back to the bed. She sighed heavily.

Seraphima touched her grandmother's wedding picture. She would bet a hundred dollars romance filled her grandparents' lives. It was what kept a couple together forever.

As her mother settled in the bed, Seraphima glanced at her sister. "Mike, what about the call from Penny? You didn't tell Mom."

Etta clenched the covers and sat rigid against the propped-up pillows. "What call? And who's Penny?"

Mike blew spiked bangs from her eyes. "Glory's friend from childhood."

"Ah, Penny Shaw. I remember her. She'd come over to our house all the time to play with Glory."

"Not all the time, Mother. Glory was grounded most of her preteen years before she high-tailed it out of town."

Etta gave Mike a steely stare. "Let's not discuss anything that remotely has to do with your father, okay?"

Mike looked away and rubbed the nape of her neck. "Yeah, okay. Sorry."

"So, what happened? What did Penny say?"

"Nothing newsworthy."

"That's not entirely true, Mike," Seraphima said. "You told me earlier today that Penny did tell you that she heard from Glory after she'd run away."

"Yeah, but she didn't give any information that would give us any clue where Glory is now. She doesn't know."

"That's all right. She may talk to Glory again," Etta said.

"Mother, that was seven years ago when Glory was living with Aunt Melina."

Etta cringed. "That hag didn't bother to tell me my daughter was alive until three years later, right after Glory left her home. I was going through hell. That woman has no empathy for people, especially her own family members."

Seraphima pursed her lips. "Can we get back to Glory, please?"

"Yeah, this is about Glory," Mike said.

Etta lowered her hands, her familiar gesture, motioning them to calm down. "Yes, of course. So, are you telling me Penny doesn't still have contact with Glory?"

"She said she didn't." Mike hooked her thumbs in the belt loops of her jeans.

Etta sighed and slumped against the pillows.

"But we've got Penny's number and she has ours, and if anything changes, she is supposed to call us," Seraphima piped up with a reassuring smile.

"I guess that's better than nothing." Etta closed her eyes.

Seraphima and her sister exchanged looks of acknowledgment. Their mother was done for the evening.

"Okay, Mom. We're going to let you sleep now. Call us tomorrow to let us know how you're doing." Mike headed toward the door.

"Good night, Mom." Seraphima kissed her mother's cheek, as Grandmother's romantic wedding and love life swirled in her mind, reminding her of Austin and their beautiful future together.

Chapter Nine

Seraphima hung her coat on one of the brass hooks on the wall in the salon and walked to the reception desk. Her friend, Belinda, appeared from the hallway to the tanning beds. Seraphima ran a hand over her newly highlighted hair. Golden streaks intermingled with dark chocolate ones. A smile of anticipation played on her taupe-painted lips. Sitting straight as a pin, with her chin lifted, Seraphima waited for Belinda to notice.

"Fima! Your hair looks fab!" Belinda squealed.

Seraphima smiled and stroked her hair. "Thank you. It came out pretty good. I've wanted to lighten my hair for so long." She examined a thick strand. "No more boring brown."

"It brings out your eyes." Belinda nodded, her own hair a sun-streaked sandy blond.

Seraphima continued to beam as her mind wandered to images of an appreciative Austin giving her a passionate kiss. But then an image in her childhood came to her when she was seven years old and she and Glory played with each other's hair. Glory had clipped her long hair back with two barrettes and brushed it over and over, making Seraphima drowsy with contentment.

Glory's voice filled her head. "You've got the best hair, Fima. It's so fun to style. Don't ever cut it short."

And she hadn't. She'd always kept it a couple of inches above her waist. She stopped smoothing out her hair. *Glory*. She had always given Seraphima encouragement. She'd been amazed at her sister's nurturing words and embraces, despite their dad's horrifying actions. Glory had never strayed from watching out for her.

Two heavyset women entered the shop and approached the counter. "We've got tanning appointments this morning," one of the women said, giving their names.

Seraphima checked the appointments on the computer screen. "Got it." She assigned the duo each a room, and they headed toward them.

Belinda set up new beauty products on the glass shelves next to the front desk. "Austin's going to love your hair." She gave Seraphima a thumbs-up.

"I think so too."

"When do you see him again?"

"Tonight."

"Really? He's not working?"

"He's got a few hours, and we're spending it at the movies and then back at his place." Seraphima smiled coyly.

"Girl, sounds like the perfect date." Belinda giggled.

Seraphima nodded.

"You two have gotten close pretty fast. Do you think he's the one?"

"Definitely. He makes me feel beautiful. It's heaven in his arms, and he's gorgeous."

"He's got the dark and handsome going, for sure. The tall part is a bit of a stretch." Belinda winked.

"He's tall enough for me." Austin was at least five inches

taller than her without heels on. Although wearing no heels was a rare occurrence for Seraphima. She looked down at her suede black boots with three-inch heels.

"And that's what counts." Belinda pulled out body lotions from an opened box and slid them onto the shelves.

"He's working really hard at the country club's golf shop. I think he'll get a raise. He never takes a sick day."

"Does he get to practice in their indoor range?"

"All the time. He practically lives there." Seraphima chuckled but didn't feel cheery as she thought about Austin's devotion to the country club and golf. It seemed like he fit her in whenever he wasn't needed there instead of the other way around—wanting to spend as much time with her on his free days as possible. The disappointment left her when images of their many dinners out and her snuggled next to him in bed filled her head. He gave her plenty of attention then and an enormous amount of love. Yes, she knew he really loved her, no matter what Mike thought. Maybe she'd even ask Austin tonight. After all, they'd been dating six months. A girl knew when a guy loved her even before that time.

"I've got to go to my station. Ms. Bedford is here for a shampoo and cut." Belinda wiggled her fingers at Seraphima and walked through the archway to the hairdressing area of the shop.

Seraphima waved back and settled in for the next eight hours of tanning appointments.

Seraphima trailed Austin through the door to his apartment. He flicked on the light switch that connected to the lamp on the end table next to the forest-green sofa. The living room bled into the area that Seraphima believed was supposed to be the dining room, but no table and chairs sat there. Three stools were tucked under the slab of bar that merged with the kitchen counter. A sofa, recliner and end table, along with a few firefighter and golf movie posters and a large fifty-inch, flat-screen television mounted on the walls. An impressive stereo cabinet filled with CDs stood in a corner.

Flipping on the television, Austin sat on the couch. "What do you want to watch?"

Seraphima sank into the couch, feeling a tinge of disappointment. They'd just sat through an hour-and-a-half movie. Now he wanted to watch something else. And why did he always turn on the TV anytime she came to his apartment? Why couldn't they just talk without the interruption of a droning program? She glanced at his profile, wondering if she should tell him to turn the TV off.

"What?" Austin gave her an innocent expression. "This show isn't violent."

"I know. I was just…"

Austin's head swiveled back to the television. "Just what, babe?"

Pushing away the uncomfortable subject, Seraphima twisted a strand of her hair. "You didn't say anything about my highlights."

Austin's stare moved from her face to her hair. "I liked it the way it was before. I'm not picky. But it does look pretty."

"Thank you."

"Sure."

She let out a nervous laugh. "Oh, that really wasn't what I wanted to talk to you about."

"Go ahead. I'm listening." But Austin didn't look at her.

On the TV screen, race cars sped around a track. The rumbling sounds of their motors ripped through the quietness of the room, with the commentators' ramblings sprinkled throughout.

"It's kind of hard to talk with the noise from the show."

Austin stared at her with mouth ajar, then at the television. "Oh. Sure. I can mute it." He smiled at her. "We don't really need the sound for this."

She slumped against the cushions, her small frame nearly enveloped in them. How would she ask him about loving her?

"Fima, what's the matter?" Austin scooped her out of the cushioned crevice and with his arm around her, scooted her against his side.

Just tell him how you feel. Swallowing, Seraphima said, "I love you, Austin."

"I know you do, babe." He kissed her forehead.

She frowned. It wasn't the answer she'd wanted to hear.

She kept focused on the mindless car racing. Her fingers began to tangle up as she tried to gain the courage to say the next words. "Do you love me?" They fell out of her mouth in a shaky voice. She winced. That wasn't how she'd wanted to sound.

Austin's body tensed against hers. A long, agonizing pause followed. She squeezed her eyes shut, wishing she'd said nothing. Fear of losing him crept into her chest.

"Uh, I-I don't know, Fima. We've only been together five or so months." His words sent queasiness through her stomach.

"Long enough to have sex and spend all our free time together, talking about our futures." There was no turning back now. She just had to make her case the best she could.

Austin looked at her as if she didn't know what she was saying. "We wanted to have sex, Fima. You told me so, and as far as our futures, I'm glad you brought it up."

Seraphima's eyes widened. "You are?"

"Yeah. You know I'm working hard at becoming a pro golfer. It takes a lot of time, energy, and focus."

She nodded.

"Well, obviously, I'm not there yet. My career is still being built, and I'm only twenty-three."

"What's wrong with that?"

"I'm not ready for something serious."

She blinked. "I thought we were already serious."

"We are... I mean, we have a great time together, and I love being with you, but I-I'm not ready for—"

"Marriage?" she blurted out, rubbing her polished nails.

He paused before answering, and she felt his stare as she looked down at her hands.

This time he laughed timorously. "Marriage? Isn't it too soon to be talking about that?"

"I don't think so. You know that I don't just randomly date someone with marriage being in the picture, if I love the person." Confidence spilled out of her, catching her off guard.

"Yeah, I know most girls want that."

"I always have."

"But I'm not ready for that, Fima."

"How long do you want to wait before you marry and have children?"

The color drained from Austin's face. "Children?"

Seraphima cringed from his reaction. Had they never discussed having children before? *Oh my God.* This *was* the first time. Her face warmed.

He ran a hand through his hair. "Children are the last things on my mind."

"You haven't thought about them?"

"Sure, I've thought about children—"

Hope resurrected in her heart, and she weaved her arm through his, clasping her hand in his. "I'm so glad to hear you say that. You *do* like children."

"Well, yeah, I like them."

"Would you want to have them with me... one day?"

Austin's brows came together. She could practically see the wheels turning in his head. He then nodded. "I hadn't really thought that far ahead. But I think if we're still together, that'd be all right."

Elation washed over Seraphima, and she hugged him. "I love you so much, Austin."

His arms wrapped around her. "I-I care for you a lot."

Leaning her head on Austin's beefy shoulder, Seraphima shut her eyes and smiled. She'd wait to hear him say he loved her. He would. When he was ready.

Chapter Ten

The following week, Seraphima sensed in her gut that Austin was avoiding her. He'd taken on extra hours at the country club and volunteered every chance he got at the fire station. Regret filtered through every pore in her body over their last conversation. He was running scared. She just knew it. Her big mouth might have ruined any chance for a future with him.

Seraphima switched off the computer on the reception desk and slumped in the chair. The large minute hand of the clock on the wall ticked over the twelve, signaling closing time. No one was left in the shop, except Eli. She heard him bustling about, cleaning beds. She'd not felt like tanning. The warm, lit pallets wouldn't relax her tonight.

"All clean on the tanning front," Eli said with a chuckle.

He stood there in his buttoned-up long-sleeved white shirt and navy jeans, with cleaning solution in one hand and a roll of paper towels in the other. His cornflower-blue eyes twinkled.

She marveled at how elated he looked after cleaning sweaty beds. A soft laugh escaped from her lips. "I'm glad cleaning the rooms makes you so happy." Although she'd been amused, her tone didn't reflect it. She'd already sunk back into her own miserable thoughts.

"It sure does. It's a job. Helps pay the bills while I'm going to college."

"Really? This job can cover your bills?"

"Some of them. My other part-time job at Home Depot is where I make the bulk of my money."

Seraphima gaped. "You work two jobs *and* go to college?"

"Yep. I've got goals I want to meet. Two more years of college left, and I'll have my teaching degree." He beamed, the dimple in his chin spreading out.

"You're going to be a teacher?"

"Yep."

"Wow. That's great. What grade are you going to teach?"

"I'm looking at middle school—seventh or eighth grade."

Grimacing, Seraphima rose from her chair. "Those are the worst years of school. Are you into torturing yourself?"

A flaxen strand of hair dangled on Eli's forehead like an inverted fishhook. He didn't use enough gel to keep it in place. "It's a challenge, but I like challenges." His hand with the spray bottle thumped against his chest. "It gives a person character."

She chortled. "I think a lot of character is needed to teach thirteen-year-olds."

"Yep." He nodded and set the cleaning supplies in the cabinet adjacent to the front desk. Eli grabbed his jacket from one of the hooks on the wall.

Sliding her arms in her coat sleeves, Seraphima glanced at the moonless sky through the front windows—another wasted night without Austin's arms around her.

"Fima, are you okay?" Eli's voice interrupted her painful ponderings.

He leaned his hand on the front door's handle with his puffy jacket encompassing him like a padded football uniform. His spindly, jean-clad legs were slightly bent as if he were getting ready to run the fifty-yard dash.

"I'm fine." Not really. She missed Austin. But what made it worse than that was the helplessness she felt. She had no control over Austin's schedule, or really Austin himself. Twisting a strand of her hair tighter and tighter, she winced as it pulled at her scalp.

Eli's brows came together. "You don't look it."

Seraphima stopped twirling her tresses, and warmth crept into her cheeks. She'd forgotten how easily her emotions were broadcasted to people.

She looked away from Eli's stare to the dimly lit parking lot. Only hers and Eli's cars sat in the paved spaces. Belinda left an hour ago for her parents' house. She needed to go home. But why did the image of her empty apartment make her stomach clench? *Loneliness.* That was it. It would be another evening of that apartment's heavy silence knocking against her chest.

"Do you want to talk? I don't have class tonight." Eli shoved his hands in his coat pockets.

Seraphima glanced at Eli again. His friendly demeanor comforted her. Conversing with him would fill the hollow hours before bedtime. "Okay."

"Great. How about going to Benny's Books? It's got books and coffee. The java kiosk's situated right between the philosophy and poetry shelves."

She pulled on her fuzzy gloves. "I love bookstores." She placed a red knit hat on her head. "Let's go."

"I have a younger sister," Eli said. "She's a pain a lot of the time, but what sibling isn't?" He sat across from Seraphima, holding a cup of steaming coffee.

Seraphima laughed. "So true. I've got two of them, both older."

"And they're bossy, right?" He grinned.

"Especially the oldest."

"Yeah, but we older siblings mean well."

"Sure you do." She snickered.

"Your second sister must be the dreaded middle child, huh?" He winked.

Glory's teenaged face materialized in Seraphima's mind. Glory, the awkward middle child. Somehow she never quite fit in. Their mother's love spread gingerly among them, but their father had shown little interest and made next to no time for her and her sisters. She believed her father secretly wanted sons and didn't know what to do with daughters.

"Okay, so your sister wasn't a dreaded middle child. Just the middle child," Eli said in a slow, careful voice.

Seraphima looked up at Eli watching her intently, his eyes gentle with concern.

"Right. She's the middle sister." Seraphima concentrated on her coffee mug.

A long silence fell between them, and Seraphima sensed Eli gauging what to say or do next.

"Are you planning to go to college?"

Seraphima shook her head. "No. I'm just working for the time being."

"Sure. It pays the bills while you decide what you want to do."

She gave him a confident smile. "I already know what I want to do."

Eli nodded. "Great. What would that be?"

"My future plans are marriage and children. I want to be a wife and mother."

He leaned back against his chair, his mouth ajar. "That's different from what I'd thought you'd say."

"Oh? What did you think I'd say?"

"I don't know. A doctor, maybe. Lawyer, perhaps. Engineer, possibly."

Seraphima giggled. "Gosh, no. I've no desire to be any of those. Besides, I'm awful at math."

An amused smile played on his lips. "Ah, that could be a real problem then."

"Yes." Seraphima took a sip of her coffee. "I've planned to be married by age twenty-three since I was thirteen."

He bent forward, folding his arms on the table. "How much time do you have?"

She gave him a faint smile. "Four years."

"Well, it's good to have goals. Do you have any prospects?"

"As a matter of fact, I do."

Eli straightened in his seat. "Uh, that does help move the plans along, doesn't it?"

Seraphima noticed the change in Eli's demeanor. He'd never expressed his feelings for her, but the disappointment in his eyes revealed his fondness, and she felt a stab of pity, replying in a shaky whisper, "Yes."

She reminded herself he brought her to the bookstore as a friend and coworker to talk and hang out. Nothing else. "Anyway, my prospects. One in particular. Austin."

Eli ran the tip of his index finger over the rim of his coffee mug. His eyes traveled from the cup to her. "Austin?"

"He's my boyfriend. We've been dating for six months. He's wonderful. He'll make a fantastic husband and father."

Tapping the cup's handle, Eli asked, "What's he do?"

"He works at the country club in its golf shop year-round, and seven months out of the year as a caddy on the golf course. He also volunteers at the local fire station."

"Busy guy."

"Yes." She frowned as her earlier thoughts resurfaced. Austin was avoiding her. She pushed the thoughts aside and focused on the man in front of her. "Just like you."

"True. I've got a pretty packed schedule."

She nodded.

"But I bet Austin makes special time for you. Who wouldn't?" Eli's face split into an earnest smile.

Averting his kind gaze, Seraphima stared at her red nails and bare fingers. Not even a promise ring to boast about. "He does see me when he's not working."

"Of course."

Quietness punctured the air between them for the next few minutes.

Eli's gaze traveled to the many bookshelves around them. "So, what types of books do you like to read?"

Relieved that he'd changed the subject, Seraphima relaxed her tense shoulders. "I like romance novels—love stories with happy endings." Why did she tell him these things—things she usually kept to herself? She really didn't know him that well. But he was so easy to talk to, so nice. Glancing at his profile as he stared at the binds of the books in the poetry section, she felt there was something about him that told her she could trust him, tell him just about anything.

"I agree happy endings are a plus." His gaze returned to her. "I like a good sci-fi story. But personally, I prefer nonfiction. I like reading biographies of historical figures, like our presidents, or people who've made great discoveries in history like Nikolai Tesla."

Not one who'd paid attention in history class, Seraphima recognized the name but didn't know exactly what the man had done. But she didn't really care enough to want to ask, so she just nodded. She checked her watch. It was already nine. "I'd better get home."

"Got other plans tonight?" He smacked his forehead with his

hand. "Of course you do. I understand. You and Austin have a date. So sorry for not catching a clue."

Grimacing, Seraphima shook her head. "No, not tonight. He's at the fire station."

"Good guy, helping others." Eli slid out of his chair and downed the last of his warm java.

Seraphima sighed quietly to herself. *Helping everyone but me.* Seraphima followed Eli toward the entrance of the store.

Eli pulled his car into the salon's parking lot next to Seraphima's. They sat in silence for a moment.

"Drive safely," he said, giving her a tight smile, as if he were in pain.

She knew deep down his behavior had something to do with her commitment to Austin, but that couldn't be helped. "Thanks for the coffee and talk. It was nice." Seraphima turned to open her door.

"Hold on. I'm a dolt." He exited the vehicle, jogged around it, and quickly opened her door.

"Thanks again." She dug in her purse for her keys.

"Sure."

She climbed into her car, started it up, and drove out of the lot, with Austin on her mind.

Chapter Eleven

"She shone like a well-polished diamond on that stage, Michaela," Etta cooed. She cupped Bailey's beaming face in her hands and rubbed noses with her granddaughter.

"You don't have to tell me. I was there. Remember?" Michaela hung up her coat in the hall closet while Doug helped Bailey out of hers.

Doug had made it to this recital—the only one since their daughter had started dance class two years ago. The first performance had been when Bailey was three. She'd been so tiny in her shiny blue dress, white stockings, black patent leather shoes, and a bow in her feather-fine, blond hair. She had gotten over her stage fright each time she'd kiss her green, lumpy frog, Frank, a stuffed toy she carried with her for good luck.

As if listening to Michaela's thoughts, Bailey lifted her dress and pulled out the plush amphibian from the elastic of her stockings around her waist. "Thanks, Frank." She grinned and mashed him against her cheek.

"You were a great support, Frank." Doug patted the plush animal.

Bailey giggled.

"Who wants cupcakes?" Etta asked, moving toward the kitchen.

"I do!" Bailey trotted after Etta, leaving Doug and Michaela alone in the foyer next to the unlit living room.

Michaela snapped on the lamp on the end table as Doug approached the bookcase and gazed at the photo of Bailey and him fishing. A smile split his face, and he tapped his finger on the glass covering the picture. "My favorite picture of us."

Michaela nodded.

"Could I take this home with me?"

Glancing at the photograph, Michaela hugged herself. "You could, but Bailey likes to look at it right there. You want her to have that memory of you here, don't you?"

Although she was happy that Doug was present for Bailey's recital, the incident with the half-drunk bottle of wine needled at the back of her mind.

Doug's eyes flicked from Michaela to the picture. "Yeah. You're right. She needs it here."

"Good. I'm glad you're putting Bailey's needs before your own."

Doug's face colored. "Of course her needs come before mine. Why wouldn't they?"

Michaela shrugged, smacking the couch cushion to plump it up. "You tend to choose alcohol over her and me. Which explains where we are today."

"Mike, you're not being fair. I told you I'm working on my drinking. Isn't that enough that I'm trying?"

"It would be if you actually showed proof of that."

Doug straightened his back and lifted his chin. "I've been doing that for the past month. Apparently, you haven't noticed."

"Oh, I've noticed." Michaela swatted the chair's cushion. "I noticed on Valentine's Day you guzzled my merlot when I was upstairs."

Doug opened his mouth to protest but then shut it and looked down, his jaw tight and forehead creased.

"Can't deny that, can you?"

"But that's all I drank that night." His hands settled on his khaki-clad hips. "Give me some freaking credit for having the control and sense to stop."

Michaela stared warily at Doug. He could be so pathetic.

"That's effort. That's progress, isn't it?"

"Progress is not drinking at all."

"Come on, Mike. You left an open bottle of wine on the counter, knowing I have a problem."

Stiffening, Michaela folded her arms across her chest. "So your problem with drinking is my fault. Is that what you're telling me?"

Doug ran a hand through his dirty-blond hair. "No, it's not your fault, but leaving an open bottle of wine sitting out isn't much help to me."

"Of course. I'll stop drinking my wine because of your problem. Because you don't have self-control."

"Yeah. Right now it's a damn struggle."

"Well, then, your moving out was for the best. No temptations."

"We just talked about one seconds ago."

"From now on, you won't have to worry. I won't leave any bottles of alcohol out when you come to visit twice a month."

Doug's mouth fell open. "Twice a month?"

"Yes. I can't trust you not to be tempted because I happen to have a glass or two of wine with my dinner."

"Yeah, you do have your wine. Seems you may have a problem too."

"I didn't say I drank wine every night."

"Mike, I've only been out of the house a couple of months."

"So?"

"So, you had a glass of wine glued to your hand just about every night of the week. I doubt that's changed."

Heat climbed up Michaela's neck. "You're full of it."

"Okay. Maybe not every night, but it sure seems like it."

"'Seems like' isn't reality."

"How about your smoking?" Doug raised his brows and gestured as if holding a cigarette and puffing on it. "That's reality."

"Mama, Daddy, please stop fighting." Bailey appeared at the arched opening to the living room, surprising them into silence. "I think you need cupcakes. They'll make you happy." She walked over and gave each of them a chocolate one.

Doug gently smoothed back Bailey's hair from her soft cheeks and forehead. "Thank you, angel."

"Yes. Thank you, baby." Michaela folded down the crinkled paper around the dessert and took a bite.

Etta clicked over in her one-inch heels, her eyes narrowed in that familiar mother's look of disapproval Michaela received too often. "It's nearly nine o'clock. Anybody going to drive me home?"

"All right, Mom." Michaela shoved more cake into her mouth and strode to the closet.

"I can take her home," Doug said, crumpling up the empty wrapper from the dessert.

Michaela glanced back at Doug as he wiped crumbs off his face. "Are you sure? Mom's house is thirty minutes in the opposite direction from your place."

"It's fine," Doug answered curtly and put on his coat.

"Mom?"

"That's okay with me." Etta took her long coat from Michaela's hands.

Bailey hugged Etta tightly around her thin waist. "Goodbye, Gramma."

"Goodbye, darling." Etta kissed Bailey's cheek. "I'll see you soon."

Bailey embraced Doug, then trotted upstairs.

Doug and her mother left a minute later.

Michaela crossed the den to the desk where a package of cigarettes lay. She shoved it into her slacks pocket just as Doug's words about her smoking came back to her. She scowled. Lecturing her when he had a real addiction. She shook the thought from her head.

Her heart softened when she leaned over to turn off the lamp and her gaze fell on Doug and Bailey sitting on the pier with their fishing poles. Would there be any more of those special moments for Bailey with her father, or was that all in the past?

She switched off the lamp, and the room descended into blackness. Michaela walked toward the staircase and looked up to see the sliver of light escaping from the crack in Bailey's bedroom door. Clutching the pack of cigarettes in her pocket, she climbed the steps with a weary sigh and a strong desire for a smoke.

Chapter Twelve

G loria sat on the bottom branch of a towering cottonwood among many blue spruces, Ponderosa pines, and not far from bleached quaking aspens.

"Glory Lofton," called Serena, Gloria's friend and coworker. She stood on a grassy incline several feet below Gloria. "I can always find you hanging out with the trees."

"Of course. You know me so well." She swung her legs back and forth as the tree's arm trembled beneath her. She inhaled deeply and took in as much of the sweet earthy aroma as she could.

Her friend trekked up the tree-splotched hill and ended up in front of Gloria's dangling shoes. Shaking her head with a spirited smile, Serena said, "I don't know anybody over the age of ten who still climbs trees."

"Sure you do. Me." Gloria winked then shimmied off the branch and down the trunk.

When her feet hit the ground, Gloria hugged the tree and gave it a chaste kiss. "Thanks, Henry."

"Henry?"

"Yes, Henry. He's always got a branch out and a hollow

groove to listen to my deepest worries and biggest dreams." She gave the rotund trunk an appreciative pat.

Serena grinned and leaned against the cottonwood. "What advice does he give you?"

"He doesn't speak so much as listen. That's the natural inclination of trees, you know."

"I kind of figured they weren't the chitchatting types."

"Very good, Serena. Maybe someday you'll press an ear to one and discover their attentiveness." Gloria walked down the grassy-patched slope with her eyes on the crown of the orange sun peeking over the silhouetted majestic peaks in the distance. She stopped. "I could stare at that sunset forever."

The mountains and sun joined in a short encounter before the sky bid farewell to the sun and welcomed the rising white moon.

Images of the local library with its room of computers came to Gloria's mind. Maybe she could have better luck this time in finding the information she had been wanting to know for the past five years.

As they reached the level ground, Serena said, "Lou and Coop are meeting us at Pam's Diner at six. You remember, right?"

She'd find something else on those computers this time. It had taken her the past four years of constantly telling herself her father's anger and actions toward her hadn't been her fault before the words had finally sunk in and stuck. She could now move forward in her search.

Serena's frustrated sigh interrupted Gloria's thoughts.

"Sorry?"

"You weren't listening." Serena folded her arms. "Henry listens better than you do."

Gloria chuckled and faced the foothills from which they'd just come. "You're right. He does." She turned toward Serena. "No, really. I heard you say something about Lou and Coop."

"It's the something you didn't listen to. The crux of what I'd said."

"Okay. I admit I missed that." Gloria swept hair from the side of her face and lifted her chin. "You can tell me now. My antenna is up and crackling."

Serena laughed. "You're such a weirdo."

Gloria hooked her arm through Serena's. "That's why you love me."

Serena glanced at Gloria, giving her a mischievous grin. "So does Coop."

Gloria stopped at the intersection of grass and asphalt road. "What? We barely know each other."

Serena halted next to her. "You haven't noticed Coop's been tagging along with Lou every time he meets up with us?"

"No." Gloria arched a brow. "That would be around three times in the past… oh, what has it been? Two months?"

"Yeah."

"And that means he loves me?" Gloria shoved her hands in her jeans pockets. "A bit premature, don't you think?"

"No." Serena shook her head. "Lou and Coop are best buds, and Lou told me he thinks Coop really likes you."

"*Likes*, Serena. That's a world of difference from *loves*."

"That's just how Lou talks. He says he likes me too, but I can tell it's more than that." Serena ran a hand over her long, burgundy-highlighted brown hair.

"You can tell." Gloria chuckled. "I guess that only matters if you 'like' him too."

Serena giggled.

Gloria glanced at her Velcro-strapped watch. "I can only stay for about an hour."

"Why?"

They reached the sidewalk.

"I've got work to do at the library."

"Going to try again to look for your old friend, huh?" Serena's brown eyes glistened with sympathy.

"Yeah."

"I don't know why you won't just get a cell phone. Then you can google her anytime you want."

"It's not in my budget. And you know I don't want one of those. I've seen how attached people are to them. They miss out on the beauty around them, closes them off from nature, and that's too valuable, too precious to lose." Gloria's heart tightened as the cool evening air brushed her face like the comforting touch of a benevolent hand that briefly took away the emptiness inside her.

She felt a squeeze of her arm. "I know, Glory." A warm smile lit up Serena's honey-hued face.

Serena *did* know. When Gloria had stepped into Summitville six years ago, searching for work, she'd met Serena at the park, watching over her younger siblings. She had been the conduit between her and their employer at Cascade Cleaning Service, and she'd worked there ever since. Serena was the first and only person Gloria had confided in about her dysfunctional and disturbing family life, and only Serena knew about the horrors and pain Gloria had expressed. Serena proved herself to be a true friend with the job connection and staying quiet about Gloria's past.

The old-fashioned streetlamps with their ivory globes flickered on as they walked down the sparsely populated street of quaint shops on either side. The settled snow, like sprinkled sugar over the mountaintops, glistened in pale coral from the sun as its last gasp of rose light tickled the rocky tips. The ebony blanket of the night pressed against the last glimmers. Gloria looked away. Evening was her least favorite time of the day. She preferred to be in the brightness of the cheerful sun. It comforted her in its warmth and lifted her spirits. Living in Colorado with over three hundred days a year of sunshine proved to be the best place for her. She'd been lucky to be born there.

They reached the glass and chrome-lined doors to Pam's Diner and entered the stuffy restaurant playing fifties music on a flashing, colorful jukebox.

Lou and Cooper leaned against the jukebox—stocky, raven-haired Lou dressed in olive-green cargo pants and a college sweatshirt, and his friend, Cooper, with spiky brown hair, a swimmer's build, wearing jeans and a black, long-sleeved T-shirt with the jagged letters of the rock band Metallica sprawled across it.

"Hey, Serena, Glory," Lou said.

"Guys, Glory can't stay long 'cause she needs to go to the library in an hour," Serena said.

Cooper shrugged one shoulder as Lou said, "That's cool. We'll eat, then jet to the library."

Why? She preferred to do her research alone. She leaned near Serena's ear. "Did you talk them into this?"

Serena laughed. "No. Now your imagination is running wild."

She poked her in the side. "That's your doing."

They found a table and ordered.

It took thirty minutes for their food to arrive, but it didn't matter. Gloria wasn't hungry. She'd only ordered a garden salad and glass of water with a wedge of lemon swimming between the ice cubes.

While she half listened to her friends talking about going to the movies after eating, Gloria took mental notes of what places to search for Penny. She hadn't any spare money for one of those websites that located people, so she'd concentrate on the white pages and social media, even though she hated the latter. Those sites were just another distraction, sucking a person into a fake, chaotic world, away from the quietness of real-life forests, the exhilaration of sitting on a boulder up nine thousand feet at Topaz Lake, embraced by the Rocky Mountains.

She hadn't looked at those sites the last time she'd surfed the internet for fear of having the urge to search for her mother and sisters and finding them. Were her sisters married? Did they still live in Parker? These questions primed the curiosity pump. But she knew if they had Facebook pages and she'd looked, there would be pictures of her father somewhere amid them. Then regret would shake her, wishing she hadn't been so curious.

Gloria had a good hunch her mother and sisters would be angry with her if she ever returned, having left years ago without contacting them. She had to be dead to them. The chance to make amends had passed, all due to her father. He'd torn her family apart. She'd lost her mother and sisters ten years ago as well as Penny, the only true friend she'd had in her childhood—the only connection to her mother and siblings.

She tried to focus on her salad by chomping on a cucumber.

"What do you think, Glory?" Serena asked.

Startled by "Runaway" playing on the jukebox, Gloria shook her head and muttered, "I'm sorry. What?"

"She's been coasting in the world of daydream," Lou said, with a snort.

"Glory, we're going to the eight-o'clock show. It's a good couple of hours before it plays. Want to come?" Serena asked.

Cooper stared at Gloria as if she were a specimen under a microscope. Why wouldn't he look somewhere else? The whisker stubbles on his jaw and round chin made him look older. How old was he anyway? Had Serena ever told her? She shifted in her seat.

"—think she likes adventure movies," she heard Lou say.

"We can see that new romantic comedy instead," Serena answered.

"I don't do chick flicks, Serena." Lou slouched against the bench seat in their booth. "You know that."

"Coop, what do you want to see?" Serena set her elbow on the table and rested her chin on her hand.

He shrugged. "Don't know."

"To be honest, I'm not really in the mood for a movie tonight. Sorry." Gloria glanced out the window. The moon shone down on the mountain's white, rugged tips and the lamplit street outside where people strolled by in no particular hurry to get to their destinations.

Those mountains would turn pink in the dawn, and they'd call to her, entice her to come tread upon their rocky soil and talk to their family of trees and gaze at their awakening wildlife tenants.

Serena frowned. "Oh."

Lou turned his attention toward Gloria. "Okay. We've got a couple of hours until the movie, so we'll hang with you at the library for a while." Lou used his thumb to wipe a drop of ketchup from the corner of his mouth.

She let out a silent sigh. She'd foolishly thought the movie would have distracted them from her library trip. What could she say to change their minds? "That's fine, but I'll be lousy company, just staring at a computer screen."

"It's okay. We don't mind. Maybe we'll be able to help you. After all, we've had more practice on a computer than you have," Serena said.

"Why don't we just use our phones to look up stuff you want to know about?" Lou asked. "It would be easier." He set his phone on the table and tapped its screen.

Ugh. Those stupid cell phones were surgically attached to just about everyone she passed on the streets in town. Gloria swallowed back the bitterness in her throat. "No, thanks. I'll sit at a desk and use a pen and paper the old-fashioned way."

"But you can save your info in my phone's notes," Lou insisted.

Gloria watched Lou twirl his phone in a tight circle on the

table. His toy. His buddy. But she raised her brows in admittance that he'd at least engaged in a conversation with them. Maybe he would be paying attention this time when she answered him. "I'd still rather do this in the quietness of the library."

"Okay, so—"

"Chill, Lou," Cooper said.

Everyone looked at Cooper. He'd been quiet since they'd arrived at the restaurant. Come to think of it, he'd been nearly mute the past three times they'd gotten together. Perhaps this was why she had vague memories of the bizarre guy.

Lou blew out a breath and looked at Gloria. "You win, O resister of technological advancements."

Serena scowled at Gloria as if she'd offended Lou.

"Tell you what. You can search to your heart's content on your phone in the library while I check on the computer's large screen." But it wouldn't be the people she was searching for. Her family was a private matter. Serena was the only exception.

"Deal." Lou waved his smartphone.

———

Gloria took a seat at the second computer in the empty room, its small space smelling of electrical cords and metal.

Lou and Serena lounged together on a red love seat outside the room, staring at their mobiles. Gloria had convinced them she could find what she needed without using their phones.

Thankful for the couple of computer classes she took in high school, Gloria could navigate through the search engine and social media sites well enough. Although she had an aversion to techno crap, she understood their usefulness and did use them on rare occasions.

She punched the name Penny Shaw in the search box, and several results filled the screen. More than one link stemmed from Facebook. Gloria clicked on the first one, and the site opened to show four people listed with the name. All had profile pictures, but only two of them were of actual people. Giving her curiosity a go, she tapped on the second profile with the picture of a dark-haired woman who looked to be around her age. When the page came up, it had her location as Aurora, Colorado. Both Gloria and Penny's families had lived in the same neighborhood in Parker, a town south of Aurora. But Gloria remembered that the last time she'd called Penny, the number was no longer in service, so it could be that Penny's family had moved to Aurora then.

The woman's square face, blunt cheekbones, and vivid gray eyes staring back at her convinced Gloria she'd found a match. She blew out a breath of satisfaction, then smiled at the screen. She scanned the information about Penny, finding no phone number. No surprise. Who'd put her phone number on the internet for all to see? Then again, why would anyone put her name and location out in the cyber universe? She sure wouldn't and knew that as well as she knew the native trees in the state.

Gloria studied Penny's face on the screen. Now that she had the city in which Penny resided, she hoped she'd find her phone number through the online white pages. Clicking a new tab in the window of the program, a fresh search page appeared, and she typed in Penny's name, city, and state. A list of Penny Shaws popped up as well as the age and state. Gloria selected the one that showed age twenty-three and living in Aurora, Colorado. The information spread across the displayed boxes with no phone numbers present. She leaned her elbow on the table, rested her chin in her hand, and drummed her fingers on the desk.

"Any luck?"

Startled, Gloria looked up at Serena. "Yes and no."

Lou held up his phone. "I'm still open."

"No, thanks," Gloria said flatly.

"What did you find?" Serena asked.

Gloria pointed at the screen. "I've got the right Penny but no phone number."

Serena craned her head toward the screen and squinted. "Okay, but you've got a full address."

A full address. Gloria looked back at the monitor, and Penny's full location stared back at her. "So I do..."

"So, why can't you just go to her house?"

Gloria rubbed her temple that had started to throb. "Several reasons. First, we haven't seen each other in a decade. I have no idea how she'll react to seeing me—"

"She'll be so happy." Serena smiled.

"Or she'll slam the door in my face. Some friend I've been. Not talking to her for the past seven years."

"Aww, I don't—"

"And how do you suggest I get to her house?"

"Well…"

"I'm not walking eighty some miles only to have her slam the door in my face, or worse yet, she's not even home. And I'm not spending a hefty chunk of bus fare to get there."

Serena slapped the back of her hand against Lou's chest. He let out a broken cough. "Lou's got a car. Remember?"

Gloria glanced at Lou as he rubbed his chest. "Oh, right."

"Yeah, I do, but it's my mom's, and I only have access to it for school and—"

"Don't worry about it. I'm not going to Penny's house." Even as Gloria said this, she'd grabbed a pen and piece of paper on the desk and jotted down Penny's information.

"Don't you want to—?" Serena snapped her mouth shut and put a hand over it.

Gloria eyed her, then exhaled. Serena knew to keep mum about Gloria's family troubles. "Yes, I do, but I need to think on it."

"That makes sense."

"It does?" Lou scrunched his face in confusion.

Serena put a finger to her puckered lips.

"So, you're done?" Lou looked around the empty room.

"Not quite. Wait for me outside where you were sitting?" Gloria glanced through the window. Cooper sat on the maroon couch reading a *National Geographic* magazine. He didn't seem fazed by his friends leaving him there or the long wait on her in the computer room. She shrugged and turned her attention back to Serena and Lou.

Lou opened his mouth to reply, only to have Serena take his hand. "See you in a few," she said and pulled Lou out the door.

Gloria retraced Penny's address with her pen. Something nagged her to open Facebook again and search for her sisters.

"Why? They've got to hate me for leaving," she said out loud.

But the urge to take a peek at their profiles only grew. Gloria gritted her teeth, smacked the pen down, settled her hand on the mouse, and clicked to the open Facebook tab. She typed in Mike's name. It brought up three matches with one that had two last names—Michaela Barstone-Morrow. The thumbnail profile picture showed a woman with very short, sandy-brown hair, a sharply defined square jaw, and intelligent hazel eyes hugging a young girl with blond hair, both of them grinning for the camera.

Despite the lack of hair and a span of ten years, Gloria knew the woman was her oldest sister through her eyes and expression. She remembered it well, when they'd played Monopoly together and she'd nearly always get the expensive blue properties and their hotels. But she also remembered Mike's bossy nature and how she'd lecture her about not doing her homework and causing undue stress to their mother and father. A flicker of resentment sparked in Gloria. Mike had already thought Gloria was a troublemaker before she had run away. Mike had even questioned her being grounded just before she had run out of the house. Her older sister would be little help to her.

With furrowed brows, Gloria tapped the search box again and typed in Fima's name. Seraphima Barstone immediately appeared, and an image of a young woman with long, chocolate-brown hair, tanned skin, and shiny, doe-brown eyes sat in the lap of a dishwater blond-haired, muscular man on a boulder, smiling contently. The familiar soft eyes, long lashes, same long hair, and sweet curve of the woman's mouth told Gloria she'd found her little sister—a sister who'd been spoiled as the youngest but sensitive with low self-esteem. Between sisterly squabbles, Fima had admired her and appreciated her encouraging talks.

Both her sisters' faces brought a dull pain to her chest. She'd left them and their father's abuse. A sudden spark of joy hit her when she saw that they were doing all right. But sorrow and fear soon overtook the joy as the haunting memories of the terror of their father lashing out at her blotted out everything else.

Gloria swallowed and blinked back tears. How could this pain still affect her so strongly? Her head fell into her hands. With eyes closed, she willed herself to erase those past images that played in her mind like a TV show rerun.

Raking her hands through her hair, Gloria forced herself to look at her younger sister again. Her hand settled on the mouse once more, and holding her breath, she clicked on Fima's profile. Fima's last post was two hours ago—something about never giving up on love. Gloria's heart tightened. She hadn't been there through Fima's dating experiences to give her support and guidance. A snort escaped from her lips. What dating advice could she possibly give? With the exception of a handful of dinner dates with one guy in high school, her love life was nonexistent. She'd never had a great desire to pursue it.

Gloria tapped the About tab on the page, and it displayed Fima's name, city, state, with whom she was in a relationship, a favorite quote about true love never ends, and a cell phone number. A cell number! Exhilaration shot through Gloria but drained quickly from her as the incessant pain of the past swallowed it up. At the same time, the big sister in her wanted to reprimand Fima for revealing too much of herself on social media, with her head in the stars.

Gloria slumped in her chair, the information on the screen glowing at her. What should she do? It had been so many years of no contact. Would Fima be pleased or upset if she called? Would she hang up on her? Would her sister help her learn what was going on with their father? Although Gloria was grown up, fear of her father had never lessened. That wild, vicious glint that often shone in his hard, gray eyes punctured her memories like a hot, pulsating branding iron.

Fima was a better possibility than Mike. Penny was Gloria's first choice since she'd helped Gloria in the past. Picking up the pen, she wrote down Fima's cell number. She then closed all the windows on the computer, folded up the sheet of paper, shoved it in her jeans pocket, and headed for the door.

She peeked around the corner. Her friends still sat on the couch, absorbed in Lou's phone, and Cooper in his magazine.

"Um… I'm headed back home. I'll catch you guys later." Before they could respond, she slid past the lounge area and hurried toward the library's entrance.

Chapter Thirteen

Grimacing, Gloria held Serena's cell phone while butterflies flitted around in her belly. She and Serena sat between the chunky roots of the cottonwood.

"Go on. Call her," Serena said.

Sometimes her friend pushed too much. With the thoughts of her sisters keeping her awake last night and dominating her thoughts through a granola breakfast, a decision finally came to her. Why was she even going this route first? She set the phone in Serena's lap.

"What'd you do that for?"

"I'm not calling her. It's insane to even think of doing that."

"Why?"

"Because I was a terrible sister. I'd been the one who gave her encouragement, listened to her when she needed to talk, and always tried to bring her out of her own self-doubts."

"That's a good thing."

Gloria turned toward her friend. "Yeah, it was, until I abandoned her."

Serena's face puckered. "But your sisters know you didn't leave because of them."

"I'm sure that was easily forgotten when I didn't come back home the next day, next week, next year. If I were Fima, I'd hate me and want nothing to do with me. I didn't even leave her a letter. Nothing."

"But you said you couldn't leave them letters because they'd tell your mom, and then your dad would find out."

Gloria waved a hand. "Maybe I was wrong to have said it."

"Glory, you were thirteen years old. You couldn't have known how to deal with it all then."

Gloria sighed. "Okay, you're probably right about that."

"Yeah."

"But I still don't want to call her."

"Then what are you going to do?"

Gloria shifted on the ground, knowing her friend would be surprised at her answer, considering how she'd talked last night about not wanting to drive to Penny's house.

"Well?" Serena said, wrapping her arms around her knees.

"I'm going to go see Penny."

"Good."

Gloria shrugged and patted a thick root hugging her side. "But I'm not sure I have enough money scraped up for the bus ticket."

"We'll find a way to collect the bus money or borrow a car."

Gloria glanced at Serena. "Borrow a car?"

"Yeah. You know? Like Lou's or my mom's."

"I don't want you and Lou to go out of your way for me. The bus should be fine."

"Quit being so stubborn, Glory." Serena poked Gloria's arm and grinned. "Whatever we figure out, you'll get to Penny's house."

Gloria managed a smile. "Thank you."

She picked up a book leaning against one of Henry's roots and set it on her lap.

"Are you reading that book again?" Serena asked with a faint laugh.

"I'm always reading it. Stories with happy endings never get old." Gloria gently swept her hand over the beige and dusty pink book cover. "Even though I'm too much of a realist to believe happy endings are the norm in life, sometimes I like a good escape."

"You can be happy too, Glory." Serena unfolded her arms and put one around Gloria's shoulders.

Gloria gazed through Henry's many arms. "I don't know."

"You deserve happiness just like anyone."

"I suppose anything's possible."

Serena leaned against the trunk.

Gloria did the same and stared up at the purple-pink firmament with the rugged tipped silhouette of the Rocky Mountains reaching toward it. "You're close to your family, aren't you?"

"Yeah. My parents, brothers, and sisters mean a lot to me. But I am closest to my *abuela*."

"I only saw my grandmother a few times when I was a child." Gloria held the book with care. "This book belonged to her."

Serena smiled. "That makes it extraspecial."

Gloria nodded. "My mom said my grandmother was very religious. She had a bunch of religious things in her keepsake box. The times she'd visit us and I sat on her lap, she'd held this book and read to me all the amazing stories in it. I took it before I left the house." She thumbed through the pages.

She then touched a black-knotted bracelet encircling her wrist. "And this. Mom never mentioned anything about Grandmother's book, or the weaved rope she wore on her wrist. I thought it was a unique bracelet, but Grandmother had told me when she last visited it was actually used for saying certain prayers. I never learned what they were, but Grandmother would close her eyes, touch each knot in the rope bracelet, and move her lips. She seemed to be in some kind of trance. Dad didn't like her influence on Mom and us. He'd said her hocus-pocus practices were corrupting our minds. We never saw her after that. She died two months before I left."

Serena frowned. "That's awful. Your grandmother sounded so sweet, and that rope sounds like a rosary that my *abuela* uses to pray with." Her full lips tightened. "Some people are so cruel."

Gloria brushed the book's cover, then looked at Serena. "So your grandmother is still alive?"

The tight line curved into a smile on Serena's blemish-free, brown face. "Yep, and she lives close to my parents' house about ten minutes away."

"It's got to be great living close by and getting to see them whenever you want."

Serena nodded. "Yeah, it is."

"That must feel so good." Gloria leaned her elbow on her bent knee and gazed through Henry's branches again, to the indigo sky. Things would have been so different had her family been like Serena's. But it never would be, and it was silly to even ponder it. She didn't live in fantasy, but reality. And cleaning vacation cabins, hiking the mountain trails, and meeting up with Serena were her reality. It could be worse, and she knew it. She was lucky to be where she was even if her heart still ached for the maternal embrace of her mother and the fun and squabbles with her sisters.

Serena patted Gloria's arm and gave her a sympathetic smile. "It does feel good." She then poked Gloria's side. "Now, why'd you dump us last night at the library?"

Gloria sat up. "I'm sorry. Didn't think you'd mind. You guys were going to the movies after all, and I'd already told you I wasn't up to going."

"Coop was crushed."

"What?" Gloria wrinkled her nose. "You're lying."

Serena shook her head. "I could tell when we found out you had left the building, he looked totally disappointed."

A rustling sound in the grass a few feet away startled Gloria. She clutched Serena's arm as they stood and looked in the direction of the noise. Two familiar male figures, one in jeans and a bulky sports coat and the other in cargo pants and a sweatshirt, appeared against the rising three-quarter moon.

"Hey, Lou. Coop," Gloria said.

"Just get off work?" Serena asked.

"Yeah," said Lou. "Thought we'd find you two here." He strolled over to them with his hands in his pockets.

Cooper trailed behind him with his eyes on Gloria.

She looked away and cleared her throat. "Just hanging out with Henry."

"Henry?" Cooper said, arching a dark brow.

Gloria's stare flicked to Cooper. He'd spoken again. Wow. She smiled in amusement and inhaled the cool, arid night air.

"Yeah. Who's Henry?" Lou asked.

Gloria gave the men a mischievous grin. "He's tall and sometimes shady."

The men exchanged worried glances.

"But no worries," Gloria said, putting up a palm. "He's all bark and no bite."

Serena giggled as the men shifted themselves.

"Are you sure you should be hanging out with this dude?" Lou asked.

Cooper bowed his head in agreement.

"Oh, yeah. He's a true friend. One that'll never leave us." Gloria laughed under her breath.

Serena snorted and nudged Gloria, then jutted her chin toward Lou. "It's a freaking tree, Lou. Relax." She howled in laughter.

"Looks like they got us good," Cooper said, one side of his mouth lifting.

Gloria draped an arm around Serena and smiled at Henry.

"Moving on." Lou grabbed the corners of his coat collar. "Do you want to go to the bowling alley?"

Lou's adoring gaze fell squarely on Serena. Gloria had noticed his fawning looks toward Serena several times since the two had met three months ago. She grinned, hoping her friends would finally spill how they felt about each other while they were together tonight.

Serena checked her watch. "It's eight. I don't know."

She shrugged. "Go on. I've got some reading to do."

"You don't want to come?" Serena asked.

"You and Lou go have fun." Gloria shooed her friends away.

Serena and Lou beamed at each other.

"Well, okay," Serena said.

They turned and strolled toward town.

Cooper still stood in the same spot, gazing at her with his head tilted to the side.

"You aren't going with them?" Gloria leaned against Henry.

"I'd just be the odd man out." He chuckled.

She bent and picked up the book that lay between two of the tree's thick roots.

"You going to the library?"

Gloria shook her head. "I'm going home."

"This'll sound lame, but do you want me to walk you there?"

She froze. Those were foreign words to her since she'd graduated high school, and she would have been happy if they would have stayed unfamiliar. She'd gotten used to her independence.

"Hey, it's okay if you don't want me tagging along." Cooper's voice interrupted her thoughts. "I just thought 'cause it's dark out…"

"I walk around here all the time, night and day."

He shrugged. "Okay. No problem."

Guilt bit her. There wasn't any reason to be rude to the man. It was just a walk home… with a stranger. She glanced at him. His chiseled features glowed in the moonlight. Okay. Not a total stranger. He was Lou's friend. "I'm sorry." She hugged her book. "You can walk me home. Thanks."

He said nothing, just gave her a jutting of his chin, turned on his boot heel, and waited for her to come alongside him.

As they took the first steps in the direction of her cabin, something fluttered worrisome inside her belly. She scolded herself for having said yes to Cooper and wondered what would happen at the end of the walk.

Gloria steadied her nerves by gripping one of the vertical beams on the porch. She hadn't been alone with a guy since a few dinner dates when she was in high school. She scanned the silent area surrounded by woods and mountains. Light from the moon shone on the dirt path to hers and the other cabins. A cool breeze whispered through the trees and brushed their faces. Cooper stood in the shadow of the eaves of the porch, his bulky jacket giving him an awkward, lopsided appearance. The darkness hid his facial features. He'd said nothing the whole quarter-mile walk home. Who was this man?

"So, how long have you and Lou been friends?" she asked.

"About three years."

She leaned against the cabin's door. "What do you do for a living?"

"Landscaping, odds and ends jobs."

She nodded. "Sounds like interesting work."

The jacket rustled, and his shoulders rose in a shrug.

Uneasiness settled in her chest. Socializing and Cooper didn't go together. She slipped her hand in her jeans pocket and pulled out her key. "Well, I'm going in now."

He grunted and shifted against the railing. "Okay."

His *okay* had a tone of sadness. She sensed he needed to talk. How she knew that was a mystery to her.

She unlocked the door and pushed it open. "Thanks for the walk home." She twisted at the waist toward his silhouette against the moonlight as he walked down the steps.

He stopped at the bottom of the stairs with his back still to her. "Sure."

Cooper began walking again.

Clutching the doorknob, Gloria sputtered out, "Hey, Coop."

He halted on the dirt path and turned to look at her, his face still masked by the shadows with the moonlight behind his head.

"Do you want to come in a while and talk?"

Only the gentle breeze answered. He stood still as a statue.

She tentatively stepped onto the porch and strained to see his body language or hear anything coming out of his mouth.

After what seemed like forever, Cooper's arm rose. "It's late. Night."

He turned again and ambled down the path.

Pressing a hand to her chest and frowning, Gloria watched him disappear from view. She entered her cabin and shut the door. "What is wrong with that guy?"

A familiar soft burning filled her chest. This warmth had nestled in her heart every so often the past four years, and it seemed to emerge whenever she'd gotten the desire to learn more about her grandmother's faith and more about the peace she encountered in the mountains and forests that nurtured and embraced her. Why did Cooper's aloofness trigger this kindling inside her? It didn't make sense but stoked determination within her to find an answer.

Chapter Fourteen

I n her apartment the following week, Seraphima examined the monthly packet of her birth control pills. She'd taken the inactive ones for the week she should have had her period, but it never appeared, only the cramps that usually lead up to it. Seraphima had never missed a menstrual cycle since she'd started on the Pill two years ago. She tapped her index finger to her chin. With all the emotional stress she'd been under with Austin, the absence of her period didn't seem out of the realm of possibilities.

A sudden thought struck her. What if she was pregnant? She could be carrying Austin's baby. A spark of excitement and joy lit her heart, but it was doused by dismay. Seraphima clutched her stomach. Austin hadn't called her since their last awkward discussion, and the few times she'd called, she'd received his voice mail.

What if she had to raise this baby on her own? Icy fear gripped her. *Stop it. You're not pregnant. You've missed your period because you've been worried and upset about Austin. That's all. It'll show up soon.* Besides, the order was all wrong—marriage *and then* children. That had been her mantra for years. She sighed. She really wanted to talk to Austin.

Setting the pill case on the kitchen table, Seraphima picked up her cell phone and called him. Maybe he wouldn't be volunteering tonight and they could spend the evening together. Four rings resonated through the earpiece before Austin's voice mail kicked on. Frustrated, she gripped the phone and said, "Austin, I was hoping you'd have some time to spend with me tonight. Call me if you do." She ended the call, grabbed her purse, and left her apartment.

———

The next afternoon at lunch, Seraphima sat with Belinda and Eli at the Subway sandwich shop two doors down from the salon.

"March is the start of spring, and I can see it and feel it," Belinda said.

"It's not technically spring until the twenty-second of March, depending on the equinox in a given year," Eli pointed out.

"So, it's two days until the official date. Spring has already sprung," Belinda insisted, giving him a lopsided grin.

"Okay, okay. I can't deny that. My poppy mallows are already starting to bud."

Seraphima's interest piqued. "Poppy mallows? Are they flowers? You have a flower garden?"

"Yes, and a vegetable garden." Eli stuffed potato chips in his mouth.

"Where do you have room for a garden?" Belinda asked what Seraphima had been thinking.

"In my backyard."

Seraphima leaned back against her chair, astonished. She glanced at Belinda, whose expression mimicked hers.

"Backyard," they said nearly in unison.

"Yeah."

"So, you must live in a townhome," Belinda said.

Eli shook his blond head. "Uh-uh."

"Don't tell me you live in a trailer park?" Belinda snorted.

Seraphima continued to watch Eli. She'd never known a man interested in flowers and gardens before. The men she knew yammered on about monster trucks, car races, football, grilling, bars with big TV screens, and pool tables.

"I live in a house with my dad and sister."

"You still live with your parents?" Belinda asked with a hint of disapproval in her voice.

Seraphima tapped her foot on top of Belinda's under the table and scowled at her friend.

"My dad's in a wheelchair. I take care of him. My sister helps too."

Belinda's cheeks reddened.

Seraphima reached out her hand toward Eli but then laced it with her other on her lap. She wouldn't show Belinda how she was feeling. Her friend would mistake her caring gesture for something much more than that, and she wanted no confusion on who she was devoted to. She turned her attention back to Eli. "Where's your mom?"

Eli's large cornflower-blue eyes shone sadness before shifting his gaze to look out the window. "She died when I was fourteen."

"I'm sorry about your mom, Eli. It must have been really hard on you and your family," Seraphima said. This time she couldn't stifle her concern and extended her hand and touched his arm.

Belinda didn't seem to notice. She was busy chewing on her soda straw.

Eli covered her hand with his and patted hers. "Thank you. It was."

She nodded with a sympathetic frown.

A dull cramp pulsated through her abdomen. Her hand

instinctively slid to her stomach. Her period was aching to start anytime now.

"Hey, are you okay, Fima?" Eli asked.

"What?" Belinda's stare bounced from Eli to Seraphima and back to Eli. "What happened?"

Rubbing the pain away, Seraphima said, "I'm fine. It's nothing." She gave them a faint smile.

Belinda took a sip of soda, then glanced at Eli. "It's cool that you have gardens." She then looked at her watch. "I've got to go back. I took off fifteen minutes before you guys joined me." She left the table with the remnants from her lunch, tossed them in the nearest trash can, then waved at them before leaving the shop.

"Are you sure you're okay? You still look a little pale," Eli said.

Startled by Eli's astute observation, Seraphima touched her belly again. "I had a little cramp that we women get monthly." She laughed as her face warmed.

"Woman issues. Got it. It must have been a doozy, because you still don't look very well."

Seraphima shifted in her seat, feeling his eyes on her, like he could read her mind. She forced a smile. "Really, it's nothing. I'm used to it." She picked up her turkey sub, and nausea swam in her stomach. She set it down and took a sip of her bottled water; the coolness of it refreshed her.

Eli wadded up his sub wrapper into a ball. A gentle smile split his face. "All right. No more prying into your personal business."

"Thank you." Seraphima bit off a small section of her sandwich and swallowed as relentless worry rattled around in her chest.

The next evening, Seraphima tapped Austin's number on her phone and waited for the several rings she'd usually get. He stunned her, answering on the second ring. "Fima."

"I can't believe you answered," she said.

"Yeah. It's time to get some things figured out."

"I agree." She sensed disappointment looming, and fear rose from her chest to close her throat.

"We need to slow down, take a break. We need space."

"Space?" She echoed the word no person in a romantic relationship wanted to hear.

"Yeah. We're moving too fast. I've got lots of stuff to focus on... my golfing... my firefighting."

Seraphima sat motionless, listening to her boyfriend, lover, and future husband break off their relationship.

"I need to concentrate on my career and goals. I don't have time for a serious relationship right now, or anytime soon."

She nodded numbly.

"Okay?"

She nodded again as tears dropped from her eyes.

"Fima, are you there?"

She blinked and muttered, "Yes."

"Okay. So you heard me."

"Yes."

"Okay, good... I've got to go. It's time for me to head to the fire station."

"Right," she replied robotically.

He sounded far away as her emotions threatened to drown her.

"Great. Bye."

The phone disconnected before Seraphima could respond. She dropped the cell on the couch cushion, planted her head in her hands, and let torrential tears rain from her eyes.

Seraphima woke in her bed with swollen eyes, a clogged nose, and a headache. She called in sick and fell back on her pillow. In a crystal-clear blue sky, the sun shone brightly through her bedroom window as birds chirped incessantly. She gripped her pillow with tight fists and squeezed her eyes shut. How could the world be carrying on after the devastating quake Austin shook her with last night? The birds didn't get the message.

Throwing off the pillow and covers, Seraphima sat up. Her hair fell like a curtain around her shoulders and achy face. She pushed back the strands from her temples and rubbed them, the headache pulsing through her fingers.

Seraphima slid out of bed, staggered to the bathroom, and fumbled for pain medicine. After downing the pills, she returned to her bedroom and grabbed the remote on the nightstand. She clicked on the twenty-four-inch TV mounted on the wall above her dresser. She crawled back into bed, settling in the warm covers, leaning against the pillows to watch whatever took her mind off Austin. It didn't work. The car races and adventure movies she'd clicked through only made her think of him more.

Biting her lip to stop its quivering, she went to the DVD stand, plucked out a comedy, and stuck it in the player on the bureau. Settling back into her bed, she focused hard on the movie and ate chocolate and pretzels she kept stashed in her nightstand.

Chapter Fifteen

M ichaela tapped Fima's phone number on her cell's screen again. She'd tried calling her sister this morning and early afternoon, receiving voice mail. It was now nearly four o'clock, an hour before they and their mother were to meet up at Michaela's house.

On the fourth ring, Fima's hoarse voice mumbled, "Yeah, hello, Mike."

Fima's depressed tone and sniffle caught Michaela's attention. "Hey, are you sick?"

"Yes... Well, no."

"Which is it, Fima?" Michaela sat down on the wooden bench swing on her front porch. The late-afternoon sun peeked from between two fluffy white clouds, giving off a hint of warmth. The smoky aroma of grilled meat permeated the air. Michaela's neighbor two houses down loved to grill every chance he got, even in March.

Fima responded with a faint sigh.

"If you're not well, stay home. We can meet in a day or two when you're better."

"I'll never be better." Fima's voice was drenched in sorrow.

Michaela sighed. Everything was a huge dilemma to her little sister. Michaela puffed on a cigarette and blew out the smoke with squinted eyes.

"Okay, Fima. You want to tell me what you're talking about? Never get better?"

"Well, it just feels like that."

"Yeah, I gathered. So what happened?"

"Austin broke up with me." Her voice cracked.

What did I say? Michaela rubbed her puckered lips with two fingers. She'd warned her sister just a couple of weeks ago about getting her hopes up with this guy who was more interested in golf clubs and sand pits than her. But she worked to stifle the urge to tell Fima this. Her sister was hurting, no matter if it was her own doing.

"Oh no. Why'd he break up with you?"

"He said he's not ready for a serious relationship and that he's got goals for his career to work on."

"Well, you have to admit he didn't really seem as interested in your relationship as you did."

"Yes, he did, especially the first month."

"Men always act on their best behavior those first few weeks and months. Then you find out who they really are—assholes." Michaela ground out her cigarette on the floor with her shoe as Doug's face popped into her mind. She hadn't heard from him since Bailey's dance recital. She'd recalled telling him he'd only see Bailey once a month or something along those lines when she'd been aggravated with him over the Valentine's Day wine bottle incident.

"He seemed different."

"They're all the same. The sooner you get that, the less heartache you'll suffer, because you'll detect their games from the start."

Fima didn't answer, only woeful silence.

Closing her eyes as she felt her sister's pain, Michaela rubbed her forehead. "Do you want me to come and get you? You can stay here tonight."

A long pause followed before Fima muttered, "Thanks, Mike. That'd be great."

"Sure."

"I'll get some things packed up."

"Okay. I'll be by in a half hour."

"All right."

"After all, we were going to spend the evening together anyway, right?" Michaela said, trying to sound upbeat.

"I'd forgotten about that," Fima said. "See you soon."

Etta and Fima sat on the sofa next to Michaela as she cracked open her laptop.

"What are we looking for this time?" Etta asked.

"Not sure. I was hoping you or Fima had some ideas," Michaela replied.

Twirling a long strand of her hair, Fima nodded. "I do have one, and I think it's a good one."

Michaela and Etta looked expectantly at Fima.

"Okay, what you got?" Michaela asked.

"Maybe Glory changed her last name."

"To what?" Michaela said.

"Mom's maiden name."

"Yes." Etta clapped her hands together. "That's brilliant."

Michaela thought about that. What better way for Glory to rid herself of anything related to their dad? She hated him. Their dad had been harsh, unbending, and Michaela admitted, struggled with showing love to his daughters. They rarely, if ever, heard him say he loved any of them, especially Glory. But that didn't matter now. Their father was dead. Glory needed to be found, if she was still alive. That thought hadn't completely left her. Yet this new possibility of using their mother's maiden name gave her a sense of real hope.

Michaela brought up the search engine on her computer and typed in Glory Lofton. Three names popped up—one with an address in Summitville, Colorado, but no phone number was listed. That was forty miles from her aunt's place and at least sixty-five miles from theirs. The other two were not in Colorado.

"We've got one in Summitville," she said.

"That's it." Etta leaned forward with her face drawn in a pleading expression. "That's got to be her."

"Sounds like it could be her," Fima answered, still twisting her hair, looking contemplative. "I sure hope it is."

"Well, let's check Facebook and Twitter and see if she's got accounts there so we can match up the face with the name." Michaela clicked on Facebook in her bookmarks and typed in Glory's name. "Nothing on Facebook," she said, closing the application and clicking on the Twitter link. She searched for Glory there but found nothing. "She's not on social media."

"I was really hoping she'd be," Fima said with a frown. "That would make it so much easier."

"Yes, well your sister was always the outdoorsy type, skipping TV shows and video games to be outside climbing trees and walking in the woods. I'm not too surprised she isn't on social media," Etta said, raising a glass of wine to her lips and taking a sip.

Why hadn't Michaela thought of that? Then the reason came to her. She hadn't paid much attention to what Glory was doing most of the time. She'd been wrapped up in community college activities, homework, and dating.

"Yes, you're right, Mom. Glory loved being outside. She'd sleep in a tent in the backyard almost all the time," Fima added.

"So what are we going to do with this information?" Michaela flicked a finger toward the computer screen, then shrugged. "Drive to the place?"

"We could do that," Etta replied.

"Can we?" Fima sat up in a snap, as if ready to pop.

"Maybe we should let her be. After all, she knows where we are and hasn't bothered to come home to see us all these years." Michaela closed the lid to her laptop. "She obviously doesn't want to."

"I don't believe that," Fima said.

"You don't believe she wants to come home?" Etta sipped her wine.

"Yeah, I don't believe it." Michaela smacked her palms on her thighs. "Isn't it obvious since she hasn't been here all this time?"

Etta shook her head. "She ran away because of your father."

Michaela eyed her mother. "I'm well aware of that."

"Well, then you'd know that she didn't leave because of you and your sister or even me."

"I knew that," Fima interjected with a satisfied smile.

Michaela scowled at her mother and Fima ganging up on her. "Yeah, I know. But stay away this long?"

Etta tsked. "She doesn't know we'd divorced and that your father died."

"Right, because Aunt Melina didn't know about all of this, and Glory was already gone from her house when these things happened," Fima said.

"Don't remind me about your aunt's keeping Glory's whereabouts a secret for years," Etta grumbled.

Fima patted Etta's arm. "Sorry, Mom."

What her mother and sister said made a lot of sense. That meant someone had to tell Glory these things, but resentment picked at the back of her brain—resentment for Glory's fleeing, not having the endurance to bear their father's anger and physical lashes when they had. Granted, both she and Fima could count on one hand how many times their father had spanked them. The cold aloofness from their father had struck her and Fima more. But Glory had been so headstrong and rebellious. If she'd done what their father had said, surely he wouldn't have lost his temper so often. Michaela was left to take care of her mother and little sister.

"So, what are we going to do?" Fima asked.

Michaela massaged her tight jaw with her fingers. "Don't know. What do you think, Mom?"

"What do I think?" Etta clucked and set her glass on the coffee table. "I think we should go see her, of course."

"Yes." Fima clasped her hands together and grinned.

Michaela placed her laptop on the coffee table. She sat on the edge of the couch and rubbed her thighs. "Okay. When are we taking this road trip?"

Light thumps on the stairs sounded before Bailey appeared, and she trotted over to them.

"Gramma, look what I drew?" She presented a piece of paper showing a fat orange figure that resembled a cat. "It's Sylvester. Can't you tell?"

"Oh, yes, my love." Etta kissed Bailey's cheek, then took the drawing from her hands. "And he looks beautiful."

Bailey beamed. "Hang it up in your house."

"I most certainly will, darling." Etta squeezed her arm.

"I've got more things to draw." Bailey skipped out of the room.

Bailey was born after Glory had run away. She didn't know she had a niece. She would have if she'd stayed. Michaela had mentioned Glory a few times to her daughter, but it did little to give Bailey any sense of connection to her other aunt. She didn't even have a current picture of her to show Bailey.

"Sunday afternoon you both are off work," Etta said.

"That's a perfect time," Fima agreed.

"All right. I'll call Lena so she can watch Bailey while we're gone." Michaela stood up. "We'll meet here at one and go from there in my car."

"We'll finally see Glory. It will be a wondrous day," Etta said, rising from the sofa.

"I can't wait." Fima got up from her spot on the couch, with her hand on her abdomen and her face pinched.

"Hey, are you okay?" Michaela asked, touching her sister's arm.

Fima nodded with a tight smile. "It's that time of the month coming on. That's all."

"Aunt Flo's unwelcome visit, huh?" Michaela chuckled.

Etta and Fima walked ahead of her toward the kitchen. *Aunt Flo. That's the only other aunt that'll be stopping at this house anytime soon.* Michaela grabbed a pack of cigarettes off the foyer table before following them into the kitchen.

Chapter Sixteen

On Saturday morning, Michaela watched Doug's gray sedan pull up to the curb in front of her house. Two figures sat in the vehicle in the shadow of its roof, hidden from the sun's dull rays.

Who was with him? Michaela stood on the porch with hands on her hips.

The doors opened, and Doug emerged first, followed by a woman with shoulder-length, ash-blond hair and a petite body. Michaela's lips pressed together as she folded her arms across her chest. Where had he picked her up? Her jaw tightened as they strolled up the cement walk.

"Mike," Doug said. He reached the porch steps and gave her a cordial smile as he squinted from the glare of the late-morning sun.

"Doug," Michaela answered, not moving. "Who's this?"

"Tina. My partner."

The word hit her like a punch in the gut. "Partner?" She fumbled for the pack of cigarettes and lighter sitting on top of the brick porch ledge.

"Hello." Tina thrust out her hand for Michaela to shake.

After lighting her cigarette, Michaela set the package and lighter back on the ledge, reluctantly took the outstretched hand, and gripped it tightly. "Hello," she echoed in a monotone voice.

"Tina's my accountability partner and I'm hers," Doug said.

"Oh." Michaela let go of Tina's hand. Was that all she was?

Tina wiggled the hand she had shaken with Michaela, as if trying to get rid of a cramp. Michaela couldn't help but snicker under her breath. The woman had wilted from a handshake.

Opening the screen door, Michaela yelled, "Bailey, your dad is here!"

She knew Doug had planned to take Bailey to the skating rink, but he'd said nothing about this woman tagging along. What kind of message was he sending to their daughter?

Bailey's pattering down the stairs carried to the porch. She appeared at the screen door. "Daddy!" She held up her roller skates. "I'm ready!"

"Great. Let's go, Bailey bug." Doug opened his arms as Bailey pushed the door open and ran to hug him. It wasn't until after they'd broken their embrace that Bailey noticed the woman next to him. She squinted at Tina.

"Hi, Bailey. I'm Tina, your dad's good friend."

Good friend. Sure she was. Michaela eyed her as a tinge of jealousy coursed through her. Tina's tiny but curvy figure made Michaela feel like a giant with her five-foot eight-inch, boyish frame.

"Hi." Bailey smiled shyly at the woman.

"Do you mind if I come with you and your dad?"

Pulling hard on her cigarette, Michaela raised her brows at her daughter when she looked at her for guidance. Tilting her head up to blow out smoke, Michaela smiled curtly. "It's up to you, sweetheart."

"She's very nice, Bailey, and she loves to skate," Doug said in a gentle, encouraging voice.

After several stares back and forth from Doug to Michaela, Bailey nodded. "Okay."

"Excellent." Doug put his fist up for Bailey to bump with hers. She obliged with a giggle.

They headed toward his car.

"What time will you have her back here?" Michaela asked, snubbing out her cigarette on the cement floor of the porch.

Opening the back door for Bailey to climb in, Doug glanced at Michaela. "We'll be back by supper time."

"It was nice to meet you." Tina wiggled her fingers at Michaela and got into the vehicle.

"It was a drag meeting you," she said under her breath. Waving joylessly, Michaela leaned her elbow on the ledge and watched the sedan roll away.

"Mommy, we're home!" Bailey stepped into the foyer and hugged Michaela.

"Hey, sweetie. Did you have fun skating?"

"Yeah. Tina skates really good." Bailey beamed at Tina and, releasing Michaela, wrapped her arms around Doug's waist. "Thanks, Daddy." She skipped to the kitchen.

Staring at Doug and Tina in awkward silence, Michaela wanted to shut the door in their faces.

"I'm going to use the bathroom before we head out," Doug announced and walked toward the door under the stairs.

"Your daughter is a doll, Michaela." Tina's made-up face, with her button nose and gray blue eyes, spread into a grin.

"Yeah, I know. Thank you. She's also very smart," Michaela said, returning a tight smile.

"Doug's a fabulous father."

"Is he?" The sarcasm in the question slipped from Michaela's lips.

"Oh yes. He's so gentle and caring toward Bailey. He's a real gentleman." Tina ran a hand over her sprayed, perfectly styled hair.

"That's what I used to think." Michaela eyed Tina. She knew Doug much better than this bimbo.

"That's a shame," Tina said, "giving up on such a great guy. I know I wouldn't have made that mistake." She puckered her lips and examined her nails.

The tension between them shot up. Michaela couldn't believe the woman's audacity. "You don't know him," she said, her tone acidic.

"I think I know him quite well." Tina raised her pointy chin.

Michaela's lips spread into a thin, cold smile. "You know zilch."

Tina straightened her short frame. "Now I see what he'd been putting up with. No wonder he drank."

Heat streaked through Michaela, and she pointed to the door. "Get out of my house."

"I see what he's suffered and how he's been working to get himself sober. Instead of helping him through it, you abandoned him. It's only natural he'd eventually find someone who truly cares about him."

Michaela jerked the screen door open. "I said get out!"

Doug appeared at the bathroom door and walked toward them. "Mike, what's going on?"

Michaela kept her eyes on Tina, her mouth a tight, thin line.

"Michaela is upset because I told her the truth."

"What truth?" Doug's brows came together, and he put his hands on his hips.

The woman had no scruples, no tact. "You mean lies." Michaela stabbed an index finger in the direction of the street. "Out!"

Tina shrugged with a smug grin on her face and walked out the door.

Doug eyed Michaela with suspicion. "I don't know what happened—"

"I'm sure your *good friend* and *partner* will fill you in." Michaela tapped her fingers on the doorknob, waiting for Doug to follow Tina. He groaned, then crossed the threshold and walked toward his car where Tina waited.

Slamming the door, Michaela stomped to the kitchen. "Good friend, my ass."

Chapter Seventeen

Seraphima climbed into the back seat of Mike's car as their mother took the front passenger seat.

"We should be there by two thirty or so." Mike started the car.

They headed toward Summitville and Glory.

Soon they'd see her after all these years. What would she look like? What would she say when she saw them? Seraphima clasped her hands together as anticipation and elation pumped through her body. She imagined their encounter filled with happy tears and hugs. They could finally catch up on everything they'd been doing. She smiled at the idea and leaned her head on the headrest of the seat.

The weather was perfect for their trip. The temperature would hit sixty-five degrees with sunshine and light winds all day. Just right to meet up with Glory in the mountains.

"I hope she's there. Otherwise, I've wasted a quarter tank of gas," Mike grumbled.

Her sister was in a sour mood today, but why? Mike hadn't seen fit to share what was bothering her. She tended to keep her personal problems to herself, which frustrated Seraphima. She wanted to share the dilemmas they faced, a way of bonding with her sister. At least when Glory had still been around, she'd been more open with her feelings and more accommodating than Mike. Maybe the ten-year age difference between her and Mike was too big a gap to close.

"Of course she'll be there," Etta said. "It's Sunday afternoon. Most people relax on Sundays at their homes."

"I wonder what type of home she lives in," Seraphima said.

"Probably a low-rent apartment," Mike said.

"Why low rent?"

"Because she didn't finish high school."

"We don't know that, Michaela. Your inconsiderate aunt said Gloria had attended the local high school while living with her." Etta stared at herself in the visor mirror and ran a finger over her eyebrow.

"Aunt Melina said Glory left the summer before her senior year. Remember?"

"Oh, I suppose I'd forgotten."

"I hope she's doing well anyway," Seraphima said.

She turned her attention back to the window, the highway and foothills in the distance. She had her cell phone with her in case Austin changed his mind. He might miss their lovemaking and call her, pleading to get back together. Their bond was too beautiful and strong to break. He just needed some time to come to that realization.

Seraphima's hand slid across her stomach. Her period hadn't come, and the premenstrual symptoms had faded except for the cramping that still surfaced sporadically. Next week she'd purchase a pregnancy kit. Better to take the test to rule it out and settle her nerves.

"We all hope Gloria's well, dear," Etta said, glancing back at Seraphima with an affectionate smile.

An hour and a half later, their car rolled up to the tiny cabin near a larger one with a wooden plank above its front door that read CASCADE CLEANING SERVICE. Pines surrounded the cabins with stony outcrops behind them, leading to the jagged tips of the Rocky Mountains.

Mike turned off the engine, and they stepped out of the vehicle and looked around. Seraphima crossed the gravel dirt path to Glory's cabin and eagerly rapped on the door.

"Couldn't wait for us, could you?" Mike teased with a lopsided grin.

Seraphima bit her lip. "No one's answering." She cupped her hands on either side of her face and peered in a window to the left of the front door.

"Do you see anything?" Etta craned her neck to get a glimpse through the window.

"No." Seraphima shook her head as disappointment set in. Her sister wasn't home. There was no way to know where she was.

"What'd I say?" Mike threw her hands in the air and rolled her eyes. "Wasted gas."

"Hush, daughter. It was hardly a waste to make the effort to see your sister."

"But we didn't *see* her, Mother." Mike turned from the house, headed back to the car, and threw the driver's side door open.

Birds sang in the trees, and the distant roar of a rushing stream sweetened the thin air. Mike's grumpiness couldn't ruin the majestic sights and sounds around them.

A heavyset, dark-haired woman came out the front door of the larger cabin, carrying a bag and keys.

"Hello," Etta called to the woman who was descending the four steps to the small porch.

"Oh, hello." The woman gave them a friendly smile.

Excitement built in Seraphima as she rushed over to the woman. "Hi. We're here to see Glory. We tried knocking on her door but got no answer."

The woman frowned and glanced at Glory's cabin. "Glory

doesn't get many visitors. It's a shame she's not here to see you." She pointed to her ample chest. "I'm Ruby. Glory works for my husband and me. We own Cascade Cleaning Service." She gestured a waving hand at the cabin behind her.

"I'm Seraphima, Glory's sister. It's nice to meet you."

"Sister?" Ruby's face lit up. "Oh, how wonderful. I didn't know she had a sister."

"And I'm Etta, Gloria's mother." Etta presented her hand for Ruby to shake.

Ruby grinned. "Glory's mother?"

"Yes."

While they'd been conversing, Mike had quietly strolled over to them.

"This is Gloria's older sister, Michaela," Etta said, touching Mike's arm.

"I had no idea," Ruby said, her pink face beaming.

"Do you know where Glory is?" Seraphima asked. "Maybe she'll be back soon and we can wait?"

The lady shook her head. "I'm sorry. I don't keep tabs on my employees on their days off."

"Oh." Seraphima slouched as her spirits sank.

"Of course." Etta frowned. "We understand, but I'd appreciate it if you'd give me my daughter's phone number."

"I'm afraid she doesn't have a phone."

"No phone?" Seraphima clutched her cell. How did anyone live without a phone?

"Well, could you please tell her we stopped by to see her?" Etta asked.

"I'd be happy to." The woman adjusted the strap of her large purse on her shoulder. "It was very nice meeting you all." She ambled to her tiny vehicle.

"Even maids have cell phones." Mike jerked a thumb in the direction of the cabin. "Doesn't sound like she has any interest in getting in touch with us."

Etta's face pinched. "Michaela, we don't know that."

Seraphima gazed at the modest wooden house. "At least we know she *does* live here."

"Yes." Etta walked toward it once more. "We know for certain she is alive and well. This is peace of mind to a mother's heart." Her voice cracked as she laid a hand on the front door and lowered her head as if in prayer.

"That's true, Mom." Mike put a hand on Etta's shoulder. "No more wondering and worrying."

"Yes," Seraphima added and rubbed her mother's back.

"I guess that alone made the trip worthwhile," Mike admitted.

Startled and thrilled by Mike's softened demeanor, Seraphima hugged her sister. "Yes. I feel closer to her just standing here. And closer to you and Mom."

Mike smoothed down Seraphima's hair as they embraced. Letting go, she asked, "So, what's next?"

"Let's give it at least an hour," Etta said, taking a seat on the first step leading to the porch and gazing at the gorgeous landscape. "We have time to spend here."

Seraphima sat next to her mother. "I know, and it's beautiful."

An hour later, with no sign of Glory, they climbed in Mike's car and rolled out of Summitville. Yet Seraphima was hopeful after seeing and touching her sister's home that she'd see her soon. She smiled and put her fingers on the window as she pictured Glory climbing one of the pine trees.

Chapter Eighteen

That same afternoon, Gloria sat next to Serena in her mother's compact car as it rolled to a stop in front of a two-story stucco home in a middle-class neighborhood in Aurora.

Gloria checked the address scribbled down on the piece of paper in her hands for the third time. "Twenty-three, twenty-two Gulch Drive. This is it," she said, releasing her seat belt.

"Yep." Serena did the same. She turned toward Gloria. "You nervous?"

Gloria gripped the door handle. Would Penny be home? And if Penny was home, would her fears of having the door slammed in her face come to pass? "A little, but it'll be fine. Let's go." She opened her door and climbed out of the vehicle.

Serena joined Gloria on the sidewalk leading to the house. The early March day gave off a gentle breeze in the temperate air. The gruff bark of a dog in the distance and faint sounds of children playing floated by them, making Gloria smile.

An image of her and her sisters in their backyard, swinging or climbing the rope ladder to their tree house, materialized. Mike had been the captain of the house that they often pretended was a ship on the ocean, and she and Fima were their oldest sister's crew, guarding the fort from pirates and other nefarious invaders. Sometimes Penny would join them on their naval adventures, making colorful flags cut from old bedsheets with anchors or marine life painted on them. A nostalgic laugh escaped her lips.

The smell of garden soil and flowers drifted along the mild flutter of the wind.

They approached the small porch with a rocking chair and two pots of pansies flanking the front door. Standing in the shade under the eave, Gloria took a deep breath, ebullience and apprehension rolling inside her. If Penny was home and agreed to talk to her, would she know anything about Gloria's family?

"You going to knock?" Serena asked.

Without answering her friend, Gloria rapped on the door. While waiting for the chirring sound of the door to open, she stared out at the noiseless street.

"Maybe you should knock again," Serena said, just as the door pulled slowly open.

Penny appeared at the doorway, her gray eyes wide, mouth ajar. "Glory?"

Gloria grinned. "How'd you guess?"

They embraced with squeals and laughter. "I can't believe you're here!" Penny pushed the door wide open. "Come in."

They entered Penny's home with its tile foyer and long, dangling light fixture hanging from the fifteen-foot, lofty ceiling above them.

Gloria touched Penny's arm. "This is my friend, Serena. Serena, Penny."

"Hi. Nice to meet you," Penny said with a welcoming smile.

Serena returned the kind gesture. "Same here."

Gloria admired the ornately carved cherrywood banister bordering the stairs ascending to the rooms on the second floor. "Your house is beautiful."

"Thanks." Penny pointed at Gloria. "Your sister, Mike, called me a few weeks ago asking about you, and here you are."

Gloria froze. "She did?"

"Yes." Penny clasped her hands together. "I never would've thought you'd show up here." She touched Gloria's shoulder. "How'd you find me?"

"The online white pages at my local library."

Gloria continued to take in the large, decorative house. She visually inspected the windows, their sills, the mahogany furniture and lace drapes for dust. Everything in the house was immaculate. She presumed her friend hired professionals to clean her house. She rolled her eyes. After five years cleaning houses, she could never just look at rooms without scanning for dust and grime. Gloria pursed her lips. Never mind that.

"Why did Mike call you?"

"She said your mother was wanting to see you."

Hope lit inside Gloria like a Fourth of July sparkler. "She does?"

"Yes."

Did Mike really care, or was she just doing this out of duty to their mother? Nevertheless, they were asking about her. At least her mother still loved her. But there was her father to deal with —the real obstacle preventing her and her mother from reuniting.

"I'm sorry to keep asking questions."

"No, it's fine." Penny led them into the living room. "I get it. You've been away from your family for so many years. Must be so hard on all of you."

"It has been for me." Gloria followed her with Serena trailing behind. "Did Mike say anything about my father?"

"No."

That left Gloria where she'd been for a decade. Was her father still with her mother? She fidgeted next to the red sofa. "Look, I have to be honest with you. I came here to find out if you had any contact in the past few years with my family."

Penny's face fell. "Oh. I see." Her expression took on a wounded look mixed with displeasure. "That's all, huh?"

Crap. That hadn't come out right. She draped an arm around Penny and pulled her close. "I'm sorry. That's definitely not the only reason."

Penny gave her an expectant sideways glance.

"I've been missing you and trying to find you for years."

Serena nodded. "She has. I saw her on the library's computers a few times searching for you." She mimicked typing, with her fingers punching the air.

Penny's expression softened, and she patted Gloria's back. "You don't have a phone to just google me on social media?"

Gloria flopped on the sofa with a sigh. "No. I hate mobile phones."

"But it would have made your search so much easier."

"Glory is anti-tech. One of her best friends is a tree," Serena said with a giggle.

Penny tilted her head to the side as the corner of her mouth twitched. "A tree?"

Gloria nodded. "Henry." She held out her arms. "A large, magnificent cottonwood."

"She climbs it all the time," Serena added.

"You still climb trees?" Penny's eyes bugged out before she let out a laugh.

"Of course." Gloria grinned.

Serena placed her hands on her wide hips. "That's what makes Glory, Glory."

They all laughed.

Penny jerked a thumb toward the kitchen. "Let me get you something to drink. Soda, water, or iced tea?"

"Water's fine for me, thanks," Gloria replied, as she gazed at a large bookcase across from her. *Wow.* So many books. If she had those in her cabin, she'd be reading through the classics in Henry's arms.

"I'll take iced tea, please," Serena said.

Penny headed toward the kitchen and returned a minute later, handing them their beverages. "Please sit down and tell me how I can help—although I'm not sure I can."

Gloria sank into the sofa again as Serena sat in the chair next to her.

"I'd really like to know anything you can tell me about my family. My sisters, mother... my father..."

"Until Mike's call, I didn't know anything about your family. Still don't know that much. As for your father, I know even less."

"I get that. I wouldn't have wanted to pay attention to him either if I were you."

Penny leaned back against her chair. "It's not that. My family moved from the neighborhood a couple of years later. So I've been out of touch with them as much as you have."

Gloria frowned. "Oh." She slumped against the couch cushion and ran her fingers down the glass in her hands. "I've been hoping for years to find out if my father's still with my mom."

Penny took a sip of iced tea, then said, "Does it really matter? You're a grown woman. He can't hurt you anymore."

"Being a grown woman wouldn't stop him. The man holds grudges forever."

"I guess being a prosecuting attorney fits him well, huh?" Serena smirked.

"Yes," Gloria said.

"Well, the only thing Mike told me was to call her if I heard from you," Penny said.

Gloria set down her drink with one hand and raised the other. "Let's hold off telling her you spoke to me."

Penny's brows met.

"Would you call her and ask about the whereabouts of my dad in some way that doesn't make my sister suspicious?"

Penny's head tilted to the side. "How do I do that?"

"You could bring up something regarding his job, like a current trial going on in the news. You know. Find a way to casually link those together."

Doubt shone in Penny's eyes before she shrugged. "All right. I'll try."

"When do you think you'll be able to contact her?"

"I'm heading out tomorrow morning for a business trip, but I'll be back Friday night, so I'll try calling Mike on Saturday."

Gloria blew out a breath. "I can't thank you enough, Penny."

Penny waved a hand. "So, tell me. How have you been?"

"Good. How about you?"

"I'm doing well, working at a bank. I'm a loan officer."

"Sounds interesting." Although Gloria had done all right in math, she'd never cared for the subject, but Penny had excelled at it. She'd even helped Gloria with some of the more complex math problems.

"What about you? Where do you work?"

Gloria's cheeks flushed. She'd not had to discuss or confess her job to anybody from her past, a past in which they'd lived in upper-middle-class neighborhoods. But things changed when she'd run away with only five hundred dollars in her pocket.

Just tell her. Trust she's still the gracious Penny you knew years ago. Gloria straightened her posture and cleared her throat. "After I left my aunt's place, I headed for the mountains in hopes of finding work there. I got my GED a couple of months after settling in Summitville. Couldn't afford college, but I didn't want to pursue that route anyway." She took a breath, then released it. "I clean rental cabins in a resort town."

Silence followed as Penny's face transformed from stupefied to acceptance. "What a great place to work, in a resort town." She smiled. "I know you've always loved the outdoors."

"Yeah, I have and do. I live simply."

Penny nodded, and a wide smile brightened her face. "You always have. I envy your free spirit and easy lifestyle."

"It has its perks." Gloria lifted her chin and grinned.

They reminisced for another hour before Penny led Gloria and Serena to the front door.

Gloria embraced Penny. "Thanks so much."

"You're welcome. It's great seeing you again." Penny pulled out her mobile phone from her pants pocket. "Don't lose touch this time."

"I won't, but remember, I don't have a cell phone."

"Oh, right."

Gloria took out the paper with Penny's address on it from her jeans pocket. "Do you have a pen?"

"In my purse." Penny dug in her purse sitting on the foyer table.

Gloria took the pen Penny offered, ripped off a section of the sheet, and wrote down the office number of Cascade Cleaning Service. "Here's the number where you can reach me. Ruby will give me the message you called." She then wrote down Penny's phone number. "Talk to you soon."

Chapter Nineteen

Monday evening, Seraphima studied the testing stick, waiting for the pregnancy result to appear. Though she felt a tiny spark of joy at the possibility of being pregnant with Austin's baby, fear struck her. Uncertainty of what to do if she was pregnant made her stomach clench.

Tugging on a fat strand of hair, Seraphima watched a faint pink line materialize in the result window. The instructions had explained one line meant not pregnant while two meant pregnant. As the fuchsia line darkened, relief washed over her. Then a faint pink line to the left of the darker one surfaced like a bad dream. Seraphima's heart nearly stopped beating. The clearer and more pronounced the line became, the more anxiety-ridden she felt. The line wasn't fading. The lines were blatantly there like two pulsing, bright pink towers.

Seraphima dropped onto the toilet lid and grimaced at the plastic stick. How could this be? She'd never missed taking a birth control pill. She set the test on the sink counter. What was the purpose of taking the Pill if it failed to prevent pregnancies from happening?

She was pregnant. She had to face it.

Seraphima padded to the coffee table in the living room where her cell phone lay. She sat on the couch and tapped Austin's phone number, doubting he'd answer.

But on the third ring, he did.

"Austin," Seraphima said too quietly.

"Hello?"

She cleared her throat and forced herself to speak louder and with some assertiveness. "Austin, it's me, Fima."

"Fima, why are you calling? I thought I made it clear where I stood."

"You did, but something's happened, and I need to tell you."

"Okay, but make it quick. I'm on call here at the station."

She clutched her knotted stomach. The lack of affection or warmth in his voice made her sick. *Don't tell him. It's not the right time.* She bit her lip. *When would it be the right time?*

"Fima, come on," he said with a loud sigh.

"I-I'm pregnant." Even she could barely hear her own voice.

"What?"

"I'm pregnant," she shouted, shaking and sinking into the couch cushions.

Dead silence answered.

She squeezed her eyes shut, bracing herself for the sound of a click, disconnecting the call.

"You're pregnant?" he finally said.

"Y-yes."

"You said you were on the Pill."

"I am."

"Then what the hell happened?" His voice grew louder and higher pitched.

"I don't know. I didn't miss any days taking them."

A short pause came before his response. "Damn it, Fima, did you do this on purpose?"

"What?" Stunned, she barely got the word out of her mouth.

"You did, didn't you?"

"No! Why would I do that?"

"You told me you wanted to have children now."

"I didn't say that."

"Yeah, you did."

"No, I said I wanted to get married soon."

"And this was your way to speed that soon to now."

Frozen in place, ready to break, she grappled with her wracked emotions. "How could you think I'd do this on purpose? I told you I wanted children *after* we married."

"I never knew you could be so manipulative."

"I'm not!"

"You never showed this side of you."

A short pause followed while Seraphima swallowed down nausea as she tried to digest his rapid-fire insults.

"It's an ugly side."

Her throat closed as her heart sank in her chest. "B-but I didn't do that."

"I told you I don't want to get married anytime soon."

Tears leaked from Seraphima's eyes. "I know—"

"Then you pull this stunt."

"Stunt? We love each other and this baby is the result of it. Don't you care about your own baby?" She wiped her wet cheeks.

"Don't try to soften me up. It just adds leverage to your manipulative game."

This man had changed in a snap, unrecognizable to Seraphima. He wasn't the man she'd met six months ago with whom she'd shared her heart, body, and soul. This man was heartless with no compassion, no love.

"I've never played any games with you, Austin."

"You have now."

"Don't you think I'm not thrilled over being pregnant?"

"Why? That's what you wanted."

"Not now! I told you I wanted to be married first."

"You won't break my heart if you don't keep it."

The blood running through Seraphima turned ice cold. "What are you saying?"

"Have an abortion. Plenty of women do that with no problem. It's early enough."

The thought of killing her baby left her numb. "It's your baby and you want to kill it?"

"It's early. I'm not marrying you, Fima, especially after this deception."

Fima sat up straight. "I didn't deceive you. I told you what happened, and it's the truth."

"It's your doing and your problem. Don't call me again."

The click Seraphima had been afraid to hear at the beginning of the conversation sounded, and a dial tone pulsed in her ear. She threw down the phone and burst into tears.

Seraphima lay awake all night wondering what to do. Rubbing her abdomen, she couldn't bear losing the life inside her. But how was she going to take care of the little one? What would her family say? Mike would berate her with "I told you so," and her mother would probably chide her for being foolish.

Glory wouldn't.

She'd have hugged her and helped her through this. Seraphima knew she would. Cramps hit her again, and she curled into a fetal position until the sun peeked through the window and her alarm blared.

She had to go to work. Seraphima dragged herself out of bed and headed for the bathroom.

By lunchtime, Belinda knew about Seraphima's pregnancy.

"Holy crap, Fima. What are you going to do?" she said, leaning her elbows on the table at the local restaurant a block down from the salon.

"I'm not sure."

"Are you going to keep it?"

She pursed her lips. Not the type of question she expected from her friend. "Yes. It's my baby."

"Well, yeah, but what about the expense? Babies are expensive."

She wished she'd never told Belinda. She'd needed support, not lectures on how costly babies were. "Yes, I know," was all she could say.

Eli walked into the restaurant and headed toward them. "Hey, ladies."

"Hey," Seraphima said, clasping her shaking hands together in her lap.

Belinda gave her a look of pity and got up from her seat. "Got to get back to the salon. I'll see you later."

Seraphima nodded.

She noticed Eli observing her closely with knitted brows.

"Fima, you've been quiet all morning, and you don't look so good."

She let out a depreciative laugh. "Thanks."

He laid a hand on her arm. "No, I didn't mean it like that. You seem really upset."

Eli always perceived her feelings, like her sisters and mother. She couldn't deny what he'd said.

She sighed. "You're right."

After sipping from a can of soda he'd brought with him, he gazed at her.

You can tell him. He'd become a good friend. He had a comforting aura about him. *You can trust him.* Seraphima picked at her house salad. *He's not going to judge you.*

Eli toggled the cap on his tin can, as he appeared to be

patiently waiting for her to speak.

Looking around to make sure no one was within earshot, she said, "I found out something last night. Something big."

Eli pushed his soda to the side.

Glancing around again at the busy room with chattering knots of people, Seraphima hesitated. This wasn't the place to reveal her dilemma. "Can we talk about this after work?"

Eli raised his brows before responding. "All right, but I have class tonight."

"Oh." Seraphima slumped in the booth.

"I don't have school tomorrow night. Would that work better for you?"

An extra day would be good, giving her time to better explain her predicament to Eli. "That's fine. Would you be okay with stopping by my apartment?"

Eli shrugged. "Sure. That'll be fine."

"Good." She pulled out her phone. "What's your number? I'll give you mine." He rattled off his number after she'd given him hers. "I'll text you my address. Meet me at my place at eight."

"Got it." Eli smiled and took a sip of his soft drink.

After work, Seraphima sat at her kitchen table, pressing Mike's cell number in her phone. She needed to at least talk to her sister.

"What's up, Fima?" Mike said after the second ring.

"Mike, something's happened."

"Oh my God. What? Have you been in an accident?"

"No. Nothing like that."

"Whew." Mike blew out a breath that hissed in Seraphima's ear. "Then why scare the crap out of me?" She snorted.

Chuckling and silently thanking her sister for a light moment in the midst of the heavy situation she faced, Seraphima didn't bother formulating a gentle segue into the subject. "I'm pregnant."

"You're what?"

"Pregnant."

"Jesus, Fima. How'd that happen?"

"I—"

"Strike that. Stupid question."

"I found out last night."

"You did a pregnancy test?"

"Yes."

"Those things aren't always accurate, you know."

"I missed my period, and I don't know how since I'm taking the Pill."

"Nothing's a hundred percent foolproof."

"Except if I hadn't had sex." Regret pricked at Seraphima.

"Well, sure. That's foolproof all right."

"This is all wrong. I wanted to have children *after* marriage."

"Did you tell Austin?"

"Yes, last night."

"Did he freak out?"

"No, he was more angry than freaked." The painful words he'd said came back to her. She swallowed hard. "He told me to get rid of the baby."

"Easy for him to say. Asshole."

Seraphima winced. "Mike, please."

"Yeah, yeah. I know you don't like cursing, but that's what he is."

"He was so cold to me."

"Not surprised."

"He even accused me of getting pregnant on purpose."

"Asshole."

"Mike."

"Sorry, sis."

"It was as if I was speaking to a stranger."

"Remember what I said about men morphing from great to rotten within a few weeks or months?"

Seraphima had forgotten about her sister's remarks until now. She'd blown them off as stemming from Mike's bitterness over separation from Doug. Now she realized her sister had been right. "Yes. Yes, I do."

"Listen, you need to go to your gynecologist and have them do the pregnancy test there to confirm."

"Okay." Seraphima pictured her mother's dismayed reaction from the news. "Oh, and please don't tell Mom about this."

"Sure, but you realize she'll figure it out in a few months."

"Yes, I know. Just for right now, please—"

"I won't. I've got to go. Bailey needs help with her homework. Hang in there."

"Thanks. I'll call you when I've got the results from the doctor."

"Good."

Fima hit the End button on her phone and exhaled in relief. Calling her sister had been worth it. She had Mike's support, and that mattered so much right now.

Chapter Twenty

After work, on a cool late afternoon, Gloria packed a bologna sandwich, apple, a bottled water, and her grandmother's book in her backpack. She threw the bag on her back, grabbed the walking stick leaning against the wall near her rocking chair, and stepped out onto the porch, breathing in the clean, light air. The bright sun hung low in the sky, making its way toward the jagged, snow-covered peaks.

The sun's white rays obscured the three figures approaching the group of cabins on the dirt path. Gloria shaded her eyes with her hands, but it didn't help. One of the people waved. As they drew nearer, Serena, Lou, and Coop came into focus. Serena and Lou's hands were intertwined, and they were grinning at each other. She hadn't seen Coop since that night he walked her home, and something hadn't been right with him. With Lou and Serena absorbed in each other, she might get the chance to talk to Coop alone.

"Hey, Glory," Serena said when they all reached the steps to her home.

"Hey." Gloria gripped the backpack's straps looped through her arms. "Didn't I just see you about an hour ago?" She winked.

Serena sniggered. "Yeah, you did. And now you get to again."

"It's a good thing I never tire of seeing your face." Gloria smiled and descended the three steps from her porch.

"Neither do I," Lou added, then kissed Serena on the cheek. She giggled.

"What are you guys doing today?" Gloria asked.

"We're going to Otter Lake," Serena said.

Serena gazed up at Lou. They couldn't keep their eyes or hands off each other. So much had changed in only a few days. Serena had told her while cleaning one of the cabins yesterday that she and Lou had finally confessed their love for each other. A smile broke on Gloria's face. *Good for them.*

Coop fiddled with a twig.

"What about you?" she asked.

He looked at her through squinted eyes from the sun. "What about me?"

"Are you going with them, or do you have other plans?"

He shrugged. "Not sure."

Lou slapped Coop on the shoulder. "No offense, bud, but the lake excursion is a trip for two." His snicker mingled with Serena's giggles.

"See you later," Serena said.

The lovebirds walked off with hands clasped together.

"Where you going?" Coop asked, as Gloria took a few steps toward the dirt and gravel road.

"I've got a date with Henry." She played with the knotted bracelet around her wrist.

He didn't reply for a few seconds. "Oh, right. The tree."

Gloria tilted her head up. "Yep. Do you want to come?"

He shoved his hands in his pockets. "Okay."

She waited for him to come alongside her, then they headed to the main road.

Gloria sat on Henry's thick, outstretched branch while Coop leaned against his trunk.

"I can't stay here too long. I usually visit Henry before my daily hikes," Gloria said, gently swinging her legs.

"Okay." He thrust his body off the tree and stood with hands in his pockets. He narrowed his eyes at her. "You ever feel like there's more to life than the shitty one you got?"

Gloria's legs stopped swinging, and she slid off the branch. She eyed him closely. He was ready to talk. "Sometimes."

Coop leaned his hand against Henry's side. "Yeah?"

"Yeah. But I haven't quite figured out what it is."

"I hate it here." He looked around the copse of trees and the lofty Rockies behind them.

"Hate nature or Summitville?"

"Summitville. Jobs suck here. Aren't any."

Gloria frowned. "But you said you do landscaping and other handyman jobs."

Coop raised his head as if surprised by her comment. "They're not steady work."

"Do you want to do something else?"

He scratched his cheek. "Can't afford college, so I'm stuck with them."

"Doesn't a landscaper get paid pretty well?" Gloria rolled her grandmother's bracelet back and forth on her wrist.

He shrugged. "I guess."

"You guess? Don't you know?"

He kicked one of Henry's fat roots. "It doesn't matter. Nothing matters."

"Why?" Gloria cringed as he continued to smack his boot against Henry. "Hey, can you stop kicking Henry?"

"It's a friggin' tree," he snapped.

Gloria stepped back and grasped her backpack's straps with shaky hands. "It's a living thing."

"Who the hell cares?" Coop's crimson face twisted in anger.

Fear swept through her. "Look, Coop. What's wrong? Why are you so angry?"

He closed the two feet between them, shot his hands out, and clamped them on her shoulders. "Why are you asking me so many friggin' questions?"

Haunting images of her father beating her flashed in her mind. Trembling, Gloria wiggled out of his hold. "I-I'm sorry. I thought you wanted to talk."

"There's nothing to talk about."

"Then why are you here with me?"

All anger left his features, and he ran a hand over his face. "Glory, life sucks. I don't even know why I'm alive." He sat on the ground, propped his elbows on his knees, and rested his head between his hands.

Gloria lowered herself to the ground and sat next to him. "Whoa. Life isn't that bad for you to wonder such a thing."

He turned his head toward her, his azure eyes glistening. "She's gone."

Gloria placed her hand on his back. "Who's gone?"

"Without her, life is nothing." He buried his head in his hands again.

"What happened? Who is this woman?"

He stomped one of his black boots. "Sarah."

"Was she your girlfriend?"

"Wife."

Gloria froze. His wife? "What happened to her?"

"She left me."

"She divorced you?"

"No."

"What happened to her?"

"She died in a hit-and-run three months ago. She was carrying our child."

Gloria gaped. "My God, Coop. I'm so sorry." She hugged him.

His eyes were on hers again. "You look a lot like her."

Everything Serena had said came rushing back to her like a rapidly flowing stream. *He likes you,* she'd said. The intense stare he gave her at the restaurant and his walking her home.

His hand touched her cheek. "Her eyes were emerald green like yours."

Uneasiness fluttered in her chest. "How long were you married?"

His hand dropped. "Four years."

How old was he? Did he get married right out of high school? "Married young?"

He shrugged. "I guess."

"I haven't much experience in dating, let alone marriage. Serena told me guys don't marry until they're around thirty."

He chuckled, and the uneasiness in her chest lessened.

"Yeah, that's probably right. But Sarah and I knew each other since middle school, went together through high school. Still, I know it's bizarre we got married that young. We're freaks."

She laughed.

He turned his head toward her, serious again. "Our baby would've been born last month."

Gloria frowned as her heart ached for Coop's loss. "I don't know what to say."

Coop shook his head. "Nothing to say. Life sucks."

Gloria stayed quiet. Life *did* suck for Coop. It was a cruel fate. How did a person cope with such a loss?

"I should've been with her." His words brought Gloria out of her own thoughts.

"No."

He bobbed his head. "Yeah. I should've died with them. Then I wouldn't have to feel the pain every damn day."

She rubbed his back again. "You'll get through this."

His head swiveled around, his blue eyes nearly black. "No, I won't. Are you freakin' insane? I can't deal with it. It's only gotten worse." He shot up from the ground, yanked on his short, spiky hair, and pounded his boots into the earth.

A thought came to her that made her feel like a hypocrite. She never got counseling for her pain and trauma. How could she give him any advice? Before she could say anything, he stormed away.

Great. She hadn't done anything for him. She sighed. But what could she have done? She wasn't an expert on those issues. She got up. Why hadn't Serena or Lou told her about this? They had to know. Maybe they didn't. She glanced at the inviting forest but turned her back to it and headed toward Otter Lake.

Chapter Twenty-One

Gloria stepped over the large, smooth boulders to where Serena and Lou sat wrapped in each other's arms, staring out at the crystal-clear water of Otter Lake. Their heads turned in her direction as she approached them.

"Hey, Glory. Didn't expect to see you here. I thought you were going for a hike." Serena tilted her head to the side and tented her face with her hand from the sun's rosy rays.

Gloria rested a well-worn hiking boot on the big rock in front of her. "Sorry to bother you guys, but I need to talk to you about Coop."

Lou and Serena glanced at each other with impish grins on their faces.

"Coming to us for dating advice?" Serena poked Gloria's leg with an amused expression.

"Hardly." Gloria shook off Serena's playful fingers. "Coop's in bad shape."

Lou sat up, alert. "What happened?"

Sensing Lou's awareness, Gloria said, "He's not coping well with his—"

Lou shot up, put a finger to his mouth, and shook his head.

Gloria removed her shoe from the rock and stood evenly on the ground. "What?"

"It's private—his stuff." Lou flashed a concerned glance at Serena.

Serena looked from Gloria to Lou. "Private stuff?"

Lou folded in his lips.

"Stuff you can't share with me?" She gave him a wounded look.

"It wasn't my stuff to share," Lou said.

Gloria bit her lip. "Look, I'm sorry. I just wanted to help Coop. We were talking near Henry, and he stormed off."

Lou nodded with a grim expression. "No, you did the right thing. I've gotta jet. Need to find him and talk to him." He reached over and squeezed Serena's rounded shoulders. "I promise I'll be back soon."

Gloria wrung her hands. Serena didn't look happy. "Do you want me to walk with you back to town?"

Serena shook her head. "No, it's okay." She swatted a hand in Lou's direction. "Go and do what you have to do. I'm going home." She leaped over the rocks and marched down the walking path.

What a mess I've made. Gloria slouched and plodded toward the way she'd come. At least Lou would be there for Coop.

As Gloria's hiking boots crunched the gravelly trail, the pink shaft of the sunset poured over her and through the gaps in the trees on her right. She'd reached the trail she'd wanted to take and had been on it for the past quarter of a mile. A chilly breeze cut through the crisp air and fluttered her hair and jacket.

Stopping to pull out her water bottle and take a drink, her

gaze fell on another path to her right that led to a clearing peeking over the slight incline in the trail a few feet away. Always up for a new adventure in nature, she pivoted in that direction and walked toward the opening.

At the bottom of the incline, straight ahead only about thirty yards away, stood three buildings. One looked like a three-story dorm, one a dome-roofed chapel with a cross on top, and the other a greenhouse. A swath of tilled land extended to the greenhouse with little sprouting to show in March.

Curious, she walked toward the church. Its outer walls were beige and its dome, gold. Reaching the door to the structure, she looked around and listened for people. She didn't hear anything but knocked on the door anyway. Seconds later, the door opened, and a woman who appeared to be in her thirties dressed in a black robe and head covering smiled sweetly. A black-knotted bracelet just like Gloria's circled her wrist. Was this the type of church her grandmother had gone to? A kindle of hope sparked in her.

"Hello. Have you come for the *Paraklesis* service?" the woman asked in a lyrical tone.

Gloria squinted in confusion. "I don't know what that is." She glanced up at the large painting tacked over the arched doorway. A woman in red and blue robes held a baby in her lap. Golden halos circled both the figures' heads.

The woman chuckled softly. "That's all right." She pulled the door all the way open and stood to the side. "It's a prayer service to the Theotokos."

Gloria wrinkled her nose. "*Theo* what?"

"The Mother of God." The woman said, then added, "The Virgin Mary."

"Oh. Okay."

A large smile split the woman's kind face. "Come." She gestured for Gloria to enter the dark foyer.

Gloria stepped inside, and the woman shut the door behind her.

The woman passed her and stood by a stand with a round top filled with sand and a handful of candles standing in it. She pressed a hand to her chest. "I'm Sister Elizabeth."

"Glory." She gazed at the flickering candles, then at the large painting hanging on the wall to the left of the candles. An old man with white hair and beard on an oblong, sober face, donned in yellow and red robes stared back at her from the picture. He, too, had a halo around his head.

"Glory. What a beautiful name," Sister Elizabeth said. She pointed to the candles. "This is where a person lights a candle for herself or someone she wants to pray for."

Gloria nodded, but she'd already moved her gaze to other paintings on the walls in the small, darkened space. Warmth filled the area, and a faint scent of something flowery and sweet wafted in the air. A sense of peace settled in her soul—one she'd rarely felt all the years of her life.

Sister Elizabeth walked toward a set of doors ahead of them. She turned and waved at Gloria. "Come in. You can watch and listen to our prayer service."

Gloria followed the nun into the larger space with no pews or chairs in the area where she'd thought most churches would have them. Only a maroon oriental rug covered the middle portion of the wood floor. Five nuns stood huddled by a chestnut podium that held open books. A bell-shaped light fixture suspended from the ceiling dangled over them, its glow spreading over the group.

Next to them, a carved wooden barrier with an archway in its center covered the whole space in front of Gloria. More paintings of people sat in recessed portions of the partition.

The nuns started to sing, and the room filled with angelic voices in a very different melodic tone. The words and melody certainly didn't sound like anything modern. The chanting transported her back to an ancient era she'd read about in her high school history courses. She closed her eyes, taking it all in. How had she not seen this place in any of her walks through the mountains?

They sang in English and another language she couldn't decipher. But it didn't matter. The sounds, the smells, the quietude among them, as well as the beautiful art surrounding her, made her want to stay there forever.

An hour later, one of the nuns clicked off the overhead light, opened a short door in the podium, placed the books inside, and all of them filed past her to the doors in which she'd come. They gave her nods and friendly smiles before gathering in the foyer and talking quietly.

She spotted Sister Elizabeth in the group. The nun gestured her toward them. "Come," she said.

Gloria obeyed and stopped in front of the handful of nuns.

"Sisters, this is Glory. She came to visit us," Sister Elizabeth said.

Faces beamed back at Gloria. The woman farthest on her left who looked to be in her midforties pointed to herself. "I'm Sister Catherine." She then laid a hand on the young woman's shoulder next to her. "And this is Sister Gabriella."

The nun next to Sister Gabriella gave Gloria a toothy welcome. "I'm Sister Angelica."

Sister Elizabeth gestured to the older woman who looked to be in her sixties with a round face and childlike, chubby cheeks. Her blue-green eyes shone wisdom. "And this is our abbess, Mother Maria," Sister Elizabeth said.

"Nice to meet everyone." Gloria bowed her head.

"This is your first visit here," Mother Maria said.

"Yeah... yes. I didn't know this place even existed in Summitville, or anywhere." Gloria laughed, her cheeks warming.

The nuns chuckled, and three exited the church in a perfect

line. Only Sister Elizabeth and Mother Maria remained before Gloria.

Mother Maria raised her head toward the ceiling and walls of the foyer. "This monastery has been here for seven years. We've truly been blessed."

Monastery. Was that what this was called? "You mean you're not a convent? I thought women lived in convents."

"Convent is also correct. Although, in our tradition, it's called a women's monastery," Mother Maria explained, tucking her hands inside the layers of her robes.

Gloria nodded and rolled her knotted bracelet on her wrist. "It's a beautiful church."

"Thank you." The abbess's gaze fell on Gloria's wrist. "Ah, you have a prayer rope. You pray the Jesus Prayer?"

"Jesus Prayer?" Gloria shook her head. She didn't remember that prayer in Grandmother's book.

The abbess pulled out a longer knotted rope with three red beads separating sections of the knots with a tassel-like end to the material. "It's a simple prayer we pray every minute of the day. It's also quite popular for many Orthodox Christian laypeople." Mother Maria bowed, then glided to the candle stand and blew out the flames.

Elizabeth touched Gloria's arm. "We must go to the dining hall and eat our evening meal now." She leaned toward Gloria. "Would you like to join us?"

Gloria's heart swelled at the thought of dining with the nuns, but it was late, and she needed to get home. "Maybe another time?"

"Of course. We have services Mondays, Wednesdays, Fridays, Saturdays, and Sundays, and we also have tours Tuesdays and Thursdays from eight a.m. to three p.m."

"Thank you. That's good to know."

"It was a pleasure to meet you, Glory," Mother Maria said and stepped out the open door.

"Thank you for coming to visit us," Sister Elizabeth said, and guided Gloria out of the church.

"Thanks. I'm so glad I found your monastery." Gloria reluctantly walked away, as a comforting blaze of peace penetrated her heart. *I'll be back soon.*

Chapter Twenty-Two

After dinner the same evening, Michaela called Doug to confirm his plans with Bailey on Saturday.

"Hello?" a female voice answered.

"Hello?" Michaela echoed. Who was this woman answering Doug's phone?

"Oh, hello, Michaela."

She recognized Tina's condescending voice. Only her mother called her by her full and given name. Did Tina think she was of the same caliber as Etta? Michaela clucked her tongue. *Think again.*

"You answer Doug's cell phone now?"

"I just happened to be closest to it."

"I see." Michaela stifled the itching jealousy and anger growing inside her. "I need to speak to my husband."

"Your husband, hmm."

"Yes, my husband."

"It's funny, because you haven't seen fit to think of Doug as your husband in a very long time."

Heat burned Michaela's cheeks. "What business is that of yours? You've known Doug but a few weeks, maybe a month."

An arrogant cackle rang through the earpiece. "We spend a lot of time together. I practically live here."

Nearly crushing the mobile in her hand, Michaela snapped, "Do you always steal women's husbands?"

"There's been no stealing involved. You kicked him out, remember?"

"Get Doug on the damn phone. We have a daughter to discuss."

"Hey, relax. No need to go ballistic."

Michaela breathed loudly, holding her tongue as she heard Tina say, "Michaela is on the phone apparently throwing a fit over the fact that I answered. She wants to talk to you."

Why did Michaela feel like a third wheel instead of the other way around? This shrew made her feel like a petulant child. Wiping her damp palms on her thighs, Michaela took in three calming breaths. *Don't let her get under your skin anymore.*

"Mike?" Doug's voice brought welcome relief to Michaela, despite her fury.

"Doug, your *partner* and *good friend* is a pain in the ass."

"Is that why you called? To bad-mouth Tina?"

Michaela sighed. She needed to forget about that woman. "No. I called to confirm your outing with Bailey at Pinewood Park on Saturday."

"Oh, right. I'll be there to pick her up at eleven."

"Okay."

"Is that all?"

Michaela began to long for the days when Doug begged her to allow him to move back in their home. He'd lost interest in calling her every few days like he did the first month they'd separated, and Michaela swore it was because of *that woman.* But he was out because of his alcohol addiction. She couldn't get soft and forget that.

The urge to bring up his and Tina's relationship and its effects on Bailey couldn't be kept at bay. "I can't believe you're practically living with another woman already. Have you thought about how this looks to Bailey and how she may be feeling seeing her dad with another woman?"

"Living together?" Doug laughed. "Don't be ridiculous, Mike."

"That's what—"

"We're friends, all right? See you on Saturday."

"Uh-huh." How naive did he think she was? Michaela ended the call and set the phone on the kitchen counter. Snatching a sponge by the sink, she flung open the fridge door and began to feverishly scrub the glass shelves.

Chapter Twenty-Three

Seraphima sat on her sofa next to Eli, as the TV screen flashed a black-and-white movie on low volume.

"It was nice of you to come," she said.

"Hey, we agreed to this. Remember?"

"I know. I'm just grateful you didn't change your mind." Seraphima curled on the left side of the couch and faced Eli.

"Why would I?" Eli smiled kindly and leaned back against the cushions. "Now, what did you want to talk about?"

"After talking to my sister, I'm not sure I should tell you without it being fact."

With a furrowed brow, Eli rubbed his chin.

"I'd rather not say anything until I find out for sure."

He scratched his blond head and said, "Okay." He rose and gestured toward the door. "Do you want me to go?"

"No, please stay. It'd be silly to leave when you just got here."

"To be honest, I can only stay half an hour. I've got to help my dad get ready for bed." He sat down slowly, rubbing his hands on his jeans.

Seraphima had forgotten about Eli's father. She had only been thinking about her own dilemma. "Oh, I'm sorry."

"There's nothing to be sorry about. It's all good." He leaned his elbows on his knees and turned his head toward her.

Seraphima smiled.

He pointed at the TV. "What's playing?"

"It's an old movie."

"Yeah, I got that." He chuckled.

"It's the start of *Talk of the Town* with Cary Grant. I love old movies." Seraphima clasped her hands around her knees. "My mom played them all the time when I was growing up."

"Same here. I'm a huge Bogart fan."

"Really?" How many men had Seraphima known who actually liked classic movies? None. They all liked action adventures. If she'd named an old film, they'd look at her as if she'd spoken a foreign language.

"Yep. *The Maltese Falcon* is my favorite." He pointed casually at the TV. "There are some movies I've seen with Grant, like *Arsenic and Old Lace*. Hysterical. Great script writing back then."

She stared wide-eyed at Eli. Every time she had a conversation with him, she learned something unexpected about him. She chuckled. "Yes, it's hilarious."

Seraphima reflexively stroked her stomach. Even though Mike had said home pregnancy tests weren't very accurate, she could tell she was pregnant. She felt different, especially in her abdomen. There was something in there. A dull ache and mild cramps told her so, as if her uterus was trying to expand for its new resident.

"Are you not feeling well, Fima?"

"Oh, no. I'm fine."

"You were rubbing your stomach. I wasn't sure if you were feeling sick."

"I'm fine," she repeated, giving him a confident smile even

though fear of this pregnancy hung over her like a dangling anvil.

"Good." He watched TV for the next few minutes, leaving Seraphima to debate with herself on whether to go ahead and tell Eli what the pregnancy test revealed. It was already Wednesday, and she doubted she'd get in to see the gynecologist for a blood test before Monday.

Studying Eli's profile with his Roman nose, sunken, large eyes, long lashes, and rounded chin, she'd felt a real friendship with him. He'd shown her nothing but kindness. She needed to tell him. Surely he'd understand and empathize with her. She hoped so. Seraphima needed friends to support her. Something Belinda hadn't really done.

"Eli, Austin broke up with me last week." She shook her head. "To be honest, I think he'd already done so before that."

Eli turned toward her. "I'm sorry. I know how much you cared for him."

"Loved him," she muttered, grasping a lock of her hair and twisting it.

He nodded with a sympathetic frown.

"I'm going to tell you what I thought I wouldn't until later."

He waited attentively.

"I found out last night that I'm pregnant."

His mouth fell open.

"And Austin wants me to get rid of our baby." With those words, Seraphima looked away, not wanting to see Eli's expression.

"Not cool. How could he not want to keep his own child?"

"He's not ready for marriage and a family. I discovered this a couple of weeks ago. Stupid me." She knocked her knuckles against her forehead as tears stung her eyes. "Stupid, stupid, stupid."

"Fima." Eli leaned over and embraced her, his gaunt chest

pressing against her petite one, with his wiry arms holding her close. "You're not stupid. You were in love."

"I should have found out about his intentions before sleeping with him." Seraphima buried her wet face in Eli's bony shoulder. "It's just we had such chemistry, such attraction for each other. It felt so right, like we were meant to be together. And when he'd wanted to take that next intimate step, I thought that meant he loved me too. Since then, I've craved his touch, the smell of him… God, I'm sorry for going on like this," she whimpered in his arms.

She heard him huff while gently rubbing her back. "I'm sorry he did this to you."

They separated, and she wiped her damp face.

Eli stood up and walked toward the doors in the tiny hallway. "Which one's the bathroom?"

"The first door on the right."

He came back with a box of tissues and set it on the coffee table. Seraphima plucked one, dabbed her eyes, then blew her nose.

Sitting back down, he said, "What are you going to do?"

"I'm going to my gynecologist hopefully next week so they can do a pregnancy test there to verify."

"That's good."

She nodded.

Eli rested his hand on Seraphima's shoulder. "Don't worry. You won't go through this alone."

His kind words were a salve on her broken heart, and his soft blue eyes, filled with empathy, lessened the weight on her shoulders. "Thank you."

Chapter Twenty-Four

Monday during her lunch break, Seraphima sat in an exam room of the gynecology clinic, waiting for the results of her pregnancy test. In addition to the urine sample, the nurse had drawn blood to check her hormone levels.

Feeling anxious, Seraphima reapplied her maroon lipstick, checking herself in her compact mirror. Did she look any differently now that she may be pregnant? Wiping away invisible stray mascara crumbs, Seraphima stared into her own eyes. She could be a mother in less than a year. She shuddered in terror by the thought, but she didn't allow it to linger. She closed her compact, shoved it back into her large black purse, and pulled out her phone to play a game.

A minute later, the nurse returned, smiling with compassion. Seraphima glanced at her name tag dangling from around her neck. It read ALICE.

"Seraphima, you are pregnant."

Dread and joy in one tumultuous wave washed over her. She held on to the sides of the chair to anchor herself.

"Congratulations," the nurse said.

Looking up at Alice, Seraphima planted her shaking hands on her thighs. "Thanks."

"You'll need to come back on Wednesday for another blood test to check your HCG levels again."

"What's that?"

"Human chorionic gonadotropin."

"Human what?" Seraphima wrung her hands.

"It's a hormone that's produced by the embryo when it's implanted in the uterus. We look at the levels to make sure the pregnancy is a healthy one and to discover any problems early on."

Seraphima's stomach somersaulted. "Problems?"

"There's no need to worry. It's a regular precautionary measure." The nurse patted Seraphima's hands tangled together in her lap.

"Okay." She blew out a breath.

"Wednesday at noon again. Will that work for you?"

"Yes."

Seraphima walked out of the building still grappling with her mixed emotions. She needed to talk to someone. She tapped her sister's number in the list of contacts in her phone. Voice mail answered. It was Mike's lunch break. Why wasn't she answering her phone?

Seraphima bit her lip and continued walking to her car.

Eli stood next to Seraphima by her car in the parking lot of the salon. All she could think of since the nurse confirmed her pregnancy was Austin. She was carrying his baby—their baby. A baby they had created out of love. And he didn't want her or it. Instead of this being a time of happiness, it was filled with sorrow and apprehension.

"I'm pregnant." Seraphima glanced up at Eli and found him studying her closely.

"Are you okay? I'm not sure if I'm supposed to congratulate you."

Seraphima gave him a faint smile. "I don't know either." Her eyes welled with tears as a lump formed in her throat. She hugged herself, biting down on her lip to stop its quivering.

Eli's arms encircled her, and she wept against his chest.

It seemed like an hour they had stayed in that position. Eli didn't offer any words, and Seraphima was grateful for it. His consoling embrace was enough. When she thought about the months ahead, cold fear gripped her. How would she do this without Austin? The hurtful words from Austin had stung her heart. She clung tighter to Eli's thin frame, wondering when her tears would stop flowing.

"Do you want me to drive you home?" Eli asked in a quiet voice.

Pulling away from him, she shook her head. "That's okay." A cramp pinched her abdomen. She winced and covered her stomach with her hands.

Eli bent his knees to stand at eye level with her. "Are you sure you're all right?"

The pain subsided. What was going on inside her? What if her pregnancy wasn't normal? Seraphima shook her head. *Stop thinking like that.* "Just a cramp." She straightened her shoulders and licked her dry lips.

She used her car fob to unlock her car's doors.

Eli opened the driver's side door. "What do you need me to do to help?"

"Nothing right now." She gave him a weak smile.

Eli pulled out his cell phone and held it up. "You've got my number from work. Please text me if and when you need anything."

Nodding, Seraphima slipped into the seat. Eli closed it and waved at her while she drove away.

Wednesday at noon, Seraphima waited in the gynecologist's exam room for the blood test results. Cramps had revisited her the past two days, but the pain was manageable.

Since finding out that she was pregnant, Seraphima had resisted the strong urge to call Austin. Part of her wanted to share the incredible news with the father of their baby, but the other part of her remembered their argument, and the hurt returned. She'd begun to realize he never truly knew her or she him. That scared her but also awoke her to the mistakes she'd made, quickly giving into Austin's caresses and ultimately losing her virginity. Shame and sorrow sat heavy in her chest and burned her cheeks as the events replayed like a movie reel in her mind.

The door opened, and Alice entered the room. "All right, Seraphima." The nurse stood over her as she sat with shoulders slouched and knees pressed together on the fabric-covered chair. "Your HCG levels did not double. They're lagging behind."

Seraphima froze. "Is that bad?"

"Remember I told you on Monday about these hormone levels?"

"I think so."

The nurse smiled and sat in the chair next to her. "We'll need to do another blood test on Friday before Dr. Willis decides the next step forward."

"Next step?"

"She'll probably have an ultrasound ordered for you to check the location of the implanted egg."

"Oh." Where else would it be but in her uterus? Seraphima frowned. Why was Alice confusing her?

Alice's hand touched her arm. "I know it's all a bit overwhelming, but we'll keep you informed every step of the way. Don't worry."

How could she *not*? Seraphima exhaled away her troublesome thoughts. "Okay. I'll try not to."

"Can you return on Friday at the same time?"

Not even thinking to check her schedule, Seraphima said numbly, "Yes."

"Okay. We'll see you then. Take care."

The nurse left, leaving Seraphima in the empty room. *What's going to happen to me and my baby?*

Chapter Twenty-Five

Seraphima waited in a plastic chair across from the examination table with its stirrups. She smelled the usual clinic cleaners and listened to the low-decibel, soft rock music drifting through the ceiling's two small speakers.

Alice slipped quietly into the room.

Biting her lip, Seraphima watched the nurse intently. What were the results today?

"Unfortunately, the HCG levels haven't doubled. Dr. Willis has ordered an ultrasound to check the location of the embryo."

"The location? Shouldn't it be in my uterus?"

Alice sat on a stool next to her, tapping a computer's keyboard. "Yes, but there's something abnormal about the numbers. So the doctor will need to see what's going on inside you."

Seraphima fidgeted in her seat. "What does that mean?" She wished she'd brought her sister or Eli along this time. She'd hoped and prayed so hard that these results would have been normal.

Alice turned her head away from the computer screen to

answer her. "It means it's possible that you have an abnormal pregnancy. Possibly an ectopic one."

"What's that?" Seraphima pulled gently on strands of her hair.

"It's when the fertilized egg implants outside of the uterus, usually in one of the fallopian tubes."

Seraphima wrung her hands. "What will happen to me and the baby?"

Alice's brows drew together, and she frowned. "Let's wait and see what the ultrasound shows."

Irritation and panic coursed through her. She wanted to know what was going on right now. She needed to have the full picture of what to expect next. "How long before I can get that done?"

Staring at the screen again, Alice said, "In a half hour. Not too long." She gave Seraphima another compassionate smile.

She slumped in her chair as the same horrible thoughts she'd had since she found out the results of her blood tests invaded her head. Her stomach twisted in a queasy knot. Silence blanketed the room with only the sounds of her heart thumping in her ears and the clicking of Alice's fingers on the keyboard. Whatever music had been playing had vaporized from the cold, clinical space.

When Alice had finished typing, she rose from the stool. "You can wait in here if you're more comfortable. The ultrasound tech will come when it's time."

"Okay." Seraphima blew out a shaky breath, wiping her damp palms on her pants.

For the past half hour, Seraphima lay on her back with her legs bent and slightly apart as the ultrasound wand probed around the opening to her uterus. She watched the screen as the tech tapped on the computer's keyboard every few minutes with her free hand. Seraphima wasn't certain where the embryo was. It was hard to tell. There were a handful of splotches and dark spots sprinkled across the monitor.

Finally the tech withdrew the wand and said, "We're all done. You can get dressed." She typed something, and the screen went blank. The tech then headed out of the room, shutting the door noiselessly behind her.

She sat up. What did the tech find?

Peeling off the hospital's gown, Seraphima got dressed quickly. She brushed hair from her eyes and whispered, "God, I hope the baby's in my uterus."

She had only been sitting for five minutes when Alice came into the room and waved a hand.

"Follow me."

Seraphima trailed behind Alice into Dr. Willis's office.

"Dr. Willis will be in soon to give you the results." Alice nodded, then closed the door behind her, leaving Seraphima alone.

Chilled by what was happening, Seraphima rubbed her arms, scrunching her shoulders to her ears. What was the doctor going to tell her about her baby? She didn't know if she could stand hearing what Dr. Willis had to say. A sharp pain stabbed her scalp. She'd twirled her hair into a tight, rolled-up knot with her finger imprisoned in it. Using both hands to unweave the intricate swirl, Seraphima felt the coiled hair release. She quickly slid out her finger and raked her hand through the messy lump, breaking up the woven tresses.

The door opened, and Dr. Willis, a tall woman with frosted hair, large round glasses, and a motherly smile walked in. "Hello, Seraphima." She carried a manila folder.

"Hello." Seraphima forced a smile.

Dr. Willis sat at the desk and laid the folder on its surface. "It appears that the ultrasound didn't show the implanted egg in the uterus. It's most likely the embryo is in one of your fallopian tubes. And from the information you gave Alice at your first visit for the pregnancy test confirmation," she said, now flipping open the folder with paperwork in it, "you're at eight weeks, which allows for the option of a shot instead of surgery in order to save your tube."

Shot? With her mind still trying to absorb the news that her baby wasn't in her uterus, a weight sat on Seraphima's chest as her heartbeat pulsed in her head. In the midst of this discombobulated state, Seraphima realized Dr. Willis was studying her with her mouth turned down.

"The shot of methotrexate will dissolve the pregnancy." The doctor closed the folder. "Do you understand? Do you have any questions?"

Stunned, Seraphima shook her head. "I don't know…"

"This shot will save your fallopian tube. One dose should be enough, but we do a follow-up blood test a few days afterward to make sure. If any remnants are left, a D and C will be performed."

What was a D and C? Seraphima's mouth quivered as she swallowed hard. *I can't handle all of this.*

"I'm sorry, Seraphima. I know this is a lot to digest. Ectopic pregnancies occur in about one in every fifty pregnancies. There is a greater risk of having another ectopic pregnancy after having a previous one, but the majority of women go on to have healthy pregnancies and give birth to healthy babies." She clasped her hands on the desk. "The sooner this pregnancy is terminated, the less likely your tube will burst or that you'll need surgery."

The fog dissipated from Seraphima's mind and alarm took over. *My tube may burst? Oh my God.* "When do I get the shot?"

"Wait in the exam room you were just in, and Alice will be in shortly."

How long would she have to wait? Seraphima moved on shaky legs out of the office toward the exam room.

"The shot will be administered in one of your buttocks," Alice explained, preparing the needle as Seraphima stood with her yoga pants and underwear around her thighs, facing the wall. "It may feel a little sore afterward. Tylenol or ibuprofen can be taken to alleviate it. The soreness should be gone by tomorrow."

Alice rubbed a cold, moist cotton ball smelling of alcohol on a spot on her rear. A slight sting followed.

"All done," Alice said. "You can get dressed."

Seraphima immediately yanked up her underwear with her pants.

"We'll need you to return next week for another blood test to check the progress of the medication. You can make your appointment up front." The nurse dropped the needle in the orange box hanging on the wall, peeled off and discarded her rubber gloves, then left the room.

Seraphima walked out with wobbly legs, hoping this horror would all be over soon. How long would she have to wait until the medication worked and her fallopian tube would be saved? Anxiety riddled her insides as she tugged on a strand of her hair and approached the appointment desk.

Chapter Twenty-Six

Bailey skipped into the foyer. "Mama, Tina taught me how to skate backward."

Biting back irritation every time she heard that woman's name, Michaela caressed Bailey's head, smoothing her hair away from her face. "How fun."

"I fell down three times, but I always got back up and kept on trying. Didn't I, Tina?"

Despite Michaela's brittle argument with Tina over the phone a few days ago, the shrew had been surprisingly cordial to her today. She glanced at Doug, who was squatting in front of their daughter and kissing her on the cheek. He must have chastised Tina for her caustic behavior.

"You sure did." Tina nodded and gave Bailey a fist to bump. Bailey touched her fist to Tina's and giggled.

Doug stood up. "We better go. It's late." He blew a kiss to Bailey. "We'll see you next Saturday for our trip to the zoo with Gramma."

Michaela had caved in the past week, allowing Doug to visit Bailey every Saturday instead of twice a month. She couldn't deprive Bailey of her desire to spend time with her dad, but she continued to monitor his behavior, checking for any signs of drunkenness. So far, he'd appeared sober.

"I can't wait!" Bailey hugged Doug, then bounded up the stairs.

"Bye, Mike. See you then." Doug smiled, and her heart tightened. The anger she'd barely been able to contain the past several months had eased, and she had started to wonder what to do about it.

He stepped onto the porch, and Tina trailed behind him, waving at Michaela but saying nothing. Yes, Doug had tamed the serpent's tongue. Guess that showed he still cared about her and her feelings, at least some. But would it last?

As the door clicked shut and Michaela locked it, her cell phone rang from the living room. She flipped on the overhead light and picked up the mobile from the desk. "Hello?"

"Mike? This is Penny."

She paused near the bookcase. "Penny, it's been a while. Do you have some news on Glory?"

"Well, no, but I was calling to see if maybe you had heard something," she said with a jittery laugh.

Michaela ran her finger over a shelf. She lifted her hand, and a thin layer of dust covered the tip of her finger. She rubbed her fingers together as she considered Penny's words. She had nothing to report but expected something from her. Of course, being Glory's best friend from childhood, she'd want to know anything new on Glory too. But here Michaela thought Penny would be the person with all the answers. Ironically, this time around, Michaela had a couple.

"You're in luck," she said. "We found out last week that Glory changed her last name to our mother's maiden name."

"Oh?"

"And we visited her cabin in Summitville last Sunday, but she wasn't there. She's alive and well, and we now know where she lives."

"That's awesome news. Will you try to visit her again this weekend?"

"My mother hasn't mentioned plans for visiting this weekend. It sure would be easier if we had her phone number."

There was a short pause before Penny said, "Yes. That would really help."

"But I suspect my mother will want to visit Glory in the next week or two."

"What about your father? Didn't he go with you?"

Michaela blinked. Penny didn't know about her father's death. How could she? "Our father died two years ago this past January."

"Oh." Penny's shrill response rang in her ear. She didn't speak for another few seconds but then replied, "I'm sorry," as if saying it in passing.

Michaela pursed her lips. Penny only knew her father by the information relayed to her from Glory. Michaela was certain her sister had only shared the bad experiences.

"Hey, would you mind giving me your address in case Glory calls and she asks for it?" Penny inquired in a hesitant tone.

"I can't believe she hasn't called you," Michaela retorted with a laugh, half teasing, half serious. This whole call seemed strange, as if Penny wasn't being totally honest.

Another few seconds passed before Penny answered her. "I know, but I'm still hoping she will soon."

"Yeah, I'm sure." Michaela told Penny her address. Had Glory really not contacted Penny? This thought continued to nag at Michaela.

"Thanks. Could I get Glory's address too? I'd love to ride out to Summitville and see her. I miss her."

Michaela rattled off her sister's address. "It's online, just to let you know."

"Oh, well, thanks for saving me the internet search. Also, thanks for the great news about Glory."

"Sure."

"I've got to go now. Dinner is done. Bye."

Michaela ended the call, tapped the top of her phone against her chin, and leaned her hip on the edge of the desk. Did Penny really not have any contact with Glory all this time? She didn't sound convincing enough to her. In any case, thanks to her, Penny now had a way to contact Glory. Maybe her mother would get her wish sooner rather than later.

Chapter Twenty-Seven

A fter a hearty hour walk in the early, crisp dawn, Gloria arrived at the monastery's chapel just in time to hear the bell tower clang. The double wooden doors opened, and the five nuns congregated on the small cement court that ran between the church and the dorm building.

Gloria spotted Sister Elizabeth in the knot of black robes. The nun turned her head in Gloria's direction, and with a knowing nod, she approached her.

Sister Elizabeth straightened her ebony head covering. "Glory. How nice to see you again." Her smooth, makeup-free face brightened. "Would you like to take a tour of the grounds?"

"Yes, I would. Thanks."

The other four nuns strolled into the dorm building.

Sister Elizabeth bowed. "Very good. Follow me." She flicked a hand at Gloria and swung around facing the greenhouse and garden. "It's such a beautiful day. We'll start with the gardens and cemetery."

Twenty minutes later, they walked the quiet halls of the dorm. "This is where we sleep, cook, do household chores, and mind the gift shop. We just had a group of high school girls with their parish priest and his wife visit last weekend. Pilgrims stay in the west wing of the building. They attend our services and take on a variety of chores to help maintain our monastery."

Gloria surveyed the area where two hallways led to the rooms the nun mentioned and another two branched off to what she imagined were the dining hall and kitchen. The floors and furniture glistened with the caring touch of the nuns. She saw herself sleeping in one of the dorm rooms, cleaning the floors and windows, pulling weeds, and watering the garden. *A perfect place to stay and use my polish and shine skills.*

Fervor flooded her as she walked down the main hallway to the open arched room on their left, which revealed the gift shop. As soon as Gloria saw the books, she hurried over to them. "I love to read, and I'd love to learn about my grandmother's religion."

Sister Elizabeth pointed to a shelf on their right. "There are many books on our Orthodox Christian faith, as well as the lives of the saints."

Gloria pulled out a book and gazed at its cover of priests inside a dimly lit, magnificent church. She then browsed the numerous tomes on saints before spying one with a nun on the front surrounded by a foggy veil of incense. "How about this one?" she asked, tapping the front cover facing them, tucked between the spines of other books. The title read *The Scent of Holiness: Lessons from a Women's Monastery.* The warmth in her heart had returned since she'd first discovered the monastery. And she wanted to learn more about these women's lives. She slid the other book back in its original spot.

"Splendid. This is a wonderful choice," Sister Elizabeth said, touching the book with care.

They walked to the counter.

Gloria dug in her pockets for money. She had a crumpled twenty-dollar bill, five dollars short of the cost of the hardback book. She frowned and showed the nun her money. "I don't have enough." With reluctance, Gloria shoved the bill back in her pocket.

Before she could take a step back to the bookshelf, Sister Elizabeth held up a palm and smiled. "It's all right. We accept what you can afford."

"Really?" Gloria hugged the book to her chest.

"Of course." She gestured to Sister Catherine behind the counter. "Go ahead and check out."

"Thank you so much." Gloria paid the nun and happily carried the book out of the shop. She couldn't wait to read it.

Outside the building, Sister Elizabeth stood with clasped hands.

Gloria looked around the area with the white sunshine shedding generous warmth and light on her and the monastery. "Thank you for the tour."

"You're welcome." The sister smiled. "Please come again."

"I will."

"Good." Sister Elizabeth bowed.

The dorm rooms came back to Gloria. "If I wanted to stay overnight or for a couple of days, what would I need to do?"

"Usually, you'd need to let us know at least a week in advance. But it will be Pascha soon, so it would have to be after the feast day. Then we will be able to accommodate your visit most assuredly."

"I'm sorry, but what is Pascha?"

"It's our Orthodox Easter."

Gloria nodded. "Thanks again."

She waved goodbye to the nun and walked onto the dirt path to begin the hour-long trek home.

That afternoon when Gloria traipsed the gravel path to her cabin and stepped onto the stoop, the door to the large office opened, and Ruby came out wagging her hand with a sheet of paper in it. "Glory!" she called as she lumbered down the steps and hurried over to her.

Gloria turned toward her employer. "Yes?"

"You've got a phone message." Ruby handed her the note.

"Thanks."

"You're welcome. Gotta run." Ruby flashed a wide smile, then skittered to her car and drove off.

Gloria glanced down at the sheet scribbled with Penny's name and phone number. She went to the office and called Penny.

"Glory, I called Mike yesterday."

"What did you find out?"

There was a pause before Penny hesitated, then said, "Your dad is dead. He died two years ago."

Gloria's mouth went dry and her legs weakened. She fell into the chair next to the desk. Images formed in her head. Images of her father pushing her on her tricycle, helping her pitch a tent on one of their rare camping trips when she was very little. Then the picture turned dark with his beet-red face yelling at her over her failing grades in science and math, followed by countless brutal instances that had left bruises on her arms, blood on her face, and burning on her butt. Her father would grab whatever he could get his hands on to punish her—his leather belt, wooden paddle, a prickly tree branch. The last time she'd seen him, he'd pummeled her. She'd run out of the house, ignoring her bloody lip and the searing pain on her butt, and hadn't looked back.

Why did she feel as if she'd lost something? He'd never told her he'd loved her. He'd been cruel to her. But then relief washed over her, and she shed the fear stashed deep within her all these years. She was free to reunite with her mother and sisters. But what would the reunion be like? Her sisters knew of their father's death two years ago. Did they think she didn't care about them for not returning home after that? Did they know she hadn't known about his death?

"Glory?"

"I'm here." Gloria bounced her knee up and down, wrestling with her conflicting emotions.

"What are you going to do?"

"I'm still thinking on that."

"I'm not sure if I should tell you I'm sorry because I know your relationship with your dad wasn't a good one."

"No problem. Don't worry about it." Gloria glanced out the window at the sunshine spreading across the rocky ridges jutting toward the azure sky.

"I'll contact them…"

"I got Mike's address."

"You do? What is it?"

Penny relayed the information.

"Thanks for all your help. We'll have to get together sometime soon."

"I'll come visit you this time. Just let me know when."

"Will do."

Gloria's outlook on her family and future had just become an expansive canyon of possibilities. Her mother wanted to see her, and that would be the segue to her reunion with not only her mother but also her sisters. This was her chance to try to reconnect, and she would.

Chapter Twenty-Eight

Michaela sat on the couch with her mother and Fima. "Doug and *his partner* will be here in a half hour to pick you and Bailey up, and you'll see how this woman operates," Michaela said.

"I'll be observing her while we're at the zoo. See what her motives are," Etta said, digging in her purse.

"I already know what her motives are." Michaela folded her arms and pressed her lips into a thin, tight line. "She wants Doug."

"How do you know that?" Fima asked, her face pale.

Yesterday, Fima had called her about the ectopic pregnancy, and it had obviously and rightly upset her little sister. Michaela would make sure to talk to her after their mother and Bailey left for the zoo.

"I know. She hasn't exactly been cryptic in her remarks to me."

"Well, Michaela, my dear, you made Doug available. You opened the door to this when you told Doug to leave the house." Etta applied a pale pink lipstick to her puckered lips.

As if painting her face was the most important thing. "You're not helping, Mother."

Etta rubbed her lips together. "I'm sorry, dear, but I'm just pointing out what is plain to see."

"You'd rather I'd allowed him to stay and continue to expose Bailey to his drunken behavior?"

"No, of course not. You did the right thing for you and Bailey."

Michaela peered out the large living room window that was cracked open, facing the quiet, deserted street. The overcast sky threatened a rain shower. The smell of it, mingled with the aroma of barbequed meat, drifted into the room. The glaring gray shafts of light from outside funneled into the den. Bailey and the others would probably end up walking through the inside animal exhibits the majority of their time at the zoo. That was fine. It would be a shorter outing with Tina, and Bailey would be home earlier. Michaela would take her daughter to the zoo later in warmer, sunny weather.

"I want to visit Gloria again. Tomorrow," Etta announced.

Michaela turned from the window. "What makes you think she'll be there this time?"

"Well, I don't, but I need to keep trying to connect with her."

"I don't—"

"She's my daughter and your sister, Michaela."

"Yeah, I know, but—"

"Don't you want us back together again?"

Michaela stuffed her hands in her pockets. *How do I know she won't take off again and leave us in the lurch?* She pushed back the thought. "Sure."

At that moment, three knocks sounded at the front door. Michaela checked her watch and crossed the room. "He's early."

She pulled on the door, opened her mouth to inform her husband of his early arrival, only to have the words lodge in her throat. Her mouth stayed ajar as she stared at her younger sister on the other side of the screen door. Her hair, the color of golden, sandy beaches, splayed across her rounded shoulders. She stood half a foot shorter than Michaela and wore faded jeans, a blue T-shirt, and tattered sneakers. She looked thinner than Michaela remembered.

"Hi, Mike," she said with a hint of a quivering smile, just enough to reveal that snaggletooth she'd always had.

Michaela gripped the doorknob as she wrestled with her feelings. She didn't look too bad after dumping them years ago. Why was she here now? But, hell, she had to admit. It was good to see the little rat. "Glory," she said, pushing the screen door open.

"Gloria?" Etta squealed from the living room.

Seconds later, Etta and Fima flanked Michaela.

Etta grabbed Glory before she crossed the threshold. "Gloria! My baby!" she cried.

Fima hugged Glory, and the three were a knot of weeping elation.

"Let her breathe," Michaela said. "And she's still on the porch." She flicked her wrist. "Move so she can come in."

"Oh." Etta broke from the embrace and wiped her eyes. "Yes, come in, honey."

"I can't believe you're here." Fima threaded her arm through Glory's. "The timing couldn't have been better."

Glory's mouth hung open.

Michaela eyed her sister. Was she stunned by their mother and Fima's reactions? Maybe she finally realized the rebellious crap she pulled and the hurt she caused their mother and all of them.

Michaela gestured toward the couch. "Sit down and tell us what you've been doing with yourself for the past ten years. Actually, the past seven. We got the first three years from Aunt Melina." Michaela sat on the chair kitty-corner to the sofa.

Glory sat between Fima and their mother on the couch, with arms around each other.

"There isn't too much to tell. I've been working in Summitville since then."

"Oh, yes. Last Sunday, we talked to your boss. We came to visit you, but you weren't there," Etta explained.

"You came to visit me?"

Michaela's brows knitted. Was she playing dumb, or did the boss lady not tell her they'd stopped by?

"Didn't your boss tell you?" Fima asked.

"No. But she's been out of town until yesterday."

"She still didn't bother to tell you after she returned?" Michaela studied Glory with narrowed eyes. *Come on, tell the truth.*

Glory shrugged. "I don't know why, other than she was incredibly busy when she got back. She's been scarce around the office and cabins since she came home."

"Sounds like you have an absentminded boss." Michaela shook her head.

"It doesn't matter. You're here now," Etta cooed and squeezed Glory. "You saved us the road trip we were planning to take again tomorrow."

"Yes, you're here now, and that's all that counts," Fima said, holding on to Glory.

"I'm all for saving on gas," Michaela said.

Etta tsked then took Glory's hand. "I'm sorry you felt the need to run away—"

Fima shook her head and waved a hand. "Tell us what you do now. What you've been up to. We missed you so much."

Glory's cheeks reddened. "I clean cabins." She lowered her eyes.

Michaela rubbed her chin. Glory expected them to be surprised she was a maid. What job did she think she'd get with no high school diploma?

Fima smiled. "It must be awesome working in a mountain resort."

Glory faced their sister. "It is. You'd love the town. It's nestled at the foot of the Rockies with wildlife everywhere and pure air to breathe."

Fima closed her eyes and grinned. "It was so beautiful when we were there looking for you."

Having fun in the mountains while Mom worried day and night about you. Michaela raised her chin, looking down on Glory. "So, you didn't come back home because you liked cleaning cabins in Summitville?"

Glory sighed, a mild reaction from her once spunky and headstrong sister. Maybe she'd finally confess her selfish behavior the past ten years.

"Michaela," Etta chided, giving her a tight-lipped frown.

"No, it's okay. I'd expected these types of questions. Frankly, I'm amazed you've been so forgiving of me."

Michaela nodded. She was going to come clean now.

"I must admit, it was hard when you left." Etta put a hand to her chest, lowering her gaze.

"Yep." Michaela folded her arms.

"But, honey, we love you, and we're just so happy to see you here, alive and well." Etta rubbed Glory's back.

Fima held Glory's hand, her shoulders raised and face beaming.

Another knock came at the door. Michaela glanced at the clock on the desk. Ten o'clock. Right on time. She left the couch and opened the door. Doug and Tina stood on the porch, staring at her.

"Come in," Michaela said, and swung toward the stairs. "Bailey, come down. Your dad is here." She gave a sideways glance toward the living room. "And so is your aunt."

Bailey pattered down the steps. "Yeah, I know Aunt Fima's here."

Michaela glanced at Doug and Tina and put up a hand. "Just a minute."

Doug nodded, shoving his hands in his pants pockets while Tina folded her arms across her chest and focused on the street outside.

Michaela took Bailey's hand in hers and guided her to the den. "No. I'm talking about your Aunt Glory."

Bailey blinked, then scrunched her face.

"Remember? The one who ran away from home when your mama was going to community college?" Michaela caught Glory wince at her words. *Good.*

Glory lowered her head.

Michaela smirked. *That's right. You should feel like crap and own up to your selfish behavior. The pain you put Mom through is unforgivable.* She stood in front of Glory. "This is your Aunt Glory. Glory, this is your niece, Bailey."

Glory's face brightened, and her mouth spread into a generous smile. She took Bailey into her arms.

Bailey's stare bounced from Michaela to Glory. She slowly wrapped her arms around Glory's neck. "Hi, Aunt Glory." She smiled shyly.

"Hello, Bailey. It's so nice to have a precious niece." Glory kissed Bailey on her chubby cheek.

Etta sat forward on the couch, reaching toward Michaela, as if wanting her help for something. "Perhaps we should go to the zoo another time, since your Aunt Glory is here."

Bailey let go of Glory, frowned, and stomped her foot. "No, Gramma. You promised you'd go with Daddy and me."

"But do you really need me there?"

"Yes. You have to go." Bailey yanked on Etta's arm. "Please."

Etta let out a soft sigh and rose from the couch. She turned toward Glory. "We won't be long, honey, and we'll talk when we get back." She touched Glory's chin. "Take time to catch up with your sisters while we're gone."

177

Glory clasped their mother's hand. "I will."

Etta retrieved hers and Bailey's coats from the closet. "It's chilly. Put on your jacket."

They headed to the porch with Michaela behind them.

"Ready to go, Bailey bug?" Doug grinned.

Bailey nodded, then hugged Michaela as she pushed the screen door open for her daughter.

"We'll be here when you get back," Michaela said. She kissed Bailey's forehead as her daughter wriggled out of her arms, grabbed Etta's hand, and headed toward Doug and Tina.

"You'll have her back by dinner, right?" she asked.

"Around then," Tina replied in an impatient tone. She didn't look back at Michaela but herded Bailey to the silver hatchback parked at the curb. That wasn't Doug's car.

"Doug," Michaela called just as they reached the street.

He looked back. "Yeah?"

Michaela waved for Doug to come toward her.

He hesitated, glancing in Tina's direction but then moved back to Michaela. "What is it, Mike? We'll have Bailey home by suppertime. I always do."

"Whose car is that?" She lit a cigarette.

"It's Tina's. She offered to drive this weekend."

Michaela blew out smoke with her eyes squinted. "What's wrong with your car?"

Doug shook his head and looked at Bailey climbing into the back seat on the driver's side. Etta sat in the back seat on the passenger's side. "Nothing. She offered to drive."

"Come on, Dougie," Tina yelled just before she lowered herself into the vehicle.

Michaela grimaced. "Is that what she calls you?"

Doug's eyes met Michaela's. "That's just her nickname for me."

"Nickname," Michaela said under her breath.

She held her gaze with his to the point where their

surroundings melted away, and she could see the old Doug inside those once kind and sober eyes she'd fallen in love with eight years ago. What had happened to them?

Doug turned away from her, said, "See you later," and walked to the rumbling car.

Taking a long drag on her cigarette, Michaela, for the first time, regretted kicking him out. *But what about the drinking? Bailey? Don't grow soft, Michaela. You did what was right for Bailey and for you.* As much as she tried to convince herself of this, a gnawing sensation of foreboding sank deep inside her chest.

Chapter Twenty-Nine

Seraphima sat on the toilet lid in her sister's bathroom. The medication had taken effect. She hadn't truly realized she'd been carrying a baby and that she'd just lost it until now, as the pain subsided and the numbness dissipated, knocking horrific sobriety into her. She slumped over, her body wracked with grieving tears.

She barely heard the raps on the bathroom door.

"Fima, honey, let us in," Glory said in a soft voice.

"Open the door, Fima," Mike said.

"Mike told me what you've been going through," Glory said. "You shouldn't be alone. Let us help."

"Go away," she replied, resting her head in her hands. "I want to be alone." Her voice cracked.

"Come on. She'll come out when she's ready," Mike said.

Footsteps creaked on the floor outside the bathroom door, then faded.

Seraphima sat up, wiping her drenched, swollen face. She plucked three tissues from the box on the toilet tank, and with one of them, blew her nose.

Her cell phone lay on the sink's gray granite counter. Austin came to her mind. Anger burned through her, mixing with grief.

Standing up slowly, she grabbed the phone, pressed his number, and waited for him to answer. But she should have known he wouldn't. His voice mail came on. Her mouth pinched as she listened to his usual monotone message.

When the beep sounded, she hissed, "You got your wish, Austin. Our baby is gone. Lucky you. Did you hear that? Our baby is dead and gone." She smashed her finger on the End Call button and threw the phone on the tile floor, sending a crack through its screen as it skittered to a stop a few feet away.

Another wave of weeping overtook her, and she collapsed onto the floor, curled into a fetal position.

Gloria turned from the bookcase in Mike's den. "We shouldn't have left her alone."

Although it had been a decade since Fima had come to her with her childhood concerns, it was as if no time had passed. Gloria had taken up the counselor mantle for her little sister. It didn't matter that she'd had no experience in what Fima had been through. A natural sisterly mechanism had kicked in, and Gloria was ready to receive her sobbing sister into her loving embrace. Here was her chance to be there for her, yet Fima wouldn't let her.

"She didn't want us there. You heard her," Mike said. She stood by the desk, flipping open and closed the lid to her package of cigarettes.

"I hope she's okay up there."

"She'll get through it." Mike clutched the box of cigarettes and the lighter next to it. "If she gets her emotions in check."

Gloria stared at her sister. What was the matter with her? "She's just lost her baby. Show a little compassion." She frowned.

Oh, I forgot. You've always been hard as granite. When will your outer shell crumble? What will it take for you to soften?

"Spare me the high-and-mighty attitude." Mike shoved the package and lighter into her jeans pocket. She stood erect and stiff as a steel beam. "You know nothing about this, so don't try to dole out advice."

"This isn't the time to be piling on me and my mistakes. Our main focus should be—"

"I know," Mike snapped. "I've been the sister who's been there for Fima. *And* the daughter there for Mom, for that matter. When Fima needed help on her math assignments, I was there. When she fractured her wrist, I was there. When you ran off, leaving Mom in tears every day for years, shredding her heart, I was there to help put her back together to the extent I could. When Mom was hospitalized with pneumonia, I was there. When Fima's asshole boyfriend dumped her, I was there. Where were you?"

Gloria winced. Her sister's words stabbed at her heart. She'd known she'd have to contend with Mike when she'd decided to take the bus to her house and knock on her front door. But how could she argue with what Mike said? She had to acknowledge that Mike was there for their mother and sister and she hadn't been. But how could she have been?

"You think everything was great after you left?" Mike glared at her and pressed a finger to her chest. "I was blamed for your running away. Dad thought I'd conspired with your escape, no matter how many times I tried to tell him I hadn't. Got a nice stinging slap across the face for that." She shook her head. "Things weren't better after you left."

Swallowing hard, Gloria steadied herself. "It wasn't easy for me to leave Mom and you and Fima." She sighed. "But you're right. I wasn't there, and I'm sorry Dad blamed you."

"Lost that rebellious streak you'd been loaded with in your

teens, haven't you?" Mike put her hands on her hips and raised her eyebrows. "That's good."

"People grow out of their awkward teen years."

Mike headed to the front door. "I'm going out on the porch for a smoke. Get me when Fima comes downstairs."

Without waiting for her to answer, Mike opened the door, pushed the screen door aside, and disappeared from her view.

Gloria stood by the filthy, smudge-laden picture window, observing the conglomerate of wood and brick houses and the busy street. She spied the foothills in the distance. Her sister lived far away from nature, too far for Gloria's liking. The distinct sound of car horns and rumbling motors with the occasional guttural screech of a Harley were some things she could never get used to. No one could think clearly with all that noise pollution, and one was robbed of the unobstructed majestic view of the Rockies. But this town and the ones nearby were where she'd grown up. This was where her family had lived for generations. Yet she had lived in Summitville for nearly as long as she had in suburbia, and she felt confident that her time in Summitville would eventually surpass her childhood years in Parker.

"Glory." Fima's quiet voice filled the silent room.

Gloria pivoted in the direction she'd heard her name. Her sister stood slouched, combing her fingers through her long, wet sable hair. Despite the obvious attempt to cover up her previous crying, red blotches stamped her face, and puffy lids hooded her bloodshot eyes.

Gloria's heart hurt, seeing her sister in raw pain. She hurried over to Fima, embraced her, and led her to the sofa. They sat down. Fima leaned her head on Gloria's shoulder.

No words came to Gloria's mind, so she just held Fima.

"The baby is gone," Fima muttered and let out an exhaustive sigh.

Mike entered the house and strode toward them, sitting next to Fima. "You feeling okay now?"

"No."

Couldn't Mike see Fima wasn't okay? Gloria frowned.

Mike shook her head. "I meant physically, Fima, honey. Are you feeling okay?" She patted Fima's thigh.

Fima shrugged without looking at Mike and continued to lean on Gloria's shoulder.

"I can't imagine what you've been through, but I'm here for you," Gloria said, interlacing her fingers with Fima's.

"You know I'm here too, Fima," Mike interjected with a firm nod.

Fima sat up. "I know you guys are. I'm so lucky to have both of you."

"Of course I've always been here for you." Mike patted Fima's leg again and leaned back against the couch's cushions.

Gloria grimaced. Mike's icy remark pricked at her heart. She didn't know if she could break through Mike's hardened heart and animosity toward her, but she wasn't going to give up trying.

Fima didn't reply to Mike but turned toward Gloria. "I had a boyfriend who turned out to be a jerk. I probably wouldn't have dated him if you'd been around, Glory. You've always been a great judge of character."

Gloria avoided looking at Mike and ignored the faint sigh coming from her.

"I'm sorry I wasn't." Gloria put an arm around Fima's small shoulders. "The truth is, I was selfish, partly, not trying to reach you and Mike and Mom sooner, but I let fear own me. Fear of what you would say or do if I—"

"Then what made you decide to show up today?" Mike interrupted.

"Penny told me Dad died two years ago. He was my biggest fear. I didn't want to come back home to his abuse."

Mike's brows rose. "Penny told you." She grumbled something inaudible.

Fima nodded. "I understand, Glory."

Mike scowled. "You could have fixed that by minding Dad all those years ago instead of riling him up. Faced your faults and stayed, dealt with his spankings like we had to."

Gloria's spine stiffened, and her face warmed. Mike couldn't be that dense. She'd witnessed their father's abusive tirades too. "I was beaten black, blue, and blistered by Dad's fist, his belt, paddle, whatever he got his hands on. Those weren't simple spankings."

Mike peered at her, as if gauging the validity of her comments. "Fima and I got the belt a couple of times." She then raised her chin. "Dad *did* take it too far sometimes."

Sometimes. Well, she supposed she should be grateful that at least Mike was starting to acknowledge her side. "And I didn't do anything to deserve that."

"We know you didn't," Fima said and glowered at Mike. "Don't we?"

Mike cocked her head to the side but said nothing.

Gloria turned her attention to Fima. "Never mind me. You're what's important here. What can we do to help you?"

"You can stay the weekend with us. Better yet, you can stay with me," Fima said, lacing her fingers with Gloria's again.

"All right. I'm not due back at work until Tuesday afternoon."

Fima kissed Gloria's cheek.

"You're welcome to stay here if you want." Mike pointed to the couch. "That's a sofa bed." She then eyed her watch.

"Thanks, but I'll stay with Fima."

Mike gave Gloria a sideways glance. "Don't you want to spend time with your niece?"

She gave a weak smile and clasped her hands between her knees. "Of course I do. I just figured there'd be more room at Fima's place since it's just her."

"Sure, okay." Mike checked her watch again. "Where are they? They should have been home twenty minutes ago." She left the couch and crossed to the front door, still open from when she'd come in earlier. "He's never been this late."

"Maybe there was a traffic holdup," Gloria said.

Mike smacked her forehead. "She's driving. Can't believe I forgot that." She ran a hand through her short hair. "Maybe she got lost." She snorted.

Gloria chuckled. "Could have."

"Yeah, and she could be stalling, just to irritate you," Fima pointed out.

Mike glanced at Fima. "That sounds like her." She walked back over to them, fell into a chair, and leaned back, staring at the shadowed ceiling. She swung an arm in Gloria's direction. "Switch on that lamp, would you?"

Gloria turned on the light, and the gray-shaded room morphed into a warm, yellow one.

"What happens now for you?" Gloria asked, her gaze on Fima's belly.

Fima touched her stomach. "I go back on Monday for a blood test to check that the pregnancy has been terminated... I hate that word."

"I hate it too." Gloria laid a hand on Fima's shoulder. "I'll go with you on Monday."

Fima gave her a grateful grin. "Thanks so much."

"I've got to work. Inventory day and meetings. Sorry I can't be there," Mike muttered, staring past them to the large window and then back at her watch.

"Mike, why don't you try calling Doug?" Fima suggested.

"Yeah, I should do that. This isn't normal."

"Do you need any help starting dinner?" Gloria asked.

Mike shook her head. "I'm ordering pizza tonight." She stood and headed toward the kitchen. "Left my phone on the table."

Gloria could sense Mike's concern over Bailey, their mother, and Doug. She had no idea what Mike's schedules of Doug's visitations with Bailey were normally, but she was hoping to learn what she could to help her sister. A hand covered hers.

"You're worried about Mike too, huh?" Fima stared at her with discerning doe eyes.

Gloria smiled faintly. "Yes, I am."

"I got his voice mail," Mike said, marching into the living room with a brooding expression. "Where the hell are they?"

"Maybe they got a late start leaving the zoo," Gloria said.

Mike tapped her fingers on her thighs.

"Let's just give it some time to see if Doug calls back." Gloria glanced at the wall clock above the desk. It was nearly six o'clock, a half hour later than what Mike had said was their usual time for returning home.

The three sisters sat in silence.

After two tense hours of trying to reach Doug, Etta, and calling the local hospital, there was a knock at the front door. Mike shot up from her chair and hustled to the door. Swinging it open, she froze.

Oh, no. What's happened? Gloria exchanged a worried look with Fima before they both scrambled over to Mike and peered out the screen door at the face of a police officer.

Chapter Thirty

M ichaela and her sisters burst through the emergency room doors of Saint Matthew's Hospital and rushed to the reception counter. Still reeling from the news delivered by the police officer, Michaela pressed her palm on the countertop. "Excuse me. Our mother, my husband, and daughter were brought here after a car accident a little while ago."

One of the two nurses behind the desk glanced up from her computer. "What are the names?"

"Etta Barstone. Doug and Bailey Morrow."

"And Tina," Fima added.

The nurse looked at Fima. "Do you have a last name?"

Fima frowned. "No. I'm sorry."

Michaela held up a hand. "She was with them." She pointed at the computer. "Can you tell us what rooms they're in?"

The nurse typed in the information, then turned to face them again. "Ms. Barstone and Mr. Morrow are in surgery. Bailey is in room 220 on the second floor. I'll need a last name for me to locate Tina."

Surgery. Michaela's heartbeat thudded in her chest, and she flicked a worried stare at her sisters whose expressions echoed her feelings. But Bailey was in a room. This had to be good news for her baby. "You two wait here for any word on Mom or Doug. I'm going to go see Bailey."

"Okay. We'll try to visit her later," Fima said.

"Yes. Go see your daughter," Glory said, shooing her away.

Michaela ran to the elevators.

Michaela pushed open the door to room 220 where Bailey lay asleep on the bed in one of those ugly hospital gowns with the equally hideous clinical white sheet and blanket covering her up to midchest. Monitors were suspended from the wall behind her and one sitting on a moving stand beeped.

A couple of small bruises marred the right side of her face. Leads snaked out from her chest and connected to the machines. But she had no oxygen tube in her nose. That had to be a good sign.

Michaela scrambled to the side of the bed. "Baby, it's Mama." She ran her hand gently against the left side of Bailey's angelic, pale face.

Bailey's eyes fluttered open and focused on Michaela. "Mama?" she said in a weak voice.

Michaela's throat closed as her eyes stung with tears. She kissed Bailey's forehead, then smiled. "Yes, baby. It's Mama."

Bailey's dry lips curved upward. Then she frowned.

"What is it?" Michaela scanned Bailey's body then touched her cheek. "Are you hurting somewhere?"

Bailey squeezed her eyes shut, bunching up her face. "I screamed and screamed for Gramma."

Her heart breaking, Michaela bent nearer to Bailey. "It's all right, sweetheart. Gramma is in this hospital, along with your daddy, getting worked on by the doctors."

"Scary sounds." Bailey covered her face with both hands and whimpered out soft sobs.

Fighting back her own tears, Michaela carefully slid into the bed, under the covers next to her daughter. She put an arm above her head and wrapped her other arm around Bailey's torso, gently drawing her nearer. "Everything will be all right. The scary crash is over." She kissed Bailey's temple. "Just rest."

Bailey let out tired breaths, then slipped back into slumber.

Michaela closed her eyes and swallowed hard, her stomach a clenched knot. *My God, what happened in that accident?*

Forty minutes later, Michaela and her sisters huddled at the lobby's counter.

"When were our mother and the others brought into the ER?" Glory asked.

An auburn-haired nurse straightened documents on the table in front of her and glanced at her computer screen. "Five-o-three."

They'd been due home around five thirty. Michaela checked her watch. Nearly nine o'clock. "How long are the surgeries expected to take?"

The nurse shook her head. "Can't say for sure." She glanced at the clock. "They arrived on Flight for Life helicopters, and we have little information on their injuries." She frowned. "I'm sorry I can't be of more help at this time."

Flight for Life? Jesus. Why hadn't the cop told them that? Choking back tears, Michaela grabbed Fima's shaking hand as her youngest sister looked ready to crumble into pieces.

Glory sniffled and put an arm around her and Fima.

"If you'd like to go to the surgical waiting room until your family members come out of surgery, it's on the third floor," the nurse said. "When you exit the elevators, it's down the hall on your right."

"Thanks," Glory said.

Fima wiped her cheeks, then tapped Michaela's arm. "Maybe we ought to get some dinner. We'll be here most of the night—"

"All night," Michaela added with a nod.

"Where's the cafeteria?" Fima asked.

Fima and her blood sugar issues. Michaela had nearly forgotten with all that was happening. She rubbed her forehead.

The nurse pointed past them. "Take that hall straight ahead and follow the signs. The cafeteria will be on your left."

Fima gave the nurse a weak smile. "Thank you."

"You two go ahead without me." Michaela waved them on. "I'm going back to be with Bailey."

"Do you want us to bring you back anything?" Glory asked.

"I'll get something later." Food was the last thing on Michaela's mind. She dreaded what could be looming ahead but focused on her daughter, as she headed toward Bailey's floor.

Chapter Thirty-One

A hand on Seraphima's shoulder shook her awake.

"Surgery's done," Mike said. "They've moved Mom to ICU." She stood over Seraphima with tired eyes, tousled hair, in her disheveled shirt and jeans.

They'd been there for hours. How did Mike have so much energy? Seraphima ran a hand over her face. At least she ate before falling asleep.

Mike left Seraphima and went to the nurses' station. A moment later, she was back. "Doug's just come out of surgery too. Heading to ICU."

Glory sat in the chair next to Seraphima, with her elbow on the armrest and head in her hand, asleep.

Before she could reach over to wake Glory, Mike said, "Same floor, down a couple of rooms. Let's go."

Seraphima's stomach churned. What was their mom going to look like? Biting her lip, she tapped her sister's shoulder. "Glory."

Glory's head came up slowly as her eyes opened.

"We've got to go to ICU now."

Glory nodded.

Mike headed toward the hall on their left.

Seraphima stood and gestured toward Glory. "Come on."

Glory checked her watch and yawned. "Just after twelve thirty."

"So late." With a tired sigh, Seraphima brushed hair out of her face and waited for Glory to join her before they followed their older sister.

They reached the ICU's nurses' station. "Hi. We were told Etta Barstone and Doug Morrow came out of surgery and were moved here," Mike said, raking a hand through her hair.

One of the nurses, a chubby woman with false eyelashes, came around the counter smiling. "Come this way." She headed down the corridor of glass rooms on their right.

Seraphima and her sisters followed the nurse to the third room. Mike entered before her and Glory. Seraphima stepped to the side of Mike.

In the bed lay their mother nearly unrecognizable. Gauze circled her head, and a breathing tube protruded from her mouth. Monitor leads flowed out of her hospital gown like spider legs. An IV covered in tape sat in the crook of her arm. Blue bruises and faint splotches of old blood covered parts of her forehead, cheeks, and nose. The bruises and lacerations ran between her skinny shoulder and neck and against her collarbone. Their mother looked so fragile, as if only a wisp of her lay there, reliant on the machines beeping and humming life into her.

"She's been in a coma since her arrival. There's been some trauma to her head and organs. But she pulled through the surgery." The nurse gave Seraphima and her sisters a tender smile.

Trauma to her head? A coma? Seraphima couldn't move her feet forward and hugged herself as cold fear ran through her.

"She can hear us though, right?" Glory asked, rolling a knotted bracelet on her right wrist.

Grandmother's prayer bracelet. She did take it. Looks like it's giving her comfort. Seraphima wished she could be comforted that easily. She needed more than a bracelet. Images of Austin filled her head. She frowned. *I'll never have his comfort again.* She pressed a hand to her abdomen. There was nothing left inside her womb or her heart.

The nurse glanced at Etta. "Most likely, Ms. Barstone can hear you."

Mike walked to the side of the bed and took their mother's hand without the IV. "Mom, we're here. Me and Fima."

Seraphima wrung her hands. She didn't know what to say to her mother.

"Me too, Mom," Glory added.

Seraphima felt Glory's hand grasp hers and give it a squeeze.

Mike touched their mother's skinny shoulder while looking at the nurse. "How long does the doctor think she'll be in a coma?"

"He couldn't say for sure," the nurse said, eyeing the blood pressure reading on the machine next to the bed.

Seraphima bit her quivering lip. "She doesn't look very good."

Glory put an arm around her, then turned toward the nurse. "Is the doctor going to come by tonight or this morning?"

The nurse recorded the blood pressure reading on her tablet, then nodded. "The doctor and his team will stop in in the next hour or so to check on her. They will also be by when they do their rounds at six o'clock."

Seraphima frowned. "That's a while from now."

The nurse slipped the tablet's pen in her pants pocket. "You're free to stay here for the night, but only one person at a time in the room."

Mike pointed at Seraphima. "Do you want to stay with Mom? I'm going to sleep with Bailey tonight."

Seraphima swallowed the icy fear lodged in her throat. The

pale, broken figure of their mother lay in front of her, and the machines beeped out the clinical sounds of Etta's heartbeat. "I-I can't sleep here." She fought the urge to flee the room. "I'll go home and come back at five thirty."

Mike's lips folded between her teeth. "Okay."

Glory moved to a chair near the left side of the bed. "I'll stay with Mom."

Mike's brows lifted. "All right." She walked to the doorframe. "I'm going to find out where Doug is, then stay with Bailey. Meet you here at six."

Seraphima took one last look at their mother, then left the room and hurried out of the ICU. She couldn't get out of the hospital fast enough before the tears fell and her body shook in horror. Would her mother recover? She took in gulps of the cold night air and jogged to her car.

At five thirty that morning, Michaela walked into the ICU room three down from her mother's. Doug lay in the bed, mirroring the visual injuries of Etta's, except his neck was wrapped in a cushioned brace. Still, he looked strong—his six-foot-three supine body with its broad shoulders and chest and toned, athletic arms. Thank God for his obsession with exercise, considering he sat at a desk, crunching numbers every day. If only her mother's wiry figure she'd seen hours ago showed a shadow of durability. But she needed to concentrate on Doug now.

She moved to the side of his bed and dragged the chair closer to her husband. Covering his hand with hers, she said, "Hey, you big lug. Pulled through surgery like a champ." She squeezed his hand. "Now you just need to recover and escape this antiseptic prison ASAP."

Doug's eyelids didn't flutter, his mouth didn't twitch, and his hand didn't press against hers.

Michaela bowed her head as she worked through all of what she'd taken in overnight. He'd just gotten out of surgery a few hours ago. He was in ICU. Of course he wouldn't be responding just yet.

She nodded in acceptance, then gazed at his ashen, bruised face. "Don't try to talk or move. Just rest." She patted his hand. "Do what I say for once, because I know you can hear me."

A small, redheaded nurse entered the room and checked the machines as well as his near-empty IV bag. "I'm Peggy." She pointed to her name tag.

"Michaela. Doug's wife."

The nurse nodded. "He's been in a coma since they flew him here. But he's a tough one, surviving the accident."

Michaela raised her chin. "And he pulled through surgery."

"Indeed, he did." Peggy removed the drained IV bag and hung a fresh one, hooking it up to Doug's IV line.

"Will the doctor be coming around soon?"

"Yes." Peggy wrote something on her tablet, then looked at Michaela again. "Your family's friend is on the same floor as your daughter, if you were wanting to visit her."

"Tina?"

"Yes, Ms. Burns."

"Good to know. Thanks." Michaela now knew Tina's last name. And Tina lay in a regular patient room, not ICU like her husband and mother. *Lucky her.* Michaela narrowed her eyes. Had Doug's *partner* carelessly caused this tragic accident?

She rose from the chair as intimate images of Doug with Tina ran through her head. She frowned at Doug and let go of his hand. If only he'd not gotten involved with that vile woman. Then Doug, Bailey, and her mother wouldn't be lying in broken pieces in the hospital.

Peggy padded out of the room, leaving Michaela in the midst of the humming machines and Doug somewhere inside himself.

Before she headed to the door, two doctors and a nurse filled the doorframe to the room. They entered, and one of the doctors with silver-streaked hair, round wire-framed glasses, and gentle gray eyes gave Michaela a smile and offered his hand.

"Hello, Mrs. Morrow, I'm Dr. Curtis."

Michaela gave the doctor a firm handshake. "Doctor."

Dr. Curtis gestured to the stocky man with a goatee and thinning hair. "This is Dr. Brock." Dr. Curtis nodded toward the blond-haired, petite nurse. "This is Kathy Porter, nurse practitioner."

Michaela nodded, shook their hands, then looked at her husband. "What's going on with Doug?"

Dr. Curtis slid the pen in his hand into his white coat pocket. "He nearly took the impact directly. He suffered a broken leg, collarbone, two broken ribs, spinal cord injury, and multiple contusions over the right side of his body." The doctor raised his gray, full eyebrows. "It's really a miracle he survived the accident."

Every word the doctor said made Michaela's stomach hurt. But she straightened her back and smoothed out her shirt. "The nurse said he's in a coma. When do you think he'll come out of that? How long will it take for him to heal?"

Dr. Brock stepped forward. "Weeks, could be a month or two, if he comes out of the coma."

"If?" Michaela's legs weakened. She backed up, teetering, and sat in the chair.

"He'll be monitored closely for any changes," Dr. Brock said.

"What would those changes look like, so maybe I could keep an eye out for them?" Michaela said, gripping the chair's arms.

"If he opens his eyes, speaks, or moves any body part," Dr. Curtis said.

"Okay." With a determined jaw, Michaela glanced at Doug.

"One more thing…" Dr. Curtis paused, avoiding Michaela's stare. He looked at the outlines of Doug's long legs. The doctor's gaze returned to Michaela. "We did an MRI and sensory test on his legs and feet." He tapped his hand on the bed's footboard. "The MRI showed the spinal cord injury, and his legs and feet didn't respond to any stimulation."

Michaela's mouth fell open, as she slowly stood on wobbly legs. "He can't feel anything in his legs or feet?"

The doctor gave her a sympathetic shake of his head.

She pointed to Doug's lower half. "Is he freaking paralyzed?"

The doctor held up a hand. "It's due to a partially severed spinal cord. His feeling may return."

"Partially severed spinal cord?" Michaela grabbed the bedside railing to steady herself. *"Jesus."*

"Yes, but there's a chance for that to heal. We're going to do all we can for Mr. Morrow," Dr. Brock said.

Michaela could only nod, as the doctor's words swam in her head.

"Nurse Porter will be around if you have further questions. We've got to move to other patients now," Dr. Curtis said and pivoted out the door, followed by his entourage.

Her mother. They'd be on their way to her mother's room in a little while. Michaela moved closer to Doug. "Hang in there. I've got to go see Mom and get the lowdown on her." She bent, kissed Doug's forehead, then walked out of the room.

Gloria laid a hand on top of Etta's. "I think the doctors will be here any minute, Mom. I hear some people in the hallway." She glanced toward the doorway where Fima stood tugging on her hair.

Mike whisked into the room. "Sorry," she said. "The doctors stopped by Doug's room a few minutes ago."

Was Doug in the same horrific shape as their mother? "How's he doing?" Gloria asked.

Mike shrugged and shoved her hands in the back pockets of her jeans. "He's in a coma like Mom." She frowned, looking at the wall as if something on it would give her answers. "His body's a mess."

"I'm so sorry, Mike," Fima said, clinging to the doorframe.

She must be in so much pain. Gloria hugged Mike. Fima joined them, huddled together.

Two doctors and a nurse entered the room and approached Mike. "Mrs. Morrow."

Mike nodded, glanced at Etta, then gestured toward her and Fima. "Our mother."

Dr. Curtis gave her a sympathetic bow. "I see." He turned his attention to Gloria and Fima and held out his hand. "Dr. Curtis." He then introduced his colleagues, and they exchanged handshakes.

"How's our mother?" Gloria asked.

"Is she about the same as Doug?" Mike asked.

The doctor lowered his gaze to the bed. "I'm afraid her injuries are worse. Blunt force trauma to her head from the impact. Her shoulder, collarbone, and pelvic bones are broken, and she has a fractured right femur. Her organs have been affected also. Her intestines were pushed up and to the left side of her torso, which we moved back into place. Lacerated liver and bronchi, as well, which is why she's on a breathing tube."

Gloria and her sisters stood speechless. The litany of injuries was too much for Gloria to digest all at once. She took hold of Fima's shaking hand and squeezed it as much to comfort herself as Fima.

The doctor cleared his throat and observed the fragile woman in the bed. "Mrs. Barstone took the brunt of the crash. We stopped the bleeding in her head, but we're not certain what kind of damage that's done to her brain. The MRI showed lack of neural activity on the right side of her brain."

"Is that why she's in a coma?" Fima asked, inching backward toward the doorway.

"Yes, and the trauma of the accident," Dr. Brock said.

"Did you have any questions for us before we go about our rounds?" asked Dr. Curtis.

Gloria took two cleansing breaths. "Will she survive?"

"I don't know at this ti—"

"You have no idea when she'll come out of the coma?" Mike asked.

"I'm sorry, no," Dr. Brock said. "If that's all, we'll be moving to the next patient." He shuffled to the door with Dr. Curtis and the nurse but stopped before stepping out of the room. "We'll be back around the same time tomorrow morning."

The group left, and Fima collapsed in the chair Gloria had slept in. Mike paced the floor.

Gloria returned to her mother's bedside and ran her fingers over Etta's pale cheek. She thought back to yesterday afternoon and whispered, "The bus ride to Mike's gave me time to sort out my feelings and prepare myself for our reunion. Mike is still sporting that confidence about her that I've always admired. And you and Fima showed me such forgiveness and love. I'll never forget it."

She stared intently at her mother's high cheekbones, long lashes, and bruised face. She and Etta had gotten the opportunity to talk to each other for just a moment before she'd left for the zoo with Bailey and the others. Would she get the opportunity to speak to her again? Find out what her mother wanted to tell her before she'd left the house? Their reunion couldn't be cut short. She had so many years to catch up on with her mother.

"I need to go be with Bailey."

Mike's voice broke through Gloria's thoughts.

Gloria nodded. "Of course."

Fima trailed after Mike. "I'm going to get something to eat. Want anything?"

"Just a cup of tea, if they have any, and whatever pastry you can find," Gloria replied as she took hold of their mother's frail hand.

"Got it." Fima walked out the doorway after Mike.

"You need to get better so we can talk some more, make up for lost time," Gloria said to Etta.

Only the machine's beeps answered her, but she knew her mother could hear her, and she'd keep talking to her, hoping her encouraging words would bring Etta out of her coma.

Chapter Thirty-Two

Michaela entered Tina's hospital room and found her awake and sitting up. Tina's mouth twitched when she saw Michaela.

"Michaela. You're the last person I'd expected to see." She ran a hand over her tousled hair, then adjusted her ugly gown so that it covered her shoulders evenly.

Michaela raised a brow. The woman still obsessed over her appearance even while lying in a hospital bed with a big bruise on her collarbone, heart monitor leads peeking from under the gown, and an IV in the crook of her arm.

She came to the side of the bed. "You don't look too busted up."

"Disappointed?"

"Just an observation."

Tina cocked her head to the side. "How's Doug?"

"Busted up." Michaela folded her arms. "I heard briefly from the police officer and the doctors on what happened. Now I want to hear it from you."

Tina's eyes widened. "Why? Their versions aren't good enough?"

"I didn't get any details." Michaela bent over, leaned her fisted hands on the edge of the bed. "You were driving. How'd it happen?"

Tina straightened in the bed. "Someone ran a red light and T-boned us while I was crossing the intersection. I heard there was drinking involved."

Michaela moved from the bed and paced the floor while taking in what Tina had said. She turned on her heel to face her. "No drinking from your end, right?"

"For God's sake, Michaela. I was driving."

"So was the person in the other car."

Tina's face flushed. "I don't drink and drive."

Michaela slowly nodded.

"Look, I don't know what you're getting—"

"I wanted to confirm you weren't responsible for turning my mother into a box of scattered jigsaw puzzle pieces, clinging to life." Michaela moved back to the bedside. "Or for my husband lying in a coma, paralyzed. Or for my baby lying in a room down the hall with bruises and cuts on her little body."

Tina's face drained of color. "I-I had no idea."

"Of course. You've been in here the whole time."

Tina's gaze lowered to her hands in her lap. "I'm so sorry."

The blond woman's words and reaction seemed genuine to Michaela. She sank into a chair next to the bed.

"Doug's in a coma? He's paralyzed?"

"That's what the docs said."

"Will he recov—?"

"I don't know," Michaela snapped.

She gripped the chair's armrests. "It's hard looking at my husband broken and unconscious, aching for him, but at the same time, remembering you'd taken him away from me. Lured him… God knows how." Michaela glared at Tina while she swallowed back bitterness.

Tina didn't respond, only stared at the covers, sucking on her bottom lip.

"He may never recover, leaving me and Bailey behind. Leaving us in shambles, unable to work anything out. Or he may at least pull through the coma, and you'll be waiting with open, deceptive arms." Her own words cut her. She closed her eyes to steady herself. "Either way, I've lost him." As the words had fallen from her mouth, Michaela hated herself for saying them, showing vulnerability in front of her rival, the home wrecker.

"Michaela…" Tina's voice was no more than a whisper.

"Nothing you say will make a damn bit of difference, so save it."

"I think it will."

Michaela sighed and leaned back against the chair's cushion. "You have to argue with me over everything, don't you?" She stared at the ceiling, feeling exhausted. "What is it? You get some tiny thrill one upping me every chance you get?"

"No. That's not it."

Michaela sat up and looked at Tina sitting straight as a pin with dead seriousness etched in her face. "Then how is it?"

Tina wrung her hands, then slid down against the pillows. "Doug and I are friends."

"This is the big news that's supposed to make a difference?" Michaela scoffed.

"Let me finish," Tina said in a sharp tone.

Michaela shrugged and sank back in the cushion.

"That's all we've ever been."

Michaela sat up. "What?"

Tina's cheeks reddened as she averted Michaela's piercing stare. "I exaggerated Doug's and my relationship."

Michaela rose from the chair. "Exaggerated?"

Tina messed with her stupid, dyed-an-unnatural-blond-colored hair. "Yes, exaggerated a bit."

"How much is a bit?" Michaela stood by the bed with arms crossed and mouth in a firm line.

"Okay, a lot."

"Now it's a lot."

Tina smacked a palm on her covered lap. "Listen, nothing ever happened between us. I just made it up to get your goat."

Michaela narrowed her eyes at the tiny woman—a disgrace to the female species. She leaned over the bed and clutched the middle of Tina's flimsy hospital gown. "You're as low as the earth's mantle."

Tina's eyes bugged out, fear flashing through them. "I know you're right."

"Damn straight."

"I'm sorry."

Michaela let go of the gown and rested her hands on her hips. "If this hadn't happened, were you ever going to tell me the truth?"

Tina shrugged. "I think eventually."

"Uh-huh." Michaela strode toward the door. Before opening it, she turned back. "Well, at least I know now... now that Doug may never come back to me." She glowered at Tina. "Did anyone ever tell you you're a nasty bitch?"

Tina frowned, then her lips spread into a knowing smile. "Yes."

Michaela yanked the door open and headed for her daughter's room.

Chapter Thirty-Three

Seraphima lay curled on one of the sofas in the lounge area outside the ICU. She hadn't slept well in days. Not only did she have the nightmare news of the horrible crash to deal with, but also her body was still healing from the loss of her baby, her abdomen still swollen. A part of her felt cheated of the grieving process.

She rubbed her belly as tears that seemed to come every other hour fell down her cheeks. She squeezed her eyes shut. It was all too much.

She glimpsed Glory coming out of their mother's room. She and Glory had had no time for a sibling reunion. No time for Glory to comfort her. All the ideas and plans she'd made in her mind when she'd first seen Glory standing on Mike's porch hadn't taken place. Everything was chaos in her life. Everyone she needed wasn't available.

But didn't her sisters have a good reason they couldn't be there for her now? What about her friends? Belinda? She rolled her eyes, feeling a headache developing above her brows. That woman had never proved to be a true friend. If Seraphima was honest with herself, she had no friends. So-called friends in the past had talked behind her back every chance they got. And she'd never done anything to make them hate her or treat her like trash. She'd tried so hard to get along with people over the years, but now she'd put up the walls, protecting her heart.

Glory sat next to her. "Hey, how're you doing?"

Her emotions stirred up, Seraphima could only shake her head.

Glory slid her arm around Seraphima's shoulders and hugged her close. "I know it's been a whirlwind of calamities since yesterday."

Seraphima leaned her head on Glory's soft shoulder, accepting her sister's comfort wholeheartedly. "Yeah." She placed a hand on her abdomen, empty of life.

Glory's hand covered hers. "You haven't had time to process it all."

Seraphima closed her eyes. Her sister understood. She'd been away ten years, but she still understood her.

Glory squeezed her hand. "Looks like that guy is coming toward us."

Seraphima raised her head and focused on the hall to the ICU.

Eli walked over to them and squatted in front of Seraphima. "Linda told me what happened. I'm so sorry."

"Thanks." Seraphima glanced at her sister. "Glory, this is Eli. Eli, this is my sister Glory."

"Hi." Eli waved. "I'm sorry we have to meet under these circumstances."

"Hey, it's okay. It can't be helped." Glory stood and gestured to Eli to take her seat on the sofa, then turned her attention to Seraphima. "I'm going back to be with Mom. Come get me if you need me."

Seraphima nodded.

Eli sat next to Seraphima and brushed a lock of hair from her tear-swollen face.

"Thank you for coming." She managed a smile.

"I wanted to be here for you. Came on my lunch break." He glanced down the hall. "Have you eaten?"

As if on cue, Seraphima's stomach growled, feeling hollow. She couldn't remember when she'd last eaten. The weakness in her body and the growing wave of nausea told her she needed to now. "No, but I need to."

"I'll go with you to the cafeteria."

He held out his hand for her to take, and he gently helped her up.

She let go of his hand and brushed hair off her shoulder. "Thank you."

As they stood, Austin strode down the hall toward them. He reached Seraphima and pulled her into his meaty arms. "Babe, I'm so sorry. I couldn't reach you on your cell, so I called the tanning salon. Your boss told me where to find you. Told me about your mom and niece." He kissed her forehead.

Stunned, Seraphima couldn't move. Austin had come to see her, held her in his arms. He was back in her life. Elation filled her. Her body shook with excitement. She wrapped her arms around his muscular torso, leaning her head on his strong, comforting chest. Everything around her melted away as she clung to the man she loved more than life. He'd come right when she needed him. He'd rescued her from her sorrow, her loss, her pain.

"We haven't met."

Eli? Was he still here?

"I'm Eli."

Austin shifted and shook Eli's hand. "Austin."

Seraphima gazed up at Austin's gorgeous face.

Eli gave Austin an amiable grin. "I'm a friend of Fima's. We both work at the salon."

Austin nodded. "Cool."

Eli waved a hand toward the corridor in which Austin had

just come. "We were about to head to the cafeteria. Seraphima needs to eat lunch." Eli's compassionate gaze fell on her.

Austin clasped Seraphima's hand. "Sounds good. I haven't eaten anything yet." He held up a hand when Eli moved to go with them. "No offense, Eli, but we need time to talk, work out some things."

A crease formed between Eli's brows. He scratched the back of his head. A tight smile formed on his face. "Sure. I understand." He slid his hands in his pockets and walked past them. "Catch you later, Fima."

Austin squeezed her hand, and her body tingled. He was really there. They moved together down the hall.

Sitting across from Austin, Seraphima nibbled on a burger while he dug into a chicken salad sandwich with chips and a soda.

He took a gulp of his drink, then reached for one of her hands. "Babe, how're you feeling?"

"A little better now that I've gotten food in me." Seraphima smiled. She still couldn't believe he was sitting with her. Their last conversation had been horrible, his tone so cruel. What had made him change?

He patted her small hand with his big one. "Good."

She finished a fry, then peeked at him while he bit into the last half of his sandwich. "Did you get my voice message from yesterday?"

He looked up at her and set his sandwich down. She couldn't read his expression. His eyes didn't hold sorrow or anger. "Yeah... yeah, I did."

She nodded, lowering her gaze, her hand absently moving to cover her abdomen.

"Look, I'm sorry about what happened."

"Our fight or the loss of our baby?"

"Both." He wiped his mouth with a napkin, then cleared his throat. "I shouldn't have cut us off. You were willing to wait for me, understood I needed time to reach my goals."

Seraphima's heart lifted, and she felt his words touch every part of her. "I'm so happy you want to give us another chance."

He held up a hand, lowered his chin. "But you know for sure now where I stand on marrying and having kids."

She picked off a piece of the burger bun, rolling it between her fingers. "You said you wanted to wait?"

"Yeah. And that may be two or three years from now, maybe even longer."

She twisted a strand of her hair with a shaky hand. *How far out would that be? How old will I be by the time I can have my three children?* Her plan was to be married by twenty-three and have the first child by age twenty-five. Maybe a couple of years difference wouldn't hurt? After all, she'd have him in the end.

Austin's hand covered hers. "Fima, you with me?"

She straightened in her chair and took in a breath, then released it evenly. "Yes. I understand. It's fine."

He gave her a winning grin, melting her heart. "Good."

She smiled and ate some more fries.

"What are you planning to do after we're done here?"

"I've got to visit my mom, brother-in-law, and niece."

He ate the last bite of his sandwich and set his napkin on the plate. "How long do you think you'll stay?" He glanced around the room half-filled with patients and family members. His eyes flicked back to her. "Because, you know, I've got to get back to the country club in a bit."

"That's okay." She took a sip of lemonade. "I'll be home tonight. I don't stay overnight here. My sister, Glory, does."

He smiled as if she'd just told him he'd won the lottery." Great. Then I'll be by around eight."

Seraphima beamed as warmth flowed through her. *We're back together.*

Chapter Thirty-Four

M ichaela snuggled with Bailey in her hospital bed. Her daughter looked better than she had yesterday—color had returned to her cheeks.

Earlier, she'd run home and grabbed Bailey's lucky Beanie frog, Frank. "Look who's here." She handed him to Bailey.

Bailey stroked the plush amphibian and rubbed him against her cheek before gazing up at Michaela with her big, blue eyes. "Mama, I wanna go home."

"I know, baby." She brushed strands of her daughter's hair away from her face.

The door to the room opened, and a doctor and nurse entered. Michaela sat up.

"Hello, Mrs. Morrow, I'm Dr. Gibbons." He stood near the bed and held out his hand.

Michaela slipped out of the bed and clasped his hand. "Doctor."

Dr. Gibbons turned his attention to Bailey. "Hi there, Bailey. How are you feeling today?"

Bailey peeked through her lowered lashes, smiling. "Fine."

The doctor moved to the side of the bed, took out a tiny

flashlight, and shined it in her eyes. He had her follow his finger. He wrapped up the exam by putting his stethoscope to her chest and listening to her heart. Hanging the stethoscope back around his neck, he gave Bailey a thumbs-up. "Very good."

Bailey lifted her chin. "I wanna go home."

The doctor chuckled. "Well, you're about to get your wish."

Bailey gaped and sat up. "Honest?"

"Honest." The doctor ran his finger across his chest in the shape of an X.

Michaela smiled and touched her daughter's cheek. "How cool is that?"

Bailey shot her arms up in the air. "Way cool!"

Dr. Gibbons looked at Michaela. "I'll have the release forms signed, and the nurse will have them ready for you in the next few hours." He glanced back at Bailey. "She'll be able to go home later this afternoon."

"Yea!" Bailey squealed.

Michaela's heart swelled. She bent down and embraced Bailey. "Woohoo!"

The doctor pumped his fist, joining in the celebrating before he left the room.

Midafternoon, Gloria sat in the cafeteria with Fima. She'd pushed her own sorrow aside in the hopes of helping Fima with hers. But she'd noticed her sister's remarkable change in mood since she left her with Eli. Was he her boyfriend? Something about his unpretentious demeanor gave her the impression that he was a nice man.

"I'm glad you're feeling better. You look like you've just gotten off your favorite amusement park ride." She chortled.

Fima grinned. "Remember Elitch Gardens, when we rode the Twister together?"

The memory of that fun day came back to her, and she smiled. "Yeah. Mike was off riding one of the looping roller coasters." She ate a bite of pizza.

Fima grimaced. "I'm so glad I was too young for that crazy ride." The grimace turned into a smile. "But our coaster ride was a lot of fun."

"Sure was."

"One of two times we got to go there when Dad had been in one of his rare good moods."

Gloria frowned, as an image of her father gripping her arm and throwing her on the floor flashed through her mind. "Yeah."

Fima touched her hand. "I'm sorry. I shouldn't have brought up Dad."

She shook her head and squeezed Fima's hand. "It's okay."

"No, it's not. I didn't think."

"Never mind that." She let go of Fima's hand and took a sip of soda. "Tell me about Eli."

"Eli?"

"Yeah. Wasn't that his name?"

Fima blinked at her.

"The blond-haired guy who came to see you this morning."

"Oh, right." Fima nodded. "He's a friend and coworker of mine at the salon."

"Oh. I thought he might have been your boyfriend. He seemed to really care about you."

Fima flashed a brief smile. "He does. He's a nice guy, but he isn't my boyfriend."

Gloria wiped her mouth with a napkin. Then why had her mood changed so drastically?

Fima straightened in her seat and beamed at her, as if she'd just reached the top of a summit. "Austin's my boyfriend."

"Austin." Gloria's brows came together. "I haven't met him, right?"

"Right." Fima leaned her elbow on the table and rested her

chin in her hand. "He came by after you went back to be with Mom."

"Okay."

"We just made up."

"What happened?"

Fima pursed her lips together as if she'd tasted something sour. "Never mind. It's all patched up now. He's sorry, and we're back together, better than ever."

Gloria nodded slowly. *Something isn't right here, but she's not telling me. Maybe she will when she's ready. I hope so.*

"He's coming by tonight to spend time with me." Fima grinned, a look of mischief in her dark eyes.

"Oh, I won't be in your way. I'll be here with Mom."

"I know."

"Okay, then." Gloria checked her watch. "We should get back to Mom."

Gloria gathered her tray while Fima grabbed her empty soda container, and they headed out of the cafeteria.

When Gloria and Fima reached their mother's room, Dr. Curtis and Dr. Brock, Kathy the nurse practitioner, and another nurse crowded around their mother, moving about with urgency. Gloria's heart leaped to her throat. *What's going on?*

Fima latched onto her arm, the color draining from her face.

One of the nurses at the station, whose name tag said PEGGY, jogged over to them just as Mike came down the hall from the elevator.

"What's happened?" Gloria asked, her body tense.

The nurse waited for Mike to reach them, then said, "Your mother had a stroke."

"Oh my God!" Fima shrieked and held on to Glory's arm as if her hands were vise grips.

Peggy pointed to the medical group hovering around her mother. "The doctors are working on her right now."

"How'd that happen?" Mike snapped but didn't wait for Peggy to answer. She stormed to the doorway and entered the packed room.

Peggy ran after her and escorted her out. "I'm sorry, but only the medical team can be in there. You'll have to wait out here."

With Fima still attached to her arm, Gloria walked with cautious steps toward the doorway and stood aside, out of the medical team's way.

Machines beeped, hummed, the breathing tube's heavy pants of breath, along with the din of the doctors talking in foreign medical jargon to each other crashed over her like a devastating tsunami.

Mike stood next to Gloria, yelling in her raspy, commanding voice, "Why the hell did our mother have a stroke?"

Gloria buried her face in her hands. Fima whimpered and slipped off her arm. She searched blindly for Fima, then pulled her close.

"Why is this happening?" Fima said between sniffles.

"I don't know." Gloria blinked back tears. *How could I have stayed away from you all these years?*

"She's going to be all right, isn't she?" Fima asked.

"I don't know."

"You don't know?" Fima's voice rose. "She has to."

Gloria shook her head, battling with the shameful decision she made ten years ago.

"I can't watch anymore of this," Fima cried. "I've got to get out of here." She bolted down the corridor toward the elevators.

Gloria plodded to the set of chairs in the lounge area outside the ICU rooms. She sat, planted her elbows on her knees and rested her forehead against the heels of her hands.

"They're taking Mom for an MRI to check her brain."

Mike's voice startled her. She looked up and found her sister standing in front of her, hands on hips with a set jaw and burning eyes.

"This is all her fault," Mike hissed.

"Whose fault?"

"Tina's." Mike folded her arms with the quick, sharp movements of a high school drill team member.

Who's Tina? She shook her head, swarming with past memories of her tumultuous childhood.

"If Mom doesn't pull through this, I'm going to kick that shrew's ass." Mike stomped out of the lounge toward the elevators.

Sighing, Gloria leaned back against the chair's cushion and stared at the white ceiling. Her hand moved to her wrist where the prayer bracelet was. What had she learned from the nuns? She closed her eyes and prayed for her mother's healing. The action felt awkward and unfamiliar, but she didn't care. She was desperate for help from this God, who Sister Elizabeth and the other sisters sang about in the services she had attended back in Summitville.

Didn't they say prayer was how a person got to know God? Prayer was nothing more than talking to Him. A stirring warmth in her heart told her she needed to know more. Glancing at her mother's empty room, Gloria promised herself she would.

Forty-five minutes later, the medical personnel wheeled Etta back into her ICU room. Gloria stood with her sisters outside the doorway, waiting for the doctors to give them news.

Dr. Curtis and Dr. Brock stepped out of the room, their faces sober and weary. Gloria knew a stroke was serious, but something about their demeanor told her the situation with her mother was truly dire. But she kept those feelings to herself and tried to temper the rising ripple of guilt inside her.

"Well? What's going on with our mother?" Mike asked, her hands on her hips.

"Is she going to be okay?" Fima twirled a lock of her hair.

Dr. Curtis cleared his throat. "I'm afraid this stroke was massive, with much more bleeding and deprivation of oxygen to her brain."

"What?" Mike leaned toward the doctors, scowling. "Quit with the doctor speak and be straight with us."

"How much clearer does he have to be?" Gloria whispered in a shaky voice as tears stung her eyes.

"There was already loss of brain function from the car accident," Dr. Curtis explained, tugging on the ends of a stethoscope hanging loosely around his neck. "The stroke compounded it, causing more damage and loss of brain activity."

"Shit." Mike raised her face toward the ceiling and pressed a hand on the crown of her head.

"Her brain isn't working?" Fima chewed her lip.

Mom, I can't lose you now. Wanting comfort, Gloria wrapped her arm around Fima and reached for Mike's hand, but Mike pulled away.

Dr. Brock nodded with a frown. "She can't breathe without the ventilator." His eyes flickered with compassion. "I'm sorry."

Fima collapsed in Gloria's arms. She guided Fima to a chair in the lounge, then returned to her spot by the door to her mother's room.

Mike's facial features hardened. "So, basically, a machine is keeping our mother alive." She went into their mother's room while Gloria watched through the glass.

"So, there's nothing you can do to heal her?" Gloria asked.

Dr. Brock shook his head. "I'm afraid not."

"Does your mother have a living will?" Dr. Curtis asked.

Gloria's knees weakened by the doctor's words. "I-I don't know. But I would think so."

"You will want to read over it and see what her wishes are on end-of-life issues."

"All right," she answered, her body and mind numb.

"You and your sisters will eventually have to make a decision on what you want to do for your mother," Dr. Curtis said. He put a hand on her shoulder. "I'm sorry. I know this is an extremely difficult thing to go through."

Gloria swallowed hard and nodded.

The doctors muttered something more, but she hadn't heard them. They walked off, leaving her with two sisters who needed her help. Mike paced the floor in their mother's room. Would her older sister accept her assistance?

Chapter Thirty-Five

Seraphima had left the hospital and driven to her apartment, needing time to breathe and be away from the noisy machines and her withering mother. Shame filled her as she curled up, trembling in her bed. She should be there, let her mother know she was there, give her comfort with her presence. But she just couldn't. Fear had shaken her core, and her legs hadn't kept her standing. *Wimp. I'm such a wimp.* Burying her head under her pillow, Seraphima shuddered tears.

Her cell phone rang. Removing the pillow from her head and sniffling, she glanced at the digital clock on her nightstand. Five-twenty. She bit her lip, reached for her phone next to the clock. Mike's number glowed on its tiny screen. She had a good idea why her oldest sister was calling her, and she didn't want to deal with it right now. *Wimp.* Frowning, Seraphima put the phone to her ear. "Yes."

"I need you to meet me at Mom's. We've got some things to settle for her."

Her heart sank. Taking a breath and blowing it out, she scrubbed her tear-streaked face. "When?"

"Now, Fima. I'm going to get Mom's living will from the

lockbox in her study. We've got to read over her wishes on this situation."

"And Glory? Will she be there too?"

After a few seconds of dead air, Mike replied, "Yeah, Glory too."

"Okay. I'll be there soon."

Seraphima ended the call, set the phone on the mattress, and lay back down. She and her sisters were going to talk about ending their mother's life. Her body felt as heavy as a piano. She had to push herself to move and climb out of bed. Padding to the bathroom, she took out a bottle of Xanax and one of the small paper cups in the dispenser, filled it with water, and swallowed one of the pills.

She left her apartment as a hint of drowsy calmness from the sedative kicked in.

Glory and Mike were standing in the study when Seraphima walked in, her mind and body steadier.

Mike held up the stapled set of legal papers. "She wants the plug pulled if she's ever in a vegetative state."

Seraphima cringed. "God, Mike." Even in horrible moments like this, Mike didn't soften. What would it take for her sister to thaw? Their mother's death? She bit her lip. She wouldn't think about it even though it loomed ahead of her.

Mike sighed, her other hand on her hip. "I'm just telling you what Mom's will says."

Glory stood with her hands clasped and head bent. Was she crying? Seraphima went to her and slid an arm around her waist. Glory lifted her head and gazed at Seraphima. A small smile formed, but her glistening eyes shone misery. Seraphima hugged her.

"So, we need to decide when we'll be taking Mom off the ventilator."

Seraphima scowled. "You act as if doing this is like turning off the study light."

"I'm trying to do what Mom wants, Fima." Mike paced the area rug next to the desk then stopped midway and looked at her. "Somebody's got to be the responsible adult here."

Glory nodded. "You're right. This is for Mom, what she wants."

Mike raised her brows, then pointed a finger at Glory but looked at Seraphima. "See? She gets it."

Seraphima folded her arms. "Am I not allowed to hate this?"

"Of course you are—" Glory began.

"Sure." Mike nodded. "After all, this whole catastrophe is Tina's doing."

Tina? Seraphima had forgotten about her. Had she driven the car? Oh, yes. She remembered Mike fussing over Tina keeping Doug, Bailey, and their mother out longer than the time on which they'd agreed.

"She's been nothing but a plague on this family," Mike said, pacing again.

"Nevertheless, we need to keep focused on Mom and what needs to be done for her," Glory pointed out, her stare moving to the papers in Mike's hands. "Does it say anything about where she wants to be buried? Does she already have a plot?"

"She does," Mike said. "Next to Dad's at Green Acres Cemetery."

"So we just need to purchase a coffin," Glory said.

Mike held up the papers again. "Already done."

"Already done?" Glory's eyes widened.

"Yeah. Don't you remember Dad was a lawyer?"

"Well—" Glory said.

"Got it all cinched up for them years before he died."

"Okay."

Mike leaned against the desk, dropped the papers on its surface, and folded her arms. "Guess it's hard to remember somebody you've erased from your mind."

Glory straightened and shook her head. "I never erased him from my mind. I couldn't."

"Sure." Mike tapped the papers. "Let's get back to Mom."

"Gladly," Glory said, sliding her hands into her jeans pockets.

Seraphima couldn't believe their exchange. Her body simmered with anger. "How can you two discuss this like it's nothing? Like it's just a bill to pay? A pet to neuter?"

Glory turned to her. "We don't mean it to come off that way."

Mike swatted the air. "First we've got business to take care of." She smacked the desk with her palm. "Then we can fall apart."

"What if I can't take care of business?" Seraphima held back tears. Her medication didn't stop her from feeling.

Glory laid a hand on Fima's arm. "I know it's hard."

Mike pushed her body from the desk. "We do what we can." She picked up the papers. "So, when do we want to tell the doctors Mom's wishes?"

Seraphima shook her head and said, "I'm not ready," just as Glory did.

Seraphima braced herself for Mike's overbearing response, but it didn't come. Her oldest sister only nodded her head with her mouth turned down. "Okay. Understand."

Glory rubbed her temple. "I think we need some time to absorb all of this."

"I know I do," Seraphima agreed.

"Right. Let's give it twenty-four hours and see where we are by this time tomorrow." Mike folded the papers and shoved them in her purse.

"Twenty-four hours?" Seraphima's eyes widened. "We're supposed to have this all figured out in twenty-four hours?"

Mike headed to the study doorway. "We'll see where we are

tomorrow. That's all I said." She left the room with quick strides.

Seraphima sank into a floral love seat. Letting out a sigh, she looked up at Glory. "It's too much."

Glory sat next to her and put an arm around her shoulders. "I know it is. I've got a lot of feelings I'm dealing with too."

"Like what?"

"Like feeling like a jerk for running away ten years ago." Glory stared ahead at nothing, as if in a trance. "All those wasted years."

Glory was feeling guilty. Seraphima hadn't even considered her feelings. She shifted on the sofa. *How could I? I just lost my baby, and now I'm told a breathing machine is the only thing keeping Mom alive.* She slumped against the back cushion. "I'm sorry," she mumbled, closing her eyes, wanting to disappear between the love seat's cushions.

She felt Glory's hand on her knee, then her leaving the sofa. "I need some time to think. I'll see you back at the hospital this evening."

Seraphima raised her head. "I won't be there. Austin's coming over tonight."

Glory stood by the doorway and frowned. "You're not going to be with Mom tonight knowing what little time we have left with her?"

Seraphima shook her head. "I promised Austin I'd be at home tonight."

"But surely he understands the seriousness of our situation?"

Seraphima rose and brushed hair from her shoulder. "He does. He cares. That's why he wants to spend time with me." She wrung her hands. "I need him right now."

Glory gave her a slow nod with disappointment showing in her eyes before turning and leaving the room. Her sister didn't understand her and Austin's relationship. A part of Seraphima felt sorry for her sister. Glory had no man in her life, something Seraphima couldn't comprehend.

Chapter Thirty-Six

A fter signing Bailey's discharge papers, Michaela guided her to Doug's room.

As they approached his door, Tina and a man were standing near it. She was decked out in gray slacks, black heels, and a pink silk blouse. To top off the gaudy outfit, she'd painted her face. Michaela raised her brows. Was this all for Doug? He wouldn't see her anyway.

Tina smiled as if everything was fine in the world. "Michaela."

Michaela rolled her tight shoulders to release the tension. For Bailey's sake, she needed to stave off the anger rising inside her. "Tina," she said through clenched teeth. "I see you've been discharged too."

"Yes." Another exaggerated smile split Tina's face. She then tapped the man's shoulder next to her. "This is my brother, Alan." His sandy-brown hair cut hovered above a small forehead, beady brown eyes, and a pug nose.

He held out his hand. Michaela hesitated, then shook it.

"Nice to meet you." He bobbed his head.

I hope he's nothing like his manipulative, lying sister. "Nice of you to visit Tina."

"He's my ride home," Tina said. "My car was totaled, as I'm sure you could've guessed."

"Right." Michaela raked her short hair behind her ears. Images of her mother and Doug, as well as the conversation with her sisters in their mother's study, came to her mind. "How could I forget?"

"So, I thought I'd stop by and see Doug before heading home. Haven't seen him since before the crash."

She let the sarcasm slip from her lips. "Haven't you?"

Tina shook her head.

Michaela pointed through the doorway. "Take a good look at him. See what you've caused." *Damn it.* She'd wanted to wait to deal with Tina when Bailey wasn't with her.

Tina's tongue rolled against her cheek. "Nice, Michaela." But her irritated look vanished when she saw Doug. Her mouth fell open, and she edged to the right side of his bed. "Doug."

Bailey tugged on Michaela's arm. "Mama, I wanna see Daddy."

Michaela tore her eyes from Tina and looked down at her daughter. "Of course, baby." She led Bailey into the room and to the left side of the bed.

Alan stood near the doorway with his hands clasped behind his back and his feet apart, as if guarding the room.

Bailey pet Doug's forearm. "You got a needle in your arm like I had." She frowned at him, then looked up at Michaela. "He's sleeping."

Michaela smoothed down Bailey's blond tresses. "Yes, he is. He needs a lot of sleep to get better."

Bailey nodded. She leaned forward and kissed her father's arm, then stretched toward his face but couldn't reach. Michaela lifted her, and she gave Doug a long kiss on the cheek. "Love you, Daddy." She stroked the side of Doug's swollen face. "You sleep lots and lots so when you're all better, we can go skating again."

Michaela blinked back tears and swallowed hard. *Damn it.* Why did Bailey have to see her father like this? Why did he have to be lying there in pieces? Her stare traveled to Tina, who smiled at Bailey.

"Anything to say?" she asked Tina.

Tina ran her finger horizontally back and forth under her nose. She didn't answer, just shook her head.

Alan moved to her side and put a hand on her shoulder. "You okay?"

Tina reached for her brother's hand and patted it. "I'm fine." She then touched Doug's shoulder. "Get better, bud. I'll come visit you soon." Without looking at Michaela or Bailey, Tina sniffed and strode out of the room, her chin lifted.

Alan walked out after her.

Bailey tapped Michaela's hip. "Can we go see Gramma now?"

"Yes, baby." Michaela took her daughter's hand, and with one last gaze at her broken husband, Michaela whispered, "We'll see you soon."

She led Bailey out of the room.

Thank God Bailey would be staying at Lena's house tonight. Lena had been the best friend Michaela ever had. She pushed back the dread spreading through her as she thought about how she would eventually have to tell her daughter about her grandmother's impending death.

At eight-forty that evening, Seraphima slouched against the couch cushions in her apartment, her finger twirling a lock of hair as she stared at the front door, waiting for Austin to come through it. *Why isn't he here already?* She froze. *Did he get called to the station?* She sighed. *Couldn't they find other volunteers to take his place?* They'd just patched up their relationship. Why couldn't they get a break?

A knock sounded on the door before it swung open. Austin's six-foot-two stocky figure filled the doorframe as he entered and shut the door behind him. He was on the couch next to her in seconds, his scrumptious cologne teasing her, making her body weak. He swept her into his lap and smothered her with hot kisses, only taking a breath to say, "So sorry I'm late, babe. Firefighter stuff."

Her head swam, her whole body soft as a marshmallow, floating, eagerly taking in his kisses and caresses. How she'd missed his touch, missed him, missed them. Everything came together like a well-crocheted blanket—cozy, warm, secure, united. When he'd lifted her as if she weighed nothing and carried her to the bedroom, her heart soared as her body took flight, anticipating their bodies coming together in one hot, explosive merger like they'd always had before the breakup, a breakup that seemed a lifetime ago. She felt the bed's mattress against her back. Austin covered her body with his, as she wrapped her arms around his thick neck, ardently prepared for a sensuous journey toward ecstasy.

Seraphima woke naked in bed, tangled in the sheets that were now cool. She reached over to touch Austin, but he wasn't there. Her digital clock read two a.m. A folded note sat like an A-framed tent next to the clock. Moving over to the nightstand, she plucked the paper and opened it. The moonlight flowing through the window above the bed gave ample brightness to the scrawled handwriting.

Babe,

Emergency. Called in. Two-alarm fire. Sorry.

The makeup sex was freaking amazing. See you when I can.

Austin

She sighed, rolled onto her back, and pulled the covers over her chest. Usually she'd have pouted, complained at his taking off once again to answer a fire. But he'd assuaged her, quenched her thirst, calmed her spirit. Her body remained spongy and light with the faint musky scent of his cologne still lingering in the warm air.

With the moonlight bathing her face, Seraphima closed her eyes, the memory of their lovemaking lulling her back to sleep.

Chapter Thirty-Seven

Gloria met with Mike and Fima outside their mother's room later that afternoon. She hadn't slept well last night, waking every half hour with the buzzing of the machines and occasional noise of nurses checking Etta's IV bag, catheter bag, and machine output. With every hour that passed, Gloria knew, with a sickness in her stomach, that the time drew nearer to her mother's leaving her and her sisters. Leaving her without having had the conversation Etta had wanted so much. And Gloria had no idea what Etta had wanted to tell her. Would she ever know? She glanced at her sisters. Maybe they knew. She hoped so.

"—had time to decide when you wanted to do this?" Mike asked, pacing the floor.

Fima bit her lip and looked at Gloria with pleading eyes. "Maybe the doctors are wrong. Maybe Mom will be fine. Start breathing on her own." She nodded her head with vigor. "Yes, I'm sure it's possible."

Mike stopped pacing and stood with arms crossed. "Fima, Mom's brain is basically dead. How the hell do you think she's going to come out of that?"

Fima scowled. "The doctors are wrong. She will get better. She has to."

"We don't have time for your emotional fits," Mike snapped.

Gloria winced. Mike was moodier than usual, but could she blame her?

"We've got to make a decision soon," Mike said.

"Why? Mom's not going anywhere." Fima pointed to their mother through the glass. "We can't make a snap decision when this could give her time to heal."

Mike grabbed Fima by the shoulders and shook her. "Wake up, Fima! Mom is dead without that ventilator."

Fima groaned and burst into tears. "Stop it!"

Startled by Mike's actions, Gloria put an arm around each sister. "Let's calm down. We do have time to talk some more."

Mike's eyes narrowed, and she shoved Glory's arm off her shoulders. "Easy for you to be so damn calm. You've been AWOL for ten friggin' years."

Gloria cringed. *She's upset. Let it go.* She swallowed back the sour taste of guilt in her mouth.

Fima dug her hands into her long hair, holding her head as if she were in pain. "Quit yelling. Mom will hear you."

Before Mike could lash out again, Gloria moved her hand in a slicing motion between the two sisters. "Time out."

"Time, time, time! I don't want to hear that word again," Fima cried and stomped toward the lounge.

Gloria blew out a breath. "Okay, why don't we sit in the lounge for a minute." She caught up with Fima, took her elbow, and led her to a chair while Mike went back to pacing the floor.

"I was doing just fine until Mike opened her big mouth, spewing hateful things," Fima said, dropping into the chair with an angry thump.

"She's just upset."

Fima swiveled her head to face Gloria. "And I'm not?"

"We all are." Gloria rubbed her temple.

"She messed up my mood." Fima leaned against the cushions, folded her arms, and glared at their sister.

"Well, we were supposed to talk about what we were going to do about Mom today," Gloria said.

Fima huffed. "You're taking her side."

Gloria rolled her eyes, her patience waning. "For God's sake, Fima. I just want us to work on this together."

Fima sighed and looked up at the ceiling. "I had the most wonderful night with Austin. He made me forget all about…" She waved her hand around. "This."

"Reality will always return. If there's anything I've learned lately is you've got to face your problems, not run from them."

"You don't understand. You've never had a boyfriend, have you?" Fima's tone wasn't altogether harsh but rather mixed with curiosity. Her eyes softened as she looked at Gloria.

"I did go on a few dates in twelfth grade, but other than that, no. I've never really cared for dating."

"Why not?"

"It's just never been a priority. Nature interests me, like Henry—"

"Henry?"

Gloria glanced at Fima and smiled. "A grand cottonwood."

"Cottonwood." Fima stared ahead as if she'd been given a trivia question. "Is that a tree?"

Gloria patted her sister's arm. "Yes."

"A tree." Fima's bewildered stare turned to her. "You're drawn to a tree?"

"Yes, and all of nature." She leaned back in her chair and laced her hands over her chest. "Stunning sunsets, majestic Rockies, beautiful wildlife, vivid and colorful wildflowers—"

Fima smacked her thigh with the palm of her hand. "I knew that. I remember you used to camp outside in the backyard as much as Mom and Dad would let you, and you were always riding your bike and climbing trees."

"Still do." She chuckled. "I love to hike through the Rockies every day after work and on my days off."

Fima brushed a strand of hair off her shoulder. "Sounds like you get lots of exercise."

"I do, but it's not about that. It fills my heart with everything good and beautiful in the world."

"Must be quiet there."

"Not really, but the sounds aren't white noise. They're the symphony of the rushing river and amazing sounds of wildlife. Makes you realize how alive the world is around you."

Fima sighed and stared at the ceiling. "That sounds nice."

"So, dating hasn't crossed my mind much."

"Well, it's worth it if you find the right guy. One that sweeps you off your feet, makes your knees buckle, your bones melt, your head swim."

Gloria chortled. "How do you function in that state?"

"You don't have to. You drink in those feelings and bask in that awesome heaven."

"Heaven. You think it's like heaven?"

Fima looked at her and grinned. "Oh, yeah. It's the most wonderful feeling ever. You feel totally free and happy and loved."

"Huh." Gloria puckered her mouth. What her sister described didn't sound like dating but an afternoon spent walking the trails, embraced by the pines and refreshed by the gurgling, clean streams. "Must be quite an experience."

"Yeah. That's why I told you if you understood how that felt, then you'd see why being with my man is so important to me."

"Right." Gloria scratched her chin. The book on a women's monastery hadn't quite talked about what heaven was like but how they experienced God, and she wondered if they were one and the same. But she couldn't quite correlate the infatuations of a romantic relationship with the soaring joy of encountering God, if she understood what she'd read.

She'd little desire to find out what Fima was describing. Was there something wrong with her? Glory frowned. Everyone she knew marked romantic relationships at the top of his or her priority list, except her. No. The peace she found in the foothills, gravelly trails, and visiting the monastery were real and satisfying. A man was incongruous to her simple lifestyle.

Mike marched over to them. She glanced at her watch. "Listen, the doctors will probably come by soon since I told them we needed to talk."

Fima rose from her seat. "You told them we'd made a decision?"

Mike's lips pursed. "No. I didn't say that. Just that we needed to talk, see if there was a time limit on this."

Gloria nodded. "Okay. So, we stay here until they show up?"

"Yep." Mike walked the carpeted floor in the lounge. She stopped midway in front of her and Fima and held up a finger. "But we should discuss this as we'd planned."

Fima flopped in the chair again and blew out a breath. "I don't want to take her off the ventilator."

Mike shot out a hip and put her hand on it. "I think you made that annoyingly clear earlier." She turned her attention to Gloria. "What do you think?"

Gloria gripped the arms of her chair. "I was hoping to talk to her, find out what she'd wanted to tell me, but I know now that's impossible."

"Anything's possible," Fima said, folding her arms.

If only what Fima said were true. Gloria swallowed hard.

Mike looked at Fima as if she were a misbehaving child. Her stare then came back to Gloria. "So, what's your answer?"

All the years away from her mother swept over Gloria, like the painful pummels of a hailstorm. Her shoulders slumped as she lowered her gaze. She'd never get to make up for those lost years. Never.

"Glory," Mike said.

Gloria went to the doorway of their mother's room and gazed at Etta's supine body with the breathing tube lodged in her throat. Her mother looked all but dead. No movement. No life in her. Tears stung her eyes as she heard Mike's sneakers smacking against the floor, growing louder until she stood next to her.

"This is no way to live, and she said in her will she didn't want to live this way," Mike said, running a hand through her hair.

Gloria nodded. "I know."

"So, what do you want to do?"

"What our mother wants."

Mike rubbed her chin. "All right. We'll let the doctors know when they come by."

Gloria turned toward her sister. "What about Fima?"

Mike shook her head. "She's got to be told again this is what Mom wants."

Gloria glanced at Fima still sitting in the lounge, twirling a lock of her hair.

During the discussion with the doctors, Seraphima frowned and said nothing. She'd given them a reluctant nod of acceptance when Glory and Mike had explained their mother's wishes. She hadn't spoken since their talk an hour ago, and she blotted out the conversation with the doctors. A strong urge in her prodded her to flee, but she waited until Dr. Brock walked off and Dr. Curtis entered their mother's room, heading toward the ventilator machine. She wouldn't watch him remove the breathing tube, watch her mother fade away, succumb to death.

"Fima, you coming in?" Glory asked.

Mike gave Seraphima a stern look. "You're going to be with Mom, aren't you?"

Seraphima looked from Mike to their mother's fragile body. She shook her head and backed away from Mike and Glory. "No. I-I can't." She spun around and scurried past the lounge, down the hall to the side door to the stairs, pushed it open, raced down the three flights of stairs, and burst into the corridor on the ground floor. Taking in gulps of air, she ran out the lobby's glass doors, away from the hospital, away from death.

Seraphima slammed her apartment's front door and strode to the cordless phone next to the couch. She called Austin but got his answering machine. "Come on, Austin. I need you." She curled on the sofa, bit her lip, and waited for the beep. "Austin, I need you. My mom is being taken off the ventilator. I'm at home. Come as soon as you can."

She put the phone back on its base, then went to the bathroom. A hot shower would do her good. She stripped off her clothes, turned on the showerhead, stepped under it, and let her tears merge with the water streaming over her face.

Chapter Thirty-Eight

F ear and impending grief ached inside Gloria as she sat on the left side of their mother's bed, holding her cool, dry hand. Mike sat on the other side, her head lowered, holding their mother's other hand.

The doctor removed the breathing tube and told Gloria and Mike their mother would likely pass within the hour. He left them alone, the room eerily silent, with the heart rate monitor's sound muted.

Gloria's childhood ran like a filmstrip through her head—images of her mother gently pushing her on a park swing, helping her put together a floor puzzle. Gloria peeking her head out of a tent in the backyard, her mother holding back the flap, mouth wide with laughter. "I'll never know," she heard herself say out loud.

"Never know what?" Mike's raspy voice brought her back to the present.

She shook her head. "We never got to talk."

"Sure you did."

"No, she said we'd talk when she came home from the zoo." She glanced at Mike.

Mike frowned, and pain flashed through her eyes. "The zoo. Right." Her sister's eyes glazed over as if in a trance but only for a second before Mike's mouth tightened and her eyes narrowed. "Tina."

"Let's not talk about Tina now… with Mom here… for a little while longer."

"We're losing her because of that woman. And Doug." Mike leaned her elbow on the bed and head in her hand. "My God. What if I lose Doug too?"

Gloria hadn't seen this vulnerable side of her sister before. She swallowed and reached for Mike's arm. "He'll recover."

Mike didn't answer, just slowly shook her head. She then looked at her, a smile tugging at one side of her mouth. "Remember when she made that lopsided and underbaked yellow cake for your ninth birthday?"

Gloria chuckled, seeing her mother set the wobbly cake on the table, pushing candles into it. The candles wouldn't stay in place, falling over into the goo. "Yeah."

"She should have stuck with ordering one." Mike let out a hoarse laugh.

"I know. But at least we had the gallon of chocolate ice cream to eat." Gloria wiped her nose with the heel of her hand and smiled at their mother's ashen face. "She'd tried. That's what counted."

Mike patted Etta's bony shoulder. "Gotta give her that."

Their mother's last words to Gloria came back to her. "But we'll never have that talk."

Mike glanced at her. "You keep saying that. What talk?"

"I told you. She said she had something she wanted to talk to me about before she left for the zoo."

Mike's forehead wrinkled as her brows came together, but she said nothing.

"Do you know what she wanted to talk to me about?"

"She only wanted me to find you." She tilted her head to the side. "Come to think of it, she did say she needed to talk to you, but she didn't say about what."

Gloria bowed her head. Guilt and curiosity ate at her, but she pushed the feelings aside and focused on her mother.

She and Mike said nothing for the next half hour, with only the whispers of the nurses' chatter and movements from their station drifting into the room.

Gloria glanced at her sister, who seemed to be staring at nothing. She reached for Mike's hand lying on top of their mothers when a sound came from Etta.

She moved toward the head of the bed, bent close to Etta's left shoulder, with Mike doing the same on the other side of the bed.

Rattles and gurgles sputtered from Etta's slightly open mouth.

Gloria exchanged a worried stare with Mike, then peered at the heart rate monitor. She looked at Mike again before turning her attention back to their mother.

"Mom," Mike whispered.

"We're here," Gloria squeezed Etta's hand.

Etta let out a weak sigh. Then the muted heart rate monitor's vertical jagged line slid horizontally across the screen. Glory's heart nearly stopped as her throat closed. She slumped against crushing sorrow rolling over her.

The nurse, Peggy, came into the room and checked the monitor then Etta. She turned toward Gloria and Mike and gave them a sympathetic frown. "She's gone."

"Christ," Mike muttered, leaning her forehead on the palm of her hand and laying a hand on her mother's torso.

Gloria kept holding Etta's limp hand as tears fell from her eyes. "I love you, Mom." Had she managed to say that before the accident? She couldn't remember. Her body weighed down with misery, and her mind filled with regret. She rested her forehead on her mother's, and her hands and shoulders shook as the tears continued to cascade down her face.

Lost in her own pain, she didn't hear Mike get up, only felt her hand on her shoulder. She turned and looked up into her sister's eyes, wet with dark glimmers of agony. Mike opened her arms, and Gloria stood and embraced her, both of them weeping in hushed sniffles resonating in the room.

"Mommy?"

Gloria and Mike turned toward the door where Fima held on to its frame as if it was the only thing keeping her from collapsing. Her face was chalk white, her large, dark eyes reflecting a little girl of five. Tears streaked her cheeks.

Gloria moved with Mike toward Fima and gathered her in their arms. Gloria held on to her sisters. The familiar sibling bond from years ago flowed through her, the first time since they were children, and it gave her a small measure of comfort in her anguish.

Mike sniffed, raised her head, and gave Gloria and Fima a sober stare, her face looking old, tired. "I'll talk to the nurse. Tomorrow we'll plan the funeral." Her gaze flicked to Fima but came back to Gloria. "Take her home and stay with her for the night."

"Of course." She wiped her nose with the back of her hand. "Just let me say goodbye."

Mike nodded, folded her arms, and began to pace the floor.

Gloria approached Etta's body, brushed a hand across her mother's forehead, then kissed it. "I'll miss you so much. I already do. Love you."

She directed her distraught younger sister to their mother. Fima slid into bed next to Etta, putting an arm around her torso and leaning her head on Etta's shoulder. Her body shuddered, and she kissed her mother's cheek. Gloria believed Fima would have lain there all night if Mike hadn't patted Fima's slouched shoulder.

"Fima, Glory's going to take you home and stay with you."

Fima rose as if she were a zombie and plodded out of the room. Gloria followed her out, glancing back before crossing the doorway. Mike stood strong, her mouth in a tight smile of encouragement, her eyes glowing in anguish. Tonight Gloria sensed Etta's death had changed something between Mike and her. No more running away. Gloria vowed to be with her sisters, to recover and heal with them.

Chapter Thirty-Nine

As her mother's casket was showered with shoveled chunks of earth, Gloria wiped her eyes, her heart aching. She walked toward Mike's car, with her sisters behind her.

Ahead of her, Aunt Melina stood in all black near a large Ponderosa pine. Gloria caught her breath and rushed toward her aunt. Mike and Fima seemed to have noticed their aunt as well and followed her.

Aunt Melina opened her arms, and Gloria embraced her. "It's so good to see you." She frowned. "Even though it's at such a sad time."

Mike and Fima reached them.

"Aunt Melina, we didn't see you," Fima said, mopping her tear-streaked face. "Were you here for the whole funeral?"

Aunt Melina used a tissue to dab under her wet eyes. "Yes."

Mike's face colored. "Why didn't you stand with your family?"

"You know why, Michaela." Aunt Melina sniffed. "I haven't been welcome in your family for years."

"Well, you can't blame Mom for not wanting anything to do

with you after keeping Glory's whereabouts a secret." Mike crossed her arms.

Their aunt's eyes narrowed. "I'll never be sorry for keeping Gloria away from your monstrous father."

Mike lifted her chin. "Both our parents are gone. It'd be nice if you'd show some respect for the dead."

Aunt Melina shrugged. "I'm here."

Before Mike could respond, Fima put an arm through hers. "Well, it was nice of you to come. Are you going to the wake?"

"No. I've done what I came to do."

"Are you sure you don't want to stay for the wake?" Gloria frowned. "It's been so long since we've seen each other."

"Don't push her, Glory," Mike grumbled. "I've got to get everything ready for the wake." She removed Fima's arm and strode toward her car.

Fima gave their aunt a hug. "Thanks for being here." She then ran after Mike.

"I'm sorry," Gloria said. "Mom's death has been so hard on us."

Aunt Melina laid a hand on the side of Gloria's face. "I know, sweetheart." She glanced at Mike. "Unfortunately, your big sister hasn't changed after all these years."

Gloria clasped her hands together. "She's trying. It's hard…"

Her aunt nodded. "I didn't know your father had died too."

"I just recently found out. He died two years ago."

"Is that why you returned home?"

"Yes."

"Well, I hope you were able to make amends with your mother."

Gloria's heart tightened. "There wasn't much time."

Aunt Melina's mouth turned down. "I'm sorry." She folded Gloria in another hug. "Know your mother loved you very much."

Tears stung Gloria's eyes. Maybe her aunt knew what her

mother had wanted to tell her. When her aunt let her go, she wiped her nose.

"Mom wanted to tell me something that seemed so important, but she didn't get the chance before she died."

Her aunt's brows came together, and she tilted her head to the side.

"Do you have any idea what she could've wanted to tell me?"

"No. Sorry. We weren't very close ever since she married Gil."

Gloria's shoulders slumped, and she nodded.

"My parents and I were against her marrying that creep. Could see right through him. His arrogance and short temper were obvious to everyone but lovesick Etta." She rolled her eyes. "Oh, what a fool she'd been."

"Please, be easy on Mom. She had it rough."

"Of her own doing." Her aunt wiped her nose with the tissue in her hand. "But of course, I'm not totally heartless. I tried to keep in touch with her for the first year or so of her marriage, but she had little interest in contacting me or our parents. Then again, it could've been that overbearing brute didn't allow her to."

"You're probably right that Dad didn't let her. I don't remember seeing anybody come over to visit her when I was still at home."

Aunt Melina shoved the tissue in her slacks pocket. "Such a shame." She gazed at the ground where Etta's casket lay deep beneath the soil. "I suppose there's some satisfaction knowing she had a couple of good years without having that jerk in her life."

Gloria swallowed hard. Her mother had gone through so much.

"Check in with me when you think about it, Gloria." Aunt

Melina squeezed her shoulder before walking toward a black Acura parked by the curb.

Gloria glanced over her shoulder at the resting place of her mother one last time. *Goodbye, Mom. I love you.*

———

A dozen people mingled and wandered through Etta Barstone's living and dining room, conversing and consuming the potpourri of assorted pastries, cold cuts, and bite-sized cheese blocks spread on the table.

Seraphima sat on the edge of a chair in the living room, watching the front door. Mike had notified all family and friends of their mother's death, so Aunt Melina's presence at the funeral wasn't too surprising to Seraphima. And the attendance of Seraphima's boss, Linda, didn't startle her. Her boss had always shown compassion for her. She couldn't ask for a better person to work for. But the absence of Austin from both her mother's funeral and this gathering afterward made her stomach churn.

On the ride from the cemetery to her mother's home, Seraphima sobbed for her mother, and she wrung her hands as worry ate at her over Austin's disappearance. He hadn't called her since the night he'd made love to her and left her early in the morning. Was it too much to expect him to let her know he wouldn't make the funeral? Wouldn't make the wake? She rubbed the wetness off her face as she walked to the drink table and grabbed one of the prefilled cups of spring water. She gulped it down and threw the cup in the trash can next to the table.

The doorbell rang, and Glory opened the door. Eli walked in, his stringy legs like a spider's donned in gray khakis that sprouted from beneath his bulky jacket. His windswept, blond hair bounced against his forehead as he approached Seraphima.

He spread out his arms. "Fima, I'm so sorry I missed the funeral."

She embraced him.

"My dad needed me to finish up the new wheelchair ramp for the front porch." He still held her, and she clung to him, taking in the comfort emanating from him.

"Hope you can forgive me."

She sniffled and smiled. "Of course."

He looked around the room. "Your mother has a nice house."

Seraphima surveyed the space. "Yes, I know. I lived here with her until last summer after I graduated high school."

Eli nodded. "Where's Austin?"

Her cheeks warmed. The love of her life wasn't standing next to her. "Well, he said..." What story could she make up that didn't make her look stupid? Nothing came. She sighed and lowered her gaze. "I-I don't know where he is."

"Fighting a fire?"

She shrugged. Lumbering through burning buildings did seem to be where Austin tended to be most of the time. "Probably."

"At least he's got a good reason he didn't make it then, right?"

"Right." But she didn't know where Austin was, really. He usually called and told her when he had to volunteer. He hadn't called at all, and anxiety pressed on her chest. Was he breaking up with her again?

"Have you eaten anything?"

She grimaced. "No, not yet."

"You should eat. It'll give you strength."

"Okay." Her stomach somersaulted when she looked at the trays of food. "Maybe later." She waved a hand. "You go ahead."

Eli walked to the table and gathered up a modest amount of roast beef slices and cheese on his plate. He returned to where she stood and took a bite of cheese. "May your mother rest in peace."

"Thanks." Seraphima moved to the Victorian-style couch and sat down.

Eli sat beside her. "How're you holding up?" He ate a piece of meat and set his plate on the table next to the sofa.

Etta's placid expression on her embalmed face floated in Seraphima's mind. "Not very well."

Eli removed his coat and put an arm around her slouched shoulders.

She leaned against him. "It's hard, you know?"

"Yeah, I know."

Eli's words from another time came back to her. He'd lost his mother when he was a teen. He truly *did* know.

"It's unbelievably hard," he said, squeezing her against his side.

"I'm sorry. I'd almost forgotten about you losing your mom."

Eli nodded and rubbed her arm with affection. "It's okay. I didn't expect you to remember, especially right now."

Seraphima closed her eyes. Maybe Austin would show up soon and take her away from this place. He had a way of easing her pain. He'd be here soon. He had to.

Gloria spied Bailey sitting with knees drawn to her chest and arms wrapped around them under the buffet table situated against the wall. The shadows of the table darkened Bailey's frowning, pinched face.

Gloria lowered to her hands and knees and peeked under the buffet. "Hey, honey."

Bailey's frown deepened, and she lowered her head to her knees. "Go away."

Gloria sat back on her heels. "Only if you're going to be okay."

Bailey spoke in a muffled voice. "I want Gramma."

Gloria swallowed down the sorrow clogging her throat. What could she say? Her heart hurt all around, for her niece, sisters, herself. She wanted "Gramma" back too. "I know you do, sweetie. We all do."

"Why'd she have to die?"

"Well—"

Bailey lifted her chin. "I didn't, so why did she?"

Gloria rolled her head to loosen the muscles in her craning neck. She slid onto her side on the floor and leaned her head against her outstretched arm. "Gramma's head was hurt really bad, and..."

Did she really want to tell her five-year-old niece all the gory details of her grandmother's death? She squeezed her eyes shut and took in a few breaths with long exhales. The monastery came to her mind. But before she could speak, Bailey crawled toward her. The little blond-haired cherub peered at her on hands and knees.

"Is Gramma in heaven?"

Gloria sat up, crossing her legs. "You know about heaven?"

Bailey wiped her nose with the back of her hand, then nodded. "There's a prayer book in my great-gramma's special box with lots of stories of people who pray all kinds of things. I looked at the pages. It had pretty pictures of red, blue, and black birds in it with flowers and stuff. And on one page with a really shiny sun and blue sky was this prayer about somebody going to heaven to be with God. I know it says that 'cause I asked Gramma to read it to me. She did. I asked Gramma what heaven was, and she said it's a happy place where good people go."

Gloria smiled. "I've heard the same thing."

Bailey came out from under the table and sat next to her. She laid her small hand on Gloria's forearm. "Gramma's a good person, so she's in heaven, right?"

Clueless as to whether this was true or not didn't matter to Gloria now. Her niece needed it to be true. "Yes. That's where Gramma went."

Bailey pointed to the ceiling. "She's somewhere up there happy?"

Gloria glanced skyward. "Yeah. I'm sure she is."

"She's never coming back. I know 'cause the story said people stay up there."

Gloria nodded, feeling completely inept for this discussion.

Bailey pointed a finger at her chest. "I'm a good girl, so I can go up there when I die, right?"

"Of course." Gloria swept a strand of hair behind Bailey's ear.

"Then I'll see Gramma."

"Yes, yes you will." Had her niece figured this all out on her own? She wished she had such faith.

Bailey reached over and kissed Gloria's cheek. "Thanks, Aunt Glory. I don't feel so sad now." She sniffled, got to her feet, and wandered toward the kitchen.

Agreeing with her grandmother about heaven was worth it, seeing her niece's sorrow lessen. Gloria stood and went to the nearest window facing the large backyard with its white gazebo, flowers, and shrubs. In the distant background glistened the Rockies. Such beauty. Such perfection. Those mountains had always given her comfort—her own piece of heaven.

Michaela embraced her daughter and kissed the top of her head.

Bailey gazed up at her. "Can I go play with Sylvester?"

Michaela lifted Bailey's little chin and smiled. "Go for it."

Her daughter scrambled out of the kitchen.

She sighed. At least her daughter appeared to be handling Etta's death all right. But she knew there would be crying spells for the next several weeks, probably months. She and Bailey would get through this. And so would Doug.

Michaela walked to the sink and looked out the garden window to the vast backyard. She'd been thinking a lot about him since they arrived at the house. She wanted to be at the hospital with him. Once this wake was over, she'd head there. He needed her, and she needed him.

She wouldn't allow herself to think negative thoughts. Too much pain had visited her and her family. But who'd brought on that pain? *Tina.* And Doug and his addiction. This mess started because of Doug. Then Tina came into the picture, and everything turned upside down. Her mother was gone because of them. If he'd just stopped drinking, she wouldn't have kicked his ass out of the house, and he wouldn't have gone crawling to that bimbo.

She pressed fingers to the side of her head. *Damn it. You're thinking negatively right now.*

Michaela caught sight of Glory walking along the slate path toward the backyard. She crossed the lawn toward the gazebo and sat on one of the benches, facing the mountains. Glory had come right smack dab in the middle of all the chaos. Michaela shook her head. Her sister's timing sucked. But Glory would have to go back to work soon. She couldn't take off indefinitely. She had her janitorial work to do back in Summitville. How she found happiness in that line of work was beyond Michaela. She tapped her chin and glanced at her sister again. With a short window of time left, what good could come out of Glory's presence here?

Michaela left the sink and walked out to the living room where Fima and a man were.

Her sister glanced up at her. "Mike, this is my friend, Eli."

Eli stood and shot out his hand. "It's really nice to meet you."

Michaela shook the man's hand, a man she'd never heard Fima talk about before. "Nice of you to come."

He looked down at Fima with a compassionate smile. "I needed to be here for Fima."

Michaela's brows rose. She hoped he wasn't using Fima's present vulnerable position to move in on her. She studied his skinny form, blue puppy-dog eyes, and wild blond hair. Totally not Fima's type. But Fima had said he was just a friend.

"I'm glad to know Fima has a caring friend."

Fima nodded, wiping under her bloodshot eyes.

Eli lifted his dimpled chin and gave Michaela a kind smile. "I'm happy to be one for her."

"Our wake will be wrapping up in a half hour."

"Oh, but..." Fima rose from the couch. "I'm waiting for Austin."

"Austin?" Michaela cocked her head to the side.

"Yes." Fima beamed. "We got back together a couple of days ago."

"You did?"

Fima nodded.

Michaela leaned her hip on the sofa's armrest. "Isn't Austin the asshole golfer?"

Fima grimaced. "My God, Mike."

Michaela glanced at Eli, whose expression seemed to agree with her assessment of Austin.

She scratched her neck. "He was supposed to be here today?"

"Well, he said he'd try if he wasn't working."

"Uh-huh."

Eli looked around and fidgeted as if he wanted to hightail it out of the house rather than listen to her and her sister's exchange.

Fima laid a hand over one of Eli's that was resting on his thigh. "Don't worry. It's just sisterly talk." Her grin quivered.

Eli glanced at her as if trying his hardest to believe her.

Michaela checked her watch. "He's got twenty minutes until we close this place up and go to the hospital to see Doug." Her stare slid to Fima. "You remember him, don't you?"

Fima gave Michaela a wounded look. "Of course I do."

"Good." Michaela rose from the armrest and joined her friend Lena in the dining room.

Fima puckered her lips as she watched her sister. Why'd her sister blurt out such awful things about Austin? And right in front of Eli. She sighed and glanced at the grandfather clock against the wall. Austin needed to show up now, but would he? Stupid Mike made her doubt him coming to their mother's wake. She glared at Mike's back.

"Have you tried calling Austin?" Eli asked.

"I'm going to call him right now." Fima pulled out her phone.

Eli nodded and went to the food table.

Austin's voice mail answered after three rings. "Austin, I was hoping you were going to be here for my mother's wake since you couldn't make the funeral. I really need you to be here. It's almost over. Please call me."

His absence had to be due to that irritating volunteer firefighting. She needed to be strong and talk him out of that. Fighting fires was dangerous, but more importantly, he had no time for her. They needed time together, especially after their contentious breakup and the loss of their baby. Yet she feared confronting him with her feelings. She'd just gotten him back. She bit her lip. Maybe it was best to wait a while until they were in a regular routine again.

Chapter Forty

Michaela led Bailey toward Doug's room and found Tina and her brother standing by the doorframe. Just the sight of the bleached-blond disaster caused Michaela to grind her teeth. She could sense her blood pressure rising with every step she took in their direction.

Tina turned and faced Michaela. She gave her an unexpected sympathetic frown. "I heard about your mother." She held out her arms as if she expected Michaela to accept her embrace. "I'm sorry."

Michaela stiffened, letting go of Bailey's hand for fear she'd crush it. She folded in her lips to stifle the vitriol she wanted to spew toward the woman. She couldn't go off in front of her daughter.

"I can't imagine what you're going through." Tina gave Michaela a suffocating squeeze.

"Hi, Tina." Bailey pointed to the man next to Tina. "Who's he?"

Tina released Michaela before she got the chance to push her away. Tina bent down and rested her hands on her knees, smiling at Bailey with her bright pink lips. "Don't you remember my brother, Alan, when we were last here to visit your daddy?" She patted Alan's arm.

Alan didn't flinch as his mouth cracked a smile that looked unnatural on his pudgy face. Michaela rubbed her chin. *Not a fan of children, are you? Figures.*

Bailey shook her head, then grinned shyly. "Hi, Alan."

"Hello." He nodded, then clasped his hands behind his back and gazed at the ceiling.

Tina smoothed out her excessively sprayed hair. She wore expensive-looking dark blue jeans that had gaudy little rhinestones on the seams of the pockets, a red blouse, and three-inch, brown-wedged shoes. "Alan, why don't you watch Bailey while we go in and visit Doug for a few minutes?"

Alan gaped, his face now pale.

Michaela balled her hands into tight fists at her sides. "I'd like to visit my husband alone."

Tina waved her comment aside. "Of course. After I leave."

Michaela planted her fists on her hips. *"After you leave?* Who croaked and made you queen?" She winced. *Damn it.* She'd let that out in the presence of her daughter just like last time they were here.

Tina only chuckled. "Nobody, silly Michaela. I just have an appointment to get to in the next half hour, so my time is limited."

Bailey tugged on the hem of Michaela's knit shirt. "Mama, don't be mean to Tina. She's really nice."

Heat rushed to Michaela's cheeks, and she kept her eyes on Bailey, not wanting to see Tina gloat. "Baby, I'm not being mean…"

Bailey stepped over to Alan and gazed up at him. "Would you take me to the waiting room with the big fish tank? I wanna look at all the pretty fish."

Oh no, daughter. Not with him. Michaela gently squeezed Bailey's shoulder. "Go to Peggy at the nurses' station, and maybe she can take you to see the fish."

Alan shot out of the room.

Michaela smirked. *You're off the hook, Alan. Good for both of us.*

Bailey hesitated, then nodded and left the room.

"I'm going in now," Tina said before Michaela could speak. "Time's ticking away." She walked through the doorway into the room.

Michaela followed her. "Have you no feelings of guilt for what happened to my mother?" She thrust her arm in the direction of Doug. "To my husband?"

"Michaela, you really need to work on your anger." Tina clucked her tongue. "You can be a real bitch."

"And you aren't?" Michaela narrowed her eyes at Tina. "You admitted to being one just the other day when you'd told me you'd lied like a Persian rug about you and Doug."

"I confessed, said I'm sorry." Tina's face clouded with annoyance, and she folded her arms across her chest. "What else do you want from me? Blood?"

"That'll do."

Tina laughed in that high-pitched, schoolgirl voice of hers that Michaela was positive would drive anyone to invest in earplugs if they had to live with her.

"God knows my mother, husband, and daughter gave enough blood due to your careless driving." Michaela closed the two feet of space between them and glared at Tina. "Why didn't you let Doug drive?"

A crease settled between Tina's expertly plucked blond eyebrows, and the edges of her mouth pulled slightly downward. "I was trying to be helpful. Give him a break from doing all the driving."

Michaela now laughed, tasting bitterness. "You see what that got you." Nostalgic images of a pregnant Etta pushing her on her bike as she struggled to steer and balance when she was five years old; Etta attending her volleyball game in sixth grade, cheering her on; Etta, Doug, and her at Bailey's last dance recital; Etta taking her last breath three rooms down from there... Tears sprang to Michaela's eyes, and she looked away.

Tina touched Michaela's shoulder. "It was an accident that I didn't cause. The man ran the red light. He was drunk." Tina sighed. "I don't know how many times I have to tell you that before you get it through that stubborn, fat head of yours."

Michaela wiped her eyes and cleared her throat. "My mother is gone. Bailey's grandmother is gone. They were very close. And my mother loved to babysit Bailey when I had to work late hours at my shop." Michaela began to pace the floor. "Thank God for Lena, or I'd have no one to watch my baby."

"I can watch her on my days off from the office."

Michaela's mouth fell open.

Tina shrugged, her expression serious. She wasn't joking.

"You want to watch my daughter?"

"Sure. She's a fantastic kid."

Michaela blinked, not knowing what to think. Instead of responding, she walked to the left side of Doug's bed, slid her hand in his and held it. They'd been quarreling all this time within hearing distance. "I'm sorry for our arguing."

Tina moved to the other side of the bed and gazed down at Doug. "Me too."

Doug's eyelids fluttered.

Michaela gasped. "Doug, are you waking up?"

Touching Doug's arm, Tina sucked on her lip, as if pleading for Doug to open his eyes.

His eyelids stilled.

Damn it. Michaela lowered her head. *He was trying to surface from the coma. I know he was.*

"He was waking up, Michaela. I could tell."

She only nodded and sank into the chair next to the bed, putting a palm on her forehead. She would never believe he wouldn't come out of the coma. But when he did, what happened then? And what about his drinking? Addictions didn't just go away. Would anything change for the good between them? She had no answers.

"I hope he comes out of this. I can't wrap my head around him dying."

Michaela glared at Tina. *He's listening, bimbo!* "Hey, watch—"

"I've got to go." Tina squeezed Doug's shoulder, then looked at Michaela. "I'll be back tomorrow after work, around five thirty."

Drained of all feeling, Michaela could only tilt her head in a half nod as Tina walked out the door.

Michaela sighed, pulled her chair closer to the bedside, and took hold of Doug's hand again. She lifted her gaze to his eyes. His eyelids moved again.

She shot up from the chair and leaned close to his face. "Doug?" She gripped his hand. "Come on, honey."

His eyelids fluttered another few seconds before they opened. He stared at her in bewilderment.

She grinned and clasped her hands together. "There you are, you big lug. What took you so long?"

His stare stayed on her.

"Waited to come back to me when we were alone, didn't you?" Michaela kissed his forehead.

His gaze finally left her face and took in the room around him without any noticeable recognition or feeling.

Michaela touched the side of his face. "I know. Not what you wanted to see when you came out of your deep sleep, but at least you've woken up."

His eyes were on hers again, large and intense, as if full of questions. His mouth twitched, but it didn't open. She held his hand with firmness, and his hand gave her a hint of response.

Michaela shrieked, "Stay right there, just like you are. I'm going to get the nurse, the doctor, the whole damn hospital!" She set his hand down and dashed out of the room.

Hot damn! He's going to recover. I know he is. Something good has finally happened to our family.

Chapter Forty-One

Gloria walked with Fima and Eli down the corridor to the ICU lounge where Bailey stood at the nurse's station. A stocky man with a buzz haircut scurried past them to the elevators. Fima and Eli moved ahead of her to the nurses' station, the two nurses there chattering as if something big had happened.

She didn't think she could take another earth-shattering event in her life. The day had drained everything out of Gloria, and the regret and guilt she'd experienced the day before had run over her like a steamroller when she'd gazed at her mother one final time before the casket lid was closed and she was lowered into the ground, the smell of the gardenias set on her gravestone by Mike, still lingering in her olfactory senses. The fragrant white beauties were Etta's favorite flowers. Gloria would always remember her mother any time she saw or smelled gardenias.

Would the awful guilt ever leave her? The heaviness in her heart gave her little confidence. But she'd let it go for today. Tomorrow would be a chance to look ahead and see where her heart led her.

She reached the group just as Mike came jogging out of Doug's room; her face lit up like Gloria remembered seeing her on Christmas mornings when they were children.

"He's come out of the coma!" Mike stood straight as a pin with hands on hips, beaming. "I'm waiting for the doctors."

Bailey gazed up at Mike with a perplexed expression on her face. "Mama, what's a coma?"

Mike covered her mouth, then squatted in front of Bailey. "Baby, that means Daddy's woke up from sleeping."

Bailey's mouth formed an *O*, and she jumped up and down before wrapping her arms around Mike. "I wanna see Daddy!"

Mike scooped her up. "Right away, Miss Bailey." She carried Bailey back to Doug's room.

"That's wonderful news about Doug," Fima said with a smile.

"Yes, very," Gloria said. Maybe some joy would enter Mike's heart with this news, chiseling away some of her sharp, stony exterior.

Eli pointed to two men in white coats approaching them. "Looks like the doctors are here."

"Hello, Ms. Lofton, Ms. Barstone," Dr. Curtis said and headed toward Doug's room.

"I'll wait here," Eli said, leaning his forearm on the counter.

Peggy hurried past them into the room.

Gloria came alongside Fima outside the doorway to Doug's room. When they entered, Mike was holding Bailey, who was reaching for Doug's face. She kissed his cheek.

Dr. Curtis and Dr. Brock approached on either side of the bed, and Mike and Bailey moved toward Glory and Fima.

Mike waved a finger in Doug's direction. "His eyes are open. See?"

Dr. Curtis nodded, pulled out a light pen and shined it in Doug's alert eyes. Doug blinked.

Dr. Brock held a tablet and wrote on it with its pen. He looked at Doug. "Can you speak?"

Doug's stare traveled to Dr. Brock. His mouth worked, twitched, his dry lips flattening and puckering before they parted, but only a sigh came out.

"It's okay." Dr. Brock raised his chin. "Give it some time. No rush."

Dr. Curtis cleared his throat. "Mr. Morrow, look at me, please. I want to finish checking your eyes."

Doug followed the doctor's command.

Dr. Curtis tucked away his light in his coat pocket, then removed the stethoscope from around his neck and listened to Doug's heart. After a minute, he hung the instrument around his neck again. "You followed the light well, and your heart sounds good."

"Did you hear that?" Mike asked Gloria and Fima.

Fima nodded.

Gloria smiled. It warmed her heart to see her sister in good spirits for a change. "Yes. That's such good news."

The doctors pivoted from beside the bed and walked toward them. Dr. Curtis looked at them with furrowed brows. "It *is* good that Mr. Morrow has come out of the coma. We will continue focusing on tests and treatments for his back injury."

Bailey tugged on Mike's shirt. "Mama, what's he talking about?"

Peggy put a hand on Bailey's shoulder. Bailey gazed up at the nurse, who took her hand. "Come with me. I've got something for you at the nurses' station. Then we'll come right back, okay?"

Bailey's confused stare darted from Peggy to her mother.

Mike glanced down at Bailey and gave her a nod. "Go on, baby. It's fine."

Peggy led Bailey out of the room.

Mike's attention went back to the doctors. "What tests and treatments?"

Dr. Curtis lifted the blanket and sheet from Doug's legs from the knee down. He then pulled out a reflex instrument and a metal object the width and length of a pencil with a pointed tip. He knocked the reflex instrument against Doug's knees. Nothing happened. He then ran the metal object up the soles of Doug's feet. His feet didn't move.

Oh no. This doesn't look good. Glory chewed her lip and peered from her peripheral at Mike, who was staring intently at the doctors.

Dr. Curtis slid the instruments back in his coat pockets and turned to face Gloria and her sisters. "It's going to take some time and more rest of his spinal column in the coming days and probably weeks before we know for sure the status of the paralysis."

Mike massaged her forehead, frowning. "Crap. I got caught up in the coma... so much like Mom's..." She tapped her forehead with two fingers, the creases around her downturned mouth deepening. "How the hell did I forget about this?"

Gloria laid a hand on Mike's shoulder. "So much has happened in the past few days it's understandable you couldn't remember it all."

Mike flashed her a look of annoyance. "You don't need to remind me."

Gloria sighed. *I can't reach her, and whatever I say isn't right. Just like when I'd tried to talk to Dad.*

A hand squeezed hers. "Mike's got to deal with this in her own way," Fima said.

Gloria nodded.

Fima pointed toward Eli by the nurses' station. "Eli and I are going home. Coming with us?"

"Go on. I'll catch up with you in a few minutes."

"Okay, meet you at my car in the lot."

Gloria followed Fima out of the room, passed her, and ducked through a door to the stairwell. With the loss of her mother pressing like a lead weight on her chest, Gloria gripped the railing. She glanced back at the door while she descended the stairs, her sneakers smacking the cement steps, echoing through the space.

Nothing had truly changed between her and Mike. Her older sister still didn't want her around. Both Mike and Fima had given Gloria the impression neither of them needed her there. Mike had her husband and daughter to concentrate on. Fima had her boyfriend to comfort her. She no longer needed Gloria's sisterly encouragement or advice.

Why had Gloria come there? *You needed to see your mother and sisters. And you were with your mother when she died. Yes, but I'll never know what she wanted to tell me.*

She frowned and checked her watch. Nearly five o'clock. Ruby would still be at the office, wrapping up for the day. She'd call her if Fima would allow her to use her landline and give her an update. Her mother was buried, and her sisters were busy with their lives. She'd buy a bus ticket tomorrow morning and catch the bus back to Summitville. She had a job, home, and the mountains to return to that she knew would welcome her.

Gloria stepped out into the cool evening air and headed to Fima's car.

Chapter Forty-Two

Gloria picked up Fima's landline phone.

"You can call whoever you want." Fima slipped into the bathroom, fidgeting. "I hate using public bathrooms. I always hold it till I'm home." She closed the door.

Gloria made the call to her employer and told her she'd be back to work the day after tomorrow. She dug through her purse for change for the bus ride. Thankfully, she'd put back some of her earnings for emergencies. Her small wad of paper money was sufficient for her trip back home.

Fima came out of the bathroom. "I need to call Austin." She went into her bedroom and closed the door.

Gloria picked up their grandmother's book she'd taken with her that was sitting on the end table. She thumbed through the pages, finding her favorite story about a woman who reunited with her sister after four years separated by the effects of World War II. She needed this sliver of light to brighten the sorrow in her heart.

Before she finished reading the first page, Fima shuffled out of her bedroom, her eyes wet, her mouth turned down.

Gloria set her book down. "What happened?"

Fima folded her arms and sucked on her bottom lip. "He wasn't there."

"Maybe he's working."

Fima dropped on the sofa next to her. "He didn't let me know."

Gloria rested her arm on the top of the sofa, facing Fima. "Too busy?"

"He shouldn't be." Fima fingered her pearl stud earrings. "It only takes a second to call me."

"I'm sure he'll call you soon, let you know what's going on."

Fima nodded, hugging her knees to her chest and staring ahead at nothing.

Gloria scooted over and put her arm around her sister, smoothing her hair out of her eyes. "Try not to worry. I know it's hard not to, him being a firefighter and all."

Fima's eyes met hers, and her mouth puckered as if she'd been sucking on a lemon. "I hate his firefighting job."

Gloria nodded. "It must be har—"

"His hours are so unpredictable, and he never has time for me."

"Hazards of the job, it seems."

Fima lowered her legs and placed her hands on her thighs. "You know, I've been through a lot lately, and you would think he'd make some time for me. To be with me, help me through all of this."

Gloria hugged Fima. "I'm here."

"I know, but…"

Gloria sighed and let go of her sister. "But I'm not Austin."

Fima sat up straight. "I didn't mean—"

Gloria patted Fima's leg. "It's okay." She rose from the sofa. "It's too late for me to be the sister you'd had growing up. I've been gone too long."

Fima's face pinched as if in pain. "No, that's not true."

Gloria gave her an understanding smile, even as her heart hurt. "I'll be going back home tomorrow morning."

"What?" Fima got up. "Why so soon?"

"Well, I've got work."

"Oh." Fima looked at her hands clasped together and wrung them. "I forgot about that."

"You'll be fine." Gloria picked up their grandmother's book and hugged it to her chest. "You've got Austin and Mike. Oh, and Eli."

Fima's bottom lip protruded. "But you're my sister, Glory."

"Yes, I am." She touched Fima's chin as if she were a delicate porcelain doll. "And I always will be."

Fima smiled and took Gloria's hand in hers.

Gloria returned a weak smile, then pointed to the bathroom. "I'm going to go brush my teeth and go to sleep."

"But it's early. What about dinner?"

Gloria walked toward the bathroom, then looked back at her sister. "I'm not hungry. Just tired." She entered the bathroom and quietly closed the door as tears gathered in her eyes. *I'll miss you, Fima.*

The Rockies rose to greet Gloria as she stepped off the bus and walked the mile to her cabin. The sounds of nature and the whisper of the cool mountain breeze consoled her. She breathed in the dusty earth, pungent pine, and clean air as sunshine wrapped her in warmth.

"Glory!"

She turned toward her friend's voice.

Serena ran over to her from the road and embraced her. "I've missed you."

Gloria rested her chin on her friend's shoulder. "Missed you too."

Serena took Gloria's hand in hers and swung them. "Tell me all about your trip and don't leave anything out." She giggled.

Gloria had little left in her to rehash all she'd been through. Not now. Not yet. She needed to grab her backpack and take to the mountain trails, feel the dirt and gravel under her shoes, hear the birds singing and the stream coursing with life. She worked her mouth into a faint smile. "Later."

Serena's face fell. "My God, Glory, what happened there?"

Gloria shook her head. "Later, please." She walked on without her friend, unlocked the cabin door, stepped inside, and shut the door behind her. She gathered up her usual items for her hike and headed back out.

Serena still stood in the same spot, but Lou and Coop had joined her. She tented her eyes with her hand. He was back. She hoped he was better than he'd been the last time she'd seen him.

"Hi," she said, stepping down the stairs to her porch.

"Hey, Glory," Lou said.

"Hey," Coop said.

Lou's stare darted from Serena to Coop then to her. "Good to see you back."

Gloria raised a hand in acknowledgment. "Thanks." She walked toward the line of trees in between hers and Ruby's cabin. "I'm going on a hike. I'll catch you all later."

"Promise?" Serena called.

Gloria faced them as she continued to step backward. "Promise."

Serena smiled and waved.

Gloria waved in return, then trekked onto the rocky trail, her spirits lifting.

Chapter Forty-Three

Around eight o'clock that morning, as Michaela turned on her coffee maker, someone knocked several times on her front door. *Who the hell is stupid enough to come soliciting at this hour?* Michaela sighed and opened the door to Fima fidgeting on her porch.

"I was planning to call you after work."

Fima opened the screen door and scuttled inside. "Glory's gone."

Michaela shut the door. "Gone where?"

Fima grimaced. "Back home."

Michaela returned to the kitchen with Fima on her heels. She poured herself a cup of coffee, then leaned her rear against the kitchen counter. "She's run off again. What a surprise." She sipped her hot beverage. Glory was predictable, hadn't changed. When things got tough, she bolted. Never knew how to face tough situations.

Fima wrung her hands. "I think we hurt her feelings."

Michaela feigned a look of pity. "Aww. Did we?"

"Mike." Fima stomped her high-heeled boot. "I'm serious."

"I'm sure you are."

Fima tsked. "Don't you care?"

"Glory's a grown woman. She makes her own choices."

Fima sucked her bottom lip as Michaela set her cup on the counter. "Although she might have waited long enough to hear Mom's last will and testament."

"She didn't know we were meeting today for that." Fima twirled a lock of hair. "I think we forgot to tell her."

Michaela's brows rose. "We might have." She shook her head. "I can't be everywhere at once. I do have a husband to visit, a daughter to take care of, and we had a mother to bury."

Fima nodded.

Michaela pointed at Fima. "Why didn't you tell her? Must I be in charge of everything?"

"But you like it that way—"

"Yeah, well, sometimes I need a breather." Michaela passed Fima and headed for the living room where she drew the ivory curtain from the large window, letting the bright morning sunlight fill the shadowed room. She slid open the window, and refreshing, cool air swept in on a gentle breeze.

Fima stood next to one of the chairs in the room and rested her hands on it. "So, what are we going to do?" She laid a hand on her chest. "I think she didn't feel wanted, like she didn't count."

Michaela's mind filled with the image of her and Glory at their mother's bedside just before she'd died. Glory had been upset about something. What was it? Michaela bowed her head and tapped her temple, willing the conversation to come back to her.

"What is it? What are you thinking?" Fima asked, interrupting Michaela's train of thought.

"Hush for a minute." She crossed her arms and stared out the window to an empty street, quiet houses, and azure sky. On either side of her house, two maple trees' leaves fluttered. She closed her eyes, and Glory's words came to her. "Mom wanted to tell Glory something, but neither of us knew what that was. Looked like Glory was bothered by this, but my mind was on Mom and Doug and hadn't really given it much thought."

"Maybe what Mom wanted to tell Glory is in her will."

Michaela shrugged. "Have no idea."

"But why would Glory leave if she wanted to find out what Mom said?"

"Probably thought the earth-shattering news from Mom died with her." Michaela ran her fingers over the curtain. "And knowing Mom, it was probably nothing big." She flicked her wrist in Fima's direction. "You know what a hypochondriac Mom was."

Fima's face fell. "Yeah. But she'd been right after all. She was dying soon."

Michaela pursed her lips. Her little sister believed everything she heard. "Mom's not friggin' psychic, Fima." She shook her head. "That accident wasn't planned, no matter what I think about that shrew Tina."

Fima's mouth formed an *O*, and she raised a finger. "I've got an idea."

Michaela smirked in amusement. "Congratulations."

Fima rolled her eyes. "No, I mean, we can call Penny to get a message to Glory so she can come back here for Mom's will reading."

"What if she doesn't want to come back?"

"Don't start that again, Mike. You said that last time, but she showed up and proved you wrong."

"She's proving me correct, right now."

Fima tapped her shoe on the tile floor. "Come on. Call Penny."

Michaela looked at her watch. "Not right now. I've got to get to work."

"What about after work?"

Michaela walked toward the staircase, then turned to face Fima who'd followed her. "Fine. I'll call her tonight."

Fima bounced on the balls of her feet, her slender heels tapping the hardwood floor. "Great. I hope she comes back tomorrow."

"We'll see." Michaela gestured toward the door. "You've got work, too, little sister."

Fima flung her arms around Michaela. "I know, I know." She kissed Michaela's cheek. "Thanks, sis."

"Yeah, sure. I'll keep you in the loop whenever I reach Penny."

Fima nodded and left the house.

Would their mother's supposed big secret be in her will? And why hadn't she shared her secret with Fima and her all those years Glory was away? Curiosity ate at Michaela. She'd find out soon enough if Fima was right.

Chapter Forty-Four

Gloria trekked down the dirt path toward Henry. The late morning smelled of earth and nature's fragrant floral beauty, glistening in the sunshine. She patted his trunk. "Hey." She smiled at the cottonwood. "It's been too long, my friend." She tilted her head downward and touched her forehead to Henry's sturdy form. She needed this connection, as it helped assuage the loss and missing her mother.

A branch snapped to her right. Coop appeared from behind a nearby Ponderosa pine. He gave her a quick wave and cracked a half smile.

"Hey, Coop."

He shrugged and stuck his hands in his jeans pockets. "Hey."

"You came back."

He squinted at her.

"Lou said you left town a while ago."

He acknowledged her with a tilt of his head. "Yeah."

"Why did you come back?"

He spun around, nearly tripping over his own foot, and pointed toward town. "I was hired on for some landscaping work at one of the hotels for the next couple of months."

Gloria leaned against Henry. "That's great news. I'm happy for you."

He lurched toward her, his eyes on hers. She tensed, her back pushing against Henry's trunk.

"Thanks." He stopped only a few inches from her. His gaze traveled over her face, landing on her pursed lips. "How you been?"

"O-Okay." Why did he have to be right in her face? She looked away and scrunched up her shoulders. "I was visiting family."

He brushed his hand through her hair. "Cool."

She grimaced. "I lost my mother a few days ago."

His hand dropped to his side. "I'm sorry."

She nodded, staring at the ground.

His hand lifted her chin. "Maybe we could comfort each other."

The smell of alcohol came from his mouth. Nausea swam in her stomach, as images of her drunken father's face floated in her head. It always started with the drinking, then the thrashings…

She swallowed down bile and turned her head to the side so his hand was no longer on her face. "I need to sort things out on my own, and so do you."

"I did that while I was away." He placed his arms on either side of her, his hands pressing against Henry's trunk. "Let me look at your eyes. They're pretty."

Her breath caught. He had her boxed in. She flicked a stare at him, then gazed at the mountains, wishing she'd stayed on the hiking trail. Whatever burning she'd been having in her heart didn't have anything to do with Coop. Her fingers grasped Henry's barky veins. Her mind was dizzy, struggling to figure out a way to escape from him.

"Come on." He turned her face toward him. "Show me those green eyes."

Gloria squeezed her eyes shut against her fear. "You've been drinking."

"Just some beer." He ran a hand over her downturned mouth.

She straightened her spine, gathered strength, and opened her eyes. "Coop, you're still griev—"

"Shut up, won't you?" He leaned his head down, closing his eyes, his mouth seeking hers.

She pushed him away. "Stop it."

His eyes sprang open, wild and confused. "What's wrong?"

"Just leave me alone." She hurried toward one of the hiking paths.

She didn't look back but scrambled down the familiar trail, her heart thumping. Her pace quickened to the point of running along the dirt and gravel between the line of trees. The sun's rays peeked through the many branches above her head, its light and warmth giving her little comfort.

Ahead of her rose the monastery, and she jogged toward it.

She knocked on the door to the church. No one answered. She turned the knob, found it unlocked, and stepped inside the shadowed foyer. A single thick candle stood in the square box filled with sand. The people in the paintings on the walls stared at her as she moved toward the opening to the sanctuary. On the wooden screen several feet in front of her, a hanging lamp in front of the Virgin Mary with baby Jesus flickered at her. Silence filled the room so thick she could get lost in it. She hugged herself, needing to immerse herself in the dense quietude.

Images of her mother minutes before dying in her hospital bed surfaced in her mind. A picture of her and her sisters holding each other, crying, and the pain she'd felt came back to her in a heavy tidal wave, threatening to bowl her over. She collapsed to her knees on the rug beneath her, covered her face, and wept. She hadn't truly connected with her sisters. She'd lost her mother only hours after talking to her after ten long years, never again to feel her mother's warm embrace or hear her nurturing voice. Whatever her mother had wanted to share with her was gone with her, tucked away for eternity.

"Glory, my child." A familiar woman's voice came from behind her.

Gloria scrubbed her face clean and turned. Mother Maria stood like an angelic but imposing figure in her black robes and head covering. With outstretched arms, the abbess approached Gloria as if floating over the floor, her shoes hidden under her habit. Gloria rose from the carpet as the abbess gathered her to her bosom. Fresh tears fell from Gloria's eyes as she hung on to the nun who was now the only mother figure with whom she could find solace.

"What has happened that I find you here, crying?"

Gloria sniffled. "I finally saw my mom and sisters. I just got back home this morning."

Mother Maria released her and took a step back to look into Gloria's eyes. "You haven't seen your family for a long time?"

Gloria wiped her nose. "Ten years."

"Oh my." Mother Maria placed a hand on her chest. "You must have missed them terribly."

"I did." Gloria pushed her hair from the sides of her face. "But they didn't need me there."

The abbess's eyebrows came together. "They didn't need you there?"

Gloria shook her head. "And while I was there, my mother died."

Mother Maria frowned and embraced Gloria once more. "I'm sorry, child. Was she sick?"

"She was in a car accident, along with my brother-in-law and niece."

"Lord, have mercy." Mother Maria crossed herself.

"Mom told me she had something to tell me, but she never got the chance." Gloria bowed her head as the pain of loss pulsated in her. "And my sisters don't know what Mom wanted to tell me."

The abbess gestured toward two chairs against the wall. "Please, sit down."

They both sat, and Mother Maria took Gloria's hand in hers. "Why did you leave so soon after your mother's repose? And your sisters must also be grieving."

Gloria stared at their hands. "Like I said a minute ago, they didn't need me there."

"Why do you think that?"

"Because they didn't say so... Well, at least Mike didn't."

"Mike?"

"My older sister, Michaela. Mike's her nickname."

Mother Maria nodded. "Ah."

"They are busy with their own lives. There's no room for me." Gloria wiped her nose with the palm of her other hand. "Really, I don't deserve to be included since I ran away ten years ago."

The abbess squeezed Gloria's hand. "My child, why did you run away?"

Gloria's cheeks burned as her dysfunctional family swam in her head.

"Every family has its difficulties."

Can she see inside my head? My heart? "My family was... is still a mess."

A soft chuckle came from the abbess, and she patted Gloria's hand. "This is nothing I've not heard before, my dear Glory." Her gaze rose to the screen of paintings. "God knows the struggles of each family in this world. No family is without them."

Gloria focused on the rug. "My dad beat me when I was a child."

Mother Maria smoothed down Gloria's hair. "You had no help to stop his abuse?"

"None." Gloria sighed. "My mother and younger sister didn't have the strength. Mike wasn't helpful either." She glanced at Mother Maria. "My father beat my mother too. A few times my sisters were spanked… Nothing like what he did to me." She shook her head. "I couldn't do anything right."

"Where did you go after you left your home?"

Gloria told the abbess where she'd been the past ten years.

Mother Maria patted Gloria's hand again. "And you eventually found our little monastery."

Gloria nodded then winced. "Sorry for bringing all my troubles here."

The abbess smiled. "This place is for the broken."

"But you aren't broken."

The abbess continued to smile. "We all are."

Gloria gaped.

Mother Maria released Gloria's hand and rose. "My dear, go back to your family."

"But—"

"They do, indeed, need you."

Do they? Gloria gripped the hem of her shirt.

"I must see to my daughters and go to my cell to pray." She waved an arm around the room. "Please stay as long as you need to collect yourself. He is everywhere, especially here."

Gloria stood as the abbess walked out of the chapel. She gazed at the lit vigil lamp before leaving the church. The heaviness on her heart when she'd entered the church had lifted.

Chapter Forty-Five

That evening, Michaela sat on her living room sofa next to Fima. "You know I just got home, so I haven't had a chance to call Penny yet."

"I know." Fima rubbed her polished fingernails. "I just wanted to be here when you did."

Michaela got up from the couch and grabbed her cell phone from the desk. Before she could check her phone for Penny's number, a knock sounded at her front door. "Now what?"

Fima shrugged.

Michaela walked to the door and opened it to find Glory standing on her porch. "What is this? Déjà vu?"

Glory only smiled, showing, once again, that snaggletooth of hers.

Michaela pivoted on her heel and walked back to the living room as Glory came inside the house and closed the front door.

"Glory!" Fima ran to her and hugged her. "I'm so glad you came back."

"Me too." Glory rubbed Fima's back.

Michaela flicked a hand at Glory. "Well, you saved me a call to Penny."

"You were going to call Penny?"

Michaela sank into a chair by the desk. "It's the only way we can get in touch with you since you don't have any phones."

Glory's eyes widened. "You wanted to call me?"

Michaela gave Glory a sideways glance. *Guess Fima was right about Glory feeling unwanted.* But who's fault was that? Certainly not hers when she'd been dealing with their mother's death, just as much, if not more, than Glory had, and she had Doug and Bailey to take care of. "Well, yeah. You ran away again, and there's unfinished business with Mom."

Taking the seat next to Fima, Glory leaned forward, beaming. "So, you found out what Mom wanted to tell me?"

Michaela waved away Glory's question. "No. Not that."

Glory frowned and sat back against the cushions. "Oh."

"It's about Mom's will," Michaela said. "We all should be there for the reading."

"Didn't you get a copy of her will before she died?" Glory asked.

"No. She kept it squirreled away. I think her lawyer kept it while Dad was still alive. She obviously forgot to dig it out and share it with us before she died, which isn't like her."

"True. Mom was always up on legal stuff in case she died unexpectedly." Fima nodded.

"Yeah." Michaela swung her legs over the arm of the chair. "Anyway, I'd postponed the reading with Doug's predicament and burying Mom, but we're going to Mom's house tomorrow after work to meet with her lawyer to find out what her will says."

"Dad didn't leave us anything." Fima pouted. "Mom said he spent most of his money on himself, and whatever he had left, he gave to his cousin, Erwin."

"Yeah, well, Mom isn't Dad," Michaela said.

"I know, but if he didn't leave her anything, what will she have to give us?"

Glory folded her arms. "Do we need to get anything from Mom?"

Michaela shrugged. "Nothing wrong with getting a couple of family heirlooms and some money. I know the extra bucks would help me out... help all of us."

Glory shook her head. "I don't want her money."

Michaela laughed to herself. Glory had the gall to boast as if she were the Queen of England while she lived on the cusp of squalor. "Of course not. You're living the good life scrubbing toilets."

"There's nothing wrong with cleaning resort cabins." Glory crossed her legs and brushed off invisible lint from her jeans.

Michaela rolled her eyes. "My mistake."

"Okay, Mike. Come on," Fima said, raising her splayed hands. "What time are we going to meet at Mom's house tomorrow?"

"Six o'clock," Michaela said.

Fima frowned. "I still can't believe she's gone."

Glory put an arm around Fima's shoulders. "I know. Me neither."

"It happened so fast it's hard to absorb it all." Michaela rose. "Speaking of which, Bailey and I are going to visit Doug now."

"How's he doing?" Glory asked, getting up from the couch.

Michaela snatched a package of cigarettes and lighter off the desk. "About the same." She headed to the front door. "I'm going to have a smoke before we go. What are you guys planning to do?"

"I'm going to see Austin," Fima said, leaving the sofa and following Michaela and Glory to the front porch. She turned toward Glory. "You can stay with me again."

"Thanks." Glory smiled.

Michaela walked onto the porch as her sisters headed to Fima's car. She lit her cigarette and took a long drag, preparing herself to face Doug, immobile and mute. Would he ever fully recover, or had she lost forever the Doug she'd known the past eight years?

Chapter Forty-Six

Seraphima walked up to Austin's first-floor apartment and rang the doorbell. Why hadn't she done this earlier when she couldn't reach him on the phone? He couldn't ignore her in person. She pressed the button again. The thought of seeing Austin's muscular body, mesmerizing eyes, and gorgeous smile sent a warm tingle through her.

The door opened, and a gorgeous, buttery-blond-haired woman appeared with a friendly smile. "Hello. Please tell me you're not selling something."

Stunned, Seraphima tensed, her shoes planted on the ground, unable to move. *Who is this woman?*

The woman's loose sweater hung off one of her artificially tanned shoulders, covering large breasts. Her miniskirt's zipper was off-center as if she'd slept in it or had pulled it on in a hurry. She wore no shoes, showing off her diamond ankle bracelet and polished pink, expertly manicured toenails on small feet. The woman possessed everything Seraphima had always wished for. Jealousy ate at her, and she bit down hard on her lower lip, willing the feeling to go away.

The woman's nose wrinkled. "Oh no. You are, aren't you?"

Seraphima shook her head as she grasped at words that wouldn't come.

"Are you lost?"

"N-no." Seraphima's hands and knees shook. *What's she doing at Austin's place?*

The woman took a step toward her, leaving little space between them. The smell of sex and musky perfume wafted off the woman.

Oh God, no. Dizziness seized Seraphima, and she struggled to keep her knees from buckling.

The woman placed a hand on her hip. "Well then, what do you want?"

Seraphima cleared her throat and pressed a hand to her chest, feeling her heart drumming against her palm. "I'm here to see Austin."

"Who's there, Kayla?" Austin's voice came from somewhere inside the apartment. A second later, he appeared next to Kayla, stuffing his shirt into his unzipped pants. He ran a hand through his hair and frowned when his stare fell on Seraphima.

Seraphima took an unsteady step back, putting a hand to her nauseous stomach.

Austin's jaw twitched, and his brow furrowed. "Fima, what are you doing here?"

"That's what I asked," Kayla said, with both hands on her hips now.

"I-I wanted to talk to you."

Kayla's stare bounced from Seraphima to Austin. "Who is she?"

Seraphima sucked in a breath. "I'm his girlfriend."

Kayla cackled as if Seraphima had told the best joke she'd heard in years. She slapped Austin's bulky chest. "Come on. What kind of gag are you playing here, Austin?"

Anger flashed in Austin's eyes as his face darkened a crimson color. "I'll take care of this." He pushed Kayla inside the apartment.

"Hey," she said but didn't come back out.

Austin folded his meaty arms across his chest. "I'm busy."

Seraphima's shoulders slouched, and she trembled as he glared down at her. "Was this what you meant every time you told me you were busy?"

His features softened, and he opened his arms. "Of course not, babe." He wrapped his arms around her shaking body.

Bile rose in Seraphima's throat. "Who's Kayla?" She felt his body stiffen.

"She's a friend. That's all."

Lies. Seraphima wriggled out of his arms and forced herself to look him in the eyes. "Just a friend?"

He raised his brows while his mouth turned down. "Okay. She was my girlfriend before you."

"What are you talking about?" Kayla's voice came from behind him. "I've been your girlfriend since last summer."

"Is she right?" Seraphima asked, even though she knew in the depths of her being Kayla spoke the truth.

Austin shrugged. "She knows how to have fun, doesn't nag me to marry her. Doesn't get in the way of my career goals."

Kayla's arms encircled his waist, and she peeked from behind one of his beefy arms, smiling as if she knew the secret code to a bank vault.

Seraphima swallowed hard, her eyes stinging with tears. *I can't stay here any longer.* She spun around on wobbly legs and ran away from Austin's apartment back to her car. She crawled into the front seat and glimpsed Austin, expressionless, shutting his door. Pushing the driver's door all the way open, Seraphima vomited on the asphalt. She closed the door with trembling hands and let go wracking sobs.

Gloria sat on the sofa, reading one of the stories in her grandmother's book, when the front door clicked open. Fima plodded into the room, her face pale with cheeks covered in wet, black streaks. Fima moved as if she weighed five hundred pounds. Gloria sprung from the couch and caught Fima before she collapsed to the floor.

"My God, Fima, what happened?" Gloria led Fima to the couch, helped her to sit, then sat next to her. She brushed the curtain of hair from Fima's face.

Fima stared as if in a daze. "He's had a girlfriend this whole time."

"Who has?"

"Austin."

Gloria frowned. "I thought he was your boyfriend."

Fima nodded as if it took all her strength. "Me too."

Some boyfriend. Gloria's jaw tightened. "He was two-timing you. The jerk."

Her sister didn't answer, only lowered her head.

Gloria embraced her, rubbing her back. "I'm so sorry."

"I thought we'd get married. Have children. He was everything I'd been looking for," Fima muttered into Gloria's shoulder.

"I'm sorry. I can't imagine how much you're hurting. But I'm here for you."

Fima finally hugged her back. "I'm so glad you are."

"Always." Gloria leaned back and swept Fima's hair off her shoulder.

Fima shook her head. "I'll never find a man who makes me feel the way Austin does."

Gloria tried desperately to find the right words to assuage her sister. If only she could take Fima to the mountains, sit under Henry's many branches, taking in the fresh air and the earthy aroma around them. But Fima didn't have a relationship with nature like she did.

"Never," Fima cried.

She hugged Fima again. "There are other men out there who will treat you better."

Fima let go of Gloria and rested her elbows on her knees and forehead against the palms of her hands. "Maybe, but they won't be able to touch me and make me melt, float, feel so good I could fly."

"Maybe it'll just be a different type of good feeling with the right man." Gloria squeezed Fima's shoulder. A sense of understanding Fima's emotions came to her. Her heart tightened.

Fima shook her head again, her face pinched. "I need to be alone now." She left the couch, took a couple of steps, then stopped. She turned toward her. "Thanks for being here, Glory."

Tears welled in Gloria's eyes, and she smiled. "I'm very happy to be."

She lay back on the sofa and gazed out the window by the front door. The night sky sparkled with tiny stars. Each star was unique and beautiful. Mother Maria's words came back to her. Fima *did* need her. Their bond was growing toward a true connection. She'd hold out hope that her disjointed relationship with Mike would do the same soon.

Chapter Forty-Seven

Michaela led Bailey into Doug's new hospital room on the main floor. He'd been moved out of ICU last night. Doug lay in the same position as he'd been in ICU, but his eyes were open, and they followed Michaela then Bailey as they came closer to the bed.

Bailey bounced up and down and beamed. "Daddy, you're awake." She put her hand on Doug's forearm. "You slept a long time."

The bruises on Doug's face had faded to dime-sized, pale yellow spots, and a natural pink colored his cheeks. He was getting better.

Michaela smiled and set her hand on his, giving it a gentle squeeze. "Hey. Welcome back to the living." She chuckled.

Bailey puckered her lips at Michaela. "Mama, he was just asleep for a long, long time, like Sleeping Beauty." She looked at Michaela, then Doug. "But he didn't need you to kiss him. He woke all by himself." She frowned at Michaela. "I wish you'd kiss him anyhow."

Accustomed to her daughter's prodding regarding Doug and her, Michaela smoothed down her daughter's hair with her free hand. Before she could answer, Doug, his voice raspy and barely audible, said, "Yeah... You tell... Mama."

Bailey giggled and climbed onto the bed, settling herself next to Doug. She petted the side of his face. "I wanna give you a kiss, Daddy." She planted a loud smooch on his cheek.

Doug's face creased, his dry lips stretching into a small, joyous smile. "Thank you."

Bailey looked up at Michaela. "Now it's your turn, Mama."

How long had it been since she and Doug had last shared a loving kiss? Two or three months? Michaela shifted from her right foot to her left as she released Doug's hand and scratched her neck that was heating up. *Look at you. You're acting like a schoolgirl, as if you don't know the man you've spent the past eight years with.*

Before Michaela could talk herself into giving Doug a kiss, a short, pudgy nurse walked over to the machines by the right side of the bed. She flashed Michaela a smile. "Good evening."

"Hi." Michaela nodded.

"Is Daddy gonna come home tomorrow?" Bailey asked.

Michaela shook her head. "Not tomorrow, baby."

Bailey huffed. "Why not?"

The nurse lifted a hand. "He needs a lot more rest to heal his back, sweetheart."

Bailey craned her neck and used her hands to inspect Doug's right side. "Why? What's wrong with Daddy's back, Mama?"

Doug stared at Michaela as if waiting for the answer to the question, as well.

The sound of heels clicking on the floor behind them interrupted their discussion. Michaela turned and found Tina standing in the doorway, wearing her usual gaudy clothes and shoes, her pink blouse the color of Pepto-Bismol. A part of Michaela cheered to see someone disrupt Bailey's uncomfortable line of questions, while the other part of her groaned at the sight of the female wedge between Doug's and her marriage, even if she'd said there had been nothing going on between her and Doug. The fact that Tina was one of Doug's so-called friends was unacceptable. Michaela scrutinized the blonde again with distrust swirling in her chest.

"Well, hello, Michaela." Tina grinned and strode toward her. She spotted Bailey. "And Bailey." Bailey slid off the bed and hugged Tina's legs. "I've missed you, little lady."

"Me too." Bailey tapped the toe of her shoe on the floor. "I miss skating with you."

"Don't worry. We'll go again when your daddy is up to it."

Bailey scowled at the nurse. "He's gotta sleep all the time."

The nurse clasped her hands together. "Rest is the best thing for your daddy."

Bailey glanced up at Tina with pouting lips. "See?"

Tina threw her head back as if Bailey and the nurse had just acted out a comedy skit. Michaela failed to see any punch line in their exchange.

"He'll be better before you know it." Tina tousled Bailey's hair.

Michaela's jaw tightened as she folded her arms. The woman had no idea what she was talking about. Figured. Bimbos rarely did. She hadn't been there to get the reports from his doctors. She'd been the driver in a fatal car accident, who walked away from it with barely a scratch while the rest of her passengers were battered and broken, her mother even losing her life. And now she stood there grinning like a clueless idiot. Michaela ground her teeth. "Why are you here, Tina?"

Tina messed with her bleached hair, as if trying to give it some oomph when it had none. "I came to see Doug, of course."

Michaela glanced at Doug.

His eyes moved slowly from hers to Tina's and back to hers. A crease appeared between his brows.

"Do you want to talk to Tina?"

Doug's mouth opened and moved, but no words were audible.

The nurse moved past them toward the door. She pivoted on her heel to face them. "You still have a half hour before visiting hours are over." She left the room.

"Great." Tina glided over to the right side of Doug's bed.

Michaela's cell phone buzzed in her pocket. She yanked it out and looked at the caller. Lena. "I'll be right back." She walked out of the room, hoping the call would be a quick one. The less time Tina spent with Doug, the better.

"Hey, Lena. What's up?"

"Mike, I'm sorry, but an emergency came up. My brothers need me to help my granny move into a nursing home in Wichita."

"Kansas?"

"Yeah. It's been brewing for a while, but now it's boiled over, and I've got to be there to help Granny's transition." A short pause followed. "I'm sorry I won't be around to watch Bailey."

"Things come up. God knows enough has in my life recently." Michaela sighed. "When are you leaving?"

"In the morning. It'll take a couple, maybe three weeks."

Their consignment shop and all the responsibilities, including the six employees they had, ran through her head, along with the absence of Bailey's babysitter in the evenings. Michaela would need someone to watch Bailey while she worked, figured out what to do with her mother's house, and with what lay ahead for Doug's recovery. Maybe the fate of Etta's house would be stipulated in her mother's will.

Michaela rubbed her temple. "Have a safe trip, and all the best to your granny."

"Thanks."

Sliding the phone back into her jeans pocket, Michaela reentered Doug's room.

"—owe me a vanilla shake the next time we go to the rink," Tina said.

"Me too!" Bailey piped up.

Doug's lips quivered into a weak smile.

Tina turned to look at Michaela. "Everything okay?"

"Of course." Michaela huffed. "Why wouldn't it be?"

Tina shrugged, then swatted the air. "You're right. I should know by now you wear a permanent frown."

Michaela covered her mouth with her hand. "I do not."

Tina cackled, putting witches to shame. Michaela glared at her.

"Dougie needs to rest." Tina patted his arm. "I've talked his ear off." Another cackle followed.

Michaela grimaced and turned her attention to Bailey. "Baby, Aunt Lena has to go out of town to take care of her granny, so she won't be able to watch you after work in the coming weeks."

Bailey slouched, her gaze lowering to the floor.

Tina moved to their side of the bed. She held her palms skyward. "As I said the last time we saw each other, I can watch Bailey after work."

Michaela folded her arms. The less time Bailey spent with Tina, the better. She didn't want Tina to become a permanent fixture in her family unit. The woman had told a whopping lie. She could sure as hell do it again. This time saying she wasn't sleeping with Doug when she really was. Michaela swallowed back bitterness. She glanced at Doug, who had drifted off to sleep.

She nearly laughed at her own words. He was paralyzed from the waist down. What could he possibly do?

Oh, my God. What could *he do? What about me and him?* Michaela stepped back from the bed.

"Hey, I'm not that scary." Tina smirked.

Never mind the drinking. Will we ever get fully back together?

Share that ultimate intimacy that melds us into one, if his body doesn't heal?

"Anyway, I'm available if you need me." Tina pulled out her phone. "What's your number so we can keep in touch?"

Damn it. Stop thinking the worst. Michaela blew out a breath. *It won't happen that way.*

"Nice talking to the ever-present frown, Michaela." Tina took out her small date book, opened it to the notes section, and scribbled something on it. She then ripped out the little page and thrust it toward Michaela. "Just in case."

Without thinking, Michaela grasped the paper as Tina in her four-inched heels clattered out of the room.

Chapter Forty-Eight

I n Etta's study, Gloria stood behind the lavender, wingback chair Fima sat in, and watched Mike pace the floor near the desk.

Mike checked her phone. "He's got two minutes to get here on time." She jammed her cell back in her slacks back pocket and resumed marching across the floor.

"I'm sure he'll be here any minute," Gloria said.

Fima slumped in the chair. "How long is this going to take? I'm tired."

Gloria laid a hand on her sister's small shoulder. "It shouldn't take long at all."

Mike stopped moving. "Yeah. I doubt there's much in Mom's will."

There was a knock on the front door before it creaked open, then clicked shut. Footsteps made their way into the study, and a man with salt-and-pepper hair and matching goatee stepped into the room. He wore a gray suit and carried a briefcase.

"Good evening. I'm glad you're all here."

Mike put her hands on her hips. "Of course we are. You were the only person missing."

The man flashed a curt smile and walked to the desk. He set his briefcase on its surface and opened it, pulling out a thin folder.

They're probably right about Mom. What she had was likely all in this house. Gloria scanned the room and glanced at the foyer. *I don't need anything. Don't deserve anything. Even if I did deserve something, I don't want it.* She looked at her sisters' gloomy faces. *But they do. I hope Mom has something for them.*

The man cleared his throat, stepped around the desk, and stuck out his hand to Mike. "We've not formally met." A tight smile broke on his sharply angled face. "Bob Carter."

Mike shook his hand. "Michaela Barstone-Morrow."

Mr. Carter strode to the chair and grasped Fima's hand, then Gloria's, exchanging introductions.

Mike sighed and leaned her hip on the edge of the desk. "Okay. Let's get down to business." She crossed her arms. "I've got a daughter in the living room and a husband lying in a hospital bed waiting for me."

Mr. Carter nodded, returned to the desk, and opened the folder. He removed three documents and passed them out to Gloria and her sisters. He then slid his reading glasses halfway up his thin nose. "Your mother left all of you her house and everything in it."

"We figured that much," Mike said.

He flipped through a couple of sheets. "She has three CDs with around ten thousand dollars in each of them, one for each of you. Your names are on them in a joint account with her at the Bank of Parker. The account number is noted here for you all."

Gloria's hands clutched the top of the chair's cushion. *Ten thousand dollars. So much money... money I don't want. The more money you have, the more you want.*

"Yeah," Mike said, wagging her finger back and forth between her and Fima. "We knew about the CDs. Mom set those up when we were kids."

Fima glanced at Gloria. "But Glory didn't."

"I do now."

"Ten thousand," Fima muttered, fingering her gold necklace with a dangling heart pendant on it. "That's a lot of money. Don't know what I'll do with it all."

Mike scoffed. "I sure know what I'll do with mine. Pay down my debt."

Gloria shifted from one foot to the other, wishing this talk of money was finished. "Is the reading done now?"

Mr. Carter held up a finger. "Just one more thing." He pulled out another folder from his case, opened it, and studied the single paper inside it.

Mike leaned toward him. "What is it?"

Fima got up from the chair and stepped over to Mike. Gloria didn't move but let out a faint sigh, feeling awkward, as if she didn't belong in the room, detached from the whole scene. Her mother was here and gone in a breath, and the pain and regret of being separated from her mother those many years pressed against the aching hole in her heart.

Mr. Carter cleared his throat. "It's a short letter your mother wrote and included with her will. It's rather unorthodox, but nevertheless, it was her wish that I read it after her death and read it when all her daughters were present." His stare traveled the room, locking eyes with each of the women, ending with Gloria.

Puzzled, Gloria came around to the front of the chair and sat down. Her sisters stood where they were, staring at Mr. Carter with confused expressions.

Mr. Carter flapped the paper so it stood straight in his hand. He set his reading glasses on his nose again. "First, the letter is dated five years ago, and she never gave me any updated one, so I assume it's still good." He stared at the sheet again. "This letter is specifically addressed to my second daughter, Glory." He paused to look at her.

Gloria clasped her shaking hands. *Was this a letter scolding me for running away? It's not needed. No amount of reprimanding could make me feel worse than I already do.*

"I will never believe you're dead. It would be too much for a mother to take. In my heart, I have felt you are alive somewhere, and I miss you so much."

Gloria swallowed the lump forming in her throat. The letter was even worse. The hurt and pain emanating from her mother's words punctured her heart as she brushed tears off her cheeks. She peeked at her sisters. Fima's head was bowed while Mike folded her arms, head tilted to the side, frowning at her. Gloria sucked in a breath to prevent herself from crumbling.

"If you return home when I'm already gone, I left you a small box with things important to me and you that you can find in my bedroom closet. Some things have to remain hidden with your father still around."

Some things have to remain hidden? Gloria straightened in her chair and looked from the letter to her sisters. "What does she mean?"

Mike slid her hands in her jeans pockets and shrugged. "How would I know?"

Fima shook her head, her brows knitted. "I have no clue."

Gloria stood and crossed the study floor to the lawyer. She held out her hand. "May I?"

"Of course." He gave her the paper.

Gloria read over the few words. "That's it? No other letters in your folder?"

"No." He removed his glasses and slipped them into his blazer pocket. "As I said before, she didn't give me any others."

A hand touched Gloria's shoulder. "We can find out if we go to Mom's room and look in her closet," Fima said.

Mr. Carter set the folders on the desk and closed his briefcase. He gave Gloria and her sister a brief grin. "Have a good evening, ladies." He picked up his satchel, strode toward the foyer, and walked out the front door, closing it behind him.

Mike grabbed her purse from the desk. "We can come by here on the weekend and start going through her stuff and decide what we want to keep, what we want to toss, or give away."

"What about the house?" Fima asked.

"It's paid off, for one thing," Mike said. "Dad paid it off years ago."

Fima looked around the room. "It's kind of big for one of us." She glanced at Gloria then Mike. "We wouldn't want to live here all together, would—"

"No," Mike said. "This is too far from my shop, and I love my house."

"Then what are we supposed to do with it?" Fima asked.

Mike jutted her chin toward Gloria. "Want the house?"

Gloria shook her head. Her mother's house stood in a line of dull cookie-cutter homes in a crowded subdivision. And worse than that, too many haunting memories of her father lingered in its large rooms.

Mike let out something that sounded like a sniffle and chuckle mixed together. "Ah, right. You have your little cabin and dozens of kitchen sinks to scour."

And nature. Gloria sighed, putting her fingers to her temple. "Yeah, that's right." *She'll never understand my life.*

Fima took Gloria's hand in hers. "Let's go upstairs and find that box."

"Good luck with your search." Mike gave them a farewell wave. "Bailey and I are going to visit Doug."

"Okay. See you there later." Gloria followed Fima toward the wooden staircase.

"Later."

The door thumped shut as Gloria climbed the stairs after Fima, her stomach churning. What would she find in her mother's closet?

296

Chapter Forty-Nine

F ima opened the accordion doors to their mother's bedroom closet. A bar stuffed with numerous hanging dresses dangled above four shoe racks filled with formal and informal footwear of every kind. On the shelf above the clothes were two stacks of purses and three various sized boxes lined up next to them, filling up the space.

"One of those boxes has to be it, Glory," Fima said.

Gloria stretched up on her tiptoes and grabbed the first box next to the purses. It looked like a hatbox, round and over a foot in diameter. She placed it on the floor and opened the lid. A beige sunhat rested in it. Gloria removed the hat, and two smaller ones lay in the bottom of the box—a tennis visor and a plum-colored beret.

Gloria touched the beret's soft material. "I didn't know Mom wore berets."

Fima bent down for a closer inspection. "Neither did I."

"Well, this obviously isn't the box. I doubt the things she left me were hats." Gloria put the items in the box and slid it back on the shelf.

Fima's fingertips brushed against the second square box, but she wasn't tall enough to reach it. Gloria, being a couple of inches taller, grabbed hold of the edges of the container and set it on the floor. It looked like a boot box. She opened it, and sure enough, long leather boots lay in the enclosure. Gloria sighed and put the top on the box and set it back on the shelf. Feeling disappointment looming over her, she looked at the last box—another square one, but smaller.

"Get it, Glory," Fima said, nudging her.

She brought it down to the floor and opened the lid. Sewing supplies filled the container. *Did you move it, Mom? Why?* She frowned and put it back. "Guess it's not here."

"That's crazy." Fima swayed slightly from one foot to the other. "Why would Mom say to look here if the box wasn't there?"

Gloria shook her head. "Maybe something happened in between those five years, and Mom didn't think to update her letter."

"Great. Then what are you going to do? How are you going to find whatever it is Mom left you?" Fima rubbed Gloria's back. "I mean, this has got to bother you, make you sad that you can't get what Mom wanted you to have."

Gloria sat on their mother's bed, worry and discouragement sitting like a heavy boulder in her chest. She rubbed her stomach, trying to soothe herself. "It is, but I don't know what I can do about it."

Next to Etta's vanity was a full-length mirror. Fima stepped in front of it and twisted this way and that, studying her figure. Her face lit up. "I know what I can spend that ten thousand dollars on."

"What?"

Fima laid her hands over her chest. "Breast enlargements."

"Why in the world would you do that?"

Fima cupped her breasts over her shirt. "They're too small, and men like women with large breasts."

"Real men wouldn't care," Gloria muttered. Her sister was on the wrong track—a track she was sure only led to heartache.

Fima dropped her hands and observed herself in the mirror from the side. "You don't think I'd look better with—?"

"No, I don't." Gloria stepped next to her sister, gazing in the mirror at both of them. "You're beautiful, Fima. You don't need to change anything about yourself, except your self-esteem."

"Yeah…"

"You need to get some and realize you're worth much more than guys like Austin deserve, who only want you around when it suits them."

Fima said nothing, only stared at herself. "I'll try, Glory."

Gloria hugged her.

"I really will try." Fima's voice cracked.

"That's all you can do, but it's enough." Gloria kissed her sister's cheek, then moved to the closet and closed its doors.

"Where do you go from here?"

"I don't know. I'll have to think on it." Gloria headed to the bedroom's door and waved an ushering hand at Fima. "Right now we need to be with Mike."

Hand in hand, she and Fima walked out of their mother's bedroom.

Michaela glanced at the door as her sisters, the doctors, and another woman entered the hospital room. Bailey sat on the chair across from Michaela. Doug slept soundly.

Dr. Curtis moved to the foot of Doug's bed. "We'll be doing some more tests on his spine tomorrow."

Dr. Brock wrote something on the tablet he was holding. "If

healing has begun, we'll start Mr. Morrow on physical therapy the following day."

Michaela rose from the chair she'd been sitting in. "That's good news, right?"

Dr. Curtis gave a shrug and tilted his head. "To be honest, it's too early to tell." He pointed at the woman next to him. "In any case, Joan will be working on Doug's legs while he's lying in bed."

Michaela slid her hands in her back pockets. "Okay."

Bailey left the chair and leaned her elbows against the side of the bed. "What's wrong with Daddy's legs?"

Michaela squeezed her daughter's shoulder. "Daddy's legs are still asleep. They are having a hard time waking up."

Bailey wrinkled her nose and looked at the outline of Doug's legs covered by the blanket. "Why?" She poked the leg closest to her. "Wake up. Sleep time is over."

Through the mist collecting in her eyes, Michaela let out a soft laugh that mingled with the others in the room. *If only it were that easy, my baby.*

"We'll be by later in the morning with the MRI and other test results," Dr. Curtis said.

"All right." Michaela rubbed her chin, flicked a stare at her daughter, then shut her mouth. She'd have to ask questions later when Bailey wasn't with her. But when would she not be with her? Lena left town. Who'd watch her daughter?

The doctors hovered over Doug a few more minutes before leaving the room.

"I'm going to go get something from the cafeteria." Fima held out her hand to Bailey. "Want to come with me?"

"Okay." Bailey waved to Michaela.

Michaela returned the gesture, sat back down, and rested her forehead against her palms. She felt Glory's hand on her shoulder.

"It's good they're starting the therapy."

Michaela looked up at her sister. "Yes, and I'd like to be there for every single session."

"Of course you would." Glory rubbed Michaela's back. "It's only natural you'd want to be with Doug through his healing."

Her sister was trying. Michaela had to give her that.

"Wonder how long he'll need physical therapy," Glory said.

Michaela shook her head and sat up with a sigh. "I don't know, but the main problem right now is that I can't be here the amount of time I need to be because of work and Bailey." She slid her hands down her thighs. "My babysitter is out of town for two to three weeks, and I have no one to fill her place."

"You have me."

Michaela gave her sister a sideways glance. "You?"

"Yes, me."

"How are you going to babysit Bailey for two or three weeks when you've got work to go back to."

Glory hugged herself. "Ruby understands the circumstances."

Michaela drummed her fingers on her lap. *That makes two offers. Tina's and Glory's.* Neither was her ideal choice. What did either of them know about taking care of a child? But what other choices did she have? She glanced again at Glory, who had moved to the other side of the bed and was gazing down at Doug's sleeping figure. *You know Tina's out, and Glory's your sister. Sure, she was MIA for ten years, but she's here now.* Michaela studied her sister in her T-shirt and jeans, straightening out the blanket and sheet over Doug's chest. *Bailey needs family now more than ever.*

"I understand if you want someone else to watch Bailey since she hardly knows me." Glory settled in the chair across from Michaela.

"She needs to get to know you."

Glory looked at Michaela as if she'd spoken heart-in-your-throat beautiful poetry. "Really?"

"Yeah." Michaela pointed at Glory. "You can start tomorrow. How's that?"

Glory beamed. "Great. I'm so glad I can help out."

Michaela waved a dismissive hand, leaned back in the chair, and mentally prepared for the coming weeks of work with Doug.

Chapter Fifty

Michaela woke from sleeping on the chair in Doug's hospital room, just as the door swung open and Doctors Curtis and Brock entered. She checked her watch. It was nearly eleven. Doug was still sleeping. She rubbed her eyes and rose from the seat. Dr. Curtis held a large manila envelope with a closed flap at the top.

"Dr. Curtis, you have the test results?"

He nodded with his lips folded in.

Dr. Brock stared at her with brows furrowed and a slight downturn of his mouth.

Michaela's heart sank, and she laid a hand on her clenched stomach. *Shit. Why'd they have to look so morbid?* She straightened her back and took in a breath. "Well?"

Dr. Curtis held up the envelope. "The MRI results revealed severe permanent damage to the spinal column."

Michaela froze. "What do you mean permanent damage?" Anger heated her face, and she pointed at him, shaking her head. "You never said that when you'd done the first MRI."

"The image wasn't as clear then because of all the swelling—"

"So you were wrong." Michaela huffed and began to stomp around the room. *Permanent damage to his spinal column? What the hell? Is this the end for Doug? For us?*

Dr. Brock raised a hand. "Ms. Morrow, please calm down. Dr. Curtis was just trying to explain the results."

She stopped and glared at both the doctors. "You want to tell me what this means for my husband? Is he screwed?"

"Your husband will live—"

She threw her shoulders back and raised her palms upward. "How?" She gestured in Doug's direction. "By lying in bed like a dead man the rest of his life?"

Dr. Curtis shook his head. "Oh, no. Not at all. He'll be able to sit up."

"Sit up?"

"Yes."

"And?"

"He'll be able to get around in a wheelchair."

Her words caught in her suddenly dry throat. "Wheelchair?"

"Yes."

Dr. Brock stepped toward Doug's bed and looked at him. "I know it's not the best scenario, but at least he will survive with no lasting brain damage."

Michaela gazed at Doug's placid face. *Thank God you aren't awake to hear any of this.* She ran a hand through her hair and focused on the doctors again. "There's absolutely no chance of him regaining use of his legs?"

"No, not medically that we can see," Dr. Brock replied.

"I guess that means we're left to believe in miracles?" Michaela laughed with cynicism.

"Some people find faith comforting at times like these."

"Some." Michaela moved across the floor.

The doctors exchanged somber stares.

"What about physical therapy?" she asked.

"Joan can start it up tomorrow, if you would like, to massage his legs and feet to keep good circulation, but it won't heal his spine," Dr. Curtis explained.

Michaela leaned a hand on the bed's headboard and gave the physicians another stinging stare. "You two are full of encouraging words, aren't you?"

Dr. Curtis's fingers ran up and down the large envelope in his hands. "I'm sorry. We're giving you the information as straightforward and gently as we can. We know this isn't easy for you."

"We'll get Joan set up for tomorrow afternoon," Dr. Brock said.

"And we'll be by tomorrow morning if you come up with any other questions," Dr. Curtis said, and they quietly left the room.

Michaela stood with her jumbled thoughts in the room with the heart monitor's beeping and other machines humming, breaking the silence. She glanced at her husband as her heart tightened. *What am I supposed to do with this news? Where do we go from here? Are we finished?* She shook her head, strode out of the room, and dropped in a chair in the lounge down the hall from Doug. She leaned her elbows on her thighs and head in her hands. *How do I live with a crippled man?*

"Michaela."

Tina's annoying voice broke through her depressing thoughts. She looked up at the woman who had caused all this. Her teeth and hands clenched as her body heated and shook with rage.

"You've done this. You've made him a cripple, paralyzed for life." She closed the three feet of space between them and breathed heavily into Tina's surprised face.

Tina let out a nervous laugh. "What are you talking about?"

Michaela's anger boiled to the surface, and all she saw was red. She punched Tina square in the jaw, knocking her on her rear. Her slutty stilettos clattered on the floor as she tried to get up.

"What has gotten into you?" she said, standing and rubbing her jaw. "You've lost it."

Hot blood coursed through Michaela's body as she swung at Tina again, but Tina ducked this time, shooting Michaela's anger through the roof. She kicked Tina in the shins, grabbed her bleached-blond hair, and pulled with all her might. Tina screamed.

"Mike! Mike!"

Glory's voice sounded miles away, outside a burning bubble insulated by Michaela's rage. The next thing she knew, her sister had wedged herself between her and Tina. "Stop! For God's sake, stop!"

"Mama!"

Bailey's voice punctured the simmering bubble and deflated Michaela's adrenaline. The anger crawled out of her. She fell back into the chair and fought back tears as her daughter climbed into her lap and hugged her. *Damn it, don't cry.* But the tears came anyway, and she embraced her daughter as if she were a life preserver. Glory sat next to her and put an arm around her.

"What happened?" Glory asked.

"I don't know," Tina said. "I just got here a few minutes ago to check on Doug and saw her looking miserable. Then she socked me in the face like a madwoman."

Michaela hadn't any energy left to respond to the destructive shrew. Only a sigh escaped her lips, and she sat back and looked into her daughter's calming, innocent face. "I'm sorry, baby. I let my anger get the best of me."

"Why are you mad, Mama?" Bailey ran her palm over the side of Michaela's warm, wet face.

Michaela bit her lip and glanced at Tina. She wasn't about to bring out the mess with Tina with her daughter present. "It doesn't matter now."

"But you were crying."

"I'm fine." Michaela patted Bailey's hand as the tremors in her body ceased.

Peggy approached them. "Can I take Bailey to the nurses' station? I have a treat for her." It was as if Peggy had psychic powers. She would always show up anytime Michaela needed Bailey to be absent from confrontations.

"Yes, please."

Bailey hesitated, her gaze flicking from Peggy to Michaela.

"Go on, baby."

Bailey bounced off her lap. "Okay." She took Peggy's hand and headed down the hall.

Michaela exhaled and raked her hands through her hair. She looked up at Tina. Her jaw had turned a reddish color and would probably be a nice purple hue by tomorrow. *Good. She got what she deserved.*

"Mike, tell me what happened," Glory said.

"Tell *us* what happened," Tina added, putting a hand to her chin again.

"*You* are what happened," Michaela said with a shake of her head. "Ever since you came into my family's life, you've done nothing but cause death and destruction."

Hurt swept over Tina's face. She rocked back a step. "You really know how to make a girl feel like crap, Michaela."

"Just stating the facts."

"There's more to it than the so-called facts."

Glory laid a hand on Michaela's shoulder. "Did something happen this morning to make you hit Tina?"

"That's what I'd like to know," Tina said.

Michaela glared at Tina. "I just told you."

Tina shook her head and sat in the chair on the other side of Michaela. "I don't buy it."

"There's more going on here, Mike," Glory said. "Tell us."

Tell us? Glory, you have no clue. "No way in hell." Michaela stood and planted her hands on her hips. "I don't have to tell this shrew anything."

"Shrew." Tina chuckled. "Is that my new nickname?"

Michaela gave her another glower. "It could be a hell of a lot worse."

Tina raised her brows. "Coming from you, that's definitely true."

Glory rose from her seat. "Tina, can you give us a few minutes?"

She paused, rubbing her jaw again. "Sure. I'll be at the nurses' station with Bailey."

As Tina clicked down the corridor, Glory turned to face Michaela. "Tell me what happened. Did you get the test results?"

Michaela folded and unfolded her arms, not knowing what to do with them. "I got them, all right."

Glory didn't respond, only kept her gaze on Michaela.

Michaela started pacing the floor. "The doctors basically told me my husband's a cripple for life."

"Oh no." Glory looked as if she was going to cry.

"Oh no is right." Michaela stopped pacing. "What do I do with a crippled spouse?"

Glory's eyes widened, and she touched Michaela's arm. "You love him just as you would if he weren't crippled."

Michaela glanced at Glory and her naiveté and chuckled. "Just like that, huh?"

Glory tilted her head to the side. "Well, yeah."

She truly doesn't have a clue. "You realize that Doug and I will never be able to have sex again. Can't have another child, if we wanted to."

Glory nodded slowly. "Yes, I get that."

"Then you understand that it's not that simple."

"It is if you love him."

Michaela lifted her eyes to the ceiling. *She still thinks like a child.* "It's not a matter—"

"Do you love him?"

"Of course I do."

"Then that's all that matters."

"This isn't a fairy tale, Glory."

"I know." Glory took a few steps across the floor. "But I also know when you marry someone, it's through thick and thin, in sickness and in health. That people are supposed to transcend hardships."

Michaela's marriage vows ran through her head as if she'd never heard them before. She'd certainly never heard such talk from her sister, the person who'd run away from hardship ten years ago.

Glory halted in front of her. "Think about that."

I can't right now. "Sure." She pointed in the direction of the nurses' station. "I'm going to go to Bailey now."

Michaela caught Glory's sympathetic gaze before heading down the hall.

Chapter Fifty-One

I n the salon, Seraphima grabbed her purse from under the front desk and moved to the coat hooks. The clear evening sky boasted sparkling stars spread across the indigo canopy like salt crystals poured from an overturned shaker. She imagined her mother somewhere up there gazing down at her. The pain of missing her mother squeezed her heart as she slid on her coat.

Eli emerged from the hall to the tanning rooms. "Quitting time, and I have the night off." He set down the cleaning supplies in the cabinet and put on his jacket.

Seraphima crossed the short distance from the desk to the large windows facing the parking lot. Too many losses had happened to her in the past couple of weeks—her baby, her mother, Austin. She missed her mother the most. After Austin's cheating on her, she had begun to let go of him. How could she ever trust him again, especially since he didn't feel bad about what he'd done to her? Glory's words about self-worth came back to her. Her sister had stepped back into her rightful place as encourager and supporter in Seraphima's life just as she did when they were children. Glory's return was something she'd gained, and she smiled thinking of her sister. She glanced up at the sky again. *If only you and Glory would've had more time together.*

"Fima?" Eli touched her arm.

She turned to face him. "Sorry. It's been a hard day for me." She lowered her gaze. "Missing my mom."

"You always will. But the ache will be less intense over time."

"I'm sure you're right. It's just hard now."

He put his arm around her and gave her a gentle squeeze. "I know."

Something stirred inside Seraphima's heart. Warmth filled her. She looked into Eli's kind, blue eyes. Her gaze traveled from his straight, thin nose and ended at the dimple in his chin. His blond hair swirled in rebellious waves, with the ever-present dangling strands bouncing above his eyebrows. *He's not so unattractive.*

He tilted his head to the side with his eyebrows knitted together. "What's that stare for?"

Warmth spread over her cheeks, and she laughed. "Oh, nothing."

He grinned. Had that smile always been so welcoming, so beautiful? Fear came over her. *What am I doing?* It had to be her state of mind tonight. She shook her head. *I'm not thinking straight at all.*

"If you're free, would you like to go hang out someplace?" Eli held the door open for her.

She walked through and locked it after him. The evening's breeze was cool and refreshing in the tepid night air. Spring had truly made its way to their town. She looked at Eli standing with his hands in his pants pocket, waiting for her response.

"Sure. Where would you like to go?"

Eli wagged an index finger. "No. It's where do *you* want to go?"

"Your house," she heard herself say. She covered her mouth.

Her curiosity over this man had taken over. "I'm sorry. I didn't mean that."

"It's okay. But there's not much to do there, except I do have a stellar back porch to watch the stars."

She smiled. "Sounds just about perfect."

"All right then." He opened his passenger car door. "Hop in, and we'll take off."

Seraphima slid into the seat and sat without any sense of anxiousness or discomfort. She didn't know what to make of it, other than Eli had become a good friend, and she knew she was safe with him, could trust him, something she could never have with Austin again.

"I don't see it," Seraphima said, gazing at the starry sky while sitting on Eli's porch. The crickets sang out a symphony of resonating chirps while the gentle breeze made a soft whooshing sound through the trees in Eli's backyard, carrying a fresh, pine scent.

Eli pointed to the right side of their view of the firmament. "Follow my finger."

She turned her attention at the spot in which he directed her.

"Venus is the brighter and steadier little light next to the three stars to its left."

Spying it, Seraphima nodded. "It really is brighter, isn't it? And it seems a bit bigger too."

"Yes."

She took a sip from her glass of lemonade. "Austin and I used to like to go to old drive-in theaters just so we could sit there in his car and watch the stars through the moon roof." A prick of pain and regret went through her. She'd been so wrong about him. He'd been her first. She'd given him every part of herself, and he hadn't. She'd been the secondhand dress, given a glance or two of attention when the brand name one wasn't glimmering in the spotlight. She swallowed the lump mixed with bile in her throat, then took a gulp of lemonade to wash it down.

The creak of Eli's wooden chair brought her back to the present. "Drive-in theaters are great. I haven't been to one since I was a kid."

She frowned. "I'm sorry I brought up Austin." She focused on her folded hands in her lap. "I'm sure you don't want to hear about him."

"Only because he hurt you and treated you badly." He took a sip from a can of soda. "But I'm here to listen if you need to get anything off your chest."

"He was my first love," she blurted out with a laugh of bitterness. "I know that seems ridiculous, but it's true."

"It's not. Everyone goes through first love heartaches." Eli set his can on the porch ledge, then looked contemplative. "Well, that's not totally true. Sometimes people stay with their first loves. The lucky ones." He stared at the backyard as if lost in another time.

She leaned forward in her chair. "You lost your first love too?"

He nodded. "She drowned in the ocean on one of her family's vacations to California. A freak accident."

Seraphima covered her open mouth. "Oh my God. I'm so sorry."

He nodded and sat back in his chair. "We were both eighteen. We'd been together two years. I took the news really hard, really tore me up."

"I can totally understand." She shook her head. "So very sad."

"And that was only four years after losing Mom." He ran his palms over his thighs. "My teens were a tough time."

"I'm sure it was a hard thing to get through." Seraphima slumped in her chair and gazed at the stars again.

"It was. Took me a few years." He ran a hand through his wild hair. "Just came around to totally healing a year ago."

Eli has lost so much. I don't know how he's gotten through it all. Seraphima hugged herself.

The back screen door creaked open, and a heavyset man with a head full of blond hair with streaks of gray rolled onto the porch in a wheelchair. The black-rimmed glasses he wore magnified kind, intelligent green eyes, "Hello, kids."

Eli stood. "Do you need me to help you up to the bedroom?"

"In a minute." He waved a hand in Seraphima's direction. "You haven't introduced me to your friend."

"You were reading in your study when we came inside." He nodded toward Seraphima. "Dad, this is Seraphima. She and I work at the Bronze Booth together. Seraphima, my dad."

She rose from her chair and stepped over to the man, who stuck out his hand for her to shake. She took it and smiled. "Nice to meet you."

"Same here." His stare traveled to Eli. "My son doesn't have many visitors. I like to think it has nothing to do with his sister or me."

Eli opened his mouth to speak, but his father cut him off. "Granted, we're a handful, but we don't bite. I promise." He let out a hearty laugh.

Seraphima found herself laughing alongside him.

"As you can tell, Dad's a big jokester. Ha ha." Eli chuckled, shaking his head.

"That I am." Eli's father paused, his face lighting up as if an idea had sprung to his mind. "Hey, son, did you offer Seraphima a slice of my blueberry pie?"

"I hadn't gotten around to it yet."

Eli's father grinned at Seraphima. "Clare helped me make it. I love to cook." He rolled back toward the door, and Eli held it open for him. He swiveled his head toward Seraphima. "And call me Gerald. Your name is beautiful. Named after an angel." He gave her another huge smile before moving himself into the house.

Seraphima watched him disappear around the corner to the kitchen, its light casting a warm glow in the short hallway. "Your dad is so sweet."

Eli nodded. "Yeah, he really is."

"Clare! Help me with this pie!" Gerald yelled.

Eli leaned a hip on the side of the porch ledge. "If you haven't guessed, Clare's my sister." He drank some more of his cola.

Seraphima glanced at the back door. "You're lucky to have such a great dad. Mine was awful."

Eli lowered the can of soda from his mouth. "He was?"

Seraphima took in a deep breath. "Oh yes." She walked down the three steps to the small square patio with a grill sitting on the right side of it.

Eli came up beside her.

She tapped the toe of her shoe on the edge of the cement. "My childhood was pretty rough."

"Do you want to talk about it, or is it none of my business?"

She shook her head. "I want to tell you."

"Okay."

Seraphima sat on the top step, and Eli joined her. She told him everything, then glanced back at the door. "How old is your sister?"

"Sixteen."

"Glory's twenty-three."

"I met her at the hospital that one time I came to visit you after your family's car accident, didn't I?"

A vague image came to her of Glory sitting with her in the lounge, the pain of dealing with the results of the ectopic pregnancy raw then. She searched her memory for Eli's visit, and a flash of him standing before her in the lounge surfaced but faded just as fast, invaded by Austin's appearance. All she could remember was being in Austin's arms, deliriously happy he'd taken her back. She grimaced. His feelings for her had all been lies.

"Yeah. I remember seeing her there with you in the lounge before Austin showed up."

"Yes. You're right." She twirled a strand of hair. "Glory was there with me." *She's been with me through all of the horrible things lately.* Seraphima sucked in her bottom lip. *Glory being Glory, but a more calm and reserved Glory.* Her lips spread into a smile.

"Yeah. She was very nice."

Fima played with her necklace's heart pendant. "She is."

Eli wagged a finger as if remembering something. "I think I met your older sister at the wake."

Seraphima cringed. "You did. I hope she didn't offend you with her foul mouth. She's abrasive."

Eli chuckled. "Naw. She was fine."

The back door opened again, and a teenaged girl with blond, braided hair walked onto the porch. She wore sweatpants and a gray T-shirt. "Dad wants you all to come in and try his pie." She bent over and whispered, "You won't be disappointed."

"I know we won't," Eli said, and tapped Seraphima on the arm. "Come on."

As she stood, Seraphima felt a weight lift off her. The skinny guy with his bouncing, wild hair and dancing, baby-blue eyes held the door open for her as she entered the house and inhaled the aroma of blueberry pastry.

The quaint kitchen with its old-fashioned linoleum floor, Formica countertops, white stove, daisy wallpaper, and compact table with four chairs drew her into a different world—a simple world full of true family bonds. She wanted to share those cozy feelings in that special space, and she hoped to have real family bonds with her sisters, the only family she had left.

Chapter Fifty-Two

On Michaela's lunch break, she went to the hospital. She found Dr. Curtis standing at the foot of Doug's bed. She sat next to Doug, the bed's headboard elevated, setting him in a partial sitting position. He was awake, his gray eyes alert within his frowning face, as the doctor relayed the bad news of his permanent paralysis before leaving them alone in the room.

She didn't know what to say. What could she say? The news was hard to swallow for both of them. She hadn't worked out the whole impact of it. She felt both the impulse to reach out to him and hold his hand and also withdraw herself from him. A spark of anger over her indecision ignited in her. *I hate this.* She stared at the heart monitor, listening to its beat in sync with her own heart's pattering.

Doug lips quivered. "I guess this is your lucky day, Mike."

She looked at him and folded her arms. "What are you talking about?"

"This is your chance for freedom."

"What?"

He gripped the blanket in his fists. "You have a good excuse to divorce me, cut me out of your life for good."

Michaela swallowed, shifting in her seat. "What the hell, Doug?"

He gestured toward the lower half of his body. "I'm half a man from now on." His face twisted in pain. "You're saddled with an alcoholic who's not even fully a man anymore."

He's feeling sorry for himself. But, damn it, hadn't what he'd just said crossed my mind since the doctors told me? She sank back in the chair, taking in a deep breath and letting it out as her hands clutched the armrests.

"No reason to feel guilty. You've got a legitimate way out of this." Doug stared at his legs, the frown deepening around his mouth and between his eyebrows.

Michaela's heart crumbled into pieces as she watched him struggle with this terrible news. Tears stung her eyes. Images of them at the altar exchanging their vows came to her, followed by the birth of Bailey, Doug holding her in his arms, beaming with pride and joy. The three of them playing Frisbee in the park on a hot, midsummer day.

She shook her head as the fears of his paralysis invaded those memories. *No. You're not a friggin' coward. You love the guy.* She sat up, leaned over, and took his hand in hers. "Quit talking crap, Doug."

"I'm talking facts, reality, Mike."

"You're feeling sorry for yourself, and I don't blame you. The news is shocking and hard to absorb at first, but it'll sink in, and you'll fight. You'll continue therapy—"

"What good is that going to do?" Doug pounded his fist on his lifeless leg. "I'm a damned cripple."

She shot from the chair and grabbed his hand. "Stop it. Stop it!"

He struggled against her as she wrapped her arms around him and hugged him with all her might. His body shook as he moaned, and tears wet her shoulder. She squeezed her eyes shut, taking in his pain with her own, her body joining his in shaking sobs.

When they both ceased weeping, Michaela sat back in the chair, scrubbing her face dry. She took a cleansing breath. "I will be with you through your therapy sessions, and when you're released from the hospital, you'll be coming home where you belong." She sniffled, wiping her nose with the back of her hand. "And I'll take care of you. We'll work through this together."

Doug's soft gaze glimmered with love. His face lit up, something she hadn't seen in weeks. "I love you, Mike. Always have."

She smiled. "I love you too."

The door opened, and Glory, Fima, and Bailey entered.

"Daddy!" Bailey ran to Doug and climbed into bed with him. She snuggled next to him, fitting under his armpit like a seamless garment, a part of him.

"Hi, sweetheart." He bent his head toward her but couldn't reach her face.

Bailey popped up and kissed his cheek, and he returned the gesture.

"Are you going home now?" she asked.

"I don't think—"

"Not yet, baby," Michaela said. She stood. "Daddy has some physical therapy to do to help strengthen his body."

Bailey huffed. "I'm tired of coming here. I wanna see Daddy at home."

Michaela smoothed down Bailey's hair. "You will, honey."

Bailey beamed and hugged Doug again.

Glory and Fima stood a few feet away talking. She approached them.

"What's going on?"

"It's good to see Doug awake and sitting up," Glory said.

"Yes. He's looking pretty good," Fima added.

Michaela glanced at Doug, then turned back toward her

sisters. "He's doing all right, considering he'd just gotten the news of his permanent paralysis a half hour ago."

Glory's face fell. "I can't imagine."

"Must have been so hard to hear," Fima said.

"It was…" Michaela combed a hand through her hair.

Glory and Fima stared at her as if they didn't know what else to say.

Time to change the subject. "Did you find Mom's box?"

Glory frowned. "No."

"What?"

"Yeah. It wasn't in the closet," Fima said.

"We don't know what happened to it." Glory shook her head.

Michaela studied Glory. Her green eyes shone with dismay as she clasped and unclasped her hands. Her sister had truly changed from that rebellious young teen she knew ten years ago to now. Michaela raised her brows. *Who the hell doesn't change from childhood to adulthood, especially in a span of a decade?*

Glory lowered her gaze to her hands. Those hands had been taking care of Bailey and making meals at Michaela's home. Her sister had taken care of Fima in her distraught state since the accident, and except for that moment of fleeing back to her hideaway in Summitville, she'd been a strong support for her as well.

It's time to reciprocate. "This evening, after work, let's meet at Mom's house to go through some of her things, what we want to keep for ourselves. Then we'll look for Mom's box for you."

Glory's eyes widened. "Really?"

Fima bounced on the balls of her feet and clapped her hands. "Yeah."

"Yes, really."

"Thank you." Glory embraced her, and Fima joined in.

"You're welcome." Warmth filled Michaela. She felt the torn fabric of their broken sisterly bond threading together again.

"I've got to go back to work now," Fima said.

"Me too," Michaela said.

Fima waved and walked out the door while Glory moved toward Doug's bed.

"I'll see you later at Mom's house," Michaela told Glory. Her stare traveled to Doug. "And I'll see you tomorrow for your next PT session." She pointed a chiding finger. "Don't be late."

He chuckled. "See you then."

"Later," Glory said.

Michaela flicked a hand toward her and headed out of the room. She walked down the hall with hands together as her heart swelled. *I'm going to help Doug and Glory, come hell or high water.*

Chapter Fifty-Three

Michaela entered Etta's bedroom with Glory and Fima behind her. Bailey sat at Etta's vanity with Etta's bracelets jingling on her arms and a long, pearl necklace hanging around her neck. Bailey picked up her grandmother's powder and soft blush brush, dipped it in the container, and swept it over her forehead and cheeks. She smiled at herself.

Michaela kissed the top of Bailey's head. "Don't you look pretty?"

"You look like a princess," Seraphima said, picking up a chunky diamond bracelet and setting it on Bailey's head like a crown.

"One more thing." Glory opened the jewelry box and clipped pearl earrings on Bailey's ears.

Bailey giggled. "I *do* look like a princess."

"You are *my* princess." Michaela brushed Bailey's hair off her shoulders and ran her fingers through the tresses falling to the middle of her back.

Glory looked around the room. "So, where do we start?"

"The closet's out," Fima said.

"I know, and we already looked in her nightstand and dresser drawers," Glory said.

Michaela spied Etta's diary sitting on the dresser, a black ribbon between the pages. She picked it up. "Mom's diary may have a clue."

"No!" Bailey shot off the cushioned stool and snatched the leather-bound book from Michaela's hands. She hugged the book to her chest, her eyes flashing with anger and mouth puckered in a pout. "You can't look at her diary! Diaries are private things!"

Michaela folded her arms and glanced at her sisters, who stared wide-eyed. She nodded. "Yes, diaries are usually private things."

"They always are." Bailey swayed back and forth, the book still cradled in her arms. "Hands off!"

Etta's words came back to Michaela. Her mother had told Bailey those exact words only a few weeks ago.

"Bailey, honey, we understand—" Glory started to say.

"Then no peeking." Bailey ran out of the room.

"Bailey!" Fima yelled and moved toward the door.

Michaela grabbed Fima's arm. "I'll take care of it."

Heading down the hallway, she found the bathroom door shut. She turned the handle, but it was locked. "Bailey, come out and talk to me."

"No."

"I'm not going to take the diary from you. I need you to come out of the bathroom."

The door handle rattled slightly, then opened a crack. Bailey's face appeared in the space. "Promise?"

"Yes. Now come out here and talk to me and your aunts."

Bailey pushed the door open and stepped into the hallway. Michaela guided her back to Etta's bedroom. Glory and Fima looked at her when they entered.

Michaela led Bailey back to the vanity stool. "Sit down."

Her daughter sat, still clutching the book to her chest.

Michaela squatted in front of Bailey so she was face-to-face with her daughter. "You are right. Diaries are private things. People put down their daily thoughts and feelings in them for their eyes only."

Bailey nodded, her lip protruding again.

"But when someone passes away, her diary no longer needs to be private because she isn't writing in it or reading it anymore. It's of no use to her." Michaela put a hand on Bailey's arm. "Do you understand?"

Bailey frowned as her eyes welled with tears. "Gramma can't write in it anymore." She lowered her head, and a painful whine came from her as she began to weep.

Michaela gathered her daughter in her arms and held her closely. "Shh. I know. I know." Her heart ached as she rubbed Bailey's back.

Glory and Fima encircled them, knelt down and formed a huddle, holding each other.

When they broke the family ring, Michaela gently wiped Bailey's wet cheeks. She then pointed to Glory. "Gramma left a gift for Aunt Glory, and we think she might have written about it in her diary. So we need to look through it."

Bailey's gaze lowered to the book in her arms. She grasped it in her hands and looked at Glory then Michaela. "Okay."

Michaela kissed Bailey's hand and took the book. "Thank you, baby."

Etta's cat, Sylvester, slunk into the room, his tail straight up in the form of a half hook. He moved to Bailey and rubbed against her legs. "I'm happy he's coming to live with us." She smiled, picked him up, and kissed his head. "Mama, I'm gonna go play with Sylvester."

"All right." Michaela rose from the floor and, after her daughter left the room, sat on the edge of Etta's bed with Glory and Fima flanking her.

Michaela glanced at Glory. "You ready to look?"

Glory took in a deep breath, blew it out, then nodded.

She handed Glory the leather-bound diary with the most personal, intimate feelings and events of their mother filling the gold-trimmed pages.

Chapter Fifty-Four

G loria ran her fingers over the soft brown cover as her heart fluttered. With another cleansing breath, she opened the diary. "Where should I start?"

"Wherever you want," Mike said.

"Yeah," Fima agreed.

Just as Gloria turned the first written page, a folded piece of periwinkle-colored stationery fell out of the back of the book and into Gloria's lap. She swallowed, picked it up, and flipped it open. "It's a letter to me."

Fima pushed off the bed and clapped her hands. "Read it out loud."

Gloria's eyes ran over the date—three years ago. She straightened her back.

"My dear Glory, as I write you this letter, in the depths of my heart, I know you will come home to me someday and read this. And after mulling over what I'll be writing in here, please read this with your sisters present. There are things they also need to know.

"I'd written you a letter that I tucked away with my will, telling you I'd left you a small box of special things for you. But

Gil discovered it inside the closet, took it downstairs to the living room, tore it open, and shook everything into the fire in the hearth.

"One of the items, a picture, had fallen out of the box and landed behind the chair closest to the fireplace, and Gil never found it. I discovered it after he stormed out of the room and went off wherever he always goes in the evenings, in his fancy Mercedes.

"I couldn't salvage the other photos and mementos precious to me from an earlier, most memorable and significant time in my life, aside from the birth of you and your sisters." Gloria looked to her sisters, who stared back at her, as if absorbed in their mother's every word. She returned to the letter.

"I confess, I married a bastard—a horrible husband and monstrous father. But I didn't know this until two years into the marriage, before I was pregnant with Michaela. Gil was a very possessive, jealous man who saw me as his trinket, a trophy to parade around at company parties and gatherings with friends. He had little patience for resistance or the word no from me. My marriage had felt like nothing more than being stuck in a cramped, airless cave, suffocating and bounded up."

Gloria swallowed back tears clogging her throat. She felt her sisters on either side of her, their arms around her shoulders. The warmth of them eased the fear and sorrow inside her from their mother's unbelievably inhumane situation throughout the years.

"When he decided it was time for me to produce a son for him, he didn't woo me with romantic gestures but told me it was time and raped me." Gloria sucked in a breath. "Dear God."

Mike tensed next to her with pain etched in her face.

Gloria sniffled and continued reading. "Your sister, my dear Michaela, was created that torturous night. And although I hated him with all that I had in me, I could never abort my child. Gil wouldn't have allowed it, if she'd been the precious son he'd wanted. But I was five months along when we found out we were having a daughter. Thankfully, he didn't force me to abort her or beat me when I was carrying Michaela, or any of you. For some reason a shred of decency existed in him when I was pregnant. He never knocked me around then. But in between pregnancies, he made up for it."

Gloria held on to her sisters who leaned into her, their tears mingling with hers.

"I hadn't given him the son he wanted, and it took him a few years to get over that. But things changed within my heart when Michaela was around four and I'd met Gerry, the love of my life."

Gloria covered her mouth as Fima and Mike kept their focus on the letter, their bodies still as statues.

"I met him at one of Gil's state attorneys' yearly bashes. Gerry worked for another law firm and didn't know Gil or me, and I didn't tell him Gil was my husband."

Gloria shook her head and frowned.

"Gerry was a defense lawyer for people with disabilities. He had a huge heart, something my husband sorely lacked.

"I would meet Gerry at a coffee shop in Denver and talk for hours. He and his girlfriend from college had broken up six months before meeting me, so we shared our broken relationships in mutual misery. But a couple of months later, we became very close. We were drawn to each other and cared for each other more than I can articulate here.

"Gerry still didn't know I was married. I didn't have the guts to tell him until much later, and I regret it to this day. I didn't want him to leave me. He was my only lifeline, even though at this time, Gil didn't bother Michaela or me too much. In fact, he tended to ignore us most of the time when he was home. He'd go away on cases for a few weeks at a time and rarely showed any interest in us, and I have to confess it was a blessing. Gerry and I were able to see each other while he was gone on those business trips, and it was a slice of paradise for me."

Gloria squeezed Mike's hand as Fima reached behind Glory and laid a hand on Mike's shoulder as their older sister gazed with furrowed brows at the diary sitting next to them on the bed.

"Then I got pregnant, and since it had been literally three months since Gil and I had had sex, thankfully, I knew the baby I was carrying was Gerry's, and not only was I ecstatic, I was scared out of my head. If Gil found out, he'd reverse that no-abusing-me-while-pregnant rule. That baby growing inside me was you, Glory."

Gloria lowered her hand, and the paper fluttered to the floor. She planted her face in her hands and released streams of tears rolling between and down her fingers. Her sisters' bodies encircled her as if they'd melded into one. She could almost hear their heartbeats through their warm breaths on her cheeks.

Mike picked up the letter and placed it in Gloria's lap. "You've got to finish reading it." She took to pacing the floor.

Gloria wiped her nose and nodded. "I told Gerry right away and finally broke down and told him I was married. I don't know if it was guilt or that I thought it was safe to tell him then because I was carrying his baby. Gerry was so hurt by my deception, but he stayed close to me through my pregnancy and your birth.

"Obviously, I told Gil the baby was his, that I was further along by a month or so. He believed me. And all was fine until he found one of Gerry's letters I'd stuck in one of my romance books on the nightstand. I think he had suspicions I'd been having an affair because he'd begun searching the bedroom and other areas of the house and would ask me in that low, frigid voice of his what I do when he's gone away on trips. You were not yet one at that time."

Harrowing memories swept through Gloria like a stinging wind, images flashing back to her early childhood years when she'd first witnessed her father abusing her mother, and Mike and her shaking with sobs, huddled behind their mother.

Mike leaned toward Gloria and whispered in her ear, "I remember," in a painful tone that made Gloria's stomach knot.

Fima hugged both Mike and her. "This is terrible. So much more terrible than I could have ever imagined."

Gloria smoothed out the letter. "His beatings were merciless, and as soon as you were able to walk and talk, he included you, to a lesser degree, in his abuse, that worsened as you grew, but you never knew why." Gloria sniffled again, and Fima pulled tissue from Etta's nightstand and handed it to Gloria, while wiping her own face.

"When Gil found out I'd been having an affair with Gerry, he threatened to kill him and dump you in an orphanage. Of course, this was illogical and frightening, but rage impairs a person's reasoning. Gerry told me he had to break it off for your sake. He had no regard for his own life, only yours and mine."

A sudden aching desire to know her father, to at least see a picture of him, burned in Gloria's heart.

"But I still have that photo Gil didn't manage to destroy. Look on the back inside cover of the diary, and you'll find a picture of the three of us taped to it. Gerry left when you were two years old. I never saw him again. And I can never forgive myself for having lied to him."

Gloria grabbed the diary and flipped to the back of the book. Sure enough, the picture was still there. Her sisters edged in close, their cheeks nearly touching, as she studied the photograph. Gloria, her mother, and Gerry were outside at what looked like a park with many pine trees. She was sitting on her mother's lap on a bench, and behind her, with his hands resting on her mother's shoulders, was her real father. His hair was bright blond, wavy, short. She fingered her golden-brown hair. He wore rimless eyeglasses, and his svelte body was clad in a short-sleeved blue shirt and jeans.

She brought the book closer to her face and locked eyes with his—a brilliant green, like hers. *My real father.* She touched his face. Her throat closed, and she squeezed back tears. *Where are you now?*

Fima took hold of the left side of the diary and moved it toward her for closer inspection. Her face lit in surprise, and she pointed at Gerry. "I'm not a hundred percent positive, but he looks a lot like Eli's father."

"What?" Mike said in a hoarse voice.

Gloria swung around, her heart sprinting in her chest. "Eli's father?" The name of the man sounded familiar. She thought back to the hospital after the accident, and a slender, young man with blond hair had come to visit Fima. *Yes. I'd thought he was her boyfriend, but she'd said he was just a friend.*

"Yes." Fima gave Gloria the diary. "I met him the other night. He was super sweet."

Gloria dropped the diary on the bed and took hold of Fima's hands. "Could you set up a time when you could take me to meet him?"

Fima shrugged. "Sure, but I'm not absolutely pos—"

"That's okay. I need to do this, see if he's my father."

Mike stood in front of them with hands on hips. "Yeah, she sure as hell does and has every right." The authoritative big sister had returned, but a protective, caring side poured out of her.

Fima nodded. "Right." She pulled out her cell phone from her purse on the nightstand. "I'll call Eli and set up a meeting time." She ran her finger over the mobile's screen, then paused and looked at Gloria. "If Gerry is your father... I don't know if Eli knows his father had an affair with Mom, and I doubt he would know that you... you and he were half-siblings." Fima's mouth hung open in awe.

Mike gestured for Fima to proceed with the call. "You'll find out soon enough."

Hundreds of emotions ran through Gloria like a roaring river. Her life had changed this very night. So much to take in, digest, she'd need time to do so in peace, by herself. She tapped Fima's shoulder as she put the phone to her ear. "If you can, make it Saturday evening. That gives me a couple of days to sort things out in my head."

"Okay. I get off at seven on Saturday nights, but we can meet up around seven thirty or so."

Gloria nodded, her mind already swirling with all that she'd just read from their mother and the desire growing in her for this encounter with Eli's father... Maybe her father.

Chapter Fifty-Five

Gloria followed Fima and Eli into his small but tidy den. Fima had told her she'd not given Eli any explanation as to why she wanted Glory with her when she visited him, just that she wanted her there. She'd also learned from Fima that Eli's last name was Lancaster. Apparently, Eli had had no problem with Fima's unusual request.

Fima sat on one of the two chairs in the room, rubbing her fingernails.

Taking a seat on the beige love seat with her purse in her lap, Gloria rehearsed the words she'd been practicing for the past two days. She'd wanted to be prepared both mentally and emotionally for this meeting, even though her body sat taut and her hands shook. The uncertainty of the situation knotted her stomach, and she flicked a nervous stare at the front door, a part of her wanting to dart out it and forget the whole thing.

Pushing the fear aside, she scanned the room filled with photos of Eli, a young woman, and who she believed was Eli's father on the mantel, next to a couple of small bowling trophies. Another picture of Eli's father with a strawberry-blond-haired woman standing in front of the legs of the Eiffel Tower sat at the end of the mantel, balancing out the items on the shelf. A thin layer of dust coated the space between the pictures and veiled the two table lamps and beige and blue curtains in the den. *Quit it.* She pressed her lips together. *Cleaning isn't their professions.*

Eli entered the room, walking alongside a man in a wheelchair, who pushed himself to a stop a few feet from her and Fima. The awkwardness hanging in the room faded from her senses for a moment as she caught her breath and her heart dropped into her stomach.

Yes, he was heavier and a couple of decades older, but the man sitting calmly in front of her bore a striking resemblance to the image of the man in the picture with her and her mother.

She swallowed, the sound echoing in her ears. She wondered if everyone had heard her do so.

Mr. Lancaster smiled at Gloria's sister. "Good evening, Seraphima."

"Hello, Gerald." Fima's hand curved in a half wave, her mouth quivering into a grin that flashed unnatural to Gloria.

She wiped her damp palms on her pants. *Dear Fima, don't fall apart on me.*

"Eli tells me this lovely young lady is your sister." Mr. Lancaster's large eyes behind black-framed glasses turned their gentle gaze on Gloria.

Their eyes met, and something in his glimmering green eyes reached into her soul and warmed her. Her heart tightened, and she looked away, grappling with the swirling emotions inside her.

Fima bit her lip and looked at Gloria. "Yes." She gestured to Eli. "Your son was kind enough to invite both of us over."

Mr. Lancaster gazed up at Eli and patted his arm. "He's a good kid, in spite of his father." He chuckled.

Fima blurted out too loud of a laugh and wrung her hands.

Gloria shifted on the love seat's cushion. *Oh, Fima. Please keep it together.* She took two cleansing breaths to steady her nerves.

The room fell into silence while Gloria struggled to remember the words she'd rehearsed. She glanced at her sister, who looked ready to pull the strand of hair she'd begun tugging, right out of her head.

Eli sat in the chair next to the love seat and slapped his thighs. "I'm glad you both could come." He leaned forward, his eyes on Gloria. "I know we met back at the hospital after the accident when I came by to see how Fima was doing. But it was a really bad time for you and your family, so I don't expect you remember me too well."

Gloria cleared her throat, working to keep it open and reminding herself to breathe through her nose calmly. "I do remember you visiting Fima that day."

"Oh, great." Eli grinned.

Gloria twisted her hands in her lap. The poor guy had no clue what she had to bring up in the next few minutes. She inhaled and exhaled again while straightening her back. *No more wasting time.* "My sister brought me here because I asked her to." She lowered her gaze to her hands. "I wanted to meet you and… and your father." She forced herself to look at Mr. Lancaster, who watched her with interest and a slight crease in his brow.

At this point, even Eli's expression had changed to a look of puzzlement. But quickly his mouth formed a small smile. "I don't mean to sound rude, but why?" He put up a hand and laughed. "Not that I'm not grateful Fima's sister wants to meet me and my family. I'm just a little confused."

Gloria nodded. "I know. I'll try to explain why I'm here." To give herself the push she needed, she unzipped her purse and pulled out the picture and set it on her lap, her hands covering it. She swallowed and looked at Mr. Lancaster. "My mother had a diary, and she left me a letter inside it. Her lawyer mentioned it when he read her will a week or so ago. And in her letter, she revealed a lot of things I didn't know… about my father."

Mr. Lancaster's face fell into a sympathetic frown. "Sounds like it wasn't good things."

Gloria shook her head. "I already knew how awful he was."

"Oh." Mr. Lancaster grasped the arms of his wheelchair with compassion showing in his eyes.

"I'm so sorry, Glory. Fima told me what a monster your dad was," Eli said.

Gerald leaned back against his chair, mouth open in wonder. "Glory..." His gaze fell on her, then shifted to the draped window, as if looking into a portal of another time and place.

She froze. Was he putting the pieces together before she'd barely had the chance to share the taboo connection between him and her mother?

Eli put a palm to the side of his head. "I didn't even tell Dad your name. Fima?" He looked to Gloria's sister fidgeting in her chair.

Cheeks glowing pink, her eyes darted from his to Gloria's. "Sorry."

"It's okay." *Push forward.* Gloria clutched the picture in her lap. "Our mother's name is Etta Barstone."

A gasp escaped from Mr. Lancaster's mouth, and he sat pale-faced, as if seeing a ghost. She could almost see the gears turning in his head. Fear gripped her. What was he feeling, knowing his daughter he hadn't seen in twenty years was now sitting in his living room? Was he overwhelmed with so many mixed emotions that his heart hurt and soared at the same time, like hers?

"Mom told me she fell in love with a man named Gerry about five years after she'd married Gil, my sister's father."

"Gerry," Eli repeated, looking with a pinched expression from Gloria to his father.

Fima went to Eli and put an arm around his shoulders.

"What are you trying to say?" Eli asked Gloria.

Mr. Lancaster rolled his wheelchair closer to Gloria, his knees nearly touching hers. He searched her face, then looked into her eyes, his mouth ajar. "You're my Glory."

My Glory. His tone was filled with love and amazement, and her heart swelled.

She was his.

He thrust out his arms, reached for her. She leaned into him, let him wrap his beefy arms around her and give her a gentle squeeze. In an unbelievably short period of time, this kind stranger had grown close to her. He was truly her father. She worked to absorb this and put her arms around his waist. His body slightly rocked, holding her. If he could walk, she believed he would have jumped out of the wheelchair and danced. Could this really be happening?

He moaned, the side of his head against hers, his breath warming her ear. The rocking subsided, replaced by tremors. Overwhelmed by his response, Gloria's heart wrenched, and tears poured out of her, soaking her cheeks and his shoulder. But she didn't care. She was enclosed inside a safe and cozy cocoon full of light and love, something she never thought she'd ever feel from a father. But Gil had never been her father. Gerry had always been, and she could see that, feel that in his embrace, his soft gaze, and kind words.

When she and her father had collected themselves, the questions started.

"Tell me. How is your mother?"

She's gone. The hurt throbbed inside her chest. Again, she fought back tears. He must have forgotten her mentioning Etta's will earlier. She hated having to tell her father the fate of her mother. "She... she died April third. She was in a car accident."

Anguish shown in Gerry's glistening eyes, as he slumped in his chair. His gaze lowered to his lap, and his hands gripped the chair's armrests again.

Gloria could feel his pain. She put a hand over his. "It's been really hard for all of us."

Eli stood and moved to Gloria and their father. He ran a hand midway through his hair and paused. He touched Gerry's shoulder, looking down at him. "Dad, are you saying you and Glory and Fima's mother had an affair?"

Gerry placed a hand over Eli's and patted it twice. "Yes."

Eli withdrew his hand. "Did Mom know?"

Gerry shook his head. "No, son, and this affair happened while your mother and I were not together. I didn't know Etta was married until she was pregnant with Glory." He rubbed his chin. "Your mother broke up with me after college and moved out of state for three years. I met Etta about six months after your mother left. When your mother came back, she and I made amends and got married a year later. You were born a year after that."

Eli's stare traveled to Gloria as realization bloomed in his eyes and swept over his face. "You're my half sister."

She nodded as the words seeped in.

The simmering awkwardness that had been floating in the room since she and Fima had arrived thickened. She didn't know how to respond. Everything that had transpired in this space had been a revelation for all of them. She scanned their faces and wondered what they were thinking.

Eli sat next to her and embraced her. She let out a breath, surprise stymying her ability to move.

"Even though, I admit, this whole conversation has been confusing and bizarre, I'm glad we got all of this out. Having another sister is kind of nice, even though I complain about Clare so much." He gave her a lopsided grin.

Fima laughed and swept her hand toward Gloria as if to say, *Come on, Glory, laugh.*

Her little sister was right. She needed to embrace this reunion with joy. Her father and Eli had shown nothing but kindness and love toward her. The nuns back home would call this a blessing from God. With a smile, she hugged Eli back. "Having a brother is a first, but I welcome having you in my life."

"I'm blessed beyond measure." Gerry held up his hands and looked toward the ceiling. He then rolled his chair backward and jutted his chin toward the kitchen. "Come in the kitchen and have the best blueberry pie ever, and let's talk some more."

Gloria smiled and followed her brother, sister, and father out of the little den that had held their secrets and revealed their joys.

Chapter Fifty-Six

Sunday afternoon, Seraphima skated in her rollerblades with Eli, down one of the many paths in the city's large park with its pines and aspens. In the center of it all stood a picturesque fountain erupting in a graceful arc from the mouths of frogs and fish.

They stopped by a water fountain and took turns taking sips.

Eli wiped his glistening forehead and grinned. "It's been way too long since I've done this, but I think my rustiness is history."

She laughed. "Good, 'cause there are still five more paths I want to explore."

"You're on." Eli pushed away from the fountain, striding down one of the sidewalks, his thin arms pumping like a machine.

Seraphima skated after him, her mouth set in a determined pucker as she gained on him, his skates only two feet away. "You're in trouble now, Mr. Lancaster." She reached forward, swinging her arms, but he shot ahead.

Glancing back at her, Eli snickered. "You're mistaken, Ms. Barstone." He scrambled ahead, his wheels smacking loudly on the pavement.

Laughter bubbled out of her as she raced after him, her hair streaming behind her, the wind refreshing on her face. When had she been this happy with a man? True happiness, fun, without worries of the usual awkwardness of dating, pressures of quick kisses and heated bodies rubbing together to make lasting sparks? *Never.*

Seraphima beamed and glided down the path with assured swiftness, passing a patch of brilliant purple cat's mint, a colorful tapestry of tulips, bushes, and pleasing pungent pine trees with the sun pouring its warmth over her shoulders.

She was gaining on him as he skidded to turn left with the sharpness of the path's direction, but he'd made the attempt too late and headed toward collision with a bush. He yelled an obscenity before crashing, just as she skated over and reached to grab him, but only got air. He rolled over on the grass between the bush and cement trail, breathing hard.

She bent toward him, her hands on her knees. "You okay?"

He squinted at her through the sunlight and held up his hand. "I will be, if you help me up."

"Of course." She grasped his hand and pulled, but instead, he brought her down, landing on top of him before flipping onto her back next to him.

"Can't believe you fell for that."

"Me, neither, you stinker." She swatted his arm and got on her hands and knees. "That's the thanks I get for showing good sportsmanship toward my racing opponent." She giggled under her breath and skittered to her feet.

He rose from the ground, brushing off twigs and leaves. "Okay. I admit, you did—"

"Fima."

That well-known, deep voice coming from behind her made her queasy. Had he followed her to the park? She spun on her skates and faced Austin. Eli came alongside her, hands on hips.

She clutched her upset stomach, then straightened her back

341

and flipped her hair off her shoulders. *Stand your ground. He doesn't hold your heart in his hands anymore.* "Austin."

He grimaced at Eli before turning his attention to her and pointing to the bench a few feet away. "Can I talk to you alone?"

"No."

Surprise registered on his tanned face, his dark eyes staring at her in disbelief.

She looped her arm through Eli's. "Whatever you have to say, you can say it with Eli present."

Austin clamped the nape of his neck with his hand, his gaze lowered to the ground, face pinched.

Amused by his discomfort, Seraphima smiled, feeling a confidence she hadn't had before. "Come out with it, Austin." She gestured toward her feet. "As you can see, we're in the middle of skating through the park."

His face turned pink as he licked his lips. The big, brawny guy had shrunk in size and importance right before her eyes. Why had she been so invested in him, so caught up in his looks, his allure? The old desires of the ecstatic intimate encounters slid through her, sparking warmth in her for only a second when she remembered it had all been about that. Fireworks in the bedroom, nothing else. What about ninety percent of the rest of their time together? The answer sent cold chills through her. There'd been nothing else there but hollowness, superficiality.

"Yeah, I get it." Austin scowled with heaving breaths of frustration. "I miss us, okay?"

She shrugged. "Where's Kayla?"

"She left me."

Seraphima tsked, shaking her head. "I guess you can only cheat on people so long before you're left all alone."

He brought his hands together in a pathetic, desperate gesture. "Fima, I know you love me—"

"Loved you."

"And you carried my baby."

"A baby you didn't want."

As Austin squirmed, shifting from one foot to the other, she noticed in her peripheral Eli watching her with admiration shining in his eyes.

She folded her arms and positioned her legs in a sturdy, narrow shape of an A. "Look, I gave you several chances to work things out with me, and you tossed all of them in the trash."

"I made a few mistakes."

"Yes, and I'm done." She glanced at Eli. "I'm happy where I am now. I'm not going back to you and our screwed-up relationship."

Austin huffed, with arms to his side and hands balled into fists. "Your loss."

Seraphima grabbed hold of Eli's hand. "My gain."

He gave her and Eli a look of disdain, swung around, and stomped away.

"Way to push back, show you're better than him, Fima." Eli ran a hand over the side of her face. "I'm proud of you."

Her heart swelled as she stared into his beautiful eyes, full of compassion and reverence. "Thank you. That means so much to me."

He nodded. "Well, it's true, and it was all you. You did that on your own." He stepped back and clapped his hands.

She grinned and clasped his hand again. "Just like I beat you all on my own in our last race." She tugged him toward the trail. "And we've got another race to go."

He laughed. "You're on."

Releasing his hand, Seraphima glided ahead with Eli right behind her, as they laughed along the path.

Chapter Fifty-Seven

Michaela sat on the stoop of her front porch, clutching a package of cigarettes. Tina sat next to her, coating her lips with Chapstick.

"I'm glad Doug's finally home. I know he's missed it." Tina stowed the lip balm back in her purse next to her.

Michaela glanced at Tina, the woman who had come into her family's life as seemingly a nemesis, causing havoc and perceived heartache. But in the past few days, she'd been there helping to watch Bailey, visiting Doug, bringing Michaela food from the cafeteria and to her home. She'd changed so much.

"Thank you for helping to get him in the car and for staying to help settle him in bed." Michaela flipped open her cigarette case, then smashed it shut. *I've got to make the effort to quit.* She set the box on the cement, pulled out a stick of gum from her pocket, and shoved it in her mouth.

"I wouldn't have it any other way. It's partially my fault he's in the wheelchair." Tina plucked on her mascara-filled eyelashes, pulling off crumbs.

Michaela stopped chewing her gum. The truth of the crash had been told to her for weeks, but she'd been too angry and stubborn to accept it. She would now. Blowing out a breath, she clasped Tina's hand and locked eyes with hers. "It wasn't your fault. The drunk driver killed my mother and permanently injured Doug."

Tina's eyes welled with tears, and she squeezed Michaela's hand. "Thank you for saying that. I know it wasn't easy."

"It should have been, and I should've told you ages ago." Michaela let go of Tina's hand and blew a bubble that snapped when it popped. "Sometimes I'm just too damn stubborn."

"No, really?" Tina feigned surprise, then grinned.

Michaela shoved Tina's arm before letting out a laugh. But something about Tina's metamorphosis still niggled at her. "Why did you keep talking to me? Why did you forgive me for decking you?"

Tina pushed Michaela back and cackled.

Michaela cringed, but Tina's laugh didn't bother her as much now.

"You still haven't figured that out?" Tina raised her brows.

"Obviously not. So why?"

"Unlike you—"

"Here we go—"

"I don't give up on people, especially my friends. I'm there for them when they need me and even when they think they don't." She winked.

Michaela's brows knitted. "You consider me your friend?"

"Of course."

"Why?"

"Why wouldn't I? Doug's my friend, and getting to know his spitfire wife and adorable daughter, how could you not be?"

Michaela's cheeks warmed, and she pressed her knees together. "Maybe because I wasn't exactly friendly to you."

Tina snorted. "That's a huge understatement."

"Exactly, so what the hell?"

Tina put a hand on Michaela's shoulder.

"And why do you always call me Michaela?"

"Well, speaking of hell... You and Doug have been going through it since we met. And the accident only compounded it." Tina shook her head. "I didn't expect you to be Pollyanna toward me. I got your personality from day one, and really, people react and handle terrible things in their lives in all kinds of ways. Yours was anger and blame."

Shit. She knows me better than I know myself. Michaela's cheeks burned again.

"As for calling you by your given name." Tina lifted her chin. "I like it. Your nickname sounds like a man's, and well, that's really not feminine, is it?"

"So?"

"So, I'm a woman, and I dress and look like one."

Michaela laughed. "Yeah, to the nth degree in ridiculous heels that will break an ankle one of these days."

Tina joined in her laughter. "I'll risk it."

Fima's car rolled up in front of her house. "They're here."

"Time to get Doug." Tina walked down the sidewalk, looking back. "You go ahead. I've got some things to get from my car."

Michaela nodded toward Tina then waved at her sisters before entering the house.

———

Michaela wheeled Doug into the living room where everyone congregated. Her sisters and Bailey were talking while, next to the window, Sylvester sat perched on the cat condo Bailey had gotten from the pet store the last time they visited.

"He's had his nap and is ready for socializing," Michaela announced, steering him into a spot next to the couch.

Glory and Fima hovered over him, kissing his cheeks.

"Welcome home," Glory said.

"Bet you're so glad to be home," Fima said.

"Thanks." He turned toward Fima. "More than I can say."

Michaela squeezed his shoulder. She could barely believe he was actually back home, in *their home.*

Doug looked up at her, held out his hand for her to hold, and gave her a gentle smile.

He then gazed at Glory. "We know you've got to head back home to your work tomorrow morning, but we'll miss you. I'll also miss all you did for Mike and Bailey." He leaned forward, and Glory went to him and hugged him. "Thanks so much."

"It was a pleasure, something I'll always treasure," Glory said.

Fima blew a kiss to Glory. "You helped everybody, which has always been who you are."

Glory's cheeks flushed. "Love you all."

Michaela crossed to her and put a gentle hand against Glory's cheek. "And we love you." She cupped the nape of Glory's neck and drew her into a hug.

Glory beamed. Michaela could sense Glory was feeling what she was feeling. They'd finally connected and healed their riff. Tears filled Glory's eyes as Michaela rubbed her arm.

Bailey slid in next to Michaela and hugged Glory's legs. "I love you, Aunt Glory. You are the best babysitter ever." She kissed Glory's cheek and she kissed hers.

"You're the best niece in the world." Glory embraced Bailey.

Tina stepped into the living room with several shopping bags in her hands.

"Thank goodness Tina offered to fill your place until Lena comes back," Fima pointed out.

Michaela raised her chin with a smirk. "Yeah. Sometimes she comes in handy."

"Sometimes?" Tina cackled. "More like all the time."

Michaela swatted the air. "Arrogance doesn't make you look good."

"That's what makeup, a great hair style, and a fantastic wardrobe is for."

Laughter filled the room.

"Shut up and sit down." Michaela patted a space on the couch.

Tina sat and flashed a dazzling smile. "Hi, everyone."

"Hi, Tina." Bailey hugged her.

Tina petted Bailey's head. "Hey, little one." She bent toward one of the bags lying at her feet. "I've brought you some gifts."

"How nice, Tina. Isn't it, Mike?" Fima bounced in her chair as if it were Christmas morning.

She's so unpredictable. "Yes. Very." Michaela stepped forward and craned her neck to look in one of the bags.

"Uh-uh." Tina clamped the slightly opened bags closed. "No peeking."

Michaela lifted her hands as if under arrest. "Okay, okay."

Tina rummaged through the bag closest to her. "First things first. For adorable Bailey."

Beaming, Bailey clapped her hands.

She pulled out a medium-sized Beanie Baby of an orange-striped cat and handed it to her.

Bailey gaped. "It looks just like Sylvester." She turned it every which way, then went over to Sylvester and presented it in front of his half-asleep, furry face. "See, Sylvester? He looks just like you." She kissed Sylvester's head.

Bailey ran back to Tina and hugged her. "I love it. Thanks."

"You're welcome, honey." Tina chuckled and dug in the next bag, pulled out two Tom Clancy books. She handed him one. "For you, Doug." She placed the other novel on the coffee table. "And one to follow."

"Thanks, Tina. You know I'm a fan of his books."

"Yes. And lastly." Tina stuck her hands in the second-to-last bag. She pulled out three gift cards. "Three free massages at

Holistic Massage." She handed them to Michaela. "Figured you needed those after all you've gone through." She smiled.

Michaela swallowed. "You're right." She laughed. "You've gotten to know me so well."

"Spent a lot of time with you the past month or so."

"Don't remind me." Michaela winked.

Tina stuck out her tongue.

"But really." Michaela laid a hand on Tina's shoulder. "Thanks for the thoughtful gift."

"You're welcome." Tina patted Michaela's hand.

Bailey pointed to the last bag—a brown paper bag instead of white ones like the others. "What's in there?"

Tina rested her hands on her jean-clad thighs. "Groceries so I can whip up some good dinners for you and the family in the coming days."

Michaela picked up the bag before Tina could stop her. "I'll put them away for you."

"Thanks," Tina said.

As her family chattered away, Michaela put the gallon of milk and eggs from the sack into the fridge and smiled. *Things are coming together, and I'm ready to face what lies ahead with Doug. And with the family along for the ride. Hot damn!*

Chapter Fifty-Eight

After tear-drenched hugs goodbye at Mike's house, Gloria climbed into Fima's car, and they headed to Summitville. They'd promised to visit each other monthly.

On the gravel road in front of her cabin, Gloria embraced Fima with the same amount of crying, before Fima got into her car and slowly rolled away.

Gloria waved until Fima's car was out of sight. She entered her cabin, feeling like a new person. So much had happened in the past couple of months—her family had expanded and was on the road to healing. That uneasy and difficult choice she'd made in March to go see her mother and sisters had been the correct one. A blessing, the nuns would say. *Yes*.

She smiled, stuffed her backpack, adding a few sets of extra clothing, then headed out, locking the cabin door. She breathed in the clean evergreen scent of the warm mountain air, and with the twittering of hummingbirds flitting overhead, she walked toward the foothills.

As she approached Henry, she found her friends there. Serena spied her as she drew closer.

"Glory!" She raced to her and gave her a near-suffocating hug.

Gloria laughed in jagged breaths.

Serena took a step back and studied her. "You look a hundred percent better than the last time you came home."

"I feel a hundred percent better." Gloria dropped her backpack on the ground next to her.

"Yea." Serena held up her palm, and Gloria raised hers and smacked Serena's.

Lou gave her a brief hug. "Nice to see you back."

"Thanks."

Coop stood next to Lou, giving her an intense stare. He then looked away with a furrowed brow.

He's not improved since I last saw him. Gloria approached him. "Hey, Coop."

He darted a look her way, then back to the ground. "Hey."

Serena leaned into Gloria and whispered, "He's been hot and cold since you left. Found out his dead wife, Sarah, looks a lot like you. Been causing him fits."

"I know," Gloria whispered back.

"You do?"

She shooed Serena and Lou away from her and Coop. With hesitation and exchanged looks of concern, they walked a few feet down the slope.

Gloria slid her hands in her back pockets. "How have you been?"

He shook his head. He was more uncomfortable than ever. Then it hit her. All his angst both when she'd been here and when she'd left for a while was torturing him. She was a constant reminder of his dead wife he'd never be with again. She scrutinized his haphazard appearance and exhausted face angled slightly away from her. He needed real help.

Raising a hand then shoving it back into her back pocket, she said, "Coop, I know you're still hurting over Sarah."

He rubbed his forehead. "Yeah."

"I think you should see a therapist to help you get through your grief."

He jerked his head up and glared at her. "How am I going to pay for that?"

Gloria squatted by her bag, opened it, and pulled out a tin container. She took off the top and leafed through rolls of paper money—the money her mother had left her, all ten thousand of it, because her sisters refused to take her share. She pulled out half the bills and thrust them toward Coop.

He looked at her then the money as if it were a snake. "What are you doing?"

"You need money for your therapy. I happen to have some." She took one of his hands, laid the bills in it, and closed up his hand.

"I can't—"

"Yes, you can."

"How do I pay you back?"

"You pay me back by never seeing me again until you are healed."

He squinted at her. "What? Why?"

"I'm nothing but a trigger, reminding you of Sarah. Until you get counseling and heal from losing her, I'll only spark the pain inside you every time you see me."

He didn't say anything but stared in contemplation, his free hand raking through his hair.

"I don't think you have feelings for me, but Sarah."

He didn't answer.

"And frankly, I don't have feelings for you in that way, only as a friend."

Realization flashed in his eyes, and he slowly nodded. His gaze lowered to the stack of money in his hand. "Thanks, Glory."

"You're welcome." She jerked a thumb behind her. "Now, go

join your friends and ask for their help finding a good therapist in town. They, or at least their parents, would know someone here."

He raised his head, jutted out his chin in a sign she took as determination, and he walked past her to his friends.

She waved at them. "See you in a few days."

Serena frowned. "You're leaving again?"

"I'll be in the mountains for a while."

Serena sighed with a hand to her chest. "Of course. Enjoy."

As her friends walked down the rocky hill, she laid a hand on Henry's trunk. "I'll come see you when I return. I'll have a lot to tell you."

Gloria knocked on the monastery dorm door, and it opened. Sister Elizabeth stood in the space. A smile brightened her face.

"Glory. It's so good to see you. You look well."

"Thanks. I am."

"Were you coming for a service or another tour?"

"No."

Mother Maria emerged from the chapel doors and walked over to her and Sister Elizabeth. "Glory, my child." She spread out her arms.

Gloria stepped into her embrace and inhaled the scents of linens and rosewood.

"You've worked out your family matters," the abbess said.

She'd only been stunned for a second. She'd grown accustomed to Mother Maria's foresight and wisdom.

"Yes, Mother."

"And you'd like to stay here for a while." Mother Maria turned her attention to Sister Elizabeth. "Sister, show Glory to one of the guest rooms. She'll be staying with us for the week."

"Of course."

Gloria gazed up at the abbess. "Thank you, Mother."

Mother Maria's childlike face wrinkled into a generous smile, as she touched her palm to the side of Gloria's face. "You're most welcome."

Gloria followed Sister Elizabeth into the dorm, down the shiny clean corridor, past two rooms, and entered the third one.

"Please join us for dinner in the dining hall at five o'clock." The nun bowed her head, beamed, then closed the door quietly behind her.

Gloria set her backpack on the twin bed with its white sheets and soft navy-blue blanket. A desk stood next to the bed with a Bible, pad of paper, and pen. A vase of daffodils sat on the right corner of the desk.

Above the desk hung a painting of Christ. He gave her a peaceful stare, dressed in blue and red robes, with his right hand lifted, his thumb and ring finger touching.

She gazed out the open window on the left side of the room, with blue spruces and Ponderosa pines in the foreground and the towering, jagged Rockies in the background. She turned to face the small, immaculate, and comforting space as the light mountain breeze drifted into the room, fluttering through her hair.

She sat on the bed, then pulled out her grandmother's book of inspirational stories and her prayer book Gloria had picked out of the chest when she and her sisters had gone through their mother's things before finding her letter. She then fished out the picture of her parents and her in nature, and a photo of her and her sisters taken the night before at Mike's house. She set the items, one at a time, on the desktop.

Rolling the knotted bracelet on her wrist between her fingers, she whispered, "A place for the broken *and* the healing."

The End

About the Author

Dorothea Anna's debut novel, *Passage of Promise*, was published under Dorothy Robey in May of 2020. In April 2018, her short story, *Summer Memories*, was published in Scribes Valley Publishing's anthology, *Take A Mind Trip*.

Dorothea Anna lives with her family in beautiful Colorado.

Visit Dorothea's website, Modest Musings, at https://dotluvs2write.com/.

facebook.com/dotluvs2write

twitter.com/Dotwriter3

CPSIA information can be obtained
at www.ICGtesting.com
Printed in the USA
BVHW081529220221
600778BV00001B/31